For Louise
with best
wishes
Atima

Oct 2023
London

Dark Waters

Atima Srivastava

Dark Waters

Atima Srivastava

Cover by
Dean Stockton

Published by Bite-Sized Books Limited 2023
16 High Holborn, London, WC1V 6BX England
Registered in the UK. Company Registration
No: 9395379

ISBN: 978-1-7391524-7-5

To my friend FD

Atima Srivastava

"The mind is its own place,

and in itself can make a heaven of hell,

a hell of heaven..."

John Milton
Paradise Lost

Atima Srivastava

Chapter 1

The one at home was obviously broken so she went into town to find another. There was an old-fashioned type in Boots, and she stepped on it gingerly. The clock hand shot up with a prang of such ferocity that she was taken aback. What, but it *can't* be she thought crossly, looked around and stepped off quickly. How could this happen? She hurried out of the pharmacy in a daze into brilliant sunlight which blinded her, unsteadied her. A man grabbed her elbow.

"I'm fine, fine. Just slipped. New shoes. Thank you."

"Please take care madam. Oh! My goodness, it's you! It's me Mohammed, I hope you can remember me."

"Oh yes, how are you? I'm just on my way to..."

"I always felt I didn't pay my respects properly when your parents passed. I know it was many years ago. All I *am* is because of their wonderful..."

"Yes, yes, must go".

"I have another shop as well now, in Ramsgate. Please know that you and anyone else from the school will get 10% discount there also. My son is running the one here. I am forever grateful to your parents for..."

Damn place was full of people, despite being a sleepy seaside town where people came to die. You couldn't hope to just be by yourself. You kept bumping into all and sundry, she thought. The clock face of the old-fashioned weighing machine had unsettled her. But both couldn't be broken. It had pointed to the same number as the electronic one at home. Dolefully, Kavya headed for the pub on Harbour Road.

There was a chilly wind coming in from the sea. Her heart was racing. It was not yet 11am and she wouldn't normally have gone into a Weatherspoons because you bumped into people, but it was the closest. She stood at the bar and ordered a double, downed it in one and then thinking it wasn't quite enough ordered another, and that turned out to be just what she needed. Her mind felt clear, and her heart was calm. She felt easy and hitched herself up on the stool.

The barman was wiping glasses.

"Nice bar."

"It's alright."

"I'm having a lunchtime snifter because I'm on a diet."

"Ok"

"It's almost 12," she said consulting her phone. "To be fair."

"We open at 10," he said. "A lot of people like to come early. Take the edge off."

OMG, she thought. Alkis and deadbeats. Rolling about on park benches with cans wrapped in plastic bags.

"It's all about calories in and calories out. If you have one cheeky drink, or two, then you're not hungry for the rest of the day."

"I can bring you peanuts."

"Who eats peanuts in a bar?" she said making a face.

The barman laughed. "That's true, you don't know who's touched them."

"Or where those hands have been!" said Kavya and laughed loudly. It was banter such as this that made going out for a drink so convivial.

The place was dark and smelled of bleach. It had once been a cinema and Weatherspoons had kept a lot of the old black and white photos of stars from the silver screen on the walls. ...I'll easily get rid of it, she thought breezily. Just cut out the desserts. But I never have dessert. It's the heaviest I've ever been. She pushed out her bottom lip. I'll tell Marymary don't make me any rice at all, and he can eat his fish and chips on his own and then I'll go to the gym every day and burn it all off...oh but it's not that at all. It isn't the weight that's weighing on me.

It's *him.* I'm only 39. *Only 39, that's almost 40!* Yes, but I don't look it, why did I marry again? It wasn't like I wanted another kid. I've got to get out of it, I can't stand the way he's always monitoring me. Like a surveillance camera! And why did he marry *me*? Wanted to get his hands on the properties I expect. I was quite the package. I am an *heiress* for God's sake...

A sudden thought popped into her mind. Something Shanta Acharya the village Twitter had said on the bus this morning. A *voluptuous* beauty. What, Georgia? I never noticed, she said as they watched her out the window, tottering down the street in mini skirt and heels, and Shanta Acharya said 'Well. You're not a man are you?' But when she comes to work, she's always in baggy shirts. That's why she hadn't recognised her immediately. In the cobbled street dressed like a hooker at 7.30am. Going *where* you might ask? Perhaps coming from somewhere…?

John had said only last week, I'll take you home babes don't bother with the bus. *He was always giving her lifts.* And touching her shoulder. Kavya had seen him do that more than once. And when he was courting Kavya he had said, I know you got nice legs babe but it's a shame cause I'm a boob man myself. He said it was a joke. But was it? A voluptuous beauty. Georgia certainly had a lot of what Kavya was lacking in that department.

Every night I come to bed late very late, and I don't show any interest in having sex, but he never says anything. Never complains! That's not normal. But that's why he doesn't complain! He's getting it somewhere else. It's probably been going on for ages. Under my nose. They do say the wife is the last to know! That would be so typical, so low class… and so embarrassing for me. Everyone would know he'd run off with the cleaner for god's sake…

But Kavs, he's the kindest of men. Johnny's the OG of decency.

Yeah, but he's *too* good. Ever since I met him, he's always let me have my way in everything. He prioritises my needs over his every time. *But doesn't that indicate his character?* Easily manipulated. Any woman could get him under her thumb. He's that kind of person. Heart on his sleeve. A peace-making pleaser. Probably the childrens home that made him that way.

He was handsome, blonde with blue eyes but that didn't mean he was confident. Quite the reverse. That sort of confidence, the type she had, came from being born into money and to a lesser extent, education. He would have his head easily turned by a girl like Georgia and her oversize hooters. And maybe they had more in common socially, the age gap in his favour and then they *were* both white…He could probably get her to agree to what he liked. Having sex on the beach for example, a proposition that Kavya had scoffed at. But Georgia…Yes, she could see it all now.

I used to love him, but he's ruined it all, she thought as she sipped slowly. I've got to get out of it. I should see a solicitor about the properties. I'll see one in London; everyone knows everyone here. But Johnny's never cared about money. He sold his flat and put it all in when we bought the house, even when I *told* him we should keep it 50/50, he insisted and said he'd rather put it all into our future. He didn't care about 50/50. He even offered to sign a pre-nup.

Yes, he said all that *then* but things change. There's the house and the School and Moghul House. And people promise everything when they know you're going to say no. Anyway, I don't care, I've got to simply get out of it as soon as possible. I'll talk to Naani about it. It hasn't even been a year, are you allowed to divorce before a year is up? We don't have to divorce straight away, we can do a separation, I could pay him. Pay him off! I could keep the house and buy him out. Really, if he's having an affair with Georgia, he'll be better off anyway. He'll be free and he can do what he likes. I just can't stand it anymore.

Chapter 2

Kavya took the train into London the next day on a mission.

She didn't want to drive because it would have meant asking for the keys to his precious car. On the train to steady her nerves she had a couple of V+T's. She phoned the school secretary Mrs Flinders to ask if there had been any calls or admin and there was, so she said she'd be in tomorrow. She apologised for not having come back after lunch yesterday, but she'd had a meeting to go to. And today, she was out of town and reception was sketchy, so she'd look at emails tomorrow at work.

Old Flinders had been at ISEE (International School for Excellence in English) for years and ran the place beautifully. They were getting huge numbers from China and Brazil now and would have to hire more ESOL teachers. Kavya sipped her drink as she conscientiously made a list of points to discuss at the next staff meeting. You don't have to make apologies, she thought. You work there but you're not an employee. You *own* the damn place! It wasn't entirely true. She owned only a third of the school, the other two shareholders (retired ESOL teachers) were the partners of her parents who had helped set it up. Come to that, technically she didn't even own a third. Lalita did.

When the train pulled into Euston, Kavya grimaced at the teeming concourse. Too many people! And the noise! Dear God, the unrelenting roar! Germs everywhere. Filth! Terrorist bombers, pickpockets, crazy people running amok all seemed imminent. This is London said the digital information flip boards overhead, but the words seemed like a warning not a welcome. It was strange how quickly you got used to living in Quaintsville on the Sea.

She took the Northern Line to Hampstead. When she was a teenager and they lived in Camden Town, she would often take a bus to Hampstead to visit her grandmother. Her parents were always busy with the English School they were building at the seaside and in those days, she had felt jealous of it because it took up all their time. Naani was the one she ran to; she admired her the most in the world, way above her own parents. Since she had moved out of London, Kavya had a feeling that she must consolidate her relationship with her grandmother. For practical as well as sentimental reasons.

Lalita Sharma CBE still lived on the top floor of a row of elegant red brick mansion flats built in the eighteenth century. When she became a widow, she was a young woman of 38 and a wealthy one but Lalita was not one to sit on her hands. She discovered within her a profound and passionate need to be of service, or as the Indians called it, *seva*. This philanthropic fervour turned her into a formidable champion of Asian Women's rights. She turned heads. Her poise, her beauty, her compassion, her uncompromising determination spoke loudly, and people listened.

She campaigned tirelessly to raise funds to set up the first Asian Women's Refuge in London. She personally initiated links with the police, politicians, and social services to recognise the double trap cultural and social that Asian women were in and established an organisation called Upna Ghar (Our House). It offered everything from phone advice to counselling to police witness protection, temporary refuge as well as Legal services, rehousing and continuing support in the form of stipends and assistance grants. Lalita Sharma had no truck with tokenism, she demanded the plight of Asian women be addressed fully.

When she was a teenager, Kavya would often encounter a haunted looking timid Asian woman in the Hampstead flat because in those days when an Asian woman had to leave an abusive home it was some time before she could move into a Women's Refuge. Lalita insisted the stranger stay in her spare room, eat with them, talk with them without fear and Kavya had always been impressed by how Lalita's generosity inspired courage in the broken of spirit.

In the forty years that Lalita Sharma had been involved with her causes she improved the lives of countless women and accolades a plenty had come her way. Asian Woman of the Year, Asian Medal of Excellence, the OBE and then the CBE. What Lalita treasured most of all though were the thousands of letters and cards she had received over the years from women who had survived and made good lives because of Upna Ghar.

Her political activism may have been a thing of the past but now a sprightly 82-year-old, Lalita Sharma still had an active social life with her legion of friends, ladies of a certain age who got together for drinks, Bridge, musical evenings, theatre outings.

Kavya rang the bell and Lalita buzzed her up. The lift was old fashioned and clanky but as it shot up Kavya thought back to her teenage years.

"Well, this is a surprise!" said Lalita meeting her at the door.

She was a tall slim woman dressed in an elegant silk sari and despite her years could carry off the ornate gold earrings, necklaces and rings that were her trademark. She smelled heavenly; she always had. A mixture of powder and perfume. Kavya had thought of it as 'the scent of heroism' because Lalita was truly her hero.

"Hi Naani," she said and walked in.

The gleaming mahogany sideboard in the hall, the antique Persian rugs, the large front room with the floor to ceiling windows and velvet drapes. Sunlight streamed into the room. There were three comfortable cloth covered couches with assorted silk and velvet cushions. All the art on the walls was Indian. Naani's flat had remained unchanged through the years. Quality never went out of style.

A high-backed chair stood by the fireplace, and this was Lalita's. They sat down in their respective places as they always had, and Lalita clasped her hands together looking Kavya up and down. When she was a teenager, she had to show her grandmother her nails so she could approve of them. Lalita had made her go and scrub them on more than one occasion.

"Cuckoo you've got fat since I last saw you. Why is this?"

It was like a knife in her back and Kavya immediately felt despondent. Failing in Naani's eyes was a hundredfold worse than a normal fail.

"No idea. I've joined the gym and I've gone on a diet. 16:8. The Michael Moseley one. No carbs," she said breathlessly.

"I see. Well, that's a good idea. So how is everything else going?"

Kavya let out a long sigh. "You know."

"I thought you would come with the rest yesterday, why didn't you?"

"So, they came," said Kavya grumpily.

Lalita looked at her granddaughter.

"What's that supposed to mean?"

"I told them I didn't want Milan to come but they cooked it up between them and –"

"What is wrong with Johnny bringing my greatgrand to meet me? He can come every day as far as I'm concerned. And it's nice for Marymary to come to London, the poor thing has no life."

"But you're busy," insisted Kavya, then sighed. "Anyway, no one—they never listen to anything that I want."

"And what is that?"

"Naani, I'm feeling agitated today. I have a lot on my mind. I wouldn't mind a drink to just calm down a bit."

"But you're on a diet."

"Yes, but if you have one drink it can make you less hungry, like cigarettes."

"Don't be ridiculous. Alcohol is empty calories."

Kavya closed her eyes and sat back on the couch. Why do I have to beg her for a small drink? Why do I have to...?

"Are you crying?" said Lalita sitting upright in her chair, frowning.

The Sharma women did not cry. The Sharma women, both Lalita and her daughter Mandakini had always known where they were going. Crying was for silly girls who depended on their looks and male approval. The Sharma women didn't need anyone to tell them they were Queens. They were Saraswati, they were Durga, they were Shakti, the powerful Goddesses of Hinduism!

"No," said Kavya and wiped a tear out the corner of her eye.

"What's the matter with you?"

"Sometimes I feel. What's the point if no one---"

Lalita's voice softened.

"Are you feeling blue Cuckoo? These feelings pass. You just must ride them out."

"I know but---"

"Listen to me carefully. I love you very much. I know everything you went through; it was a lot for anyone. I lost my only daughter, but you lost both of your parents. And then you became a widow at too young an age. I've always felt for you, because I was almost the same age as you when your grandfather passed. I know these things go deep but they must be got through. Otherwise, you end up becoming one of those people who are just a bundle of troubles. The therapy helped didn't it darling?"

Kavya nodded. Lalita had paid for many expensive therapists for a long time. And there had been Marymary to look after the baby and to cook comforting food. She knew she was much better off than most people and she had no right to complain or feel blue.

"And now you have a new life, a wonderful husband---"

Kavya snorted.

"I don't get why you're such a fan?" she said crossly.

Lalita smiled. "Because he loves my granddaughter with all his heart and would lay down his life for her, perhaps?"

"It's not the same as it was with Kishore."

Lalita made an impatient sound.

"Oh, the Mukherjees. All they cared about was money and how things look. Johnny is a far better human being than Kishore or his risible family ever were."

"How can you say that? You've never said that. He was from a good family! Kishore was…perfect."

"For goodness sake! I don't wish to malign the dead, but he was far from perfect."

"None of you trusted my judgement."

"No, we did not. But no one stopped you marrying him, did they? Your parents had your interest at heart when they put the properties in my name. He would have gambled away your entire inheritance! They didn't deprive you of anything."

"The Wills said I had to get *your* signature on everything! Who does that? Humiliating!"

"Those Wills were made in a rush. How were they to know that two years after you got married, they'd be dead? They would have changed them eventually and put everything in your name.

"As if I was a child!"

"So, this is what you've come for is it? You want me to rescind the Trust order on the School and Moghul house? What's the hurry? Everything of mine will be yours anyway, eventually."

"No, no of course not. No, I...But it's different now, I don't live in London and you're busy and I can't see you all the time."

"That has nothing to do with it. You just want your way. It's capriciousness. You're a forty-year-old woman. A mother. I shouldn't have to sugar coat things for you. Sometimes I think you're still that teenager mooning about, jealous of me giving my attention to a woman who needed me."

"I am 39!" shouted Kavya.

Chapter 3

Lalita smiled indulgently.

"Alright, alright. And what a beauty at that. You got your legs from your mother you know? *Her* legs were like Jane Russell's."

"Who?"

"Mandakini always refused to wear skirts above the calf, she insisted on those damn dreary academic tweeds. Used to drive me mad. Alright you got your First from Oxford, but you don't have to dress that way."

"And those horrible Help the Aged cardigans!" said Kavya laughing. "I threw one in the bin once and she went and fished it out. It was full of holes!"

"You get your sense of style from me darling. We are classic," said Lalita.

"Hmm," said Kavya, shaking her long black hair and catching a glimpse of herself in the mirror. Weight or no weight, she still had it. People were always amazed that she was 3 years older than John.

The landline rang.

Lalita looked at the Caller ID, and said, 'oh Lord' and looked at the phone sternly. It went to voicemail.

"Screening? How very rude!" said Kavya with a chuckle.

"It's your fault. Why ever did you give that woman my number? She's always phoning to pass on some dreary gossip."

"Which woman is this?"

"Your local village dragon."

"Ah," said Kavya. "Shanta Acharya. She's terribly impressed with your CBE. And where you live. An original 18th Century mansion block. *Aiii Hai.* I think she's hoping for an invitation. To further her academic architectural knowledge, you understand."

Kavya beamed with delight at her grandmother's composure. Lalita would never lower herself to say anything bad about those she considered beneath her, even when she couldn't stand them. She could imagine the hoops Lalita would go through to be polite and at the same time to deter; but there was no deterring people like Shanta Acharya. When she had news, she was faster than Usain Bolt. And unfortunately, she had a habit of picking up on things...

"Kishore was a perfectly pleasant boy," said Lalita returning to familiar territory. "But he didn't have any character. Like so many Indian boys of his class he had been spoiled to weakness all his life, by his mother, his women folk, by Marymary…"

"She was only 12 when she went to work for the Mukherjees! He would have been 5."

"Yes well, these poor girls who get taken into wealthy houses, they become attached to the babies. These poor young children are made to look after someone else's children. India is still in the 19th century in some quarters."

"Well, I liked living with Kishore. We had fun."

"You just liked the lifestyle, the Marylebone life, the flat given as a wedding present."

"I'm not that shallow!"

"And when he died, they took the flat back didn't they, so what kind of people were they?"

"No but there were reasons."

"Reasons for what?"

"I don't remember," said Kavya tilting her head. "Is that a new acquisition? I don't understand art. The point of it, I mean. This kind. Abstract stuff. I need someone to explain it to me, but then--."

"You don't have to understand it. You just have to look at it. Don't be such a deliberate philistine, it doesn't mean you're cool!"

Kavya turned her head this way and that. It was still a square with circles in it.

"Anyway, now listen I want to talk seriously to you about Marymary."

"I can't have a serious talk without a drink," said Kavya. "Especially when I'm being vilified!"

Lalita laughed.

"I know it's March, but shall we allow ourselves a Pimm's?"

"Oh yes please," said Kavya brightening up.

Lalita got up and went out to the kitchen.

“Shall I help?” said Kavya staring at the painting above the fireplace.

It was a Hussein. Priceless probably. Somehow thinking about any of the beautiful artefacts in Lalita’s flat made Kavya feel anxious. One day those artefacts would belong to her because Lalita would be gone. But she didn’t want them! Not one! She wanted Lalita to live forever. She wanted her fortitude, her resilience, her indomitable ability to make everything alright.

Several times she had had a dream where she was in the flat banging things into the wall with nails. Paintings, vases, rugs, couches. Like a crazed creature hammering away. Woke up in a cold sweat thinking if they’re all nailed in, then they can't be mine, which means she can't die.

“I need you to carry,” called Lalita and Kavya leapt to her feet.

She put the tray with the jug of Pimm’s on the table and sat down because she knew Lalita liked to be the hostess, it was a ritual they had always followed. Lalita poured out two glasses. She cut the strawberries and cucumber and popped them in with a jaunty red striped straw and sprig of mint.

“There we are,” she said handing one to Kavya. “Now I’ll come straight to the point. Marymary. As you know I’ve been paying her salary, and very happy to do it, it was needed for you and for Milan.”

"Thank you Naani," said Kavya bowing her head.

Was it a hint? She should really be paying for Marymary herself, but the money wasn't important; she felt connected to Lalita this way. She drew a healthy salary from ISEE which just went into the bank and her weekly expenses were paid for by dividends received from investments.

"Naani. Did you think John looked different yesterday?"

Lalita ignored the question and carried on.

"But the problem is the visa. I had it renewed for 5 years after Kishore's demise, with the option to extend but the Home Office won't do it. All part of the hostile environment for immigrants. So, at the end of this year, we shall have to decide whether to fight it or let her go. Marymary has said she will abide by whatever is decided. I think perhaps also she would *like* to return to India to be with her family. She hasn't been back since she came to you, too afraid they wouldn't let her back in to the UK. Six years after all. And perhaps, you might –it might be better, good for you I mean to get a bit more hands on with Milan—Johnny is so good with him..."

Kavya sipped her drink. It was too sugary, but she didn't want to be rude and ask for something else.

"Can I have another one please?" said Kavya and got up to pour herself another.

"Well alright but. Have you thought about it then?"

Kavya stuck out her bottom lip and nodded. "Yes, I knew it was coming. But what I don't understand is why you think John is such a hero. You don't really know him. I mean, he's a random man I met on the beach!" And then she added, appealing to Lalita's latent racism: A *gora!*

Because, Kavya suspected, to Lalita who would never admit it, an uneducated white working-class man who had grown up in a children's home, was close to an Untouchable, yet she operated a double standard when it came to working class Asians whom she revered and was determined to lift up.

"I like to think I'm a good judge of character," said Lalita. "Won't you miss Marymary if she has to go back? I know Milan will."

"Of course, I'll miss her. But what can I do? Everything I've ever loved has been taken away from me."

Lalita looked at her granddaughter.

"What?"

"You've always been spoiled. But I never took you to be so self-absorbed and full of self-pity that you couldn't see the lives of other people. You don't stop for a minute to imagine how *she* feels? Your mother did not raise you that way, and neither did I."

"But I've never known where I'm going. I've never amounted to anything. How could I compete with you and mummy? I feel worthless."

"But you are not worthless. You are made of good stuff. You have a lot to offer."

"I just—I wanted to talk to you today about. I want to see a solicitor."

"For what?"

"I just want to know my position regarding my net worth. I know you think the sun shines out of his backside but I want to make sure that---"

"What on earth is *wrong* with you? And where are you going?"

"I just want to top up my—"

"You've already had two. That's quite enough. Now sit down and explain to me what is going on in your mind."

Reluctantly Kavya sat down. The sentence 'self-absorbed and full of self-pity' kept stinging.

"I don't want to be married to him anymore!"

"But why ever not? He cares so much for you."

"Well, we don't sleep together!"

Lalita shrugged. "That's temporary. You can sort that out."

"You don't understand. I'm just not happy."

Lalita nodded. "No, you're not. You never have been."

"Yes, I have. When I was travelling. When I was married to Kishore…"

"No. It's never been enough. You've always been discontented. You've had all the advantages a person could have but you've never been truly happy. The tragedies that came into your life didn't break you because you don't really care about things very deeply. You don't appreciate them."

Kavya looked up.

"I was devastated when mummy and dad died. When Kishore died. How can you say----"

"Yes, you were and who wouldn't be? And I was so relieved when you met John. I was. Because I've always known you can't be alone, you need people around you. And people have always wanted to be, Cuckoo. Always. You attract people, it's a great skill you have. People want to love you, care for you. Even your son knows how to be careful about getting your approval. And yet..."

Kavya stared at her grandmother, her eyes blurred with tears. She couldn't speak.

"And yet. You're so easily bored."

Lalita got up and came to sit down next to Kavya. She put her arm around her and hugged her tight.

"I love you very much. There is no one in the world I love more. That's why I'm telling you these things."

Kavya laid her head on Lalita's shoulder.

"Yes?" said Lalita.

"Sorry."

"No, don't be sorry. Just *try* a bit more with John. He really is worth it. I know you can be happy together if you allow it."

"Me allow it?" Kavya stood up.

"Yes, my dear. Let him in. Be kind. Compromise a little."

Kavya walked to the fireplace. She didn't dare take another drink. She turned around and looked across the room at Lalita.

"You don't know what he's been doing. You've got this idea about him but believe me looks can deceive. You think he's so good, so virtuous and all the time..."

"Yes," said Lalita.

"All the time, he's been. He's been. Unfaithful to me."

"No, he hasn't."

"Yes, he has! With the cleaner of all people!"

"The…now Kavya, really. You've turned into one of those old busy bodies. Are you listening to village gossip now? Are you that bored with your life? Stop all this nonsense and get yourself in hand."

"Alright, well," Kavya looked at her watch. "I've got to go anyway. I want to avoid the rush hour."

"Don't be angry," said Lalita putting her hand on Kavya's face. "If I don't tell you the truth, who will?"

When Kavya got outside the building she was shaking. If Naani was against her, she couldn't do anything. If only she would be on her side.

Chapter 4

She went to a bar near the station and ordered a whiskey to get the sweet taste out of her mouth. The barman put a bowl of pistachios next to her drink. How Hampstead, she thought.

"No thanks. I'm on a diet."

"LCHF?" said the barman, a skinny rake.

"That's the one. You're allowed alcohol but you can make it up by subtracting the calories in the food."

"But also," said the barman. "Not everyone puts on calories if they drink. Some people drink like fishes and never put on a pound."

That's true, thought Kavya. There were people she knew who drank and were as thin as the barman. But, just have the one because later tonight you're bound to have three or four to get to sleep so you don't want to mess up the diet. What did I have today? Just coffee. And I'll skip lunch and for dinner I'll have a plate of –Her phone pinged. It was a text from J.

If you're on the 3.50 from Euston, I can pick you up at LC station. Gets in at 5.15 x

She texted back.

Cool, thanks x

His upholstery workshop was close to Lower Common Station, and they would often meet there when she was walking back from the School and walk or drive home together. From the station it was a 20-minute walk into Mamble Wafre. Kavya missed the 3.50 from Euston and sat on a bench on the platform swinging her legs till the 4.10 came. I should text him, she thought.

When the train came, she got herself a window seat with a table. She sat back in the seat and closed her eyes. She fell asleep, her face against the window and woke up self-consciously looking around because she knew she had been snoring. The carriage was empty, the sun was falling on her face, so she closed her eyes again. It was pleasant to be in a moving train, the rocking motion. She wanted to think about Georgia.

Where did I hear the gossip about Georgia and John? I can't remember. But it's probably got around by now. Everyone knows everyone in that place. What about the solicitor? Naani wouldn't even consider it. The thing is, if I divorce him and she doesn't like it, she won't let me have the School or Moghul House. And what else might she put a stop to? Marymary's wages? No, she wouldn't deprive Milan. But. No, I *have* to get her blessing for a divorce.

I just want to find out what my financial position is now. Alright, the world is full of solicitors, I'll go into Ramsgate or anywhere, just look one up on Google. The thing about Naani is, she thinks she's very cosmopolitan, but she doesn't know people like Georgia and John. Anyway, what can I do about it? Maybe I can just wait it out? Something will probably happen, one of them will make a slip up and then I'll tell Naani *see*, I told you, but you didn't believe me.

Lower Common station was deserted when she got off the train at 5.35. The sky was lavender and tiny clouds were drifting by. This part of Kent was famous for its sunsets and people would often stop their cars and watch them. Something in the air reminded her of being a teenager when no one was home, mum and dad were here, and she would go on the swing in the garden in Camden Town. I felt happy when I was alone, she thought. Naani's wrong that I need people; it's the exact opposite. I didn't even mind mummy and dad being busy all the time, I loved having the house to myself, sitting on the swing with one foot on the grass. I was probably the happiest I've ever been.

When she came out of the station John was waiting for her in the car. He had his shades on and he was looking at the radio, turning the dial. He looks so handsome, she thought. The golden light on his shoulder. His skin bronzed. A stillness to him. I always had the feeling if I was close to him nothing bad could ever happen again. There was something great and solid about him, right here, waiting for her.

"Sorry," she said hurrying towards the car. "My battery died."

He shrugged good naturedly and she got in.

"How's the old bag?"

Kavya giggled. "Same. Boring on how much she enjoyed seeing you yesterday."

"I've got a surprise for you at home."

"What is it?"

John laughed. "You know the couch---I told you this morning. I made it on commission for Darlings of Chelsea, then they cancelled it. Devaani said she'd put it in the Mowgli window and this guy saw it and loved it."

"Yeah yeah, and he's rolling in it. But you charged him the same as you'd quoted Darlings. Honest John! You've lost on the deal!"

"I didn't want to put a premium on it. I'm glad he can give it a good home."

"Does it stink? I bet it stinks of curry. And not even real curry. English people curry sauce. That's all Mowgli's is. An Indian restaurant catering to white people. Mowgli's for God's sake. It's *so* BarleyBarton-on Sea. And as for that horror."

John started laughing.

"Poor woman, you've always had it in for her."

"*Is* she a woman?" said Kavya eyebrow arched. "Sure she's not a tranny? Devaani, it's a made-up name. It means 'wild and free' in Hindi. She'd like to be seen as wild. Shame she's over 500 years old."

"I think you'll find she's all woman," laughed John. "And she's not that old."

"Ugh."

"Anyway, I took it out of the window of Mowgli's. And I gave it a clean. And it's in our living room. The guys gonna come and pick it up tomorrow. Your last chance to sit on it. I know how much you love it."

"Oh, ha ha."

When they got home Kavya got out and started stomping towards the house. The door opened and Georgia came out.

"Oh," said Kavya.

"Hiya," said Georgia.

She was dressed in tight jeans and a smock-y low cut embroidered white gypsy blouse, no bra, huge jiggling tits, big silver hoops and her hair was a spectacular nest of auburn ringlets. Bloody Hell thought Kavya. She even looks like a porn star. It was the kind of outfit that could be torn off at a moment's notice.

"I love your outfit, George."

"Cheers yeah? I'm going out, so I got changed. Hope that's ok? I did the oven today and I've kept the sheets separate from the towels. I'll do the bathroom cabinets next week yeah?"

"Yeah, no problem. Where are you off to?"

Georgia smiled. "Just to a friend's house."

"Hello babes, you look gorgeous. Lucky bloke," said John walking past both and going inside the house.

"See you tomorrow," said Georgia. "Doesn't need too much now. Just mowing and a bit of weeding."

She came twice a week, one day for the house and the other for the garden.

"Yeah, see you mate," said Kavya watching Georgia walk down the path and turn left. She watched her disappearing behind the wall of their garden and then she went inside.

John was in the kitchen looking at his iPad.

"Fancy going to Paris?"

"What? Why?"

"It's romantic. Lalita said there's some good deals on Eurostar. We could go for a couple of days this week."

"I've too much on at the school. We're getting a new curriculum and muggins must go through it. Anyway, I've *been* kissed in the rain in Paris. It's no great shakes."

"Oh," said John.

"It's just a saying! I didn't mean..anyway, I can't go."

"Another time then," he said and went out to the garden leaving Kavya alone in the kitchen.

It feels so empty, she thought. No noise, quiet as the grave.

"Where's Milan?" she said to no one in particular and walked out into the lounge.

She saw the monstrosity immediately. A three-seater low back couch covered with a thick orange brocade material. It was the kind of thing that people who wanted to make a 'statement' bought. People who didn't have any taste but wanted guests to think they were interesting. She went upstairs to the bedroom. From the window she saw John bending down to check the leaves on the rosebush. Something had made them all go yellow.

When we first got together, he couldn't wait to go to bed. We took every opportunity of the empty house and even once when Marymary and Milan were coming down the road, we did it against the wall, giggling. He was still finishing up when Marymary put her key in the door. We never do that now, she thought. He'd rather smell the roses.

Chapter 5

It was an hour before dinnertime and Kavya thought she could persuade Marymary to have an aperitif with her while they discussed the visa situation. She went downstairs into the lounge and to the cocktail cabinet. Now, she thought looking at the array of bottles. What am I in the mood for?

"Hello," said Marymary behind her and Kavya spun around and smiled.

"Hello darling, are you ok?"

She was so dainty, like a bird and always so perfectly turned out. She was 51 but she looked ageless in a way; her skin was like a baby, she wore no makeup, and her hair was a startling white, cut short with no style. Her accent was IndianIndian. She wore plain perfectly ironed clothes in different shades of beige. She was like a doddery old lady and an inquisitive child at the same time.

"It's rather wonderful, isn't it? Very expensive looking. All that golden velvet. Johnny is very clever."

"Marymary, let's have a little drink before dinner. I know it's not Sunday. An *aperitivo*. As the Italians call it."

Sunday was when Marymary allowed herself a little tipple. Usually a sherry at 6pm.

"Oooo," said Marymary, eyes bright. "Yes let's!"

Kavya plucked a bottle of gin from the row of bottles. She made two gin and tonics and then realised they were large ones, so she made another one for Marymary with less gin. One time she had made her a normal size drink and Marymary had fallen sideways in the chair and gone to sleep. Giggling, she and John had put her to bed and not spoken about it knowing how mortified she would be. Now Kavya took the drinks over and sat down next to her. They both looked at the new orange brocade covered couch in the middle of the room as if it was television.

Marymary sipped her drink tentatively.

"The tonic has qui-*nine* in it," said Kavya pronouncing it the Indian way. "It's a digestif. Gin is all the rage now you know?"

"The taste is ni--ice," said Marymary unsure.

"So listen, the visa thing. Tell me honestly, do you want to go home? But what would we do without you?"

"Well…Lalitamams said it might be trouble to renew---"

Kavya waved her hand dismissively.

"No, no it can all be arranged. Naani knows how to pull strings. The thing is Marymary do you want to stay with us? I know you miss your family in Goa. Maybe we can find a way to—"

"Oh no," said Marymary. "I don't miss them at all. My family is here. Everyone I care about lives here."

Kavya's eyes lit up.

"Awww, thank you. We care about you too. You are part of this family."

Marymary went all shy and looked at her little bird feet. She wasn't usually so open about her feelings, and it made Kavya feel good. She leaned back nursing her drink.

“Let me ask you a question.”

“Yes?”

“What do you honestly think about Georgia?”

“Well, it’s not for me to say….”

“But say. Say!” said Kavya waving her fingers.

Marymary put down her barely sipped G n T and composed herself.

“I have no issue with her work. I write down a list of tasks and she does them adequately. But I don't trust her. And I don't approve of Milan mixing with her.”

“Milan? With Georgia?”

“Oh, don't you know? She has a lock up in Mamble Wafre and she stores in it all manner of junk that she sells at car boot sales at the weekends. He goes and sorts through the things with her.”

“What?”

“Yes, he says it’s fun.”

“Where is the lock up?”

“Just ten minutes down the road, near the bakery. There are four garages there. She rents one.”

Kavya frowned.

“I suppose it’s safe enough for Milan to be there. The baker knows him..”

"Yes, it is not a question of safety."

"Hmm, and so?"

"It's a question of influence."

Kavya finished her drink and looked at Marymary expectantly.

"Is she a bad seed?"

"Well, I don't say that."

"Well, what then?"

"Something unsavoury there."

"Thief?"

"Oh no. No, no. Very honest."

"Oh," said Kavya deflated. "Then?"

"She is quite cheeky sometimes. Says things it is not her place to say. I don't mean place, I mean---"

Kavya was aware of how many conversations she had had with Naani and Marymary, and even with Shanta, that she would never, *could never*, have with English people. They would be *outraged.* Indian people were brazenly upfront about class and caste in ways that no English person would dare to be. John was different, he'd got used to it.

"Go on."

"It's more a question of…she sometimes will say something that I think is altogether too pessimistic. Misanthropic. I don't think this is a good influence on Milan."

Kavya got up and took the other drink and came back to sit down.

"Did you ban Milan from going to the lock up?"

"Oh no. I wouldn't go against Johnny's advice."

"He defends her?"

"Well, yes. He's very kind and democratic. He doesn't judge people and he thinks it's important Milan meet all kinds of people and treat them with respect. I admire that. Maybe I'm too mired in my prejudiced Indian ways."

Before Kavya could say anything, John walked in.

Chapter 6

"Spag Bol tonight. I've made it with turkey mince which apparently has less fat. And you don't have to have any parmesan if you—"

"I'm not having dinner. I told you, I'm on a diet."

"But Kavs, you have to eat *something.*"

"We'll see," she said and sipped her drink.

Marymary turned to look at John. She saw them exchange glances. She couldn't be bothered to find out why. No one spoke. An uncomfortable silence fell into the room. John was still standing there. He seemed to be waiting for something. She couldn't ask him to join them for an aperitivo because John didn't drink.

He had seen a lot of the workers in the children's home get drunk out of their minds and have fights and he had vivid memories of the smell of alcohol on their breath. It had frightened him, the unpredictability. He had fallen into a mis judged relationship with a mentally challenged violent girl and married her. Later, she was diagnosed with schizophrenia. He used to go to parties and bite the rim off pint glasses to amuse people. Then after several years that were now a blur, everything went sour, they got divorced and he ended up having to section his ex-wife for her own safety, as she had no one else. In a sense, it was the best thing to have happened to him.

He moved away and got himself an apprenticeship with an upholsterer and when he qualified, he came to BarleyBarton-on-Sea and set up a small business in Lower Common Village. And after some time, he made enough money to buy a small flat but his business stayed small and his flat was in a condemned building. When they met, Kavya had taken him in hand, told him he couldn't live like that, he deserved better. They had pooled their resources and set up home together, but John still had his old workshop with the faulty taps and the cracks in the wall. The thing with John was, he didn't have any ambition thought Kavya. He was a happy go lucky, under educated, loving type of person who would never make much of his life. But perhaps ambition was overrated? She herself had none of it, despite being a Sharma woman.

"Kavs," he said at last. "Will you try it out?"

"Yes," said Marymary smiling. "You must."

"I know it's not your style… but it's comfortable. You'll be the first to sit in it."

Kavya got up, lifted her glass at them set it down on the small table and walked towards the couch exaggerating her steps, pretending to be a tiger in slow motion creeping up on prey.

"I'm going in!" she hissed, and they both laughed.

She lowered herself and sat down in the middle. And then, she bounced a little and somehow the thing gave way underneath, and she shot down towards the hand rest. She tried to get up both arms flailing, but she couldn't get out. She was trapped.

"Hai hai!" cried Marymary. John rushed forward to help her.

"The foots collapsed. Wait, I'll -."

He pulled her out and she stood up, her knees jiggling.

"I'm so sorry. I must have damaged the foot when I carried it in—I'm so sorry babes. Are you ok, let me--"

She hated John now.

"I'm fine. I don't need anything."

"It's my fault, I---"

"I just want to go and look at something on the computer. Good night, all."

"But wait Kavs. What about dinner?"

She stalked off to the computer room and locked the door. She sat down on the swivel chair and winced. The side of her thigh was sore, but it was the humiliation that hurt more. She opened the drawer and took out the Smirnoff bottle. Her hand was shaking as she poured herself a drink. There was no mixer, but she didn't want any.

This is the end she thought. I'm only a little bit overweight but –when you've put on a few pounds you're sensitive about something like that. That bloody couch. He *forced* me to sit in it. I've hated it ever since he made it. It's gaudy and vulgar. And cheap! Screw him. That's it now. I can't stand him. It's finished between us. I can't bear to look at him

There was a knock on the door.

“Kavs..”

“Go away. I’m busy.”

“Yes, but can you let me in. Please.”

“John, I want to be alone. Respect that.”

“I know. Just five minutes. “

She sighed and put the glass in the drawer and closed it, got up and unlocked the door.

“I wanted to apologise. It was the leg, I dislodged it when I was carrying it in. I’m so sorry Kavs. Are you hurt baby?”

“John, thanks but it’s no big deal. Didn't even hurt. And I really do have to do this boring research about the curriculum because they’re coming to inspect the school.”

“Could I just. Sit in here with you for a while then?” he said.

“But—that’s weird. There’s hardly room to swing a cat as it is.”

“But I want to talk to you Kavs.”

She sighed and walked back to the desk and went around to sit on the chair. He stood on the other side of the desk. She was glad of the distance between them. It would deter any hugs. He had a concerned look on his face.

“I’m worried about you Kavs. I know you went to the quack but.”

"Yes. I went to see Dr Ali like you told me to. He said I should—just drink black coffee for breakfast and lose—why'd you keep going on about it?"

"I'm worried about you."

"I'm fine. I'm just on this *diet.* And I'm a bit stressed with the inspection. What's the problem?"

"You never eat anything. At all. And. Well, I was talking to Lalita, and she said—that you were always. That you lose interest in things. You got bored easily as a kid. And I started thinking, maybe she's bored with me."

"For God's sake! Anyway, that's not even true. Where's she got that idea from?"

"Maybe we could. Go out a bit more. Drive down to London more often if you want. And Paris? I mean we could talk about it."

Yeah, she was thinking but you won't do anything will you? It's all on me. You don't ever want to have sex, you'd rather do anything but. Because why am I like this? Because *you're* here, *you're* the problem. Watching me all the time.

"Yeah, it's a good idea. But talk tomorrow."

"Because whatever it is. We can work it out. We can work everything out."

"Yes, of course we can. We're adults for God's sake! But there's nothing."

"I love you babes."

He came around the desk and put his arms around her shoulders and kissed her forehead.

"I know John, enough with the PDA" she said wriggling free. "I'm just in a – there's nothing to sweat about. Go to bed I'll be up as soon as I've done this. Five mins max."

Chapter 7

She woke up the next day feeling a peculiar kind of nausea as though her head had become partially disconnected from her neck in the night. When she pushed back the duvet and got on her feet, her knees began to tremble to such an extent that she sat down again with a thud. In the recess of her belly there was a churning motion. I don't feel well. Sitting still for some moments she thought, this isn't a normal hangover. In any case I didn't drink that much yesterday. I was tired, I didn't need to. Nope, this is something else. Something serious.

She got to the bathroom and sat down on the loo trying to remember what she had eaten yesterday. But then, food poisoning usually took place within 30mins of eating so it couldn't be that. It wasn't that. Mustn't fall asleep. She hauled herself up and holding the wall, carefully stepped into the shower. Gingerly she clasped the shower head and saw her hand shaking uncontrollably; the water was going everywhere, and it discombobulated her so much that as she tried to turn it toward her body, it slipped from her hand and landed smack on her foot.

"Ow!" she cried and turned off the water.

Limping, she got out of the shower and wrapped herself in a big towel. She had a sudden feeling of fear. What if I can't dress myself? She breathed slowly and pulled the towel around her for comfort, feeling the throbbing pain in her foot. It could be her metatarsal which would put her out of action for 6-8 weeks. Now how on earth did she know that?

The year was 2002. She was in a cool dark narrow bar in a side street in Granada nursing a café con leche. She was 22 years old. The Sun newspaper was on the bar. The headline said: Beck us Pray. A picture of the footballer David Beckham's injured metatarsal on the front page, urging the British public to heal it by touching. An English tourist must have left it there.

On the tv above the bar there was an English report on the life of David Beckham for who's metatarsal the world was praying. 6-8 weeks was too long! The old men in the bar looked up, none of them could speak English. The football commentator was in his element:

*"The Goldstone Ground in Brighton, a League Cup second round first leg, 16,649 fans and a 17-year-old boy by the name of David Beckham taking the first steps in a career that would before long make him one of the most famous people on the planet. It was September 1992. He was wearing number 14 on his back that night. Legend has it the teenager was initially greeted with 'Who the f***ing hell are you?' chants from the Brighton fans, although they were soon drowned out by the jubilation of an equaliser... What a year, September 1992."*

In September 1992 from Delhi had come a tornado into Kavya's dull privileged private school life. Dinny was the new girl come to London for a tip top British Education, installed for the next 5 years in the house of a prim Mrs Chandresheker in Kentish Town. They had become best friends forever. They were 12 years old.

I'm going to marry a famous man called David Beckham, Dinny confided. Who? said Kavya. It's in my horoscope silly. My astrologer spelled it out. Never heard of him, said Kavya. He'll be a famous footballer and I'll be his wife, just wait and see. But won't you go back to India and have an arranged marriage, said Kavya and Dinny said *no way jose,* her older sibling would have an arranged marriage, she was going to have a ball until she met a boy called David Beckham.

Beckham was still only on an apprentice contract at the time… Beckham made full United debut when he was chosen to start a League Cup tie against Port Vale in September 1994….

But Dinny was dead by 1993 so she never met or married David Beckham. One day in July Dinny didn't come to School and no one knew why and some weeks later, Kavya couldn't remember how she'd heard, the girl had suffered a brain haemorrhage and died in a hospital bed in Delhi. When had she gone back, what had happened to her? None of it was news in the School and Kavya had kept quiet. Kavya had sat in that dark bar years later and thought of how random life was, how the connections in it were all in your head. They had been best friends forever for a total of seven months.

Back then nine years had passed, and she had but a dim memory of Dinny, and yet today seventeen years after that day of The Sun headline, the information about the metatarsal had stayed fresh. And Dinny's face was imprinted on her brain forever. Smashed, bloody, whimpering. Back in Spain, in that bar in Granada she had felt good, because the memories of Dinny had faded away. She was relieved to be free of them. The old men ordered a shot of brandy, and it came with a glass of water. They had all started talking in Spanish and waving the newspaper about, laying their gnarled hands on that front page. No one in the bar could tell Kavya wasn't Spanish because some of them in Andalusia were much darker than her. She could blend in, and no one would bother her.

No such luck here, she thought.

She forced her foot to flex back and forth because if she went downstairs with even the hint of a limp it would become the discussion of the day. Carefully and methodically, she got dressed thinking but this isn't a normal hangover. I've had plenty in the past and this isn't one. I must be delirious. I'm going to have a drink to calm me down, although I'm not sure it will help with this. Whatever this is.

The one good thing was that no one was downstairs, and she felt relieved, grateful for small mercies. The trouble was, she knew the bottle in the computer room was empty—infact she must get rid of it today—but how to get another bottle from the lounge? The cocktail cabinet was stocked but what if someone came downstairs and saw her taking out a bottle of Smirnoff? She stood uncertainly at the foot of the stairs looking into the lounge and at the cabinet. She broke out in a sweat thinking what if Marymary or John or even little Milan came down now? She felt afraid and upset.

But I must, she cried to herself. I can't go on like this, she told herself and hurried into the lounge. Inside the cabinet were some glasses and she grabbed one and poured herself a couple of inches. She took a sip and made a face. She had poured herself Gin instead of Vodka. I'm not a gin drinker!

It tasted different when I had a couple with Marymary, I don't know why. Then an idea came to her, and she set the glass down and went across into the kitchen, took out a waterbottle from the dishwasher and went back to the cabinet. Here she carefully filled it up with vodka.

With a sense of satisfaction and glee, she screwed in the sippy top and took a sip. Carrying her waterbottle by the little handle she went into the computer room and switched on the computer. She put the waterbottle down carefully next to the mug of pens. What a good idea! Now at least there wouldn't be any lectures because it was good to drink water. She knew John would soon come knocking, and he did.

He knocked and seeing the door open took his chance and walked in. Kavya was writing something on the pad.

"Hi babes,"

"Oh hii," she said. "Come in, come in. Just… reviewing the situation."

She started laughing uncontrollably and then stopped because she was snorting. She didn't know if John would have seen the film Oliver, and if he had seen it, would he have thought it was a funny song? Before she could stop herself, she started singing, doing the hand movements that Ron Moody as Fagin had done in the film:

"Better settle down and get myself a wife.
And a wife would cook and sew for me,
And come for me, and go for me,

And go for me, and nag at me,
The fingers, she will wag at me.
The money she will take from me.
A misery, she will make for me..."

She stopped in mid leer, both her hands raised.

"Babe," said John. "Were you smoking last night?"

Kavya tutted. He'd ruined it now. She looked at the ashtray next to the computer. It had two butts in it.

"Sometimes I just fancy one. Don't you?" she said.

"Yes, I do," he said.

Oh, don't say 'but I don't give in to the urge' she thought. We know how good you are.

Marymary was peeping in behind Johns shoulder.

"Did I hear singing?"

Kavya brightened.

"In my posh private school Marymary, I mean it was a very exclusive and trendy school you know? We did this musical Oliver, and they swopped the gender roles. Imagine, we were 13 years old! So the girls played..."

"Like they do in India, the Hindus do, in Raam Leela!" said Marymary nodding encouragingly.

"That's *right!*" said Kavya and took a swig of her water bottle.

"Like a pantomime," said John.

She looked at the keyboard. A volcano of fury was whirling up in her chest. No, not like a pantomime at *all* actually. He thinks I'm a joke. Undermining me. Maybe it was weird to suddenly break into a song like that? I don't know why I did it. But what's wrong with being happy? Singing a popular song. I was being spontaneous. She started peering intently at the screen as if it was displaying something vital.

"I'll be in for breakfast, or rather coffee, in a minute. I've just got to print off this thing first."

"That's alright," said Marymary, her hand on John's arm. "Come on Johnny. Milan will be down in a few minutes."

John and Marymary left the room. Kavya sat back in the swivel chair. In the first place she had managed the situation well, because no one even expected a waterbottle to be full of vodka and so no suspicion had been aroused. But the point is, normally that's not really a good thing. To drink in the morning. It's a sign of something quite serious. But the thing is I'm feeling so sick today...

And then she realised she wasn't. The clouds had cleared. The nausea had gone. Her stomach was behaving beautifully. Her legs were stable like a table. I'm on it like a bonnet, she chuckled to herself. She felt clear and calm and relieved. I've bounced back. Like a storm, it had passed, whatever it had been. Now she could start to work on the plan she had made last night.

Chapter 8

Kavya went into the kitchen. It was casual Friday, as they called it. A different or no routine for breakfast. Marymary had gone back upstairs to get ready for her Friday outing and Milan and John were sitting at the table, both their heads bowed looking at something football related. Infact they were subconsciously mirroring each other.

She noticed they both had the same shaped head even though her son had black hair and John's was blonde, they seemed connected in some familial way. John was explaining something, and Milan was nodding intently, his little fingers involuntarily tapping on the table. That's what I do, Kavya thought proudly. He's a chip off the old block. He's got my eyes too and he's long limbed like me.

"Mummy mummy, do you know the offside rule?" said Milan looking up with glee.

"Of course," she said and walked across the kitchen to the counter. She could hear them giggling behind her.

"Eggs babe?" said John. "We just had sunnyside up."

"Really good. What's not to *like*?" said Milan.

"Shut up Kardashian," said Kavya leaning back against the counter with the mug of coffee. "John, I've got an idea."

Milan started stamping his feet playfully. "You mustn't *say* shut up!"

"Milan," said Kavya, "Come here!"

Milan dutifully got out of his chair and trotted up to her nervously. She put her arms around him. The top of his head was at her waist. How long before he was taller than her? Her embrace wasn't tight, and Milan easily wriggled away.

"Mummy! I'm 6," he said and went back to sit at the table. John was smiling indulgently.

"Yes, so you should know better than to keep repeating stupid phrases you've picked up!"

"Not stupid."

"And don't sulk. It's boring!"

"Kavs, please. He's not sulking. Don't shout at him, he just wants---"

"Don't tell me about the psychology of my son! I don't want him to be a spoilt brat! You give in to everything. Kids need boundaries."

"Mate listen, do you want to go up and brush your teeth? We can carry on afterwards. I've got a few things to do first and then we can go out if you want?"

"Sorry Milan," said Kavya. "I didn't mean to shout at you. You know what I'm like."

"It's alright mummy," said Milan with a nod. "See you later. I'm going out with Marymary today."

"Yes, see you later. Off you go."

Milan went upstairs obediently. She looked at John.

"I would never tell you how to raise your son. I'm just trying to be there for him."

"Yeah. Listen so I had an idea."

"Go on."

"Now don't get big headed because you're right all the time".

"Oh this sounds good."

"I was thinking about what you said. Paris is too complicated but why don't we go to Moghul House? For the weekend."

"Really?"

"You love swimming in the sea when it's still too cold for most normals."

"True!"

"And we could have a little break. Do some bonding."

"Some shagging you say?"

"We need to get it ready for the lettings soon anyway so, I know it's a bit early, but we could? It'll be quiet too. All the restaurants will be closed. We can BBQ on the beach."

"Great idea. Maybe we can even do a long weekend?"

"Sure. Go to London on Sunday if we like, Brick Lane, Portobello. We can do what we want."

"I like it," he said smiling.

"The only thing is I've *got* to go into work this morning. The inspection. So, this is my suggestion. You go down in the car. Take Georgia with you—she's coming today for the garden anyway. Let's use her to clean up Moghul instead. She won't mind. You can open up and tell her what needs doing, all that. Then you can go swimming and chill, whatever, you can have a free day and I'll get there for dinnertime and we can have a late—in the moonlight on the beach."

"Ok, but—how will you get there?"

"No problem. I can get a taxi from the school—"

"But I can come and get you—"

"No need! I'll just hop in a taxi from work. Evening drive to Saint Dorothy's at Cliffe along the coast road as the sun goes down. Nice. I'll charge it. There are some perks to being the boss. Well, a third of a boss. What do you think?"

"Not bad."

"Take Georgia with you. I'll text her as well. We need to get the place basic clean after the winter and then once we get bookings, she can do the jujjing up. She won't mind the extra cash."

"No I think it'll be nice for her," said John.

I bet you do, thought Kavya.

"Maybe tell her to bring her car though," said John. "Because then she can be independent. She can go after she's done. I won't have to drive her anywhere,"

Kavya hadn't thought of that. Damn! It was risky. But she couldn't think of a reason to say Georgia shouldn't bring her car. I've got to get rid of John she thought suddenly, and the thought hit her like a lorry. I mean, that sounds awful. Murderous. No, no I mean, I've got to. We've got to be separated. I don't like his influence.

"Talking of Georgia, I didn't know she had a lock up. Is it a good idea to let Milan go through all her junk?"

"He finds it interesting. Aladdin's Cave. She's just trying to make a living Kavs. These car boots are her way of…finding some structure to her life I think."

Oh, boo hoo, thought Kavya.

This is what Naani doesn't understand. If she was here, if she saw what I know, then she'd understand. It's all in the subtleties. And now, to prove it to her, I've got to go through this charade. But I made the plan last night, I had to make it. Now I've got to act. When I went up he was snoring away. And when I got into bed he turned his back to me. What's the point of it all? Once it's done. Once it's done, I'll feel lighter.

"Alright. So I'm off. I'll text Georgia on the way. But sometimes she doesn't look at her phone, just tell her to come! It's 4 – 5 hours work, she'll easily manage it. But you must go as soon as she gets here! And then I'll be there in the evening, and we can—."

"Alright. Ok."

"Expect me around 7pm. I'll bring some chicken and salad stuff, don't worry about all that. You just go and chill. You deserve it, you work hard."

"Thanks babes. I'm looking forward to it. I love that little place. It's romantic."

When she got to the school it was 8.30am. She imagined John and Georgia had set off. A nice long uninterrupted day at the beach, what could be better? She sat in the office forcing herself to read through the dreary procedure information about the Inspection. It happened once a year and was just a formality and the school always passed with flying colours, but the staffers worked hard and took it seriously.

As soon as it was 11am she felt like she needed a drink so she went out and walked along Main Street to the newsagent on the corner. She never went to the newsagent close to the school because it was owned by an Asian man, who had very proudly told her he was the 'first Asian tobacconist in Kent' and then followed her with his eyes as she walked around the shop. The one on the corner was owned by a white couple, something unheard of in London.

She bought a couple of miniatures, Vodka and Tequila, and shoved them in her pocket. It was costly doing that but if she had a bottle in the drawer at work it would draw attention. When she went back into the office, it was fairly deserted as everyone tended to take lunch at the same time. She thought about locking the door before making the phone call, but it was unnecessary. She took a swig from the Vodka miniature and felt calm. Then she punched out the number.

Chapter 9

"Are you busy?" said Kavya looking around in case someone came into the office.

"I'm never busy," said Shanta Acharya. "I have my routines of Reiki Healing, babysitting for my grandchildren and television. Can I take you somewhere?"

Kavya had asked her a few times to drive her a short way and Shanta had jumped at it, assuring her she was always available, day or night. Kavya knew the generous offer was in no small measure connected to the fact that she was the granddaughter of Lalita Sharma CBE, who was the real prize, who Shanta wanted to cultivate as her best friend.

"Do you know Saint Dorothy's at Cliffe? It's a small town along from BarleyBarton. Another seaside resort."

"Yes, yes, I do. It's a charming place."

"Yes."

"And the wonderful thing about that little town is it is distinguished by the historical visit of the Maharajah of Avadh Bihar who came to the small town for his health and the locals were in awe of him because he was friendly with King George V. He loved Saint Dorothy's at Cliffe and stayed there with his entourage and wives. They built a special row of houses just for him you know. In the 19th century, I think as late as 1870. A beautiful line of houses by the shoreline. I think there's about 6 of them. And they put these domes on top to remind him of home, because India then was full of Islamic architecture. They look like onion tops, but they really are a marvellous copy of Moghul architecture. I've always been curious about who lives in those wonderful houses."

"Ahem," said Kavya.

And so she told Shanta about what they always called the Moghul House, the one on the end that her mum and dad had purchased at a steal back in the day when Saint Dorothy's at Cliffe was where they said the *parents* of the people in God's Waiting Room (Eastbourne) lived. Very English, very staid. It was an hour's drive from the more popular-with-families BarleyBarton-on-Sea, and in those days a sort of hideaway.

In later years some shops had sprung up in the town centre, but it was still mostly untouched by DFL's. (Down from London) Not trendy enough. Kavya explained they rented Moghul House out to holiday makers for the summer season who mainly used it as a base to go to other places. No one actively came to Saint Dorothy's at Cliffe for their hols. Not least because there were only a few spots where you could get mobile reception; little Saint Dorothy's at Cliffe hadn't heard of 3G, let alone 4 or 5.

"You see I thought I'd surprise John. He's gone down there to tidy up, a lot to do…and I want to give him a surprise. Turn up with lunch and whatnot. What do you think?"

"How romantic! Yes yes, I would be honoured to drive you there."

"If you're coming from Mamble Wafre it'll take—"

"Oh no bother my pleasure, I can pick you up in say 30mins? And it won't take us long, perhaps another 30. So you'll be there by 1pm. So exciting!"

"Well, that's very kind of you. And please, do have lunch with us. We can fire up the BBQ. I can show you the inside of the house."

"I should love to see the house, but I'll not dampen the romance, I shall drop you and go. Shall I come now?"

Kavya looked at the clock on the wall. 12.05pm.

Boom!

Shanta Acharya turned up in her old Renault all dressed up for her day out. She had put on a silk sari for the occasion and dabbed lipstick and two spots of rouge. She had a short lopsided bob (she may have cut it herself) and the cheap hair dye made it look too black against her sallow skin. She was 73 years old and had very few friends but in her own way she was always self-improving, cutting out articles on diets from magazines purloined from the Dentist's waiting room, and taking out six romantic novels at a time from the library. She was addicted to the Indian melodramas that she watched all day on subscription television.

"So nice of you," Kavya said getting into the passenger seat. "Oh is that ...?"

"White Musk! Body Shop! My daughter gives me the scents she's tired of. Body shop is a very ..a brand 'on trend' I've heard. And look she gave me these lovely stud diamond earrings too! Well, they're not real but not bad, not bad!"

"Sure," said Kavya. "No, they're lovely, they suit you."

Shanta's daughter sounded like a bitch; she was always dumping her kids with her and giving her cheap cast offs and yet Shanta had nothing but praise for her. Shanta was a very accepting person, thought Kavya. She was grateful for crumbs. Suddenly Kavya felt a bit bad about exploiting her but after all, it wasn't *such* a terrible thing to do…

"I'm indebted to you Shanta. It's so kind of you," she said. She knew that it would please Shanta that Kavya, the granddaughter of Lalita Sharma CBE felt in her debt.

"Oh, but it's my pleasure! It's a lovely day and I love to drive. I'm playing cupid in a sense, aren't I? Oh it's very romantic isn't it? There he'll be all on his own toiling away and you shall turn up! A sight for sore eyes. So happy he will be!"

As Shanta Acharya drove and wittered on merrily, Kavya liked her plan less and less. What if they caught them *really* doing something? *In flagrante*…But John wouldn't…not in our house. But you never know. What if her suspicion was right? What if he *was* having an affair with her for real? But he was, she was mostly sure of it…a woman knows, a wife just knows these things…and if it hadn't become something yet, it was going to. These things always did, they gathered momentum…but to see it, graphically. That would be unspeakable! And in any case, it would be enough for Shanta to see that Georgia was even *there*. That's all that was needed. She would be on the phone to Naani as soon as.

As the scenery skimmed by, Kavya put up the window and snuggled down. Images came cascading into her mind. Georgia wearing shorts and tight t shirt sitting next to John outside the house, looking at the sea, knees touching. Georgia bending over the oven cleaning it and John standing in the doorway. Kavya imagined the scene and then imagined herself telling Naani all about it— "..so humiliating…I never suspected for a minute that….and for Shanta to *see* that ….I thought I was being paranoid….it was *awful*, simply ."

If only they *could* catch them shagging, thought Kavya. At it. That would be perfect! Throw open the door of the bedroom and there they'd be…. naked!

I feel sick. To think like this. It's so low. But what can I do? Something is going on and I have to stoop to these measures to prove it, so that I can tell Naani I must have a separation. A divorce. I wouldn't have to go to all this subterfuge if she just believed me. *I'm an adult, I don't have to get her approval!* But..there's the matter of ..Marymary's salary…she pays it…and the properties and. Naani will never approve of a divorce, she'd talk me out of it and make me the unreasonable one. She could even disinherit me. Change her Will. That's the truth. She's my only connection…but the hard fact is I'm relying on her for my future security. She has to see I'm the injured party.

"My dear," said Shanta Acharya looking at Kavya for a second turning her head from the road. "If you don't mind me saying. You're looking tired."

Kavya jumped.

"Yes…couldn't sleep last night."

"Have you been to the doctor? I don't believe in sleeping pills, no, but if there is insomnia."

"Oh yes, I've been to the doctor. Dr Ali. He said..he said try the hot drinks. At night. Usually, John makes me a Horlicks. But he's been. Away."

"Away?"

"I mean, out. He's been out in the nights. Some nights."

"Where does he go in the nights?"

"I'm not sure. Maybe the beach in BarleyBarton. Anyway, by the time he comes home I'm asleep. But I'm not sleeping well at all. You're right."

Shanta Acharya pursed her lips. No doubt remembering that she had told Kavya she had seen Georgia wearing very little at the beach in BarleyBarton late at night, up to no good.

"Well why not have a little sleep? I'll wake you up when we get there."

"Good idea," said Kavya and snuggled down deeper, head against the window and closed her eyes with relief. She didn't want to talk anymore. Sunlight warmed her face as they drove on. Sleepily, she opened her eyes. There was the big wheel in the distance. The circus was in town. They were setting up the candy striped what was it called in English, it was 'shamiayana' in Hindi. They had had one for her grand wedding to Kishore. She noticed there were guests from her wedding milling about. The trapeze artists had set up their equipment. John was bare chested on one side and Georgia was in a tutu on the other side.

Everyone was looking up to see them perform their death-defying act. She couldn't see Kishore anywhere. She was wearing a heavy red brocade sari. Her head was covered. She was crying. The tears plopped and splashed on to her bare feet. And someone said 'What good is it marrying *him*? Why didn't you help me? Why didn't you *help* me?" The voice was so familiar and yet she couldn't…Oh, it was Dinny.

Kavya woke up with a start. They were in Saint Dorothy's at Cliffe town centre.

Atima Srivastava

Chapter 10

Kavya couldn't get out of the car fast enough.

"This shop. Nothing in the house. Forgot to get the .. for lunch."

"Isn't it wonderful?" said Shanta. "There's free parking in Saint Dorothy's at Cliffe. Take your time dear one. Ah the air, the air. Nothing like it. I remember the last time I was here, and I believe there is a Farmers market somewhere but I'm..."

Kavya's mouth was dry, and she licked her lips repeatedly making a smacking sound. She pushed the shop door open violently. She felt anger. It's his fault. He's *making* me do this. Her stomach was in knots. If there was any choice, she wouldn't have come into this shop but Saint Dorothy's at Cliffe was too small for choices and the Bugden supermarket was too far. And she hated this man. And his shop stank.

"Hell---ooo," said the man behind the counter. "Early in the year. Miss Kavya"

"Hello hello, and how are you?" she said and turned sharply around the corner into the narrow aisle. They constructed these mini marts with as much shelf space as possible and so you felt like a frightened little mouse shuffling up and down the narrow maze. They were the same design, stuck on every corner in London and outside London, even in small coastal towns where you couldn't find Turmeric in the shops, you could still find a mini mart to rip you off.

Next to the freezer was a tower of egg boxes. Out of date, reduced. He shouldn't be selling those, she thought disapprovingly. People like him give Indians a bad name...But she didn't dare mention it because what she wanted was two bottles of wine and a bottle of vodka, better get a Pimm's as well as that looks more convivial. So annoying because he kept all that stuff behind his cage. Suddenly she looked up and noticed a huge round concave mirror stuck in the corner above the freezer. His moon like face was peering in it, watching her every move.

"Having a party at the house today. Expecting at least five or six people. From the English School. From ISEE. We're getting an inspection and I've invited them to the house," she announced after pretending to look for something and ending up at his cage.

He lolled his head.

"Very good. I remember your dear mummy and daddy when they used to have--

"I'll have two bottles of Frascati, maybe give me also a bottle of red, any one. Oh, and they like the English drinks, so give me one bottle of Pimm's and also a bottle of the blue. That one only. And tonics."

She was always amazed at how she slipped into the broken "Indian" English accent whenever she went into one of these Asian shops. Why you chatting like Goodness Gracious Me babes, John had said once and she had to laugh. I can't help it, she'd said. I don't know why. Maybe in some way she was trying to ingratiate herself with the shopkeeper; maybe she thought he wouldn't understand her London accent? But why when she hated him?

"Busy," he said his head lolling at top speed, popping the bottles into brown paper bags.

"No! Not that one!" she cried in an aggrieved voice. "I'm not a gin drinker!"

Why had she blurted that out?

"Bumbay Sa-Pyre," he said reading the label. "It is blue! The colour of Arabian Sea. The colour of Krishna. Auspicious."

Kavya sighed. She didn't want to call attention to the Blue Smirnoff. He seemed to think the Bombay Sapphire gin had some Indian and therefore healthy properties. For God's sake, now I'm having to bow to the ignorant theories of idiot shopkeepers! She lost the will to ask him to exchange the bottles.

"Better have some of these and these," she said plucking bags of popcorn and pretzels and lobbing them in. "Put them in-between the bottles, only."

"I often think of Kishore saab," he said as he meticulously, oh so slowly, put the goods in two bags. "What a man."

Kavya squinted at him. Typical of the kind of Indian she loathed. He used to always call her Mrs Mukherjee and she was always telling him she had not changed her perfectly good surname. He had loved Kishore even though he'd only met him a few times just because of Kishore's surname.

A Brahmin was as good as a God to these people. Kishore could have been a wife beater he would still be licking his boots. And he loved mum and dad because they owned a school and three properties. Like so many of them, he measured everyone by money. It disgusted Kavya. And he was such a racist, he never even acknowledged John, even though John was always polite and friendly to him.

As she walked out with the bags, she had a sinking feeling. Shanta's like that too. Narrow minded Hindu caste-ist racist hateful snob. Once she had forwarded a WhatsApp video that said 'Muslims smell like devils because they eat too much of meat,' and Kavya had deleted it and meant to pick her up on it, but she had let it go when Shanta had said 'oh it's just a joke' which to Kavya seemed a worse kind of racism; to say something wilfully hateful and untrue and then pretend it was funny. That ignorant shopkeeper and the educated Shanta both got their news from WhatsApp family groups. Now I have to *use* her, be obligated to her…I've been forced into it. I really am indebted. The ignominy of it all. If Naani had just *listened* to me, I wouldn't have to go through all this horrible…

As they drove along the winding road and came nearer the beach, Kavya thought again, this time her heart thudding in her mouth: What if they really *are?* … But if we see it. Then I'll be free, she thought and felt her shoulders relax. I won't have to put up with him watching me, judging me, interfering in my life.

"Park here Shanta," she said. "We can walk down the steps just over there."

She got out clutching the two bags which she had placed between her feet. Shanta was looking around, her sari flapping around her, her hair blowing up to reveal the bald patch.

“Bracing, isn’t it?” she said with a smile.

The sky was a pale endless blue and the cool breeze had moisture in it, the sort of breeze you only felt at the seaside. Like wet clammy hands touching you.

“Too cold for me to go in the water. But John loves it.”

“Can I help…?”

“No no, I’m fine. Look here, we go down these steps and we’ll be in front of the house. Or rather at the back of the house. Please hold on to the railing. The stairs are a bit rickety. Ours is the one at the end.”

As they walked down the steps, Shanta talked.

“It’s really very interesting. They even built them ‘backwards’ you know? It’s what the English architects used to say about the Taj Hotel in Bombay during the Raj. It’s been built backwards. Because they didn't understand that Islamic architecture required the seclusion of a courtyard, and the buildings face into the courtyard and have their backs to the street. As it were. You see the Moghuls were a fascinating breed, one really can’t connect them to the ignorant Muslim in say East London or Bradford.”

“Really? Well, these are in a row. But yes, they’ve been built in this odd way whereby all the ‘front doors’ are facing the street, but infact everyone uses them as their ‘back door’ and almost never leaves the house from there. You tend to walk down the steps, then walk all the way around, on to the beach and enter from there.”

"So, you call your back door the front door, yes I read about that in a magazine article on Kent Architectural Follies and Intrigues," giggled Shanta.

"Yes," said Kavya. "And our actual front door to the street is sealed, so we don't even use it as a back door. It's just part of the wall. You're right, it's all a bit topsy turvy. All the Moghul houses have a very long back garden, and look on to the beach, which is private, you'll see…and we often sit in the garden and look out. There's the promenade and then the sea. Very close."

As they turned left on to the private beach Kavya's jaw dropped.

There was Georgia in her usual shapeless work clothes, on her knees weeding in the garden. And far away from her was John in his shorts sitting at the table. With Milan.

Chapter 11

"Kavs!" cried John. "What a lovely surprise. Wasn't expecting you till much later! What happened? Hiya Shanta!"

"Mummy!" cried Milan.

Georgia got up, trowel in hand and was standing squinting at them. The door into the house was ajar.

"Oi Kardashian. Why's he here?" said Kavya. "He's supposed to be out with Marymary today."

Milan giggled "Kardashian".

John shrugged. "He wanted to come."

"*What is she doing here?*" Kavya hissed in Hindi to Shanta who also looked surprised and confused. And then in English, Kavya said, "Alright, look Shanta have a seat here I'll just go and put this stuff in the kitchen. No John, it's fine, you stay there. I can manage."

"I'll fire up the BBQ. Weathers not too bad. Stay and have lunch with us Shanta. I'm sure Kavs has bought some veggie stuff for you," she heard John say behind her.

As Kavya walked up the garden path, something was gathering force inside her. She approached the front door and Georgia was standing there, staring at her with the trowel in her hand. Insolent.

"Alright George?" she said and walked past into the house.

"Want a hand?" said Georgia behind her. The girl had a way of talking that was…Kavya couldn't put her finger on it. As though she was thinking one thing and saying another.

"No, it's cool, you carry on," she said and closed the front door.

She dumped the bags by the door and raced into the bedroom and started scanning the room. Nothing to see. The bed had been recently made. Georgia! Had they used it before she'd changed the sheets? She bent down and sniffed the pillow. Georgia wore a very distinctive perfume or deodorant. It was one of those body sprays you got 3 for £10 at Superdrug but it was a nice one. Nothing, but then, she had changed the sheets.

Kavya turned her attention to the bedside table and pulled out the drawer. Book, torch, sweets, pens, yes, there it was. She took out the Boots wrapper. Inside was a 12 pack Durex. They'd bought them last time. She opened the pack and started counting how many were left in there…

"Having fun?" said Georgia behind her and she almost dropped the things.

"Gave me a heart attack!" she said crossly spinning round. "How long you been standing there?"

"What are you doing?" said Georgia.

"Nothing! What are *you* doing?"

"Garden. I changed the sheets in here and in the guest. And I've done both the bathrooms. If you want to check, there as well? For fingerprints and that."

Kavya gave a nervous giggle.

"These are probably out of date now," she said holding up the Durex pack. "I was just checking on…we bought them last summer."

She'd been caught red handed anyway, may as well try some damage limitation. Was it still snooping if it was her own house?

"I wouldn't know. Never use 'em," said Georgia with a grin.

Kavya bit her lip. Oh really? If she thinks I'm going to ask her for details…

They looked each other in the eye.

Guilty, thought Kavya.

"Why'd you come in? If you were doing the garden?" she said.

Georgia shrugged.

"Good point. I'll get on."

"Cool," said Kavya and followed her as she went to the door. "Thanks George."

"Want me to put the shopping away?"

"No, I'll do it. Have lunch with us?"

"I've got to run soon as I've done the garden. Got another job on. But thanks for asking."

"House looks nice George, thanks for coming today. Appreciate it."

"It's my pleasure," she said and gave her a wide smile and went out the door.

What a bitch, thought Kavya.

She went into the kitchen with the bags and took out the two wine bottles and put them in the fridge. Then she wrapped the brown bag and then the plastic bag around the gin and put that in the cupboard next to the bin. She debated about the red wine, and then put that in a cupboard where they kept a few tins for emergencies. She took the Pimm's and put that on the counter. Now what?

I'll make up a jug, she thought. That's pleasant. She poured out two small bottles of the tonic water in the jug, added ice, and then poured the Pimm's in. She cut up a lemon which was all there was in the fridge and threw it in. The thing about Pimm's is, it's like squash, you can offer it to guests.

She bent down and took out the gin bottle, poured herself a glass and drank it down. I'm not really a gin drinker, she thought. Time, they took off the picture of Queen Victoria, surely? She didn't rule any waves anymore and Mumbai was not the jewel in her crown. She twisted the top back on and put it back under the counter. Then she took the Pimm's jug in one hand and a bag of pretzels in the other and went out to the garden, past Georgia, and up to the table.

"oooo Pimm's," said Shanta.

"Forgot the cucumber, sorry. And the strawberries!"

"And the glasses. I'll get them," said John with an indulgent smile and got up. Kavya sat down. Shanta was sitting erect looking out to sea with her sari tail wrapped around her shoulder, taking deep yoga breaths. Kavya opened her mouth to say something bitchy about Georgia in Hindi, so Milan wouldn't understand, but it felt inappropriate, and she didn't think Shanta would be convinced. It would be mortifying if Shanta rumbled that she Kavya was trying to *insinuate* something. To speak against your own husband. Very bad manners. Low class. She pressed her lips together and kept quiet.

"You can smell the brine from here," said Shanta looking out to sea. "It's marvellous. Reminds me of going to Juhu beach in my youth. We would sit and watch the monkey man, drinking Kaala Khatta from the stall, and we were just this far from the water. Not that any one of us would dare to go into that polluted sea."

"I'm going to swim. Learn to swim," said Milan.

"Oh really," said Shanta eyebrows like trapdoors. "Today? Isn't it too cold for you?"

"He's not. Milan, you are not going to learn to swim in the sea. Forget it. In the swimming pool first. We already had that conversation."

"But the sea has natural boncy."

Shanta smiled.

"I'll give you boncy in your bonce!' said Kavya and put her fist on top of his head. Milan tittered holding his stomach.

John put down a tray of three empty glasses and 2 glasses of Orange Juice for him and Milan. He poured the Pimm's for Shanta, but Kavya put her hand over her glass.

"George," John turned and shouted. "Come and have a drink with us."

Georgia padded over and shook her head.

"Thanks, but I'll just have an orange juice. I'll get it, no worries."

She didn't put her hand on John's arm but that might be deliberate, thought Kavya. I've seen *him* put his hand on *her* arm, plenty of times. And he's given her lifts.

"No, I'll get it," said John and put his hand on her shoulder. "Sit, visit."

OMG thought Kavya.

She didn't dare look at Shanta or Georgia.

Shanta Acharya's head turned to watch John go into the house. Georgia sat down.

Now the three of them and Milan were sitting at the table.

"I don't really drink but occasionally I do like a little Pimm's. Although I suppose it's not quite the weather for it," said Shanta lifting her glass and taking a small sip. She coughed and put it down daintily.

Georgia sat there stony faced. Impassive, thought Kavya. No emotions crossed that face. She didn't seem at all uncomfortable. She doesn't think she has to make conversation. Rude, in a way.

"Not drinking?" said Kavya looking at her sideways. She went ahead and poured herself a tall one.

"Not today," said Georgia.

"Oh," said Kavya and sipped her Pimm's. It was infact disgusting. What's that supposed to mean, not today? What is she the Queen of Sheba?

John returned with a glass of orange juice for Georgia.

Kavya looked up. Now there was a redundant empty tall glass on the tray. Things had gone from bad to worse.

"Babe, where's the food?"

"What food?"

"Chicken. Salad?"

"Oh. He didn't have anything. Paki shop. Nothing fresh."

Kavya looked pointedly at Georgia to see if she had any reaction to the "P" word, but the girl was a sphinx. A sphinx who was a stranger to a bra!

"I'll go and get something from Budgens," said John. "But I've parked the car a bit further away."

"I'll take you!" cried Shanta. "My car's just here."

"Really, are you sure?"

"Very sure. Please."

Shanta took her handbag and smiled.

"I think I'll say goodbye."

"Oh, but the house tour?" said Kavya.

"Next time. I wish you a wonderful afternoon dear one. I shall take John to the supermarket and drop him off and then I'll buzz off. And you can have a lovely day together."

"Cool," said John.

The two of them went off.

Georgia was staring at the sea, her orange juice untouched.

"Milan," said Kavya. "Go inside now. You can play on the iPad for an hour. Then we'll have a late lunch."

Milan got up and trotted inside the house.

And then, there were two, thought Kavya and took a large gulp from her Pimm's. She poured herself another from the jug. Shanta's glass was untouched.

"She didn't finish her drink," said Kavya.

"Too strong innit?" said Georgia.

Kavya looked at her.

"Is it?"

Georgia scoffed.

"What?"

"Think I'm a retard?"

"You can't use that word, it's not--"

"I know what you tried to do. You got me to come down and you told him you weren't coming till later, and then you bomb up early with that old dragon. You thought she'll see me and him, put two and two together and make 5 and then put it out on the Asian hotline. So lame."

"What the? What hotline? A little bit racist…"

"I saw you," she said. "In there. Miss Marple."

"What are you on about?"

"You should ease up on the booze. It's making you dumb."

"Shut up!" said Kavya almost choking. "You're out of order George. Shut up."

Georgia smiled but it wasn't a smile, her mouth was closed.

"Yeah sure. I'll shut up. Until I start chatting."

Atima Srivastava

Chapter 12

John was walking along the beach towards the house. Kavya's hands were in fists. What's she going to do? What's she going to *say*? Is she trying to blackmail me...?

John's hair was burnished gold in the sun, and he was smiling as he approached her.

"Hey," he said gently, slipping in the seat next to her. "You, ok? Milan, ok?"

"I'm sorry I forgot to do the shopping. I'm sorry you had to go again—"

"Babe. No big deal. Georgia taken off. I noticed her mini was gone."

"Yeah, she took off. I didn't have any money to pay her. . ."

"No tragedy. She's coming tomorrow to do the garden at home. I'll give her the double bubble tomorrow. What's up, why so. . .what's wrong babes?"

"Tomorrow?" said Kavya feeling her heart quicken. "She's coming tomorrow?"

"She did a pretty good job inside and the kitchen. She's a fast worker," said John.

Too fast. Too clever. Too clever by half. How *dare* she speak to me like that? I'm her employer! O but what if she tells him. . .if John finds out that's what I did, he'll be crushed. The hurt on his face, I can't bear to. But I haven't *done* anything! There's no proof. None at all. Intention is not the same as. . .

"Shanta bought a load of stuff at the farmer's market. She's a funny old girl. Reminds me of this one 'aunty' as we had to call her, who worked at the home for some months. She was Sri Lankan I think, tiny like a sparrow. The word spinster was made for her. But she was the best one there. She was into discipline. She kept us all in line. None of that liberal nonsense with her. Everyone loved her, all the kids. We all wanted her to be proud of us I suppose. Some people just have that sort of authority."

"I was supposed to show her the house, she's got a whole bloody PhD written about it...I mean she's just all over it."

John threw back his head and laughed.

"Oh yeah, she can't get over the fact these were built for Indian royalty. Anyway, she didn't mind at all. If you ask me," John grinned and put his arm around Kavya's shoulders. "I think she enjoyed the opportunity to hang with me."

Where was Georgia now? Would she text John? And tell him what? You're crazy---

"Pardon?"

"Thing is babe, old Injun ladies they love me. Fact. There's something about me."

"Is that meant to be a joke?"

"No."

"You heard what you just said?" said Kavya crossly and John burst out laughing. He kissed her cheek.

"Babe but you're *my* old lady. That's different."

They looked at each other.

"Alright?" he said and smiled. "Don't be weird."

The sun was bright overhead, and the lapping waves made a soft sound against the sand but Kavya felt sick deep in her belly. *I've got to get him on my side.*

"Johnny," she said taking her hand from the wet glass and putting it on the back of his hand. "Take Milan out for a run or for Frisbee. Tire him out so I can put him to bed. And then we can."

"Oh," said John eyes wide.

"I'm sorry I've been. Just coming to bed so late every night. I mean. It's not that I don't want to have sex."

"I understand. It's not the end of the world."

His eyes were so sad. It was as though he was pleading for something he didn't want to say.

"No but. I want to. I'll get Milan to have his afternoon nap and we can go to bed."

While Johnny and Milan were playing on the beach Kavya went to the kitchen and took out the cooked chicken and roast ham and cheese from the bag. As usual John had done a great shop, nice bits. The BBQ idea had been abandoned. She opened the bottom cupboard and saw that there was less than half left in the Bombay Sapphire. How did that happen? I must have left the top off. That stuff vaporises. She took out the two bottles of white wine and the red wine and put them in her rucksack. Then she put the rucksack in the laundry basket in the bathroom and put a towel on top.

She went back to the kitchen and poured herself a glass of gin, and as she drank it she thought I'm not well, I shouldn't have to do this. But she felt better afterwards and it was easier to lay out the cold cuts. She watched her hands and they weren't shaking but inside she was trembling. *Until I start chatting. But to who? To whom?* She left the bottle of Pimm's on the counter and put the Bombay Sapphire away in its plastic bag in the cupboard next to the sink.

It went as she had planned. Milan napped next door while they made love in the early evening. Inexplicably, John had caught the sun. He smelled like the beach. His skin tasted of salt. Kavya straddled him and looked at his face and kissed his mouth hard. He grasped her tighter than he usually did and when he came, he held her wrist, and his eyes were closed. Johnny didn't have a sex face. It was never funny or embarrassing watching him during sex. He had the look of a surfer or a skater, deep in a kind of meditation. Afterwards she snuggled up to him, her head on his shoulder and his long fingers stroking her hair. To the victor, she thought. She could breathe now.

"Still works," he said deadpan. Men never wanted to show how happy anything made them feel, she thought. They always knocked it down to indifference. Was that all men? Kishore had never really been happy unless he had made a bonus. And even then, the accumulation of money only ever made him feel superior which was not the same as feeling happy. I didn't really know him, she thought. We used to drink voddies together. We never needed to talk.

"Johnny, I want to talk. Something's on my mind."

"Not porn again! Woman I've told you; you've got to stop with that!"

"Shut up. This is serious. Wait what do you mean porn.?"

"Joke!"

"Porn's a joke?"

"Some people. Wait, before you blow a gasket, not people I know or care to know, watch porn while they have sex."

"Disgusting!" she said. "Why?"

He pulled her close to him.

"Because they don't have someone they adore."

"Shut up! Don't be soppy!"

"Someone who was the best thing that ever happened to them," he whispered in her ear.

"Johnny, listen, there's…it's about Georgia."

"What's she done now?"

"I just don't like the way…she looks at you!"

"How's that?"

"I've seen her looking at you. And sticking her tits out. I'm not happy about it."

John laughed. "You're crazy. Why would she look at an old man like me?"

Kavya sat up.

"Well, what does that make me, if you're an old man?"

"Come on, lie down. Kavs I'm only three years younger than you. It's not a May September thing. Even if it was, it wouldn't make any difference."

"Three and a *half*!"

"Alright, just push the duvet aside so I can look at your legs while you babble."

"Anyway," she said snuggling back in, warming to her story. "I think. Ok, maybe it's a sort of crush. But you know when you like a guy, you get into fantasies. You can."

"Fantasies?"

"I'm just saying. Be careful. That's all. If she. You don't know women. You don't know the things they'll say to get you to like them. Things they'll make up. Devious you know?"

"What about going to the circus tomorrow?" said John. "We could take Milan, Marymary can have some more time to herself and."

I *can't!* I can't miss Georgia and she's coming tomorrow. I must see her. I must make sure she hasn't told anyone. I must see her.

"No, no, we can do it next weekend. Milan is back at school on Monday, he should get settled in. The circus will over stimulate him. Where the hell did Marymary go today by the way? I mean it's no problem but usually she takes Milan on her outing."

"To see a relative."

"Relative! She hasn't got any relatives who don't live in Goa!"

"Well, whatever," said John.

"I'm hungry," said Kavya getting up. "Let's have a shower. And then we can watch the sunset."

Atima Srivastava

Chapter 13

"But can't we just go for an hour? It's a trail. John said we could go!"

Kavya and Milan were sitting at the table at the end of the garden, looking at the sea. There was a soft milky light and that lovely hush filled with the soft sounds of the waves. The sea shimmered gold and blue. The sky was pale with a formation of clouds that looked like the texture of the beach when the tide had gone in.

"Not a trail. A trial. And John didn't make any promises. Don't lie Milan. You know that's a red line of mine."

Kavya picked up her glass of wine and sipped. She had put the bottle in an ice bucket and laid out cheese, ham and fruit. And fizzy water for John and Milan. She wasn't worried. They had taken a shower together and got dressed in the bedroom; there was no reason for John to go back and find her rucksack in the laundry basket. He could cook and do practical things, but John never did the laundry, ever. If it was left to him, he'd just keep buying new t shirts and pants. She was the one who did the laundry.

She looked at her son breaking the French bread expertly with his little hands and studiously filling it with ham and cheese. He cracks me up sometimes, she thought. Look at him, little Lord Snooty. He prefers Gruyere and his favourite food is Organic Hummus for God's sake. John's so right to make him be part of the real world. Otherwise he'd end up weak and useless like Kishore. His feet were dangling off the chair, rocking back and forth. She didn't feel like telling him off. There was a calm inside her.

She took another sip of the wine and gently placed her fist on top of Milan's head and tapped. For some reason this contact always made him giggle. I like making him laugh, she thought. I made him. I'm glad he doesn't look like Kishore; I don't care if it's mean to think that. He's going to be a little hunk when he's a teenager, even though he's awkward now in his body. But he's generally well behaved. Not like these feral kids you see in London.

She turned and saw John come out of the house carrying blankets. All at once she remembered her dad coming out of the house waving to them. She was 19 years old, and mum and dad had just bought Moghul House because the school was doing well. Dad's floppy hair and tortoiseshell glasses. Years later, Marymary coming out of the same door, like a bird, slow gait. That woman was tough, she just didn't do anything fast, maybe that was the secret of her youthful looks. Ah and Naani! When she came out of the door wrapped in her pashmina and a fluttering silk sari, she was regal. She walked the way you were supposed to walk in a sari. Elegant, tall, hardly moving yet moving. Kavya hadn't mastered that. Few women had. Lalita Sharma CBE owned it. John was right, some women just had that kind of quiet authority.

Being at the Moghul House was always special. It was like being on holiday in a lost place but surrounded by the people in your life. You could be alone with the sea, feel utterly alone and calm, but with the knowledge that they were all there, in the background. Was that selfish of her? Kavya liked to see someone coming out of the front door and walk towards the table, the path was long enough for it to be something to see. Characters in her life, emerging from inside. Expectation, perhaps. Whenever someone came out of the door, something would happen.

John gave Kavya a blanket and put one around Milan. Then he put Kavya's phone on the table and sat down to look at the lapping waves.

"Thanks John," she said sipping her wine.

He looked at her, that same strange look she couldn't figure. A sort of plea of helplessness or something. At any rate it irritated her.

"Well, a glass or two…I thought it would be alright."

"Very," she said and grinned.

John sighed. "I bought it for Shanta at the farmer's market. It's organic. I tried to give it to her to say thanks for driving you down but she refused to take it. She said you and Kavya must enjoy it together. I tried to tell her I don't drink but—"

Milan was listening intently.

"Shame to waste it," said Kavya taking the bottle out of the ice bucket. It made a clanging noise. She topped up her glass. "You did the right thing. Wasted on her anyway. She's the type who says oooo yes please then doesn't even drink a drink. Wasteful."

"You can put the cork in it. It'll keep," John said.

Before Kavya could say anything, her phone rang and she jumped, frowned and grabbed it.

"What the fuck? There's *never* any reception here!"

"Kavs," said John and Kavya turned to look at Milan staring at her, a look of horror on his face.

"Sorry. Delete. Erase," she said and pointed a finger at him. "Don't repeat!"

"Hello? What? The fuck? Bloody Hell?"

"Milan, listen. Can you do me a favour please?" said John quietly. "Remember those football magazines we bought down? I've left them in the front room somewhere. Can you go get them please?"

"Where are they?"

"That's the thing champ. I think by the tv, or maybe—have a look around. I'm sure you can find them."

Milan nodded, got up and walked back towards the house.

"But—are you alright?" Kavya said. "The police!"

John put the cork back in the bottle. Kavya glared at him, took out the cork, poured herself some more and carried on talking, partly in Hindi.

"Arre? Arre? *Abhi aatay hai hum.* No no, I don't want you to be alone. I know, it's temperamental sometimes, but usually it's a total dead zone. Yes, it knew it was you. Yes, now listen baaba. *Subkutch Bund, subkutch.* Sit tight. We're coming home."

She put the phone down and stared at John.

"The burglar alarm went off. Marymary was inside. She couldn't turn it off and she thought someone was in the house."

"God, what happened?"

"Well, the police got there quick she says. No forced entry. No window broken."

"Then how come?"

"Police said they do go off sometimes…"

"No," said John.

"Marymary said she thought she heard someone in the bushes. But the police gave all clear. I told her to lock herself in and we're coming home."

"Yes," said John.

Was it her, thought Kavya. Was it Georgia?

Chapter 14

They had the radio on. As a special favour, Milan was allowed to sit in front. It was dark by the time they had carried everything from the house and put it in the car. They had to take all the bits of food and milk, so it didn't go off. Kavya sat in the back with her rucksack between her feet. John looked at her in the rear view.

"She'll be fine. She's safe," he said.

"Yeah," said Kavya.

She felt responsible for Marymary. The house was a calm, serene place because of her. It had been that way in the Marylebone flat too. Marymary was like always having a piece of Lalita with her. Reassurance. I can't do without her. What if something had happened to her? What would I tell her family, I've never even met them?

For almost all her life, from the age of 11, Marymary has been part of someone else's family, never her own. She went to the Mukherjees when she was 11 for God's sake. A child herself! And then, where else? Other families. I've never asked her. All these homes she's lived in. Did they all treat her well? Does she know we all love her? Does she know how important she is to us?

Kavya sat in the back glowering as the streetlights skimmed past. Milan was singing along to the song on the radio, but he didn't know all the words, so he was humming some of them. John was tapping out the beat on the steering wheel to keep Milan's spirits up.

If Georgia had anything to do with this, thought Kavya...*I'll kill her.*

By the time they got home, it was dark. There was a crescent moon. Milan and John came out the car and went on ahead and Kavya followed, carrying her rucksack carefully like a baby. She had put a towel inside to stop the wine bottles clanking. As she came into the house she heard them in the kitchen, and she took a right turn and quickly put her rucksack on the floor in the computer room, then closed the door and walked back through the lounge and into the kitchen.

"It's alright, it's alright baaba," said Marymary when she saw Kavya's face.

"You saw someone in the bushes. Was it a man or a woman? We should get a camera installed. Tell me exactly what you saw."

"Could have been a man, so thin. I saw the shadow. But somehow—I think it was a woman."

"And you told the police."

"Why to bother the police na? What will they do?"

Marymary still had that Indian resistance to sharing anything with the police, any police, as she was convinced the more information you gave them, the more they would tie you in knots and end up arresting you. She had had first-hand experience of it with her younger brother who had been unlucky enough to be caught wandering after hours in the streets of Goa and been beaten to a pulp and the local police had just turned a blind eye.

John took a torch from the kitchen drawer and went outside. Milan was sitting contentedly at the kitchen table; he was used to long conversations that didn't include him. He also knew, without being told, that nothing was censored, and this made him feel a part of things.

"What was she doing? Was it someone you recognised? The shape I mean."

Marymary would have known Georgia's body shape immediately, no one could hide those big boobs.

"The strangest thing is…yes, I had a feeling I knew the person. Couldn't place them, and yet."

Marymary now switched to Hindi so that Milan wouldn't understand. "Ajeeb cheeze ye thi. Wo bus dekh rahi thi. Dekh rahi thi. Aur kutch nahi."

Kavya frowned as she translated in her head. Her spoken Hindi was rudimentary, but she understood perfectly, and the way she always understood it was by listening and then translating the sentence. Kind of like blind people read Braille. She had even used this experience once with the foreign students when she had taught a few classes and discovered that all bilingual people operated that way.

The strange thing was. She was just looking. Looking. Nothing else.

"All is well baaba. False alarm. Nothing. I'm safe and the house is safe. And now I'm going to put a young scamp to bed. Someone has got very excited all day!"

"Thanks, Marymary," said Kavya quietly and hugged her. "Milan, good night, don't bother Marymary too much please."

"As you know he can bother me as much as he wants," said Marymary and they both went upstairs.

Kavya was sitting with her elbows on the kitchen table, head in hands when John came in. *I'm all at sea,* she thought.

"I've checked everything outside. It was just one of those things," he said.

"I need a drink," she said. "It's alright to have a drink. Anything might have happened."

"Yeah," he said. "Want me to get you one?"

"Brandy," she said.

John went to the other room to the cocktail cabinet, poured out a small brandy in a large balloon glass, and bought it in.

He sat down opposite her.

"What did you really see?" she said.

He wrinkled his nose. "There were some footprints. Boot marks. In the earth by the trees." He shrugged. "I'll install a camera."

"It's always there isn't it?"

"What babe?"

"Threat. Dark shadows. Something frightening. The bogey man. I mean it can be terrorism or it can be a rustle in the trees. It's what makes you a coward. You can't ever properly get rid of it. Sometimes I think of it as that moment when someone comes to tell you that someone is dead, and you can't hear them because you're shaking with terror."

John looked at her. He didn't know what to say. But he knew not to make a joke.

"I think they call it triggering," she said, and he nodded.

"Because if I think of losing Marymary, I think of losing mum and dad. And losing…It's a strange hopeless sort of feeling. Like being at the bottom of a well that's run dry. But I used to feel it even when they went away for the weekend, when we lived in Camden. Sometimes even when they were at home." She took a sip of the brandy and felt it slip down her throat. "Truth is. I've always felt it. Maybe I was born that way. Anxious. Cowardly."

John put his hand on her wrist. She was holding the balloon glass with both hands.

"You're patient," she said. "You put up with a lot from me. I babble on, I know that. It must be a real drag".

"I don't put up. I like being with you. So, it's not a drag."

"Well…" She was staring expressionlessly at the table.

"Kavs. Let me help you. Please. Let me be with you. If you don't feel well, we can go to see a doctor together. Let me help you."

She looked at him with irritation.

"But I've been to a doctor. There's nothing wrong with me that a diet won't fix."

"Ok," said John and turned on the tv. The volume was low, and he watched it for a few minutes then turned it off. Kavya was staring into space.

"That show," she said. "Was from last year. Love Island. We watched the finale. You hated it. Everyone was talking about it. We were just married."

"So much for our romantic getaway this weekend," he said.

"We can do it next week. It was *quite* romantic," said Kavya and smiled at him.

Chapter 15

She wanted to stay up alone for a while and John respected that and went to bed. She bought the bottle of brandy in from the cocktail cabinet in the lounge and sat drinking for some time in the half light of the kitchen, her mind empty, staring into space. She heard footsteps and turned her head.

"Hello darling," she whispered. "Come in and sit with me."

"Are you ok?" whispered Marymary and tip toed in to the kitchen. Her eyes were shining. She was wearing a slinky black kimono that Kavya had never seen before.

"I'm going to make some Green Tea, want one?"

"No, I'm good with this," said Kavya raising her glass.

Marymary came and sat down at the kitchen table. It was dark, they could only see the glints in each other's eyes. They were comfortable with each other and sat silent for some time, lost in their own thoughts.

"Do you remember Dinny?" said Kavya.

"Who?"

Kavya laughed. Oh, *she* had given her the nickname. She'd forgotten.

"Nandini, I mean."

"The Mukherjee baby?"

They spoke in hushed tones as if not to disturb the darkness

"You must have gone to work in their house in Delhi when she was born."

"Yes. Master Kishore was five, very naughty. Yes they took me in and I helped Mukherjee Mam. Everyone was in love with that child, so much. Kishore must have told you—"

"No. He didn't even know I knew her."

Silence.

"You *knew* her?"

"She came to London. To my school. She was supposed to be there till –I don't know."

"Ah. You see I left the Mukherjees when she was three or four years old. I went to work for a nice family in Nainital, Hillstation. I stayed with them for many years. And after that I went to Goa because my own baby brother was born. I was the eldest. I was 24, or 25 years old. I had six sisters."

"You were seven sisters?"

"Yes. And now a baby boy. I left my job and I went home. So, you see I missed those years with the Mukherjees. When Nandini came to the UK, I was in Goa. And then. When she died, I was also in Goa. Terrible. Shall I put the lamp on?"

Kavya shook her head. There was a silence in which she had the feeling that Marymary understood something.

"Is that why you found Kishore? On Shaadi.com? Because he was Nandini's brother?"

"Yes. No. I don't know. I was enjoying my life, I was single for a long time, travelling aimlessly around Europe. With a whole bunch of people who all drifted away. And then I was 30 and I thought it's time to get married. Why did I go on an Indian wedding site? I never thought I'd marry an Indian guy. But he popped up. Dinny's older sibling who was expected to have an arranged marriage. We matched.

Maybe it was fate. Maybe it was chance. I thought it's meant to be."

Marymary nodded.

"God's will"

"No. Dinny's will. Perhaps. I've suddenly thought about her after all these years. She was the new girl. Sent to the UK for a good education. We were 12 years old, but we became inseparable. I was enchanted by her confidence and the things she talked about. I followed her everywhere. We'd go out. Nothing major, just to the park and have a cigarette. I don't remember, we just used to hang around together. And then we both hit 13. Teenagers at last. It was only six months after she came to my school, but it felt like a milestone. And then--"

"And then?" said Marymary.

"You see what happened was. One afternoon, we bunked off school and—it was in the park. These men set upon her. I was in the newsagents. But I came out and I saw them. I saw them. There were six of them. They were taunting her. Paki this, paki that. They started kicking her and shoving her. I just. I couldn't move. I hid in the bushes. I was afraid."

"I understand," said Marymary.

"After they'd gone, I went to help her. She was alright. She was bleeding a bit but I wiped it all off and I took her back to Mrs Chandreshaker's house in Kentish Town, where she was lodging. We said she'd fallen over in the street. She wanted me to say that. She didn't want anyone to worry."

"And there was no question of going to the police," said Marymary with a sigh.

"No. What would they do? Dinny didn't want a fuss."

"But she didn't stay on in London. Something made the Mukherjees bring her back home to Delhi."

"Yes. She never came back to school. I don't know what she said or what happened but, yes, she disappeared, and it was like London had never happened"

Marymary leant forward and Kavya saw the whites of her eyes.

"When my little brother was beaten up, the police did nothing. They almost killed him. They beat him to a pulp. He was beaten up for *nothing*. The police..the police were useless. They didn't investigate. But I said nothing to my father. We sisters kept it a secret. And my poor brother felt it was all his fault."

"I'm sorry Marymary."

"He left as soon as he could. He was 14. He left India and never came back."

"You never saw him again?"

"I never saw him again. But he lived. He lived; I know that. And that was enough."

"I think…sometimes I've thought. Maybe Dinny died because of me."

Marymary turned on the lamp. Kavya blinked. The brandy bottle was on the table, and she was holding the big glass.

"Why would you think that? She died of a brain haemorrhage some months afterwards. It was unfortunate."

"But if I'd helped her. If I'd stopped them. The *way* they hit her; it must have affected her head. Formed a blood clot. And later, the haemorrhage came as a result. A delayed reaction."

Marymary sighed and put her hand on Kavya's shoulder.

"No. The two things weren't connected at all. You have nothing to feel guilty about. It was a tragedy."

"I was a coward. That's what I couldn't get over. My repulsive cowardice. It gnawed at me for years. I wanted to be on my own so no one could see me, smell it on me. I thought that was happiness, being alone. Sounds strange I know. The Sharma women don't cower. I've never told anyone in the world. Ever. I've drunk too much tonight. I wish I hadn't said anything."

Marymary patted her hand.

"Don't worry, I've forgotten everything. Go to bed. Go to bed before it's light."

In the middle of the night Kavya woke up sweating.

She disentangled herself from Johns arms and crept downstairs feeling disorientated. Her head was throbbing. At first, she thought they were in Moghul House. Then, she couldn't remember them driving home. What time she'd gone to bed. It was all a blur. She couldn't remember. All she knew was she needed a drink and she remembered she had smuggled in bottles of wine in the rucksack.

She felt angry. It's ridiculous that I have to be furtive in my own home, just to have a drink. But I have to. I need a drink. These headaches. It's not too bad if you drink wine anyway. Kishore used to say when you drink beer it's not really drinking. Hard liquor is drinking. He wasn't very bright. I knew that when I married him. I knew it on the wedding day. That's why I was crying. As if marrying him would atone for not helping her. Stupid despicable deluded coward. What sort of Sharma woman was I? The one with no guts.

She went into the computer room and without turning on the light, picked up the rucksack. She took out one of the bottles and unscrewed the top. That was clever getting the screw top. What had happened to the organic wine? Had she finished that or had she left it in the ice bucket on the table?

A harsh white light sliced into the room from outside; it wasn't the moon; it was a street lamp. When did they change the streetlamps from yellow to white light, she thought. There was no glass in the computer room. She sat down in the leather swivel chair and drank from the bottle. It was the white wine. Warm. I should have looked and opened the red, she thought and took another draught and another. She wiped her mouth, screwed the top on tightly and put the empty bottle back in the rucksack. You fill your life with meaningless trivia. That's what Naani would say, but the trivia gave you something to hang on to. That's what people didn't get.

She felt better. She felt relieved. As she climbed the stairs, she thought I must wake up early tomorrow. Georgia's coming. She always comes early. Sometimes at 8. How does she get here on the bus that early? It's got to be at least 1.5 hours from her house in Ramsgate. She never drives when she comes to us. Yesterday was different because she knew she had to go to Saint Dorothy's at Cliffe. I mustn't grind my teeth. That's because I'm stressed.

She remembered everything now. Georgia saying I'll shut up. Until I start chatting. The insolent look. John's hand on her shoulder, no worries, babe. Every time I think about what she said…I don't want to think about it. But she said it. The teeth wear away like that. The dentist told me I should look after my teeth. They're dissolving. I had that nightmare once. Teeth dissolved inside my mouth. I've got to be fresh as a daisy when she comes. I've got to talk to her. *I've got to talk to her.*

Chapter 16

Kavya woke up. There was a note on the bedside table:

Didn't want to wake you. I'm going to work see you later J

She looked at the clock. 10am! She took a quick shower and got dressed. The house was empty. Kitchen empty. She went in the computer room and peeked out to the garden from behind the blind. Georgia was at the far end digging, her back to the house. Kavya stepped back inside. I'm not ready to talk to her yet. I need a drink.

She went to the kitchen and got the water bottle out of the dishwasher, then to the cocktail cabinet, took out a fresh bottle of Smirnoff and walked into the computer room. She poured the liquid into the water bottle and put the Blue into the drawer. She winced at glugging from the water bottle but there was no glass. She sat down on the swivel chair and composed herself. Then she got up and stood by the small window with the pulled down blind. Through the side crack she could see down to the end of the garden. She sent Georgia a text.

Come into the computer room for a minute? NTT

She watched as Georgia heard the ping, then saw the message. Slowly she put down the spade, wiped her hands on her apron and started toward the house. Kavya quickly turned on the computer and pretended to be looking at something.

A knock on the door.

"Come in!" Kavya said cheerfully.

Georgia had washed her hands in the kitchen sink. She was wearing a strange get up of a paint spattered apron. Underneath she had on jeans and t shirt. Kavya had never seen the apron before.

She stared at it.

"Been painting?"

"No."

"D'you mind shutting the door please."

Georgia shut the door. She stood on the other side of the desk. No expression on her face. Was she on drugs?

"Not touching what?"

"Eh? said Kavya.

"NTT. Not Touching That. So? Not touching what?"

"That's not what it means. NTT. Need To Talk"

"No it doesn't," said Georgia. "It means Not Touching That."

And then Georgia chuckled.

The nerve!

"So, I'm not happy about what you said yesterday."

Georgia just looked at her.

"And we had a –burglar alarm went off last night. We came home. There was a prowler."

Georgia shrugged as if to say so what?

"Wasn't you, was it? In the bushes?"

Georgia snorted.

Kavya felt her temple throb. It was like the elephant in the room. She knew and Georgia knew exactly why she had summoned her. Georgia's revolting idea that she Kavya had engineered some sort of sleazy set up...*But I did do it.* It's humiliating that she saw through it. I can't stand her! I hate her!

Finally, Georgia spoke: "You're off your nut."

"What d'you say?"

"Nothing."

"No, go on. Let's hear it. You're dying to tell me. And what did you mean by 'until I start chatting?' Who are you gonna talk to? About what? If you think John is going to listen to a word you say you're deluded. He's my husband."

"Who said I was gonna to talk to *him*?"

Kavya couldn't bring herself to ask her what she meant. She was dying for a drink. Her mouth was dry. But she had to know.

"Who then?"

Kavya was aware of her bottom lip sticking out. I'm hurt, she thought. I'm hurt by this…betrayal.

"Well, if I was gonna to tell anyone, I'd tell your grandmother."

"What, you're going to try and blackmail an old woman?"

"Who said anything about blackmail?"

"What …why?"

Georgia grinned.

"But now you mention it…"

Kavya felt as though she'd been kicked in the head. Knocked sideways. If Naani knew...if Georgia even went to her…Naani would know it was the truth. It would be worse than any blackmail. Her character would be torn to shreds. And the fact that it was being reported to Lalita by an outside party, would make it worse. For all her modernity, and for all her compassion for working class battered Asian women, Lalita Sharma was an old-fashioned snob when it came to her own kith.

To hear such things about her granddaughter, to hear she had schemed such a crude scheme, to hear that she kept bottles around the house like a common alcoholic...Kavya would fall in her grandmothers eyes forever. She knew it. Lalita wouldn't forgive it. What can I do? What can I say? Kavya squirmed in her seat. What does she want? Is it money? No, it's not money. I can't say *please* don't. She won't listen.

Georgia stared at her for a few seconds, then took out a packet of cigarettes.

"You can't smoke in here!" cried Kavya.

Georgia fished out a lighter and lit her cigarette, looking around the room with disinterest.

"What the actual hell?" shouted Kavya. "Put it out."

"You need to chill down. Before you do yourself an injury."

Kavya sat back in her chair, winded, lost for words.

"The fact is," said Georgia. "You've got a problem."

"Yeah, *you*!"

"What you did yesterday. It was actually quite sad. Lame-O. You couldn't even do it properly."

"I'm lame!"

"The alcohol's pickled your brain. Look at you. You've got everything anyone could ever want. Had it on a silver platter all your life. You've got houses and schools and money and a live-in nanny and a husband, but that's still not enough. Talk about privilege."

So that was it. *Class war!* Well screw her.

"Georgia, shut your mouth."

"You're a joke. You don't live in the real world. You're a pathetic drunk. I pity you."

"Right, that's enough. Get out."

Georgia blew a smoke ring at the ceiling.

"Here's your money. For today and yesterday. Now get lost. And don't come back. Ever. If you do, I'll report you to the police. You're a nasty little slag, everyone knows it, I did you a favour by hiring you. Now piss off. If I hear you've as much as gone near my grandmother or anyone in my family, you will live to regret it. I can promise you that. You're the scum of the earth. Pure Chav. You have no agency. You're of no importance to anyone. You're nothing."

Chapter 17

Kavya heard the front door close. She slid down in the swivel chair and didn't dare look out to the garden. She heard Georgia's footsteps go down the path, and then out through the garden gate and then she couldn't hear them.

A big boulder came rolling down the hill in her mind. *I shouldn't have sacked her.* Big big big mistake. Dumb. No...I've got to think.

She unscrewed the top of the water bottle and drank from it. It was neat vodka. I wouldn't usually...but there aren't any mixers. I need to think. Clear my mind. Her brain began to work now. Now she knew how she should have behaved. I should have been light. I should have been casual. Brushed it off, not even remembered what she said yesterday. By getting angry, I betrayed myself. I made myself vulnerable. I've put myself in jeopardy.

I've got to fix it, pronto. Make amends. Repair. Yes, that's what I'll do. I'll apologise, I'll say I was in a strange mood because of the –alright nothing happened but someone was prowling about, and the alarm went off and I was nervous, we came back early. I'll say that. I'll fix it. I'll ask her to come back. I'll tell her we can't do without her. I'll say her... her hair looks nice. Maybe I can even give her a raise? Yes, that's a good plan.

There was a knock on the door.

Come in, she said staring at the computer screen. She screwed the top back on and put her water bottle on a coaster. Everyone must drink more water, what was wrong with that?

Marymary stood beaming. Next to her was Milan in his new school clothes.

Kavya nodded appreciatively. "You look ready for tomorrow. Nice threads Milan. Why didn't you put the cap on?"

Milan frowned.

"I'm a bit stressed out," he said.

Kavya laughed.

"You're six years old. What have you got to be stressed out about? Don't be ridiculous. Where does he pick up these things?"

Kavya picked up her water bottle and sipped, then put it back. She smiled at Marymary.

"Are you fine?" said Marymary.

"Sure."

"Don't worry. I forgot all. It's all in the past."

"Ok," said Kavya.

She had no clue what Marymary was on about but she was getting on, maybe her mind was going a bit Alzheimery. How old was she, 60 something? The main thing was everything was back to normal. All was well with the world. Now I know exactly what to do, I feel much better.

Marymary said “Anyway, now we’ve given mummy the fashion show. And now let's go and take everything off and hang it up. And we’ll go out for a walk before lunch.”

“I must do some work too,” said Kavya.

Once they had gone, she checked her emails and then went into the ISEE website and worked for an hour on some of the pages. The inspection had come through with flying colours, as expected and the academic proposal put in by two of the teachers, had also been given approval. With the rolling out of Brexit, the focus of ISEE would now shift from Europe to China. New Intake Strategy would also target Brazil, Japan, Russia, Taiwan, Korea, and Vietnam. European students would still be welcome, but they would occupy a lower priority.

Alongside the New Intake Strategy, ISEE would devote a portion of the finances to promoting work with Refugees, not only teaching English for free, but also creating a course called Contemporary British Culture, where the Refugees would be taken to various places of historical interest, treated to a pub lunch and High Tea in an Olde English Tea room, taken to music venues and finally paired with a foreign student for the day to share perceptions of what Britain was like IRL, and also to be a human library for each other.

A good deal of government incentive was available for the venture and it would raise ISEE to a true Global profile.

Kavya spent an hour filling out the endless forms for the funding, ticking boxes, carefully outlining the initiative. She never minded this kind of embroidery work, it soothed her. Four hours passed. When it was 3pm, she sent a text to Georgia by WhatsApp.

Hey George, I am really sorry about what I said. Forgive me. I must have lost my mind. Please don't leave us. Come over this evening for a drink. Let me make things right. K xx

She stared at the phone waiting for the ticks to go blue. They didn't. After waiting for 15 minutes, she punched out the number to make a voice call. Continuous dialling tone. Strange. She tried again. Same. She rang Vodaphone and asked them what it meant, and the man said it meant the phone was out of order. What does that mean, it was working this morning? It can mean either the sim has been taken out or the phone has been destroyed.

Kavya got up, feeling unsteady on her feet, and went out of the house. I must eat something she thought absently. Never mind, it's good for the diet she thought as she came out of the gate and turned right. She trudged along the road, an intense churning in the pit of her stomach. The sky seemed to be pressing down, full of heavy grey matter. When she got to the line of lock up garages by the bakery she stopped.

One steel shutter was open and the lock up was empty. A man was standing nearby.

"Hello," she said. "Doesn't this lock up belong to Georgia Galton?"

He shrugged.

"Not anymore. It's mine as of this afternoon. She took all her stuff this morning."

Kavya stood rooted to the spot. She felt like when she stood on the beach barefoot and the tide went out and you were standing on a stump. She called the number three times. A long continuous tone. Georgia's gone, she thought. She's disappeared. A strange prickly frightening feeling overtook her as she turned and walked home. I don't care how much I drink now, she thought.

Chapter 18

I've gone too far this time, she thought and locked herself in the bathroom. She stared at her hands. They were shaking uncontrollably. Is this the DT's? Her entire body was shaking, and she held on to the sink. Just *stop!* Not daring to look in the mirror she kept her head down. I didn't say goodbye to Milan, she thought blankly. I didn't wish him a good first day back to school. But the thought vaporised. She was trembling, head to foot. Jesus, what is this?

A rotting stench climbed from her belly to her mouth and then slid back down into her chest and sat there like a ball of fart. She punched herself in the back, coughed and blew out three times, as if there was a candle in front. Out damn smell, out. Her knuckles were white. How am I going to face anyone in this state? If I have a drink now, I might start screaming…

She remembered climbing the stairs last night and missing one. John came out of the bedroom to help. Maybe I was abusive to him, she thought. I don't remember. I need to see a doctor. I want to die. I'd be happy if I died. If only I could die. She was losing control, falling apart...Paracetamol, she thought suddenly and opened the medicine cabinet.

Some things fell out and landed on the floor. She took a couple of the pills, swallowed them and then grimaced. They make me sick, she thought. Then remembered the house was empty. She had woken up when John was getting ready to go to work and assured him she was fine. Marymary had taken Milan to school. I'm lucky, she thought. I have help. And she put the things back in the cabinet.

There was a smell of sick coming from somewhere. Holding the banister for safety she went downstairs into the computer room and locked that door. I don't need to do that she said out loud as she opened the drawer. There's no one here. This is my home, not a prison! She took a swig from the bottle of Smirnoff Blue thinking I need help; *this* isn't going to help me. I'm too far along. No, she thought. This is all in my head.

I felt humiliated last night when John saw me on the stairs on all fours. It was undignified. I was embarrassed and I felt guilty. Anyone would. I shouldn't have had all that brandy. Cheap Spanish stuff. I had an awful sore throat babbling at Marymary, that's right she was there with her Green Tea. What were we discussing in the dark I wonder?

Falling on the stairs was bad. John finding me like that: bad. Those kinds of things can affect you physically. Nausea can be an outcome of a mental state. Of course, I feel ashamed of myself. Wasn't dignified. Yes and I've got a terrible hangover so naturally I don't feel well. But it's not that serious at all. I can fix it. Apologise and make amends. That's all anyone can do. She looked at her hands; they were not trembling, and she could feel her lips. I'm feeling better now.

She picked up the phone.

"Hi, it's me."

"Hello you."

"I know I was out of order last night. I apologise. I'm mortified. Honestly, I'd taken these pills, for my period. And they reacted badly. I don't know. Maybe it was the fish I had, no one else had fish. I literally only had a couple of glasses of wine, but I was swaying. It was a Sunday night, you know. Sunday night I keep my wits about me. You know that. I was working on the proposal…"

"It's alright Kavs."

"No but you don't understand all I had was two glasses of wine!" she said.

"It's ok, don't worry about it. These things happen. I know it wasn't the booze. It's ok."

Suddenly she remembered she had thrown up on the stairs. Oh dear God. Her shirt was half off her shoulder too. Why was that? She had missed a couple of stairs and the material must have got caught…She looked at her knees. Both with blood encrusted burns. He must have cleaned it up. Well. I'm not going *into* it now!

"John," she said. "You're very patient with me. I don't know why you put up with me. You're a good man. What can I say…?"

"You don't have to feel ashamed," he said. "We can work it out together."

Ashamed?

Who said she felt ashamed? She'd missed a stair and something had given her a gippy tummy. She hated him for using that word. How *dare* he?

She had a quick shower and ran out of the house before Marymary got back. She didn't want an interrogation about why she had not wished Milan well on his first day back to school. I'll Skype him; he loves that anyway. She couldn't bear the thought of walking, too fragile, so she got the bus. As usual it was almost empty. In the back seat, she put on her sunglasses and Skyped Milan. The phone was turned off as they asked the children to do in class. So much the better.

She left a funny message and sat back relieved. The relief didn't last long. I've got to find out where Georgia has *gone*. She looked out the window absently and remembered how she and Shanta Acharya had watched her tottering down the road so recently. Where is Georgia now? What is she doing? She could be up to anything. Would she dare to talk to Naani…is she capable of such mischief? Yes…but it's ridiculous. But I must know where she's *gone*. She's capable of anything now. Why disappear? And to clear out her lockup like that. That's sinister. Why cut off your phone? Why?

As soon as she got off the bus Kavya phoned her grandmother.

"Well, hello," said Lalita. "What brings you?"

"Just wanted to check in. Miss you love you mean it," she trilled. It wasn't her usual language. Lalita made a disapproving noise.

"These little Americanisms. What do they really mean?"

"Shorthand innit," said Kavya feeling deflated. She stuck out her bottom lip as Lalita railed on.

"I've always said it's a very silly thing to tell the people in your life you love them. Don't they already know? Americans always want to tell you, which makes me rather suspicious of the whole thing. Alright you love me, well what else? Do the dishes, help someone without asking reward. And why speak in slang? You're not a Black teenager. It's affectation."

"It's acceptable slang!" said Kavya. "Even MP's use it!"

"I rest my case."

"I did have a reason to call Naani. I wanted to know if you'd come and stay a couple of nights. At Moghul House. Tomorrow for instance. No occasion. Just the three of us, you me and John. To hang –I mean, just a cosy catch-up get together. To share Moghul moments as you call them."

Kavya felt sure Lalita had not heard anything from Georgia. But she felt better if she could get both John and Lalita in a no network zone.

"That's sounds lovely darling. Let me check my diary and I'll get back to you later today."

But *why* must you check your infernal diary? I want you to say yes now! You have to. I can't have you---

"Alright," said Kavya dejectedly. "I look forward to hearing from you."

She walked past the ISEE building, and into the cut-through for Harbour Road. Several students sailed by on bicycles. The bus took 40min to get to the sea, but the cut-through bought you there in 20. As she forged on, fat entitled sea gulls pecking at rubbish tottered away like disgruntled old men in front of her feet. Lazy birds, she thought. If you can fly, why walk? When she turned into Harbour Road, she phoned the office.

"Morning Mrs Flinders. Yes lovely isn't it? I'm going to be late in today. I've sent the proposal to your email, just spell check it and circulate. Ask for all staff feedback and additional points to be sent to me. Hopefully we can send it off tomorrow. It's in the bag anyway, well done to all etc, let them know I appreciate it won't you? Make sure you leave early today Mrs F, I know it's your 19th Century Women Writers Book Group tonight. Emma? No,I haven't but I've seen Clueless though, it's a modern reworking set in an American High School. The phrase "I'm like Hello?" was made famous from..."

Mrs Flinders efficient as usual (and far too conscientious to see the film instead of the book) had already printed the documents off and made paper copies. Everyone agreed that while it took some more time, important documents should be in hard copy as well as on the computer. ISEE was old fashioned like that and Kavya liked it. However, old school was one thing, what she needed today was cutting edge technology.

She pushed open the door of the kiosk at the end of Harbour Road.

Chapter 19

"Salaam-a-le-kum Terry Kelly," she said.

"Alekum-salaam Kavya aunty."

Tariq Ali was the 19year old son of Mohammed Ali, a refugee from Afghanistan who had attended ISEE on a government grant while still on Leave to Remain. Father and son had entered the building sheepishly, all at sea and perhaps had felt a little more at home when they saw the 'boss' had a similar colour skin to theirs.

"Saw your dad the other day. Said he'd put the lunatic in charge of the asylum," she said deadpan.

Tariq fell about laughing. She was gratified to see he had now fully embraced the 'English' sense of humour, a concept that had once been alien. To put him at ease, Kavya had coined the nom de plume of Terry Kelly, telling the boy that English people would always get his name wrong so he should be ahead of the game. She quoted her own case, where despite paying for a horribly expensive school, she had been subjected to nothing racist but still annoying. Luv Ya Luv Ya wouldnt wanna Bee Ya. Tariq only 15 at the time had lapped it up. Mo his dad went on to be lionised by the other students and the teachers for *his* name, which was a hilarious counterpoint because unlike the world-famous boxer, Mo was a short stout bald man who looked older than his 35 years.

Like so many Afghanis, Mo was painfully modest, and Kavya had told him he must be less modest, because he was in England now where the American culture was rampant;

people expected you to “big yourself up”. She had written out some choice phrases for him to read and digest. Mo’s favourite phrase was “it aint bragging if it’s true” A direct quote from the world champion himself.

Mo had passed with flying colours and established his family and opened a small phone business within three years. He fixed computers and phones and had begun to sell reconditioned ones. He credited ISEE for his good fortune and gave them a discount on all phone and computer matters. These days Mo was busy in the new Ramsgate shop and Tariq held the fort in BarleyBarton. Kavya was relieved because she didn't want Mo to be a party to her request.

“I’ve got a little job for you Tariq. A bit of a tekky challenge.”

Tariq’s eyes lit up. General repairs didn't challenge his brain, but they were the bread and butter of the business. He had hinted that he was far more advanced than his father in his understanding of technology. The kiosk was not much bigger than a large cupboard but even when it had up to four customers and there wasn't any breathing space, Tariq managed to attend to all of them. This morning thankfully, it was empty. She sat down on the stool on the other side of the counter.

“Excited,” he said. “And always at your service.”

“Ok, well this is the problem. One of our…Employees has gone missing.”

“Oh!” cried Terry Kelly. “But you know, this is my new sideline. Finding people. I call myself The Bounty Hunter of BarleyBarton.”

"Looking for chocolate bars filled with coconut? You'll have to go to Ramsgate Tesco for those.

Terry Kelly honked with laughter.

"No no Aunty, you are too funny! You see," he lowered his voice. "We have many in our Afghan community, girls, who run away from marriage arrangements. I find them. I have already found two. Now I'm ready to go into business with calling cards."

"Tariq!" said Kavya. "You mean you look for girls who have run away from forced marriages? And you bring them back for a bounty?"

Terry Kelly beamed.

"You know that's illegal?"

"Marriage arrangements?"

Kavya sighed. She didn't have time for a teaching moment but really! "Arranged marriages are not the same as forced marriages. These girls have no choice in it. Forced marriages are a crime; these girls are prisoners! Imagine the courage it takes them to run away and then you go and drag them back! Does Mo know you're doing this?"

"No, aunty. No," said Tariq bowing his head.

"Well, what if it was your sister? Or your cousin? What if it was me? The clue is in the word forced. You know the difference, don't you? Imagine it Tariq. You're a young guy. You know all this izzat, honour stuff is all bull. It's the patriarchy. The fathers who don't want to lose face selling their daughters off!"

Tariq looked confused and scratched his head.

"Alright listen. Remember that Kurdish girl that was found in the freezer in the Iceland warehouse in Minster? Chopped up? In five bin bags? What do you think *that* was all about? She ran away from a forced marriage, and someone like *you* found her, and returned her and the dad chopped her up and put her in the freezer. He was the night manager there. What kind of a brainbox does that? How do you know that doesn't happen to the girls *you* find?"

"I never knew," said Terry Kelly with genuine concern. "I thought."

"You have to *read* Tariq. Don't just listen to one person, or what they say in the Mosque or on social media. Go to the BBC news. Read an English newspaper. Don't let them brainwash you. Make up your own mind. You're young. If you don't change the future is dark. I wouldn't bother to engage with old farts like Shanta Acharya about their views, they're too ignorant, they'll never change. But Tariq, that could be your sister. Stop doing it. No more bounty hunter. Promise? I mean it Tariq."

Tariq nodded seriously.

"You have my word of honour aunty."

"Ok. Good boy. Now, about this. Employee of mine. I'm trying to locate her. I thought maybe you could...I only have her phone number though."

"Illegal without papers?"

"No, no. Native. I mean white, regular English."

"Absconded?"

"Well..."

Kavya was always surprised by Tariq's burgeoning English vocabulary. She remembered when he could only speak Pushto, Dari, Farsi, Arabic and Urdu.

"Burglarisation?"

"No, no…not theft. But, just disappeared. Yesterday. Her phone has a dead signal. She had a..garage of junk, and that too has been emptied and given up."

"No home address?"

Kavya felt sheepish. Was it crazy to have hired someone when you didn't have their home address? But Georgia was a cleaner, it was all cash in hand, casual work. But that's why I'm scared of what she might do…

"She is of no fixed abode," said Kavya. Georgia had told her she 'was looking to move.'

"Car plate?"

Kavya frowned.

"It's a Mini. Pretty old, I think. Sorry."

None of this negativity seemed to phase Tariq. He simply nodded and asked a series of questions.

"Name, age, race, profession and any other identification"

"Georgia Galton. 26. English. White. I think she's just a cleaner. Red hair."

"Address of garage"

Kavya gave it to him.

"Any social background?"

"She's originally from Hastings. Daughter of single mother. I think there are siblings but no love lost there. Left and went travelling for some years, then came back and that's when I met her. She came to the school. Asking for cleaning work. I felt sorry for her. Many had turned her down because she had no formal qualifications, or references. I didn't ask for an NI number, so I have nothing for background check. "

Tariq was nodding. It was after all common for refugees and asylum seekers to get cash in hand work and no questions asked. It was a question of limited means. Why wouldn't it be the same for poor white people?

"Any reason you can think of why she disappeared?"

Kavya bit her bottom lip and frowned as if deep in thought.

"Really can't think of anything. So, is it possible? To find someone. With just?"

Tariq smiled, eyes twinkling.

"The question is not if it is possible, but how quickly? I will call you with my results?"

Kavya stared at him.

"How long do you think it'll take?"

Tariq shrugged.

"I should have something definitive by tomorrow."

"Well," said Kavya. "Faster than the police! I haven't contacted the police by the way. I mean. Didn't seem right."

"I understand. Why involve police when no crime has been committed? Just one more thing. Do you want her just traced? Or do you want her tracked?"

Kavya brightened. Never thought of that!

"Yes trace. *And* track. Let's see where she's been and where she's going. Can you *do* that?"

She deliberately didn't add the word 'legally'.

Chapter 20

When she came out of the kiosk, she thought I'm going to have a drink now, and walked purposefully past Wetherspoons into a small bar in a side street. BarleyBarton-on-Sea had over nine pubs and bars and it was well to rotate them. This upstart thought it was a cool Soho bar like Fernandez and Wells in Lexington Street, with large serrano hams hanging off the ceiling and the offer of "charcuterie" for the younger discerning crowd.

There was a menu of cocktails. The barman placed a black square on the bar and put a small white saucer on it. She sat on the stool and ordered a James Bond 007, took out the cocktail stick with the olive, drank it down and ordered another one. She drank that and ordered another one. The drinks had proper measures of spirits she noted approvingly, unlike those trendy rip-off bars in London where things were watered down. Quaintsville on Sea had its good points.

She thought of the black curtain at the back of the pristine Mo's Phones kiosk, behind which she had once seen a mountain of tangled wires, laptops, innards of phones all piled up higgeldy piggeldy and it had led her to think of a funny comment which she had refrained from expressing because it might have been taken the wrong way. Might have sounded Islamaphobic. *When you see the bikini under the burkha, you can never not see it.* Who was she to be giving Tariq a lesson in morality, she thought? After all, she had asked him to do the same thing as those horrible men who wanted to locate and kill their runaway daughters in the name of "honour" in the name of *izzat*. But I don't want to kill Georgia. I just want to shut her up!

The three olives lay on the small white saucer and she thought I must eat something, I forgot to have breakfast. But she wasn't hungry. The green and white against the black reminded her of Marymary's never-before-seen kimono. It was silk, good quality. Racy. Where would Marymary wear such an item? Who had given it to her? There was some hidden secret there, some passion. She remembered how Marymary was always looking up to John, touching his arm timidly. Lovingly.

There was no shop in BarleyBarton or even Ramsgate that sold an item like that kimono. You'd have to go to Ann Summers for it. Or possibly Rigby and Peller, more upmarket. Hadn't John said he'd been commissioned to make that couch by Darlings of Chelsea? But they were right next door to R&P. She felt sleepy. Possibly it's good for the weight loss, she thought trying to remember how many hours it had been since she had last eaten. That was the current most popular and effective diet. Intermittent fasting. If you counted the hours, you were asleep that was quite a long fast.

After the fifth dirty martini she could feel her eyelids getting heavy and she thought it's so ridiculous that they don't have a room where you can crash out for a while on a comfortable couch. In the old days, in taverns and suchlike, they had private rooms. Her sleepiness had become a nuisance. I can't remember when I got to bed, I haven't had any sleep. Dog tired. She sighed out loud, then got up and left the bar.

And why shouldn't I have a nap in the office, she thought with annoyance? I'm the boss.

When she got to ISEE, she told Mrs Flinders she was going to do a Zoom meeting and didn't want to be disturbed for 20minutes. Then she closed the door and slumped down in front of the computer.

"Kavya," said Mrs Finders from behind the door.

For God's *sake,* she thought. I've only just.

"Hang on," she trilled and rubbed her eyes. She got up and opened the door a crack. "I'm in a Zoom. I told you 20mins".

"But it's been two hours," said Mrs Flinders. "And you've got a visitor."

"Who is it?" cried Kavya.

It was Terry Kelly.

"Come in, come in," she said. "Thanks Mrs Flinders."

She closed the door, went around the desk and sat down in the chair. Tariq stood respectfully on the other side. He was holding a folder.

"I thought I'd come over and give the information in person. I printed off some stuff. Nice to be in the old place again."

"Have you already found her?" said Kavya lowering her voice.

"Oh yes, that was easy. But I thought you should know something."

His jolly face was sombre now.

"Go on."

"Two years ago, she didn't go travelling. She was in prison."

"What?"

"For assault and GBH."

Kavya stared at him. I'm in an earthquake, she thought. A criminal.

"And…now? Where is she?" said Kavya feeling sick.

"That's why I thought I should come and tell you personally. You see. She is just across the way."

"What way, what do you mean?"

"Behind your house."

"What?"

"Behind your house in Mamble Wafre village there is a disused railway track, they call it the.."

"Picklechurch Walk yes yes yes. What about it?"

"Beyond that are a series of high-rise tower blocks. Low-income housing. She is sitting in one of those. If she uses binoculars, she can probably see into your house through the branches of the trees. But she does not use. She only sits."

Kavya didn't want to know how Tariq had found out all this information, she only wanted to flee.

"What's she *doing* there?" she cried.

"Eating."

"Eh?"

Tariq consulted his notes like a true detective.

"In the last 24 hours, there have been 4 Pizza orders and 2 Texas Fried Chicken orders. In the orders she stipulates mud pie, chocolate milk shake and Pepsi cola. No one else is there." He looked up and said. "I noticed she does not eat chillies. She specifically says 'no chillies, or hot sauce.' I *also* do not like chillies! We Afghanis don't like them, despite being over the border from Pakistan, we do not enjoy the Mughlai food. I always ask for the korma in my local Indian Takeaway. I am pukka English in that manner."

Kavya had tuned him out. Her heart was beating so hard she thought she was going to faint. Which windows faced the Picklechurch Walk? Her bedroom! And Marymary's bedroom. Not Milan, not bathroom. If only I could just…

"Tariq how can you know such detailed, details?"

He smiled ruefully.

"Everything is online these days. Easy to trace. I could tell you *your* movements yesterday, down to which items you bought and where."

"Why would you do that?" Kavya said, taken aback.

"I would not do it. It was merely an example."

"Ok…ok. Yes, I see. You've done very well Tariq. This is useful information."

"One more thing that I found curious. The garage and flat are not registered in her name. I could not find out who.

That fellow must be off grid. You can sublet a garage or a flat but I was not aware that it is possible to sub-let a car due to the insurance problems but in this case I believe the car was also…"

"I'm going away for a few days!" Kavya said abruptly.

Irrationally she suddenly wanted Tariq to leave, be out of sight.

"Thank you, Tariq, *shukria*. I have some work to do now, you see I'm going out of town. I'll look into this matter when I'm back. I appreciate your effort. Do I give you something?"

Tariq smiled and placed the folder on the desk. He put his palms together.

"Of course not. You are not consulting the Bounty Hunter of BarleyBarton *nonextant* – You are my Teacher, my Guru, my Aunty. It is my pleasure to do whatever I can for you aunty. Anything I can do to help. Do you want me to keep tabs on her?"

"No, no, I'll take it from here."

Chapter 21

She closed her eyes not to sleep but to picture her house. The thought of Georgia sitting there looking through the trees…a criminal and a liar. A loose cannon. What could she really see? Our bedroom window, that was always closed and the blind drawn. That left Marymary's room. Kavya didn't know if Marymary had the blind down, but even so, what difference did it make? All the important rooms, Milan's room, bathroom, kitchen, and front room faced the garden. And John had installed the camera round the back which they could monitor on the phone. Alright so the most important thing now was to do this.

She Skyped Lalita's number.

"Hello sweetheart."

"I don't want to bother you."

Lalita frowned. "What's wrong with your face?"

Kavya moved further back from the screen.

"Red nose," said Lalita.

Kavya hung her head. Why is she so mean to me?

"What's going on?" said Lalita.

"I just wondered if…never mind."

"Tomorrow, I'll see you. I've already texted you. I shall come for lunch. And we shall have Moghul moments."

"It's a long drive just for lunch."

"Nothing is too long a drive. Driver Jack drives."

Then why can't you come today? I've got to get her away. And John, thought Kavya miserably.

"Why are you making that noise with your mouth?"

"Thirsty."

"You seem to be drinking rather too much these days."

"No I'm not! Just wine and occasional cocktails. Everyone does. The sea air."

"Your problem is you're bored. It was always the same."

"What do you mean?"

"Even as a teenager. Maybe you were thirteen or fourteen old. There was so much *raunak* in the house, comings and goings, people talking, interesting conversations, comfort, help, music, and I found you sitting alone in a corner. Do you remember?"

"No."

"I said come on and join us. We are all in the sitting room. And you said I don't want to. I said why? You said it bores me. I remember thinking what a funny thing for a child to say."

"I must have picked up the phrase."

"May be. But the things we say start becoming the things we think. And the things we think start to inform our behaviour."

"I'm not bored at all!"

Lalita scrutinised her through the screen, unconvinced.

"I look forward to our lunch tomorrow. I hope you've turned a new chapter with John, with other things. I think you should think about learning a language or getting involved with the community. You don't have enough to do. And drinking fills the hours."

"I don't drink that much! And I'm very busy thank you. I work."

"Where I was born. In Rai Bareli. A train ride from the larger town of Lucknow in Uttar Pradesh. You never went there. I myself never went back once I'd left. I was determined to find a larger life. But in my childhood I saw many things. One was a woman called Asha. She lived in a small, it wasn't even a real house, a sort of mud construction along the path from our house. She had once been married and had children, but I don't know what happened to them. I was very young, 6, perhaps 5 when I first became aware of her. She sat on her haunches outside her house and drank moonshine till she was drunk. She would fall asleep and wake up, sometimes she would ask strangers for food. But I remember seeing her at all times of the day, and even at night, just lying outside her house."

"For God's sake," spluttered Kavya. "You're not saying I'm like this drunk?"

"Well of course not. I'm simply sharing a memory. May I?"

Kavya wasn't interested in this walk down memory lane. If Lalita wasn't going to come today, what was the point?

"I felt pity for her. Everyone did in our small town. And people tried to help her. But the thing was, she didn't want help. Sometimes, I'd see her as I came back from school with my schoolfriends. We had all been told to keep away. And I remember very clearly. She was lying outside her house, the mud construction, and she was completely naked. A dog who was diseased was lying next to her. And it frightened me because I couldn't tell the difference between the two wretched creatures."

Once Kavya had managed to get rid of Lalita, she called John.

"Hey," he said brightly. Immediately put Kavya's teeth on edge because he was always using that tone when he was feeling anxious or something with her. He thought she couldn't tell and that irritated her.

"Listen I was thinking. Let's just drop everything and go and stay in the Moghul for a couple of days. Try again, you know? It got all messed up the other day. Just us. What do you think?"

"Yes. And we can just chill out. Talk. Quality time."

"Yes, exactly."

"My car's got a funny noise coming from it though."

"No no forget that. I'll take the train from BarleyBarton and I'll meet you on the train. Get on at Over Poever Common. We can easily synchronise it. Remember how we did the sea route when we met? You said, it's not exactly jumping freight trains, but it's fun."

John laughed.

"Remember?"

"Of course I do. Yeah, it's a route they still haven't figured out at the tourist office. You need to keep changing trains and then you get to travel the entire Kent coastline as close to the sea as you like."

"Yes, but we'll stop at Saint Dorothy's at Cliffe. Stay at the Moghul. Naani's going to come for lunch tomorrow. And then we can take off. Do the rest of the sea route. Go all the way to Eastbourne. Have dinner in that tiny place near the timber yard? The Jamaican woman who runs it. Goat curry?"

"I'll have the ackee and saltfish."

"So, I'll see you later? On the train? Let's just do it. Let's not plan it too much."

"Alright babe. Whatever you say."

When she got off the phone, she felt bored. Now I'll have to spend the next 24 hours with him. It's all so pointless if Naani isn't even going to come till tomorrow. Anyway, it isn't boredom. It's fear. She couldn't tell the difference. And Georgia. She'd forgotten what she had to do about Georgia. Her anxiety about Georgia was endless, and much more intense now. She was some kind of food addict and addicts of all kinds were reckless, they could become delirious and do anything. I've got to get rid of her once and for all, thought Kavya.

It wasn't difficult to time the rendezvous because there were only five trains a day that came from Mamble Wafre and passed through BarleyBarton and Lower Common and went on to Saint Dorothy's at Cliffe. She boarded the train feeling annoyed at having to keep up the charade with John, knowing he would get on with a big smile on his face.

The train stopped at Over Poever Common.

"Hi," he said walking into the carriage. "This is nice. Great idea babes. I bought a couple of nice steaks."

"Oh, I was thinking we'd just go out, but ok."

"I'll cook, do the barbie just as we said we would."

"So, when we get there, is it ok if I just do some work on the computer for an hour, it's a meeting I've got to attend. And then you can have me all to yourself."

"Oh," said John looking at her feet.

"Oh this? Yeah, I had to bring some folders and things. I bought it today. It was on sale in The Bag shop. Nice colour, isn't it?"

John stared at her. "We can relax and talk and maybe go for a swim together. We haven't done that for ages. Just spend some quality time. Just, be quiet together."

I couldn't think of anything worse, thought Kavya. Can't bear the thought of being cooped up with him.

"Naani's coming for lunch tomorrow. She's so fussy about what she eats, I think we'll just make a salad and some bread."

"Oh, that's great. What an amazing lady she is. The three of us together, well we haven't done that for ages."

Kavya stared out the window. She had lost interest in John prattling on about nothing. It was like a waking nightmare of boredom having to be with him. And pointless too, because if Naani wasn't coming till tomorrow, Georgia could still get to her. She looked at the other passengers. They looked dull and damp and she felt like the carriage smelled of pond at the bottom of the garden. Stagnant with cold dead things inside. But it comforted her in a way, reflected her own mood.

What annoyed her the most about John was his sunny nature. He liked everything. There was no critical thinking going on there. She closed her eyes and let the sun fall on her face, hoping it would make him stop talking. It did and he became quiet. But even when he'd stopped talking, he was like a radiator. Heat, like life kept coming off him relentlessly.

Chapter 22

Saint Dorothy's at Cliffe station was deserted.

It was a marvel that trains still went through it but it was the only route to bigger seaside towns. As soon as they got off the train John tried to help her, but she hitched the rucksack on her back and moved away from him. This "gentlemanly" gesture is so tired and John you should know that I can manage! He said he couldn't help it; it had been ingrained in him. Like not hitting women and opening doors. Kavya laughed and elbowed him.

"You're a dinosaur really," she teased. "In this day and age. Johnnysaurus Rex."

"I feel it sometimes!" he said. "Hey! Look at Jimmy's, what's happened to it?"

Jimmy's Car Hire was a Saint Dorothy's at Cliffe institution from 1965. Everyone and anyone who came to Saint Dorothy's at Cliffe immediately needed a car to get the hell out, and he was open 24/7, and every day except Xmas. His Greek name was Dimitri, but he had changed it in 1965 because the English couldn't pronounce it. It said Under New Management.

"He must have retired," said John. "Nice old fella."

"But of course, it was a good thing Johnnysaurus Rex. They taught you proper manners at that children's home. Manners make character. That's what Naani always says."

They stood outside the station looking at the town.

"Smells of my childhood," he said and they started walking.

In the children's home John had grown up in - *the only one in the country that didn't have any paedos in it, just violent psychotic drunks,* as he liked to joke - the highlight of the year was when they took the kids in a coach to the seaside – never mind Cornwall or Poole, they couldn't even afford Blackpool or Eastbourne so they had come here to Deadsville, Saint Dorothy's at Cliffe. In those days there was literally just beach and one fish and chip shop and three seagulls, but John said to go into the sea was like going into Narnia.

He had told her that story when they had met on that part of the beach in BarleyBarton-on-Sea that the locals called 'sunset strip', and she had felt embarrassed to tell him that she owned a house in his Narnia, as well as other properties and a business. She had so desperately wanted him to like her for who she was. To this day he still didn't know that Lalita was the primary signatory for ISEE and Moghul House as well as an inherited portfolio of investments. All that Kavya owned outright was what she owned jointly w John, namely their house in Mamble Wafre and the dividends.

"It's a sweet little place still isn't it Kavs? The DFL's haven't taken it over. I don't think they ever will. Saint Dorothy's at Cliffe's not trendy enough for them."

"They come and make it trendy, don't they? That doesn't take long. Set up a few independent coffee shops and a farmers' market. They've already got one!" she said.

"That's true. That's true. But it's still nice, isn't it?"

What was it that she had to remember about Georgia?

As they walked along the deserted road, she was aware that he was walking too close and she yanked down both the straps of her rucksack and started striding forward.

"Fresh air," she said.

The wind took off and whipped her hair up as though she had had an electric shock. The sea in the distance was tossing and turning, glinting, and foaming. When they turned into the road that led down to the row of onion top Moghul Houses, she was suddenly horrified. The house looked like big white bones washed up on the shore, remains that had once been some sort of sea monster, now dead, long dead.

She shook her head. I'm not well, she thought.

"You alright?" said John.

"Never better. I'll just go and finish off this meeting thing and then we can…"

"Now? But we just got here."

She turned her back to the house and stared at him, the sun blazing behind him.

"Yes. I *told* you," she said raising her voice over the crashing waves.

"Ok, ok," he said. "You go and do your thing."

She turned and walked quickly into the house. For years this house had felt like a sanctuary to her yet today something about it made her fearful. She strode past the kitchen door and turned right into the bedroom, then changed her mind and came out and went left into the guest room. She locked the door and set down her rucksack. The window curtains were drawn, and it was cool and dark. She unzipped her new yellow rucksack and took out one of the two bottles she had purchased.

She took out a pink pop-up picnic plastic glass and poured the vodka in. She drank it all down and felt better. Then she put the bottle back in the rucksack and put the rucksack in the bottom of the wardrobe. Then she unlocked the door. It wouldn't do to lock the door. He was bound to come in. Then she went back to the wardrobe and took out the laptop and a plastic folder from the yellow rucksack and laid out the papers from the folder on the little desk. Then she set up the laptop there.

The blue folder that Tariq had made for her was still in the bottom of her desk at work; she hadn't even bothered to read through it. Knowing the bare facts had been enough. She sat down on the edge of the bed and took another sip from the plastic glass. She pressed her nose with a finger. Red, was it? Probably the Skype on Naani's side had a colour filter that was set too high. I'll be fine after a good night's sleep tonight. Now for Georgia.

Criminal, Liar, Blackmailer.

Thinking of Georgia bored her. But I must think about her, she told herself and sipped some more. Let her do what she wants, I just don't care anymore. Anyway, she has no agency, she can't do anything. Whatever she tries I can say the opposite. Who's going to believe her? She's a chav. She's a cleaner. She's an ex-con. Her shoulders slumped. Did I say all those things to her? Can't remember, she thought miserably. Dog tired. I need to sleep. She put the glass on the bedside table and lay down on the bed staring at the centre pendant light.

Light was coming in through the threads of the curtain. The waves outside sounded like a snoring animal. If only I could sleep. There was a magazine in the drawer of the bedside table.

Oh goody, she thought. Vogue. Let's have a look. It was from last year, but it was enjoyable to flick through the pages and move your fingertip back and forth over the glossy pictures of shoes and bags.

There was a knock on the door.

"Yeah," she said wearily. I've literally just closed my *eyes.*

John came in and he looked smudged. The light's gone off outside she thought. I mean, sunset. The sun has set on the British Empire, when once upon a time the sun was always shining somewhere in the world that belonged to Britain. These days it's the television show Friends that is always playing somewhere in the world at a given moment and thus the soft power of America…

"Are you alright?" he said.

"Yeah, I just lay down for a second. Had a funny dream. Like those old black and white newsreels. But I wasn't really sleeping. I just closed my eyes for a minute. It was one of those what do they call it, waking dreams. What do you want?"

John was standing above her, his face creased. He picked up the glass on the bedside table.

"Hey!" she shouted. "Leave that alone."

John sniffed the contents.

"Put it down now!" she shouted.

John looked like he was going to cry. He reached out and put his hand on her cheek and she wrenched it away.

"Kavs," he said in a small voice. "Let me…let please let me help you."

She stared at him. He was looking right at her. It was dark but she could see him clearly.

"Leave me alone," she said steadily. "Go away and leave me alone."

John turned and walked out of the room. She flew up and locked the door. Then she went to the wardrobe and got out the open bottle. She poured herself a large one and didn't bother to put the bottle away. He bored me, he annoyed me before, he irritated me, but now I hate him.

I hate him.

Good, now maybe he'll leave me and I won't ever have to think about it. All I want to do is go to sleep. She lay back and closed her eyes but she started coughing so badly she had to sit up. I'm having a fit, she thought, I can't breathe. Her heart was hammering dangerously. I've got to sleep, she thought. If I drink the whole bottle, maybe I can sleep.

There's something wrong with me, she thought. Something physical. Like the lungs. Lung cancer or something. My stomach hurts. My chest hurts. I need to get up. Could be the liver. But I must sleep. She got up and slowly got off the bed. Took in a deep breath. I'll go and get myself some water, she thought and unlocked the door.

She looked left and right, but the house was in darkness, except the line of light under the bedroom opposite where she had counted the Durex. Good, he was in there. She came out of the guest room and was about to go into the kitchen when the doorbell rang.

Who's that at this hour?

The bedroom door didn't open. Good, stay in there and don't come out, thought Kavya as she walked towards the front door.

Chapter 23

John came out of the bedroom. She waved a dismissive hand and went lurching towards the front door. The wind probably. The bell was pressed again and for longer this time. This was not the wind. Something's happened. She unlocked the key and opened the door.

"Youcavaria," said a demented voice in the dark. "I've come to paki you."

From the light in the hallway Kavya saw a frightful raddled old white hag dressed in jeans and a denim jacket. She had an oval face with dark shadows under dead eyes and thin wispy short hair.

"And who the hell are you?" shouted Kavya. "It's very late!"

"I've..I've mmm to pa..talki to you about Courtnee Marie."

"Who?"

"Georgia Galton"

The name sent a rocket through Kavya. It was danger. She didn't want to hear it. And she didn't want John to hear it. She took the keys and quickly stepped out, closed the door and locked it behind her. Locked him in.

"What's this about?" she said.

"You've put the police on her."

"What?"

"And I know why."

Kavya peered at the swaying woman. Classic druggie. The kind of dirty person you saw on the beach off their face in a group of similar.

“I don't know what you’re talking about. You’d better go,” said Kavya.

“She told me you sit a trap for hair. She’s told me everythin’. And ya sacked her. Forno reezin. You’ve said cruel things to her.”

“No I didn’t!”

“You triggered her.”

Kavya laughed.

“What's that supposed to even mean?”

“You live in privilege. You have no idea. Words can break people.”

“Oh boo hoo.”

She couldn’t place the accent. Russian? German?

“Call the police off. Tell them she’s innocent. Do it now! Phone them.”

“Why would I call the police on her? Go away crazy woman,” said Kavya turning to go back inside.

The woman grabbed her arm.

Kavya turned and in a shaft of moonlight saw the woman had a monkey wrench in her hand.

The mad old witch started saying something. Abuse, it was all abuse.

As she tried to put the key in the door, the wrench struck her on the forehead in a scorching blow. She spun round and struck out at the woman with a punch; her fist caught her in the neck and sent her crashing into the bushes.

"Who the hell do you think you're talking to?" bellowed Kavya.

The woman was trying to scramble up, arms flailing. Kavya saw the monkey wrench glinting in the moonlight. She grabbed it and swung it above her head. Her temple was stinging.

"Bloody racist," she shouted bearing down on the now cowering figure. Then she kicked her hard in the stomach and the woman let out a yelp. She got up on her knee and tried to stand up. Kavya stood her ground, shaking the wrench in her fist and as soon as the woman was on her feet, she slammed her on the head with it. The woman cried out and began to stagger away hunched over like an animal on all fours. Then she got up and started toward the sea.

"That's right, piss off!" shouted Kavya triumphantly, unlocked the door, went inside and locked it. She put the key in her pocket.

John was standing in the hallway.

Kavya stood with her back to the door. Everything in her was alive and righteous. She walked past him into the bathroom. She looked at her temple. It was bruised but not bleeding. The druggie had just missed her eye! She came out to the hallway.

John was standing in the same place.

"Kavs..." he said quietly. "What did Billie do?"

"What?" said Kavya.

"That's Billie. She started the group Clean Breaks. She has mental health issues."

Kavya looked at John.

"She's a racist. She attacked me."

"I'm going out to see if she's ok. Give me the key."

Kavya grabbed Johns wrist.

"Don't you dare! You're going out there to help a racist. Don't you dare."

"Calm down. She's probably just come off her meds. She's a fragile person. She's been through a lot. She started a small group for ex-offenders and gave them jobs. Georgia is like a daughter to her."

Kavya ignored him and went to the front door, took out the key and double locked it. Then she put the key back in her pocket and crossed her arms standing in front of the door, legs apart.

"Now I've heard it all."

"Let me just go and see she's alright. You're not thinking straight Kavs. Don't inflame the situation."

Kavya stood her ground, fuming.

"You're going nowhere. Sit down."

John sighed and sat down at the small table.

"All I'm saying is if she's come all the way down here, she's obviously on some kind of – mission—and she – she knows a lot of powerful people. From her past. It's another world Kavs. Please believe me. I don't want anything to come back on you. I can calm it all down, see she's ok, and leave it there."

"Oh you're so worried about me. Don't bother. That racist nutjob isn't *coming* back. I saw her off. I saw her *right* off. I stood up to her. I can handle myself. I handled it, not you. *Me*. And if she dares to come back? Watch me."

Kavya strode to the guest room and came back with the unopened bottle of Vodka. She took out two glasses and poured.

"Drink it," she commanded.

"I don't drink," said John getting up.

Kavya pushed him back down.

"Drink it."

John sighed.

"I know you've drunk alcohol in the past. You told me you used to bite the rim off the glass as a party trick. You're no tee totaller."

"A long time ago. Another life."

"Then drink."

Kavya drank down her own glass and looked at him.

"Why?"

Kavya stared at him, eyes blazing.

"Because you're my husband."

John shook his head and looked down.

"This isn't right Kavs. You're not right. Please. Just sit down. Take a minute. Let's relax. Sober up."

"I'm perfectly sober. Drink it."

John sighed.

"If it means anything to you. Our relationship. *Drink it.*"

"That doesn't even make sense," he said helplessly.

"What doesn't make sense is a racist evil bitch comes to my door and tries to kill me and you want to make sure she's ok? That's what's doing my head in John. You make one move, just one and you're gone. Don't ever come back. We're done."

John picked up the glass and drank it all. Then he put it down.

"Alright?"

He looked miserable, in pain. Kavya poured him another.

He picked up the glass and sipped it slowly. He winced and put down the empty glass.

They looked at each other across the table.

"Is that enough?" he said.

Chapter 24

"Let's go and look," said Kavya taking John's hand.

She went to the door and opened it. A gust from the sea came in and made them shiver.

"See? She's run off."

John nodded.

"You're swaying," said Kavya and put her hand on his shoulder. "Drunk again."

"I'm alright."

"Go to bed. Johnny. Go to bed. We'll double lock the door and forget this night ever happened."

"Why did she come here?" he said frowning.

"Off her meds, like you said."

"I might throw up," said John.

Kavya closed the front door and locked it.

"Go to sleep. Sleep it off," said Kavya.

He looked her in the eyes and she could tell something had changed in him.

"Alright," he said and went into the bedroom. He didn't say "Aren't you coming babes?"

"I'll sleep in the guest room tonight," she announced.

The door to the main bedroom was ajar. John nodded and lay down on the bed and turned to the wall. He wouldn't look at her. It was best to sleep separately tonight, she thought. She closed his bedroom door and padded quietly into the front room and looked out to the dark sea from the window.

The moon splintered the water. The wind was up. Kavya picked up the bottle of vodka and drank from it. I could sit here and drink it all, she thought. But it won't help. Suddenly she heard the familiar sound of John's snoring. She laughed. Men. They could sleep. He wasn't used to alcohol but even so, despite this highly charged evening, he had crashed out. She was glad.

She went to the kitchen drawer and got a torch. Then she put on a puffa jacket and pulled on her gloves. Her hands didn't shake, her mind didn't falter. She double locked the front door and started out. As she had suspected, as soon as she got past the table and chairs at the end of their garden, and out of the gate and down the step onto the sand, she saw the woman lying there motionless.

She switched on the torch.

The wretched creature was on her side and the beam picked up the haggard features of her face. Her mouth was slightly open and there was sand around her lips like sugar. Kavya switched off the torch quickly. Dead? She had to take a closer look. She walked around and bent down, lowered her head to the chest listening for a heartbeat. Nothing. She lifted the woman's bony wrist and it was clammy. That's it, she thought. That means police.

But it was self-defence, she thought. John witnessed it. And I've got a bruise on my temple.

But I don't want the police here. This woman had something to do with Georgia and I don't want *that* story to come out. She couldn't remember what the story with Georgia was. But she remembered that Georgia had threatened her and everything to do with her was the end of days, terror.

But no, I'll go back to the house and leave this woman here. Let someone else find her. I'll say I didn't even know she was there, because of the stone wall in front, you can't see anything from the house. I'll say she threatened to kill me, shouted terrible racist abuse at me and then, she ran away, got scared maybe? Then I'll say, but then she must have come back. It's got nothing to do with me, I didn't even---

But it doesn't work, she thought. Because she's outside my house.

This is the only chance you'll get to make it right, she thought. This small window. I can't go back inside and let things happen. Let someone find her. Let the police investigate. Let Georgia blab. No, I can't let those things happen. I'll never sleep.

I'm stone cold sober, she thought. It's the shock and the cold wind, but thank God for it. Whatever the reason, she felt a surge of energy flow around her body, pumping into her veins. It was the same power she had felt when she had turned around and smacked the woman on her head with the monkey wrench. It made her quick and fearless. Who asked you to come here? Who wants you here, no one? Why should I get into trouble because of you, a nobody? No one cares about you.

She scoffed at John's words. Very powerful people. Yeah, let them come. What are they going to do? Druggies only know criminals and druggies and there is no honour among thieves, that's a myth. They only look after themselves. No one gives a damn about this woman.

Kavya took hold of the woman's ankles and began to drag her down the beach. She was like a bag of bones and came easily, infact the main pain was she had to bend over quite a lot to drag her. The tide must be out because it was such a long way to the water's edge. But she got there.

It wasn't until the water reached halfway up her shins that the cold of it struck her, the bitter cold. But she went on, walking backward, dragging the woman along. If she wasn't totally dead, thought Kavya, this would wake her up. Her face and her scraggy hair were under the icy water. Only I want her to float, Kavya thought. I want her to float the fuck away from here.

She was crying now, waist deep in the icy black water and Billie just lay there on the bottom, not floating. How does it happen? They float after three days. Is it unconscious people that float? Or dead people? How does it work…? Oh god! If I can just get her into some current that will carry her away…

She dropped the woman's ankles; she waded back, behind her. She stooped and lifted her under the shoulders and dragged her farther out. But there was no current, only the gentle wash of the tide. She was growing numb with cold; the water was up to her chest. Get out! She cried and gave Billie a shove. But Billie sank like a stone.

She had to get her up. She couldn't have Billie drifting back up in front of the house when the tide turned. She peeled off her gloves, plunged down into the bitter water, and pulled the woman up by one arm. Kavya looked around in despair; only one little light in Moghul House and the stars in the sky and the eternal black water. What can I *do* with her?

What can I *do* with her?

I can't swim with my clothes on, she thought. But she could if she had to. She began to swim, pulling Billie by the arm. Until she was gasping, freezing, perishing, in the middle of the ocean. She gave the woman a push and turned back toward shore. But her strength was gone; her arms and legs moved like cotton wool. This is it, she thought. She sank under the water, and then she began to fight. She kicked out wildly, and her foot touched the bottom. In all this nightmare stretch of time, with all this herculean effort, she hadn't even got out into six feet of water.

She waded out, panting, teeth chattering, and she became aware that she was making some kind of noise, groaning, sobbing something like that. She had to stop that. She came out of the water, and the wind froze her to the marrow. The light in her own house was a hazy yellow, so far away, so forlorn. Freezing and shivering, she climbed up the beach, so exhausted that she walked like an animal on all fours, and sometimes stumbled, her palms flat on the ground.

If he hears me... she thought, in terror.

She got up on to the path, bent nearly double as she got to the front door. She wasn't stumbling when she unlocked the front door silently. What if he woke up and opened the bedroom door? Suppose he stood there staring at her. Please God, don't let him see me now, she cried inside her heart. I couldn't bear it.

Water was dripping off her all along the hallway. Never mind. Please let me get to the guest room and lock the door without seeing him. Just keep him away.

She got in there; she locked the door. Now. Now I can breathe. Let him knock on my door, let him bang on it. Let him shout and yell. I'm safe now.

Chapter 25

He was knocking. He was calling.

"Kavs.."

She sat up in bed. Just from the tone of his voice she was sure something had happened.

"Yeah, I'm up."

"It's almost eleven. Lalita's very punctual."

Although the curtain was closed, light seeped in from the bottom and bounced off the bottle of Vodka, making it sparkle. She looked at it and heard herself breathing hard. She had been in a nice deep sleep. Could have done without the interruption.

"Yeah yeah, I haven't forgotten. She'll be here at mid-day. We could order in."

"Ok," said John from behind the door.

Silence.

She had thought he might say don't be silly, I'll make a green salad and we can have it with the cold chicken. Coffee's on. Do you want breakfast? But he didn't say any of those things.

Kavya got out of bed and poured herself a drink. I opened a new bottle last night she thought. But she had needed it for God's sake. She drank standing up and peered at herself in the round mirror on the wall. Last night was crystal in her mind. She had peeled off her wet clothes and thrown them in the wardrobe, locked it and taken out the key. The rug was still wet in patches but that didn't matter; she could explain it away by saying she had spilled some water.

She put the newly opened bottle and the empty bottle back into the rucksack, and then unlocked the wardrobe and put it on the shelf above the sodden clothes and locked it. Then she went to the other wardrobe and looked through the hangers and picked out an outfit. I've got to be cool when Naani arrives, she notices every single thing. Absently, she checked her nails.

When they find that racist gorgon washed up on the beach, she thought, well ok then. What's it got to do with me? If they ask me, I'll just tell the truth. Yes she came knocking on my door in the middle of the night, off her *face,* shouting obscenities. She had a weapon! Some sort of spanner or lead piping, not sure. No, no idea who she was but I assumed she was a junkie, a drug addict. I've read about that sort of thing. Newspaper reports. Needles on the beach found.

What if they say no, she wasn't off her face? Well she was crazy, raving, abusive! That's not even a lie! She called me a…terrible racist things and it was quite terrifying. And she went crazy, started threatening to kill me. Paki this and paki that. I was scared and I slammed the door and locked it. I don't know where she went after that. I locked the door. No idea what she did or who she met. Never met her before. Totally random. Don't know who she is. Yes, I could have called the police, but what's the point? You can't prove anything…Racist abuse. You get used to it. *As a person of colour.* Happens all the time. Not to this extent but.

Buoyed up, Kavya went closer to the round mirror to examine her face. Red nose. It *was* a bit. And her face looked a bit creased. On the plus side, the bruise on the side of her forehead had healed up well. I must be healthier than I thought, if I look ok after what I went through last night...She took out her makeup bag and rubbed on foundation coverup, then added just a little eyeliner. No lipstick. Naani had a thing about lipstick how it made you look cheap if you wore it before 7pm. There was no long mirror in the guest room, but she could feel the gypsy skirt and the top looked fine.

The guest room wardrobe contained her overspill. She always kept slightly more bohemian clothes in the Moghul, kaftans which she wore in the daytime and pallazzo pants and long Greek cotton dresses for the evening, and in the hall were the raincoats and hats. Last night's wet clothes including the puffy jacket were in a heap on the floor in the locked wardrobe, and she would have to do something about them later. As long as I can do that, there'll be nothing to prove I had anything to do with dragging that hag into the water. If only I'd managed to get her further out. Now she'll probably get washed up once the tide comes in. At least she won't be outside the house though.

She wished Lalita wasn't coming today, the day on which that old hag would be bound to be discovered and questions asked. Would have been a lot easier if she wasn't around. Also, her routine was going to be severely compromised with Lalita there. If she kept popping into the guest room for a drink, she would notice. She would demand to know what she was doing, and if she said it was a zoom or a skype, she had to attend to, Lalita would want to know who with and why. And there was no way Kavya could have a casual water bottle filled with vodka in it anymore, not after last night.

If John would just keep his nose out of her business, she thought with a rush of fury. It was out of order of him to have come in here like that and pick up that pink plastic glass. *If he'd just leave me alone, I wouldn't need to drink so much.*

She put the wardrobe key in her pocket and surveyed the room. The wet clothes and the bottles were safely locked up. She walked across and opened the curtain, letting in the bright sunshine that made her eyes flutter. Then she opened the door and left it wide open. Nose around as much as you want, see if I care!

She went out into the hallway and saw the Vodka bottle there. It had enough for a few more drinks. Good. It was perfectly normal. She could even suggest a drink to Naani if she wanted it, but she doubted she would go for a Vodka before evening. But anyway, to have a bottle out for guests was what you did in your seaside beach home.

She didn't remember leaving it there or why, but she knew it was one of the ones she had bought after she bought the yellow rucksack. That's right, that's why she had to open a new one when she got back all wet and bothered last night. So now there were two in the wardrobe. One still sealed. She walked casually into the kitchen where John was taking out salad stuff from the fridge.

"Hiya," she said.

"Hi," he said.

He turned around and Kavya was shocked to see how drawn his face looked. Pale and pinched.

"Are you ok?"

"Not really."

"Oh. I'll make the salad," she said staring at him. He looked awful What was *wrong* with him? He'd better sort himself out before Naani turns up.

"Don't worry about it," said John and started chopping.

God, who died? Cheer up.

Kavya felt her mouth was all furry. She heard the noise she was making with her tongue and stopped. She went across to the coffee machine and poured herself a coffee and carried it to the other side of the kitchen where she set it down on the windowsill. She had to hurry up and get in one drink before Naani arrived. She didn't want it at all, it made her sick to think of it, but she had to have it. Especially if John was going to walk around with a long face all day.

What's wrong with him, she thought with irritation and panic. He better not be going down with the flu; Naani can't stand sick people, she'll get annoyed. She left the mug on the windowsill and went to the bathroom to brush. I look quite good really, she thought as she rinsed out with Listerine. She sprayed herself with a floral perfume, not too much. She brushed her hair next and then checked her breath and fingernails again. I can last out a bit longer, and then I'll find a way. She went out and picked up her phone. There was a spot outside by the wooden steps where you could get reception.

She walked back into the kitchen.

“Shall I order…what shall I order?”

John turned around.

“Maybe wait till she comes? She might want to go out.”

“Oh. That’s true.”

“Just making a salad in case.”

“We can have it in the evening if she doesn't want. You know what she’s like? So fussy. Are you sure you’re ok John? Want some help?”

What the hell is wrong with him? He looks like a bottle of milk.

“It’s all done,” said John and sighed.

Why’s he sighing like that? I’ve never seen him like this. Why doesn't he sort himself out? He’d better not be like this when---

The doorbell rang; Lalita had arrived.

Chapter 26

Lalita was dressed in walking shoes, navy trousers, a white polo neck and a quilted beige jacket with a hood. Her makeup was natural and impeccable, and Kavya gazed at her for a second amazed as she always was at how good her grandmother looked at the age of 82. As usual, she was dressed for the occasion.

"Hello hello!" cried Kavya hugging Lalita. "Thank you for coming Naani."

"For goodness sake, all this formality," said Lalita. "Nice to be here. Lovely old place."

"Come in, come in," said Kavya brightly. "What about your coat?"

"It's cold. I'll keep it on for bit if I may?" said Lalita and Kavya bowed her head and they went into the front room.

"Haven't turned the heating on yet—"

Lalita sat down and surveyed the room. John came in and kissed Lalita hello and sat down. Kavya got up.

"Tea?"

"Sit down, let me see you for a minute," said Lalita looking from one to the other and Kavya immediately felt as she always had when she was a teenager. Naani's gaze on you was a searchlight, a wrecking ball. Kavya was desperate for a drink but there was no point offering one. Suddenly, John got up, mumbling about having to do something and went out the front door. Kavya bit her lip. So *rude*. What was he playing at? Now how am I supposed to keep the conversation going?

"He wants to put the BBQ away. In case it rains. You know what men are like with the BBQ," she said.

"What's wrong with you two?" said Lalita ignoring the chit chat.

"Nothing, why?"

"What have you said to him? He looks like a puppy that's been kicked. You haven't got drunk and started raving?"

"What—why do you say that?"

"Because I notice that you've started to like the drink a bit. That's all."

"So unfair. I told you. At the seaside people drink a bit more, the sea air makes you thirsty, but it's nothing bad. It's perfectly normal."

"Is it? Well, he looks awful."

"And what makes you say it's *my* fault?"

"You're always dominating him."

"No, I'm not. Sexist."

"Well, what's wrong with him then?"

She knew she would have to explain John's long face; if only she could get a drink, but it was impossible.

"Let's go out for a walk," she said.

"Good idea."

"We can eat when we come back."

"I'm avoiding these days. Just a salad."

"Well, that's what there is," said Kavya gruffly. "I'll just get my purse."

Lalita nodded. Kavya went into their bedroom and found John in there opening the wardrobe.

"Thought you went outside? What are you doing in here?" she hissed. "We're going for a walk."

"Ok," he said and sat down on the edge of the bed. He was staring into space.

"Johnny! Aren't you going to be nice? She's been asking me if you're sick. She's come and see us. All the way from London…Can't you at least smile?"

"No," he said. "I can't."

Kavya looked at him and thought better of asking another question. No point getting him even more annoyed or upset whatever he was. She went into the guest room and then out to the front room and Lalita got up.

"Yes, good idea to put on slacks. You don't want your skirt blowing around."

No one knows what slacks are, she deliberately uses arcane words, thought Kavya.

They stood outside the front door looking at the path. The sky was clear and there was a stirring breeze. Everything looks like a perfect picture postcard, thought Kavya. A postcard that we've had in the family for years. It's part of our social history. Mum and dad bought it when the school took off and it cost peanuts. They used to bring the foreign students there and serve them scones and cake and tell them about how important idioms were in the English language.

Our Moghul house we called it. Milan plays here. The table and chairs at the end of the path next to the little gate, the small BBQ on the other side, the beach beyond, the sea shimmering. France over there. Seagulls overhead. It's been our sanctuary, our indulgence, our little oasis. Our glittering privilege. Kavya remembered suddenly how it had looked like the bones of a dead extinct animal. And I never want to come here again, she thought with a shudder.

"Let's walk along the sea," Lalita said.

"Oh no. Let's walk along the sea road it's much nicer."

"But I want to walk along the sea."

"But—the sea road is much better," insisted Kavya. "Trees and that."

"I've seen the sea road. We drove along it and the car is parked up there."

"Oh where's Driver Jack?"

"I told him to go and have lunch etc. I said I'd be back by 4ish. Let him have a nice day at the seaside. Now come on. We are walking along the sea!"

Alright. Alright *alright,* thought Kavya in a fury. And then you'll trip over the washed-up body of that cretin and I'll have to say it looks like that one who came to my door shouting terrible obscenities and then attacked me with a monkey wrench.

Where is that monkey wrench?

I forgot all about it. It must still be outside. That's evidence! Calm down. You're not in court, evidence of what? No crime has even been committed. That cretin came to my home with a weapon with the sole intention of killing me! If the subject even comes up. Anyway, there's nothing to fret over, nothing at all. Only, I've got to have a drink before lunch. After everything I suffered last night.

Chapter 27

Lalita put on her Gucci sunglasses. As she opened the little gate, Kavya said let's turn *right.* It's a nicer walk *that* way. Towards the lighthouse. So, they turned right, their backs to the sun and began to walk along the shore. At least she didn't have to walk the other way. Why did they say the criminal always returned to the scene of the crime? I never want to walk along that part of the beach ever again! I'm not a criminal anyway. Georgia is the criminal.

"Now, tell me what's wrong with John?" said Lalita matter of factly. "What's happened?"

Kavya fished out a crumpled pack from her coat, took out a cigarette and lit it. Behind her sunglasses she knew Lalita had one eyebrow hiked up, but the Sharma women did take a cigarette now and again, so it was a moot point of disapproval. Lalita's own mother had been a 'secret' smoker. In the large austere house, beside which lived mad alki Asha in her mud hut, Lalita's mother would disappear inside the open-to- sky toilet, five or six times a day and smoke cigarettes there.

Everyone including her husband knew of this vice that was only permitted in very low class or very upper-class women, not in middle class ones, but no one ever claimed knowledge of it, no one in the family, and not any visitor who came to the house who could clearly smell smoke and hear the coughing fits that came from the toilet. Lalita the youngest, embarrassed, and humiliated had once confiscated the saffron colour packet of Charminar hidden behind the mugga in the toilet and her mother had slapped her in front of the servants.

Far from it being a source of shame, Lalita would tell that story years later with glee in her palatial Hampstead home, to her audience of assembled waifs and strays and her daughter and granddaughter, while she smoked a long Dunhill from her silver cigarette box.

I've got to play it perfectly, thought Kavya as she blew out a smoke ring. Her mind began to work.

"You won't like it," she said.

"What won't I like?"

"The truth!"

Lalita smiled. "I thought the truth set you free. Go on."

"I sacked Georgia, and he went mad at me. Ballistic. Last night. We had an unholy row. He kept defending her. It was embarrassing. So obvious. I told you. But you refused to believe me. I told you."

"Maybe he was putting the case of unfair dismissal. You can't just sack someone like that. They're your employee!"

"You weren't there."

"But I didn't have to be there. I know that John loves you. He is kind and thoughtful. You're harsh with people."

"Why are you having a go at *me*? Why is it always my fault? It doesn't even occur to you that he might be in the wrong!"

"You're harsh with them, because you get bored."

"Not this *again.*"

"You're capricious. Once the shine rubs off, you move on."

My God, she has one script and it's repeated endlessly.

"So unfair. So unfair."

"Alright, tell me who from your university days are you still friends with?"

"It was a long time ago wasn't it, different lives. I didn't finish college, I went travelling so that makes a difference, you lose touch."

"And what of those who you went travelling around Europe with? That international crowd you were so fond of?"

Kavya said nothing and they trudged on.

"Let's sit down in this shelter," said Lalita. "I like the way they've made it so modern, a Scandinavian design. Fits nicely with the old ones from the 1930's infact. Don't you think?"

"Yeah, it's won some award," said Kavya sourly.

They sat on the wooden seat and looked back across the expanse of beach toward the line of Moghul houses. A figure came out of the last one and turned left, began walking and then stopped still like a statue. It was John, he had turned the wrong way. He was far away from the water's edge. He sat down and just looked out to sea, the wind ruffling his hair. Kavya put her sunglasses on and looked at her feet.

Lalita softened her voice.

"I hold you to a high standard because I hold myself to the same standard."

"Well, I've never been capricious with you have I?"

“No darling. You have hero worshipped me ever since you were a girl. I know. And you’ve always had my heart. But Kavya, I won't be here forever.”

“Don't say that Naani, don't say that.”

“Well it’s true. And I want to be sure that you will be alright when I’m gone. I want to---”

She didn't hear the rest of what her grandmother said because past the Moghul houses in the distance along the water’s edge she saw something. The sunlight sparkled off it. It was her Kate Spade glove. It was dark and slimy, but she recognised it immediately. It was splayed like a starfish. It was strange that she could make it out from so far away, but it was definite. And if the glove had washed up, then the body wouldn’t be far behind. She looked up and across the expanse of sea. There was nothing.

“I wanted to talk to you privately,” said Lalita. “About a rather delicate matter.”

“What?” said Kavya in terror.

Chapter 28

"There's no need to look like a rabbit in the headlights. I have hinted at it previously. It's to do with Marymary. Now, I want to be clear it is not about money. The standing order to your bank has been constant. I made myself the 'secret' employer when Kishore died, and I have never regretted it, so rest assured."

"It was very nice of you Naani," said Kavya pushing out her bottom lip.

"Now, now there is no need for waterworks. Milan is my great grandchild; it has been a privilege and an honour to pay for his full-time nanny."

"But she's not—"

"Yes, I know. She is much more. And I wanted that for you. You needed it. Several earthquakes had shattered you. And I know in many ways having Marymary there has been comforting, grounding. A stabilising influence. You have been a joint family of sorts. English people don't understand the value of these things because it is not their custom anymore. It used to be."

"Yes," said Kavya feeling impatient. As usual, Lalita took a circular route to making her point, dropping lectures as she went.

"Yes. Well, I believe it's time for it to stop. I think she should go back to Goa and be with her family."

"What? But…you can sort out her visa, you can pull some strings."

"But it's not about the visa now."

"I don't understand. She'll think badly of me. I pay her, so she thinks…and it'll be…unfair dismissal!

Lalita smiled at the irony.

"But you see, I have a reason. I'm afraid it is to do with money after all."

Kavya stared at Lalita. She didn't dare ask: You don't have enough? That would be the height of rudeness. And anyway, Lalita was loaded.

"She has been..overspending. She has taken out loans. Several loans. And don't ask me how I know. I know. I won't reveal my sources. It has been bought to my attention. And I'm afraid I don't like the feel of it."

"Well…it's her money."

"What does she need money for? For years, she saved like a good Indian and sent money home. After all, she goes nowhere, she has no hobby, her accommodation and needs and food are paid for."

"You sound like you've been surveilling her."

"I wouldn't put it quite like that," said Lalita and pursed her lips.

Kavya was desperate to look at the shoreline again, to scan it, to make sure, but she didn't dare. So, she just looked desperately at her grandmother, thinking, when, when can I get home and have a drink? This is intolerable. I can't endure it. I'm sweating.

"It started after you came here. I mean to Mamble Wafre. A few weeks in. At first it was a trickle, hardly noticeable. She had a healthy savings account. And then the money began to drain, as time went on, it's become a flood. This kind of spending is an indication of something dysfunctional. I don't imagine she has ever done anything to invite blackmail."

"Blackmail?" said Kavya looking up.

"And I'm assuming she does not hoard designer items in her room?"

Kavya thought of Marymary's spartan sparkling clean bedroom, where she had even mended things rather than ask for new ones. But there was a black kimono, and now she felt certain it had been a gift. From. A. Man.

"No, well it was a rhetorical question. You see it can only mean one of two things. Gambling or Drugs. I think she must be gambling. It is often seen in the older lady."

"She's 51!"

"She's a spinster!"

"Sexist!"

"Loneliness, a certain species of idleness, I don't know. I have no time for these character defects. But it goes from recreation to addiction very fast. And these addictions…they can lead to criminal activity. It's her life and I daresay it allows her some respite but…I don't want that near you or Milan. So, I think we need to have an exit strategy. We shall keep the façade of you being her employer, and we shall not make it about money. Rather you can say you think it's time for her to have a well-earned rest and visit the family back home for a holiday. I'll arrange it. First Class ticket. And once she is there, after some weeks, we can ease her out. Think it over. Let's talk about it again next week, ok?'

Kavya's head flopped forward. They sat motionless side by side and the waves grew tumultuous, reaching up to the glowering sky.

"Do look at this. I rather like it," said Lalita brightly pointing to a sculpture by the promenade. "Did I tell you I'll be in the area again? I'm being put up at the White Sands Boutique Hotel no less. I'm on the board of the Kent Arts Council and I'll be here for 10 days for the Asian Art Fair. You must come to see me, it'll be great fun. You should buy a piece or two, they'll rise in value. Asian Art is very collectible these days."

"Ok," said Kavya.

"Of course, this one is rather derivative of the Gormley figures but there is some brass in with the iron, and it is already turning green due to the moistness in the air. That's deliberate and rather good for sleepy Saint Dorothy's at Cliffe I thought. I saw one on the Sea Road too. Sitting reading the newspaper but looking nervously around. The same expression. Being eaten away by age and the elements. I was very keen they should encourage Asian artists but why must they only make art about rage and racism and Bollywood? Why not art for art's sake? But the silly things insisted let's make it a newspaper in Urdu, let's add a turban, to distinguish him. I can't see why young Asian artists still feel the need to..."

Kavya dragged her eyes away from the sea to look at the figure fashioned out of wrought iron. It was a man, naked except for large shorts, wearing a turban. She thought it looked cartoonish, but art had always bewildered her.

"There are nine in all apparently. Dotted around the town. Saint Dorothy's at Cliffe is coming up. You know what they say, first the artists come, then the money men come."

If only I could get a drink, Kavya thought miserably. Maybe I could pop into the pub, but how can I get rid of both?

"Oh look!" said Lalita turning away from the statue "Isn't that John? He's walking the wrong way! He won't find us there."

From behind he looked muscular and surefooted as he padded across the sand in his trainers. He was wearing just a t shirt and jeans. His dark blonde hair was fluttering in the wind. Kavya watched him with a creeping fear. He was her husband, but he could have been anyone. How well did she really know this man? His thoughts, his values, his feelings? Any second now, he would realise he was walking the wrong way. And it happened. She saw John turn around and start walking back toward the house but now along the water's edge. She saw him stop. He was looking at something at his feet. She knew what it was.

It was her glove.

Chapter 29

"I've been promising you for months and today is the day," said Lalita putting on an apron, and enthusiastically folding back her sleeves.

"Finally!" said John with a smile.

"Infact, we shall make three kinds. Onion, Potato and Cauliflower. We don't call them bhajis, we call them pakoras."

"Pakoras," said John nodding.

They were all standing in the kitchen. It was raining outside.

"I'm just going to have a little lie down," said Kavya and left before anyone could say anything.

She went into the guest room and closed the door, then locked it. They'd be too busy cooking to bother to come and try the door. She unlocked the wardrobe and took the rucksack off the shelf. It smelled musty in there because of the wet clothes below. She felt angry thinking they were probably talking about her. Saying what she didn't even care. It's been such a hard day, she thought. Horrible beyond suffering. And now, bloody pakoras.

Lalita had come up with the idea suddenly as soon as they got back to the house. She had phoned Driver Jack to go and find the one 'Continental Stores" in Saint Dorothy's at Cliffe and buy a bag of gram flour, onions, cauliflower, potatoes, and a bottle of cooking oil. Unfortunately, there was no turmeric said Driver Jack. I shall improvise, said Lalita.

Bring me Paprika! And Black Pepper. There is nothing in this kitchen. My granddaughter does not cook, Lalita had declared over the phone. I've got used to her putting me down over the years, thought Kavya as she sipped a drink. But telling her driver! Of course, Lalita had some fancy phone that would probably get reception underwater!

She could hear her droning on to John through the air vents in the wall. '…you see, when the monsoon came, we would eat fried food. It was a thing. I can remember the smell of the frying pakoras to this day, and I was just a child at the time. And you know, I remember very keenly the smell of DDT in the gram flour. It's what they put in the flour to stop it getting infested with bugs, due to the dampness caused by the monsoon. Why did we always eat fried foods in monsoon? I think it was to finish things off and to make us feel happy."

The smell of hot oil seeped in and then the whirr of the extractor fan. She can't even cook, Kavya thought as she sipped. It's a family tradition. Several times she and her mother and her grandmother had sat in a sitting room drinking Pimm's and saying, 'look at us, three generations of prime Indian womanhood and not a cooking skill between us.' Rarely did Kavya think of her mother. Now she found herself remembering her.

Dr Mandakini Sharma had been a brainbox. She had earned a First from Oxford in Languages and travelled the world giving and publishing countless papers about Education. It was true that she had dressed dowdily but she had such a presence that her long legs and slouch and bad fashion were forgotten. Her students adored her. So often that she had lost count of the times, Kavya had been stopped in the street in BarleyBarton on Sea by an ex-student, a refugee or an asylum seeker who would tell her how his or her life had been not only changed, but *made*, by Dr Sharma. She had taught them not just the bones of the English language and helped them develop a love for it, but also love and pride in themselves. For a displaced person lost and lonely in a dark place, Dr Sharma had created light. That was real money in the bank.

Mandakini had forged her own path, she never said it out loud out of respect, but Kavya had understood that she disapproved of Lalita. Her mother thought Lalita's good deeds were self-serving, and part of setting up a School of English in a small seaside town in England had been Mandakini's way of helping refugees and people in need in a constructive way. Once she taught them English, they could be independent and free and on the stage in their own right, not continuously drowning in gratitude.

And Kavya had been all too aware that Lalita did not much like her serious undemonstrative swot of a daughter; she preferred her gregarious granddaughter. For years it had been a mutual admiration society between them, revered *Naani* and beloved *Potee*, but some of the scales were falling from her eyes. Now, she thought, I could really talk to mummy about these things, but now it's too late. When she was alive I hardly bothered with her. I wish I'd shared my feelings then, when I was a teenager.

I wish I'd told her about Dinny. How scared I was. How I couldn't move or help or raise alarm. I wish I'd been brave enough to tell someone of my cowardice. Dinny died of a brain haemorrhage a few months later in India. Of course, it was connected. They had thrown her to the ground and punched her in the head. Repeatedly, over, and over. Her jaunty Royal Blue pleated school skirt yanked up to reveal her white knickers, sodden with blood and dirt. And after a while she stopped yelling.

Those men hollering, shrieking with delight. They were adults. It wasn't just…it wasn't a mugging or a fight. It was six adult men trying to kill a small girl. It was a lynching mum. I watched it all mum, it went on and on. Something human seeped out of me. I witnessed something unrepeatable. I can't forget the force of the punches and the kicks. The sound is terrifying. I never saw her again. She never contacted me. I was ghosted and I became a ghost to myself. The nightmares were vivid, my silence immense. All those overpriced Hampstead shrinks that Lalita paid for in later years were a waste of money. I had nothing to say by then. You were dead. Everyone died. I was left alive.

Lalita's voice was booming through the air vent. Fingernails on a blackboard! She talks to *me* about being harsh and whatnot, she talks to *me* about being a lady of leisure or privileged or whatever, but she thinks nothing of sending her poor driver to buy ingredients to make pakoras with! Talk about Lady Bountiful. So much for Driver Jack's nice day at the seaside. But that was Lalita. The original champagne socialist. But I don't want to think badly of her, Kavya thought suddenly. She's all I've got left.

Kavya took a few large gulps of her drink and quickly put the bottle back in the rucksack and locked the wardrobe door. Then she lay down on the bed and closed her eyes. It isn't a good thing to drink so quickly, she thought. Well, I wouldn't have had to do it if I could go to the pub. I'd rather have a long leisurely drink sitting at a table, but I'm not allowed to. I don't dare to even propose it, because there'll be all kinds of comments about me being an alki. The funny thing is, I've never had an unkind word from any of the locals, ever, but from my own family, my own flesh and blood, all I get is abuse.

Chapter 30

She couldn't sleep at all. She didn't want to. She closed her eyes and thought about The Situation. The glove. John stopping to see it. Did he see it? But how could he possibly have known it was mine? It's just that, the beach was so clean…there was nothing else there. But did *I* really see it? We were so far away. Couldn't it have been some seaweed? But she knew it wasn't. She didn't know how she had seen the sparkle of it, but it was her glove. What about the other one? She had peeled them both off frantically trying to drag that witch into the icy water….

I wish they *would* find her. I really do. Then I won't have to think about it all the time. It's making me so nervous, just waiting. The suspense is killing me, quite literally. Why did I make this plan? I wish we hadn't come out here at all. She squished up her face, trying to think. Why, what was the reason in the first place? She couldn't remember. It was something to do with Georgia. What had she called her? Courtnee Marie. What kind of stupid name was that? Sounded American. Georgia. Georgia.

Oh yes, Terry Kelly found her for me. And why. Oh yes. She told that witch I'd sacked her. That meant Georgia had started to blab. Maybe she even told her to come and look for me? It was *her* prowling outside the house, it must have been? Why, why? But what else did Georgia tell her? Oh yeah. That ridiculous story. That I tried to set her up so that it looked like she was having an affair with John behind my back. As if.

But what if?

What if Georgia came now? Did the racist have a phone? Everyone has a phone. I didn't look. Was it floating in the sea as well? What if it started to ring? From under the *water!* She could have phoned her and told her…In the gap between the time when I pushed her and I was inside the house. It was a fair amount of time. She could have phoned Georgia. And Georgia might...

I just don't want to think about it. Why do I have to be involved in all this? It's really revolting. Kavya's face began to burn. I hate it. I just don't want to be a part of it. I want it to be over. And I don't want my glove to become a clue. Will there be an investigation? Police? I'll have to take the wet clothes back home. I can't leave them here and I can't dry them, she thought wearily. I can't bury them, and I can't burn them. And the bottles. Even the empty one. I'll have to take them all back with me because—when I want to have an innocent drink there's a big drama and I have to go to these extreme measures. It's so ridiculous. Why do I have to do all this in my own home? I have to behave like a criminal, make all these plans.

The *wrench.* The wrench. I have to find it. It'll be outside. In plain sight.

Lalita was calling her.

"Come and get them! Garam garam! That's what the man in the railway station used to say you know John. We were not allowed to eat outside the home, because the 'frying medium' was not good. Oh how we children craved it. You know I really think in the bad oil, in the bits of dirt that one found in snacks fried at the railway station, there was something of what I now, decades later, think of as the taste of home. Such a strange thing. How can one think of something as home when one didn't even taste it, or live it? And yet I do."

"I know what you mean," said John. "I think of my childhood like it was warmed by the sun, how everyone was so kind to me, and how I never missed having a mum and a dad, because of all the people who took care of me. But I was lucky. Others didn't get treated so well. I think sometimes I've had a sort of guilt about it. I think I turned away from things that happened to other people. That affects you. I saw lives ruined, as I grew up. I couldn't help them then, but I felt it more as I got older. I could have done something."

"Oh Johnny. You remind me so much of my dear husband. He was always thinking of others. You couldn't have done anything for the other children. You were a child yourself. Injustice and cruelty are rife. All we can do is hold ourselves to our own standards of kindness and compassion. And you are a wonderful example of it."

Oh get a room! Kavya rolled her eyes and went out to the bathroom and washed her face quickly then went into the dining room where Lalita and John had bought in a large platter of mixed pakoras.

"Basically a fritter. I don't know why I've never tried to make them. I always order them," said John.

"But in restaurants, they're not crispy. And they use far too much flour. They don't really know how to make them, and they save money you see. Less material, more batter."

Lalita offered the platter to Kavya, who took one and bit into it. It was disgusting. Thick, greasy, uncooked and no salt.

"Lovely," she said.

John shovelled them into his mouth, dipping them in ketchup.

"No," said Lalita with a sigh. "They haven't worked. They're no good."

A silence descended over them like a sheet. Kavya felt a grudge against it. It was awkward. John was looking at his plate with a half-eaten pakora while the rest of them grew cold and congealed on the platter. Why doesn't he talk, thought Kavya angrily? After all she made them for him, he could at least say something. I can't stand this.

A woman's wailing voice rose up, followed by a loud drumbeat.

"What the--?"

Lalita chuckled. "My new text ringtone! Do you know this was the most popular Bollywood song of 2018? I love it!"

Kavya stole a glance at John, but he didn't return it. He was busy staring at the useless pakoras. At another time they would have shared an unspoken unkind word about Lalita who was always pretending to be a prole.

"Driver Jack says he is ready whenever I am. And I am."

"I wish you weren't going so soon," said Kavya.

And still, John didn't say a word. It was too much! I've apologised and I've made amends, what else am I supposed to do?

Her own phone rang unexpectedly, and she grabbed it. It had piggy backed on to Lalita's 4G.

"Hello?" she said and then kicked herself because she didn't want to get into any conversation just as Naani was leaving. "I'll call you back—oh, hello?"

"Sorry to bother you aunty. I found out something, maybe you might want to know."

"Ok."

"About the. The eater."

"Ok," said Kavya looking around. Lalita was gathering her bag and zipping up her coat.

"I found out who the feeder is," said Tariq and giggled.

"What?"

"Oh sorry. Sometimes I get the idioms wrong. Sometimes I am using slang but incorrectly. Because I watch a lot of American…"

"Yes, yes?"

"Yes. So, I found out who owns the flat that the greedy lady is sitting in ordering the takeaways from. Because she used the bank card of the person."

Kavya didn't say anything and got up, making a gesture to Lalita that indicated she "had" to take the call because it was work/important. Lalita's face was a mask of indifference, which Kavya knew was her number one expression for contempt.

"Her name is Wilhelmina Brown. It is her bank card, her flat, her garage - they call it lock up. The strange thing is—"

"What?" said Kavya a sense of foreboding pressing in her chest.

"This lady seems to have disappeared off the face of the earth."

Chapter 31

She said she would walk with Lalita to the car and get a lift to Budgens and buy some milk and fruit for tomorrow. She asked John if that was ok, which was really a way of saying don't come. He didn't. He said goodbye and that he would see her later. As soon as they got to the car, Kavya made an excuse saying she had remembered she didn't need to go to Budgens after all and would walk back.

"Thank you for coming all this way Naani," she said feeling bereft.

They hugged.

"It was nice for me too. I'm sorry it didn't turn out exactly as we would have liked. I think Johns cheered up now, don't you think, notwithstanding my terrible pakoras? And you still have the rest of the weekend, you can have some quality time together. Come up to London in the week and we can talk about the other matter."

Kavya watched the car drive off and then she turned around and walked desolately across the beach to the sea. She started walking away from Moghul house. She just kept walking. I don't want to go home, she thought in a blaze of anxiety. It'll just be the two of us and I'll have to sit and talk. I *can't.* I don't want to. Maybe I'll find that witch washed up on the shore and then. And then.

She kept walking. The sun was setting now and the water looked purple and silver. The wind was whipping up and chilly but she didn't care; she'd forgotten to get her coat. If I could only get rid of him, she thought. Maybe I could suggest a divorce, or a separation? I can deal with Lalita's objections afterwards. *It's my life!* What did he really want with her now? She could settle some money on him, if that's what he wanted? I suppose he'll be too proud but the truth of it is he hasn't got a pot to piss in, so money would give him security. I could do that after all. Would that be enough?

And then, I could leave the seaside and go back and live in London. I could sell up and buy a flat in the West End, somewhere like Rathbone Place and then I could drink whenever I wanted. Stroll into Soho to The Coach and Horses, walk across to The Nellie Dean, The Two Brewers, The John Snow, The Star, anywhere. I wouldn't have to hide bottles and lock doors, what a relief it would be.

I could get a three-bedroom flat and Marymary could have one room, Milan another and the three of us could live just fine together. Milan could go to a private school. I could hire a manager for ISEE, I don't really need to be there. Sell Moghul House too. I hate it now. I never want to come here again.

As she turned back it had grown dark and she could hear her footsteps squelching in the wet sand. She didn't bother to look for the glove. It was long gone. The dark sky was studded with stars, it was a rather magical night and from somewhere she thought she smelled a wood fire. The smell transported her to when she had been a small girl.

Mum and dad had lit a bonfire in the back garden and put potatoes wrapped up in foil in the ashes. She was sitting in her room upstairs watching them. They turned and waved and asked her to come down, but she didn't want to and they accepted it and let her be. She sat there looking at the two shadowy figures at the end of the garden, the embers of the bonfire, the sky sprinkled with stars. She felt so peaceful and happy and safe. No one was looking at her and that's how she liked it.

I used to be a gregarious child. When I was six and seven and eight I would sing and dance and whirl about aimlessly; I was flexible and bendy, a wild little jungalee, full of supernatural energy. Gregarious. That's what everyone said, a label that stuck. But the truth is, I always liked being alone, she thought. They tried to make me join girl guides and go swimming with the school but I never liked it, I didn't want to be with people. Maybe I was afraid of people. I preferred to be alone. I liked to sit by myself or go off walking, lost in my own thoughts. Maybe it became a habit with me.

I'm never alone now, she thought tearfully. I can't enjoy anything. John's always there.

As she walked back, she could see the lights were on in the house. She stopped by the side of the house and saw him moving about the kitchen. Like a prowler she stood in the shadows and stared into her own house. She knew by the time she got in he would have got rid of the ill-fated pakoras, cleaned up the kitchen and probably set the table for dinner. He would have made something simple but nice. It wasn't that she didn't like that, she did. But she was grateful for it and that was all. Grateful because if he didn't cook, she wouldn't eat and drinking on an empty stomach made you sick that's all.

All at once she thought of Marymary. She would be at home, sitting with Milan. She would have asked him to unfold the napkin properly and not make a noise when he was eating. Maybe people in Mamble Wafre thought they were strange, out of time, that Kavya was an entitled princess, she didn't care at all. She felt a great stab in her heart. I'm not the lucky one. Marymary saw every small change in him, changes that might become his habits. She walked to the hot spot by the side of Moghul house, took out her phone and called.

"Hello Kavya, dear, are you having a nice time?" said Marymary.

"Can I speak to Milan please?"

Milan came on the phone.

"Mummy has been very naughty," she said.

He giggled, "What did you do?"

"I didn't call you. I forgot. Isn't that silly? Or naughty?"

"Both!" cried Milan. Then, "Not really mummy."

"I suppose the mice have been playing while the cats away!"

He laughed. "I've been practising my magic tricks."

"Shall I come home?" she said urgently. "Don't you want to kiss me? I want to kiss you."

"Mummy!" said Milan. "Why are you being so silly?"

"Because I miss you stupid boy."

"I'm not stupid."

"No. You're very clever. And handsome. And cool."

He giggled.

"If I could, I'd fly home. Like an eagle. Do you want me to?"

"No mummy, come back when you're ready. I'm alright."

"Are you?"

"I'm six," he said.

As soon as she finished the call she thought about Georgia.

Georgia sitting in a flat across from Picklechurch Walk, watching her house, ordering takeaways. Georgia picking up a pair of binoculars and looking through the trees into my life, my house, my child, my people. She might be waiting for the phone to ring. She might come down all guns blazing and accuse me of killing that old witch. And I did kill her, she thought with a wave of amazement. It was an accident, but I did kill her. I killed her dead. And then I dragged her body into the sea.

She straightened up and walked purposefully to the gate, opened it, and walked up the path. I was in complete possession of myself, I didn't even break a sweat. That woman came and banged on my door in the middle of the night and tried to bully me. I didn't let her. I fought back. I let her know who was in control. A lesser person would have panicked, but I didn't. I met the situation with coolness. I didn't need a man to defend me.

She stopped outside the front door and looked up at the moon. It was bright and the street beyond the onion top of Moghul house was lit up, not a single soul in sight. I know this little place like the back of my hand she thought. Something like a sense of nostalgia and propriety swelled up in her chest. It made her strong. And so what if Georgia comes, *let her come.* I'll meet her too. Why should I run away from the likes of her? Let her come, let her try it. I'll look her straight in the eyes, just as I did with that old witch.

At that moment Kavya suddenly remembered the wrench. She turned around and looked for it and found it lying by the bushes. She bent down to pick it up and shoved in inside her trouser waistband; she could feel the wet and cold metal against her thigh. If Georgia comes, maybe I'll whack her with it too. Who does she think she's dealing with? She's a nobody with some sort of eating disorder. She's out of control. She's nothing. People like that have no agency, they rely on others, they depend on them.

The door opened.

"Come inside Kav, dinners all ready. Come in out of the cold," said John.

Chapter 32

"Just give me five minutes, I want to get changed. I'm all damp," she said walking past him and going into the guest room. She locked the door and unlocked the wardrobe, took out the wrench from her waistband and shoved it inside the rucksack. She took out the opened bottle and poured herself a drink. It's absurd, she thought. It's a farce like when their trousers come down every time someone comes in the door. Why should I have to do this in my own home?

Quickly, she peeled off her clothes and hung them up. She went to the other wardrobe and pulled out a Greek kaftan and flung it on. She finished her drink and looked at herself in the mirror. Long time since she'd worn this one. Everything in this wardrobe was slightly old fashioned, slightly retro (without being ironic), because that's what you wore at the beach in your house by the sea at the English seaside. You dressed down. It was another story in Spain or Italy, they dressed up over there. She scraped her hair back into a bun and put on some eyeliner, tilting it up into a doe eye. Then she put on a peach-coloured lipstick and smacked her lips.

As soon as she came out to the hallway, she felt furious. It was Johns fault, all of it. She was a prisoner. Because of him, she had to drink her drink quickly, too quickly, all the time anxious about a knock on the door. He made her nervous with his relentless judgement. She had to lock up the wardrobe door. She had to unlock the door of the room; it was like an endless locking and unlocking cacophony.

The lights were dimmed in the front room so she went into the kitchen.

John had laid the small table there and the lights under the cabinets were on. They threw a harsh bluish light which she had never liked but she didn't say anything. It was cold chicken and salad, the meal he had thought they would all have for lunch. I don't mind having it, but why is he so miserable, she thought as she watched him moving about getting a jug of water and glasses. What's the matter with him?

"I hope you threw away that crap she made," she said.

"I did," he said without a smile.

"I don't know why she bothers. The world knows she can't cook! What a waste! And getting poor Jack to---"

John was looking at his plate and he sighed.

"She was just trying to be nice," he said.

Somehow she couldn't talk, so she took a few forkfuls of pasta. She had tried to make fun of Lalita so they could have a common enemy, but John wasn't having any of it. It alarmed her in a way.

"It's lovely," she announced. "But I'm just not that hungry. Dunno why?"

He ate his pasta without saying anything.

He's thinking about my glove, she told herself. Well why doesn't he say anything? Why doesn't he say, hey you know I think I saw your Kate Spade earlier, down at the beach.

Mine? The ones with the diamantes? I doubt it, I didn't bring those down to the Moghul, they're far too nice. But he had seen them on the hall table by all the coats. No no it couldn't have been mine Johnny. My Kate Spades are at home, in my chest of drawers. For special occasions.

She was braced to face it all, answer any questions, any suspicion, but how could she when there was nothing but silence? He wouldn't meet her eyes. She forced a few more mouthfuls and then put the fork down. She couldn't taste it anyway. Was it Amatriciana or Pesto, she couldn't say, she didn't care.

"Did you hear the seagulls last night? They're really becoming quite a nuisance."

"Last night...?"

"I mean it's bad enough when they're pecking at the rubbish bags in the high street, but at night! They collect in the inlet. Like a mothers meeting!"

"Really?"

"Yes, I'm amazed you didn't hear them. There was about three or four, big ugly things. Shuffling about outside, I thought it was a burglar or something."

John was looking at her now, waiting.

"So anyway, I went out quickly putting on my coat. I dropped one of my gloves on the ground and the little beggar came and picked it up and waddled off. The other ones followed him, like he'd got a fish in his beak. I ran after him, but he lifted up, the wingspan still amazes me. Anyway, he swoops up and the others scatter and that's the last I saw of my glove. You remember the Kate Spade gloves? I knew

I should never have bought them here. Anyway, it's lost forever now. I don't know what that stupid seagull did with it. Tried to eat it maybe."

John nodded. He picked up the pasta bowls and took them to the sink.

"I'll do that," she said eagerly.

"I don't mind," he said.

"Why so quiet tonight?" she said.

"Sorry," said John. "I was thinking. Do you mind if I go back tomorrow?"

"Go back? I thought we were—going to jump trains and do the sea route."

"I don't feel like it. And anyway, I miss Milan."

She curled her lip.

"I see."

"You can stay if you want. I'll get the train back. You don't mind, do you?'

"No, I don't mind. Go home."

Locked in the guest room, she lay on her side and fell asleep instantly. In the middle of the night she woke up with a jolt, burning with resentment against John. He wants to get away from me. Leave me here alone. Good, he can piss off then. That's what I want. She could hear him moving about. The clink of cutlery. The scrape of the chairs. He was still in the kitchen, cleaning up like Mrs Mopp.

She had always been impressed by how tidy and organised he was, but tonight he got on her nerves; he seemed to be doing everything super slow. Kishore had never cooked a thing. Or emptied the dishwasher. At the time she had thought oh well, he's a man, but it had got on her nerves because Kishore had been a spoilt brat. But now, listening to John creeping about, trying not to make any disturbing noises inflamed her.

She heard him double lock the front door, switch off all the lights and then go into their bedroom. The door closed and then she heard a key turn in the lock; she heard that distinctly. She sat up in bed, alert in the dark, eyes wide open.

What's he locking his door for? He's never done that before. What's he afraid of? A tremor went through her body.

Chapter 33

Kavya woke up at 5.30am seething at John. She couldn't forgive him.

She went to the kitchen and made a pot of coffee, poured herself a mug and left the rest for him. Then she wrote a note and stuck it on the bedroom door, and tip toed back to the guest room, opened it and locked it. She left the mug of coffee on the side and opened the wardrobe where the wet clothes lay on the floor, smelling alarmingly of the sea. She had to stuff them into the rucksack with the two bottles, one empty, one full. It was exasperating having to fit them in. She sat down on the floor with the rucksack between her legs.

She took out the bottle that was empty, then shoved it back into the rucksack. She made a noise with her tongue. I can't leave it here; I've got to take an empty bottle back with me. They never left any trash behind; it was always tied up in a plastic bag and deposited into the big bins by the side of the houses and as the bin collection only happened every three weeks for the Moghul houses, it was always best not to leave anything. They usually took their perishables with them, and John had already made up the 'take away' bag.

She sighed and unscrewed the full bottle and lifted it to her mouth. It's low, drinking like this, she thought wiping her mouth with the back of her hand. Tramps in Camden Town. She had seen one once with his flies undone, sick all down his trousers, stared at his shrivelled-up penis and giggled and gone ewwww. Alkis, deadbeats, losers. Comical objects.

She got up and zipped up the rucksack and left it there. Then she went to the bathroom and had a quick shower and tiptoed back to the guest room. She noticed the note had gone. As she was getting dressed, he slipped the note back under her door. She opened it and read her own handwriting:

I'm coming back with you. There's a 10.30 train. I can't be where you're not. Don't be angry. I can't speak, I'm ashamed. Just let me know you want me to come back with you by pushing the note back under my door. Then I'll know.

Underneath it John had written: *I'll order a cab for 9.30 x*

She exhaled. The "x" was important. It was 8am. She didn't feel like going out to the kitchen where he was having breakfast. She had written the note because she didn't want to stay in the Moghul alone. She just wanted to go home. Back to the house where Marymary and Milan would be pottering about, where the heating would be on a little bit higher than it was in every other house in their English village of Mamble Wafre. Sometimes they used to call it Mumbling Wafers in Quaintsville on Sea and make each other laugh. She didn't even care about Georgia now, or about that old bag. All that was in the past.

She was going back to a normal life with people who she had known for years and who loved her and she them, people she could rely on to be a constant. I'll ignore John, she resolved. I'll just ignore him. At least until he sorts himself out, because whatever was wrong with him, he had to get over it. Misery likes company, well no! Try smiling occasionally, it won't crack your face.

She came out with her rucksack when the doorbell went. She got into the back of the taxi while John locked up. He got into the front. He spoke to the driver as they drove to the station, and it was a clear road. She leant back thinking there's no one in sleepy Saint Dorothy's at Cliffe. It was Deadsville. As they drove along the sea road, she noticed two of the iron figures, outdoor sculptures that were part of the forthcoming Asian Art Fair.

Lalita had said they were depictions of cultural alienation. It was the same man, or the same man in different –what did she say? Emotions? Stages of madness? Stages of grief? Kavya couldn't see that at all. They were just men. When they got to the station she thought suddenly 'I've always had men. I've never had a problem getting them. They've always come to me. I liked the sex but I never liked a single one of those men. Why didn't I ever have a best girl friend? It's too late now. I've become comfortable with old women.'

On the train they didn't speak. John read the paper and she looked out of the window. She was dying for a drink and before it got to the next station she said,

"Johnny, I'm going to get off at Marfleet. I'm going into the school."

"But it's..."

"Well, I do go in on Sundays sometimes, it's quiet and I can get things done."

"But Marfleet's—"

"I'll walk. Do me good, clear the cobwebs. Anyway, the Loop will probably go past, I'll hop on."

John looked alarmed. He put his hand on her arm.

"Don't Kavya. Let's go home. Together."

"I don't want to," she said. "I want to go into work. I'll be back soon. I'll get a cab, whatever. I'll be home by 6. And I'll make dinner. It's my night. Just—"

"Pasta," they both said and laughed.

"I'll make sure I have a kebab beforehand then," he said with a grin.

"Oh ha ha. You'll eat my pasta, and you'll like it!"

They smiled. It was a well-worn script. A bit, the way couples had bits. It was what she had said to him on their first date; she had invited him over to the flat that she had ended up selling because it was full of mum and dad's stuff. And he'd sold his flat and together they'd bought the big house in the village of Mamble Wafre.

It was their first date. He had eaten the tragedy she had cooked up and then he'd said, 'when we're married, I'm doing the cooking' and it had pleased and taken her aback. When you know, you know. At the time it had felt inevitable and right. This man with the blue eyes who she had met on 'sunset strip' by the lighthouse was going to make everything alright again.

Before Marfleet station came into view she got up quickly and hitched the rucksack up on her back and as the train hurtled into the station she lost balance, slipped and half fell on John. She steadied herself and without thinking, offered her hand, not her cheek or lips to him. He took her hand and pressed it. She quickly pulled it back feeling embarrassed.

"See you later Mr Bond," she said and got off the train.

She stood on the platform with her back to the train and the train sped on behind her. What's wrong with me, she thought. She started to walk out of the empty station and the embarrassment left her. Marfleet was even smaller than Saint Dorothy's at Cliffe, a strange abandoned little place and the train only stopped there on certain Sundays. It was yet another ghost town in a coastline of ghost towns.

Maybe it was a village, Kavya didn't know the distinction. It was just small. That was how a big city person thought and she would always be a big city girl. ISEE was about a 20minute walk and she began to walk. The rucksack was heavy and she could feel the wet clothes inside pressing against her back. As she trudged on, she started to make some calculations.

The problem was, she had two bottles. One empty and one more or less full. What she wanted to do was buy another bottle and get rid of the empty one. It was a main road but there was hardly any traffic on it yet it felt weird to take out the empty bottle and just put it on the roadside. What if a car went past just at that moment? There wasn't a single bin anywhere.

As if in answer to her anxiety, one then another car flew past, far too fast on that narrow road. That's how they drove out here, unencumbered by fear of traffic police or camera. Half of them couldn't drive, too stupid, the other half shouldn't, too old. She felt weighed down by her burden. It wasn't just the heaviness of the rucksack; it was a strange dark feeling in her head like water filling up a dark tank. She had no intention of walking all the way to the school so why was she walking in that direction? There had to be an Off Licence or some small shop, surely? But there was nothing, so she kept walking, thinking it was silly to be walking away from the direction of home.

And then she saw a fork in the road and a sign that said Andy's Micro Brewery. That was new. Well, she had never walked on this road before, so maybe it had been there for ages. She turned into the small road and saw to her amazement a small, secluded house. There were some people sitting in the garden on plastic chairs, smoking, drinking, chatting. She pushed the door of the house and inside it was like a dark barn. All the walls had been knocked down and replaced with bales of hay. It smelled of freshly dug earth. There was a small bar and a people sitting on stools around empty upturned beer barrels. She sat down on a stool at the bar and looked at all the beers pumps. Charming, really! Just the kind of place the salivating DFL's loved to 'discover' and proceed to ruin by invading it.

"Just beer?" she said.

"Yes," he said. "Want to try some real ales?"

"Give it a go," she said happily.

Chapter 34

The young man behind the bar told her about how Andy's came to be, and how his father and uncle, both long distance lorry drivers put out of business after Brexit had decided to buy up this ramshackle house and set up the brewery at the back and rip out all the walls and make it into a local micropub. The hay came from his other uncle's farm.

The sawdust on the floor was from the place they bought the barrels. The room at the back was given free to local community groups to hold meetings in. Andy's was a small village within a small village and named after the horse that came in netting his long distance lorrydriver uncle a cool £5k which started the scheme off in the first place, crowdfunding it to the tune of an even cooler £25k.

She nodded as he talked, sipping the various Real Ale samples. Before she settled on the Haymaker, he had given her five different tastings. He was trying to explain something to her, but she couldn't pay attention. She felt high, like she'd smoked a joint. She was floating.

"Where's the loo?"

He pointed, and then when she got off the stool, he said 'you can leave your rucksack here, no problem,' but she said no no it's ok, and then giggled apologetically and said, 'it's the Londoner in me'. When she got inside the toilet she thought, I could leave the empty bottle behind the toilet. But the trouble was, it was a Smirnoff bottle and they only made beer at Andy's, so they would know it was her. What would it matter, she'd be long gone?

But it would, what if someone came out of the toilet holding it aloft as she was leaving? Like a silent movie, she imagined someone running down the street after her with tinkling piano music playing. It was farcical, bizarre, truly absurd. What a situation to be in? She came back and ordered one more glass. This real ale was strangely satisfying, heavy yet flavoursome. The man behind the bar had been telling her something about it and she had felt too lightheaded to care. You have to drink it slowly, that's right. She lifted the glass to her lips and then the door opened.

The unmistakeable figure of Shanta Acharya walked in, white sari, desi leather sandals, dishevelled hair. Today, not dressed up.

I must be hallucinating, thought Kavya.

"Arre!" cried Shanta Acharya. "Well of all the places?"

She seemed to know everyone there.

"What are you doing here?" said Kavya.

"I come to Marfleet for Reiki."

"But this is a---"

Shanta chuckled. "I know. I don't touch it. As you know I do enjoy a little Pimm's now and again but this is too strong for my—oh but do go ahead."

"Oh, I'm just having a small one."

"They allow us to use the garage in the back. It's a fully insulated room. And they very kindly let us use it for free. Usually a few of our number drift in for a drink after wards but today—there won't be a class. I've just found out."

Kavya nodded slowly. These small towns, villages, barns whatever they were with their crazy ass English names. There was a village two villages over called Bobbins in the Beans where she thought they must all bob about like bunny rabbits. She quite liked them, these quaint little places. Everyone just chatted away endlessly as if they were in your front room or in the next garden, all the time in the world. A lack of urgency, of ambition, of speed…

"Apparently, it's closer to a tonic. It's organic."

"Did you hear?" said Shanta Acharya

"In the old days they used to give Guinness to pregnant mothers. It's not all that alcoholic."

"She's disappeared," said Shanta Acharya.

Kavya looked up from her pint.

"Who?"

"Our Reiki teacher. Wilhelmina Brown."

Kavya shrugged her shoulders.

"Never heard of her."

"We're all at a loss. The story is that she has been AWOL for two days. Hasn't been in contact and usually we always get an email before class. Oh surely---But you *must* know her. John has known her for years. She helped him set up his workshop I believe. Didn't she give him the finance for it? He trained a few of her proteges and they are all working in London now."

“I don't know her. Before my time.”

“She teaches Reiki in prisons, in schools, oh she even flies over to the Continent. She has had an incredible life, she has never allowed her shortcomings to restrict her; she should write a novel about it, I keep telling her so. Everyone in BarleyBarton knows Lady Billie Brown.”

“Not me. I’ve never heard of her…”

Shanta lowered her voice to a delicious whisper.

“Her people own rather large sections of Kent you know, but she never uses the “Lady” which of course shows breeding…she is top drawer. Of course, her real surname is *Von Braun*. Her ancestor is Werner Von Braun the aerospace engineer, or to give him his full title: Wernher Magnus Maximilian Freiherr von Braun. Oh, you must have seen her around. She was born with a cleft palate, and she has a disease that attacks her muscles so she looks bony like an anorexic. Why if she hadn't taken up Reiki, she’d be long dead. She’s 65 you know. Amazing. Her cleft palate makes her sound like she has a speech impediment. What can't that woman do? That’s German stock for you.”

“They call it Real Ale. Why, does it mean there is Fake Ale? Like fake news?” said Kavya sipping away wishing Shanta would stop talking. She was like a wind-up toy.

“Her father is a Lord, or is he an Earl? Or a Viscount? Anyway, whichever is the highest one, that's him. She counts the British Royal family as childhood friends! Oh but she never mentions it and nor must you. Considering the privilege, she had growing up it’s fascinating to know that she is also a very good car mechanic, don't ask me how! She fixed my car for me once! Imagine that, just like an ordinary mechanic! And she’d take no money! She has taught the subject of Car Maintenance at evening class. She has formed groups for ex-offenders called Clean Breaks, and she is a Reiki master. I'm surprised you haven't seen her around. Anyway, the thing is, people are worried about her, and I've been sent to do some investigations!"

"Investigation?" said Kavya. "You mean police?"

"No no. It's a little early for that. No, they've just asked me to ask around at Andy's. I'm the youngest in our class you see hee-hee-hee and I used to be an academic researcher, so they nominated me. But to be honest, I really don't have a clue. No one wants to go to the police, but I think if another day passes...Well, but it's funny I should bump into *you* here because I was hoping I'd bump into you. By the way what *are* you doing here?"

"Oh, it's a funny story. We were at the Moghul and took the train home but what happened *was* I forgot I had to do some work at the school, so I got off the train and started walking. Then I went the wrong way and changed my mind and wandered in here to wait for John. He's coming to pick me up. Soon. Thought I'd try this tonic. Why did you want to bump into me?"

"You're a young person and I expect you know about computers."

"A bit"

"Well...I wondered. You see I had this idea. There is a place in BarleyBarton-on-Sea where they fix your computer and your phone. And I thought I might – ask them to help."

"What can they do?"

"These days...can't these people do everything? I mean a simple thing like tracing her, if I give them her phone number and address. I heard they can do these things."

"Shanta, now be very careful. That sort of thing is illegal. Were you thinking of Mo's Place? The one where his son works?"

"That's right. He fixed my telephone once—"

Kavya lowered her voice. "Shanta, please be cautious. You know he is—a refugee. Infact he studied at our School. A lovely man but—well, I wouldn't get too involved there. You see, you don't know the freight that these refugees carry. Who they paid to get to the UK, who they fraternise with. Some of them have been convicted of honour killings. Remember that case of the girl in the freezer? Five bin bags."

Shanta Acharya's eyes grew big. "Honour killings?"

"You don't know who they're connected to. Gangsters and thieves. You start asking them to do something illegal…well you open the floodgates."

"To what?"

"It could lead to all kinds. Blackmail for instance."

Shanta Acharya shook her head.

"Oh, I hardly think."

"But you *should* think. I'd keep well away from Mo's place. I mean it. Infact don't even take your phone to get fixed there. Or your computer. Never go there. After all, when you think about it, why are they offering the service of 'unlocking' phones? Maybe because they have stolen phones and sim cards for sale? And who needs phones that can't be traced? Gangsters and terrorists that's who. Give that place a wide berth if you ask me. Can't trust," Kavya lowered her voice. "That type of person"

"Yes, yes, you are right dear Kavya. You never know with Muslims. Not trustworthy. You're right to warn me. It was a silly idea perhaps. But what can we do? About our dear teacher?"

"I'd just wait. People turn up, don't they? Sometimes they – well I don't know. Does she have any family?"

"Well not in BarleyBarton. I suppose she might have children or cousins, I'm not sure. There's no husband in the picture, infact I get the feeling she was quite alone."

"I'd *leave* it alone if I was you. She could have personal reasons. Don't poke a hornet's nest. Leave it alone Shanta."

"Yes, yes, I shall indeed. You are right! Can I take you somewhere? I'm going back to BarleyBarton."

"John's coming to pick me up in a half hour. I'm just waiting for him. I was going to offer you a lift."

"I'm driving. I'm sorry to miss him. Anyway, it was nice to bump into you dear Kavya, do give my regards to your esteemed grandmother Lalita*ji*."

Chapter 35

Great, thought Kavya coming out of the micro-brewery after giving Shanta a lead of 10 minutes, just *great.* This is too much, she thought. This is getting beyond a joke. The fact that the woman was a somebody was beginning to alarm her. German aristocracy connected to the British Royal Family. No one cared about a white trash drug addict, but this Billie character...people were going to do something about a Lady, this was England, they would do something to find a missing Lady.

I thought she was drunk or stoned. How am I supposed to know she had a speech impediment? Was she saying Paki? Or Kavya? Forno Reezin. I thought it was German or Russian. Was that an upper-class English accent? I don't want to think about that, Kavya told herself. As she crossed the road to go back to Marfleet station, her legs suddenly buckled. Her head was swimmy. Her knees felt as though they were getting dislodged. She put down the rucksack and steadied herself.

Shanta bloody Acharya! It was like the worst scenario, the cruellest coincidence. Much worse than any picture that had come to her mind of someone running out of the toilet waving an empty Smirnoff bottle. Relax, stay cool, stay cool, she told herself. Mo's place! That was just a coincidence. A horrible thing. No, but she won't go there, and even if she goes there Tariq won't say anything. He'll think it's fishy.

But what if she finds out that Georgia is *staying at this woman's flat* which is behind my house? Well so what, what's that to do with me? Tariq won't tell her anything and it doesn't matter if he thinks it's fishy, he won't say anything to anyone. After all he *was* taking money from those awful men. Bounty Hunter of BarleyBarton. After all, he *is* a refugee, and he *is* a Muslim and there's so much Islamophobia especially in these small towns, so he'll never want to have anything to do with any kind of controversy---She won't go. She won't.

For a long moment Kavya felt herself go numb all through her body and she was aware of her mounting hysteria. She was confused and rigmarole was running around her brain like cocaine. She felt cornered, hemmed in from every side, like a fly trapped in a spider's web, vulnerable and defenceless, surrounded by looming predators. Georgia, Terry Kelly, Bille, John, even Shanta Acharya all terrorising her and she couldn't remember why.

I've got to eat, she thought suddenly. I'm fainting with hunger. It's affecting my brain. Her knees jiggled. I can't walk anymore, she thought with alarm and stopped. Something wrong with the bones…Must eat something. Got to stop drinking. If I don't, my mind's going to get all messed up and I won't be able to think straight. I must stay sharp. I must be in touch with reality. These new worries had taken her mind off her rucksack. She was almost at Marfleet station when she saw The Sunshine Café. In she went.

It was one of those funny little places you only saw in English seaside towns, or rather, she corrected herself, not the sort of place you saw in London anymore. The walls were covered with bad 1950's jaunty paintings of Venice, and the countertop had pyramids of perfectly balanced sausage rolls, curry puffs, cakes, and breads, all too large and not Italian. Underneath the counter were plastic containers of sandwich fillings made with salad cream.

The sort of place that had been opened by an Italian immigrant possibly back in the 1950's when English people didn't entertain foreign muck, and probably in this little hellhole, they still didn't. Just like the Indian restaurants where the waiters never ate what they sold to white people; in this establishment they served overcooked macaroni cheese but privately ate pasta al dente.

"I'll have the full Monty please," she said sitting back in the chair, rucksack between her legs.

The short husband and his short wife behind the counter, dressed impeccably, stared at her.

"Breakfast is feeeneeesh," said the man. "Now itsa lunchtime. A macaronicheeesaa."

"Alright, then give me bacon, sausage, eggs for lunch! Hold the fried bread."

Grumbling, the owner bought her breakfast to the table. She wondered if he would be equally disapproving if she ordered a cappuccino, because it was after 12. But this was England and he had been the owner of this establishment for decades, what did he care? So, she ordered one and he bought her an undrinkable beverage. It was an "Instant" cappuccino from a packet.

She couldn't be bothered to complain. Instead, she concentrated on eating what she had ordered but she couldn't even eat half of it. There was nothing wrong with it, she just couldn't eat. I've got to go home, she thought in a panic. I'll get a cab and sleep all the way. I'm going to stop drinking. But I don't want to be stuck at home without any drinks. Just in case I need one. Better to do it in moderation than to go cold turkey. But where? She smiled, remembering something and wiped her mouth with the nice cloth napkin, freshly laundered and pressed.

"Excuse me," she said. Then she lowered her voice. "Do you have any wine?"

"Sure," said the man.

In London, she thought they would have whispered it, but here it was like the wild west, very little was regulated or policed.

"What do you have?" she said in a casual tone.

"Cans, vino."

"Rosso?" she said, and the man smiled, as she knew he would, because she had said the Italian word correctly with an Italian inflection. Those even slender connections with home bought a smile to the face.

"Sii."

It was just a Vin de Table that he had bought by the crate on his trips to the Calais Hypermarkets for bulk buys on toilet rolls and food provisions, but it would be drinkable. She bought two bottles and he put them in a plastic bag. Ciao she said feeling the sausage repeating in her stomach. Ciao Bella, both said waving. She walked along the street and into Marfleet station. There wasn't even anyone at the booking office, so she walked directly on to the platform and into the Ladies. It was spotless. Another thing you never saw in London.

Here she put down her rucksack, took out the empty bottle and placed it behind the toilet. Then she took out the two wine bottles from the plastic bag and shoved them in next to the full bottle of Smirnoff. The clothes were beginning to smell. She quickly zipped up the rucksack. She bent down and wrapped the empty Smirnoff bottle in the white plastic bag and put it behind the toilet again, then walked out. I don't care if someone sees me and knows I left it there. It's Marfleet.

She was standing on the platform wondering where to find a cab company when a train came dawdling in. It was going to Mamble Wafre. My lucky day, she thought and got on. She didn't have a ticket, but she had a good reason—no one at the ticket counter. There was no one on the train either except a polite subdued Somalian family further up the carriage, and she put the rucksack up in the hold. She sat down with her head against the window, suddenly feeling so sleepy that she felt she could sleep for a day. Just before she dropped off she was thinking they're safe there, with the clothes around them, they won't fall off.

As she dozed, she thought, it's another problem to be dealt with. Where am I going to dry them? Should I just throw them away? But where? I can't dry them at home, the explanations. I can't take them to the launderette because it's too far into Mamble Wafre town centre. OMG, there were no such problems in London! There was a launderette around every corner! It's all Johns' fault she thought with venom. He's made everything so tense between us. I can't ask him to help me now, it's too awkward. Ordinarily, he would have taken them to be washed, but not now! That's why I need the drinks. It's his fault, all of it.

Mamble Wafre being the end of the line meant she slept for a good while and woke refreshed with a gentle thud. The sun was warm on her face and the familiarity and greenness of Mamble Wafre was comforting. She got off the train feeling happy. Honey I'm home! Everything seemed better. All folly and mistake were far away, in another town. As she came out of the station, she felt full of energy and thought suddenly, longingly, of Milan.

She folded out the small wheels at the bottom of the rucksack. As she walked trailing the bag behind her, she remembered when he had been a baby. Kishore had bought a ridiculously expensive Scandinavian pram and the three of them had taken the baby down Marylebone High Street passing the church on the corner where Marymary went every Sunday. She met a relative there she told them, and they had whispered that maybe Marymary had a boyfriend in London and that's why she had relocated so readily.

Kishore said he was going to buy cigarettes and disappeared, and Kavya was left alone with her baby. She had scooped him up out of that monstrous ostentatious thing and cradled him. She had started to cry. She couldn't stop. Just like she had at the wedding. She wanted to take her baby and run away from Kishore.

Lalita was right about him. He was a useless person.

Why had she married him? She couldn't remember exactly. Some half-baked idea she had got attached to, some idea of redemption. But redemption from what? Dinny's life had ended. She was just a kid she'd known at school. It was almost a bad dishoom-dishoom Bollywood movie plot. She couldn't even remember their married life, only in fragments.

As she came nearer and nearer to home, she thought all she'd ever wanted was to be alone and she hadn't been for a long long time. Tears were streaming down her face as she dragged her rucksack along. She thought of Milan growing up into a boy and then a teenager and meeting a nice girl, or boy, whatever he liked. A good person who would love him once everyone had gone. We will all be gone one day but you will go on.

Chapter 36

She put her key in the door and was delighted to see Marymary sitting alone in the kitchen.

"Hello! Hello!" she cried. "Hang on, I'll be down in a minute!"

She hurried upstairs to their bedroom, opened her wardrobe, locked the rucksack in there and went downstairs again.

"Where's Milan?"

"Johnny's taken him for a stroll" said Marymary.

"Oh. Bit late."

"They like going on evening constitutionals. They talk and walk, and sometimes they just walk."

Kavya sat down at the kitchen table.

"I was just about to make some tea. Shall we have a pot together? Darjeeling, first flush?"

"Oh, well. If you can spare it?"

Marymary set about making the tea in the old fashioned "British" way. A pot of tea, a pot of hot water, two cups, and the precious tea leaves she got from India. Kavya watched her slow assured soft movements, her neat uncluttered white hair, the perfectly ironed blouse and skirt and flat shoes that she must have had for 20 years, always diligently re-heeled and soled and polished. Marymary seemed to her at once a good and moral person.

How could Lalita think of sending her back to India? She would have none of it. She'd pay her out of her own money. She'd already decided that. So, what if she had a small gambling problem or any problem. Unlike my grandmother, I'm an open and liberal person, thought Kavya. But the black silk kimono bothered her. It pointed to some secret, possibly dangerous life. Was it possible Marymary was involved in something? Was there a secret affair?

"It's a worry about Billie, isn't it?"

"Who? But I don't really..."

"She is such a fine lady. I hope they find her soon."

Find her? Does that mean the police are already on to the case? Where is she anyway? Why doesn't she get herself washed ashore and put us all out of our misery?

"Shame you could not stay longer at Saint Dorothy's at Cliffe."

"Well, we wanted to come home. It's not the same without everyone. And to be honest, I don't like Moghul house anymore. Might sell it."

"Really? But Milan loves it there. And Johnny. What about Johnny? He likes to swim."

Well, what about Johnny? Why was she so concerned suddenly? Did she have a crush on John?

"That's just because we all went when he was a baby," said Kavya. "You remember."

"Yes," said Marymary putting her hand on Kavya's shoulder. "I worry that he's forgetting his father and sometimes I think, perhaps it's good for him to forget a little, so he can bond with John."

Him again. Are you having an affair with John? But the idea was preposterous. She understands the whole thing very well, thought Kavya staring into space. She's polite and kind. She realises John is infact a terrible influence on the kid, after all he once had Kishore's parents, our grand flat in Marylebone, crazy presents, trips to the Moghul house at the seaside on a private beach. What's he got now? A stepdad who makes couches. She gets it, she was there!

If only I could just tell her everything that's happened, it would be such a relief.

"Kavya, may I please say something. You won't mind?"

"Sorry, I was miles away. Go on."

"You know there is a new doctor in the practise in Bobbin in the Beans."

"Oh, yes?"

Marymary's tone was sombre, walking on eggshells. Like John.

"I've heard she's helped a lot of people. Her name is Dr Moody. American."

"Funny name," said Kavya and burst out laughing.

Marymary's head jerked at the sound. Maybe the laugh was too loud. You've got to watch yourself these days thought Kavya. Measure your words, mind your manners, lower the volume of your laughter. Much better to sit around being miserable.

"So, I thought you could visit the Walk In Private Clinic. Tomorrow. Just to meet her why not?"

Kavya thought it was funny how she used the word "visit" as if this Moody character was some old relation that one had to pay a visit to.

"But I'm feeling much better. I was a bit rundown, and I've had to put a brake on the carbs."

"Can't do any harm can it?"

No, that's true thought Kavya. And she was feeling a bit rough, sleepy a lot of the time. Fatigue. And that Doctor Ali was no good at all. Telling her to only drink black coffee and go on a diet. Giving out pills to everyone, that's what everyone said about him, and he did. These village doctors, what did they really know, everyone said he was very serious and matter of fact; no bedside manner at all.

But I never went to see that doctor she thought with a shiver. I never did get those pills. I just talked about it.

The thing is, it's fine to tell *them* all some story, but I've got to keep the truth and the lies straight in my own mind. I'm starting to get them mixed up. I haven't seen a doctor at all. Even when we were in London, I was supposed to see the one in the –I never went. I don't get sick, I never catch the flu, I've never had any jabs. Never needed them. When was even the last time I went to a doctor?

Her phone buzzed and she jumped. Text. Kavya's jaw dropped.

"Georgia's coming around," she said to Marymary.

Somehow, she wasn't surprised.

"Oh, that's fine. So, I'll retire now for my afternoon nap. I'll see you in the evening. I've made your favourite. Think it over about Moody. Try her tomorrow."

"Good idea. Have a nice siesta, see you later."

Marymary left. Kavya waited to hear her go up the stairs, open her door and close. After a few seconds Kavya tip-toed up the stairs. I'll just have a quick drink before Georgia gets here, she'll be at least 20 mins. She stopped halfway up the stairs and held the banister. No, maybe I shouldn't have a drink, I've got to stay cool and collected.

The thing was, *the truth was*, having a few drinks gave her a clearer head, calmed the constant tremor in her hands, made her relaxed and engaged in every way. The ale had all worn off. She'd probably sweated it off. That's not right, she told herself. That's bad. I've got to stop doing it, it's dangerous.

She had her drink. Then she went through the tedious routine of locking and unlocking. They never went into each other's wardrobes at home and hers was the one with the lock, so the yellow rucksack was safe in there. She felt funny about locking it somewhere in the computer room downstairs, it didn't feel safe or protected down there. That would be the first place they'd look, she thought. Who for goodness sake?

From the top she saw Georgia standing at the foot of the stairs.

"Door was open," she said looking up.

Kavya nodded and came down.

Georgia's auburn hair was tamed into a braid, and she was in her usual dungarees and a jean jacket, no makeup. Georgia was one of those women who could look sexy, slutty even in one sort of attire but dull, almost invisible in another kind. Someone who would make a good spy, thought Kavya. The area at the foot of the stairs was bathed in a pool of late afternoon light, warm, cosy. She stood in the centre of it and had a solemn look on her face.

Kavya stood facing Georgia. I'm not inviting her into the lounge. Or the kitchen. We'll conduct business here in the hallway. She crossed her arms.

"So, you're back then?"

"Nah. I just wanted to know if you'd seen Billie."

Kavya felt irritated at Georgia's tone, the use of the "nah." She could have asked her what she'd been doing ordering takeaways three times a day and watching her house from across the Picklechurch Walk, but she didn't want to say anything. Part of her had thought maybe the girl would come begging and crawling, full of apologies…A chilly breeze flew in, and Kavya shuddered.

"Who?"

"Billie. Everyone knows her. Billy Goat Brown."

"Oh, that woman who's disappeared? I've never met her. I don't know who she is."

The front door was wide open. John and Milan were standing in the porch. They turned and walked around the side of the house. Kavya went to the front door and slammed it shut. But it was too late.

John had heard the whole thing.

Chapter 37

"Come in for a bit. You look rough," said Kavya ushering Georgia through the lounge into the computer room. She knew John and Milan would come through from the kitchen any moment and she did not want them there. They walked in and she motioned Georgia to sit down. She extended her hand to the doorknob, but something made her stop. If I close the door now, it'll look suspicious. I'm not the furtive type. I like keeping things upfront and open. She left the door open and walked around the desk to sit in her chair.

"So, I'm sorry for--- things I shouldn't have said. I didn't mean – you *know* I didn't mean it. I was out of order. I haven't got a filter."

Kavya was making amends looking at Georgia now thinking, but I can't even remember exactly what I *said*, still it's always good to apologise. Lalita had once said all you really needed to know was the word "sorry" in England and you could live a whole life.

Georgia shrugged.

"Wasn't really listening. I've forgotten it."

"Oh. Good. That's good."

Kavya sat back in her chair now feeling the slight give in the spring. Was it the right time to ask Georgia if she wanted a drink?

"But the thing is," continued Georgia.

"Yes?"

"Um. I might have said some *stuff* to Billie. She went a bit mental. I thought she might have come to read you the riot act. She's got a bee in her bonnet about social justice."

"What stuff?"

"Sort of made-up stuff. Can't remember exactly."

Kavya nodded.

"Who is she? To you I mean?"

Georgia sighed.

"Do you want a drink?" said Kavya.

"Yeah, don't mind if I do."

Kavya opened the desk drawer and pulled out the bottle.

"Secret stash," she said, with a grin. "But you know all about my secret stashes."

Georgia made a face.

"Prefer wine? I think there's..."

"No, it's ok, alcohol is alcohol."

Kavya poured out a glass each. She was aware there was no ice, but Georgia took a large gulp of hers. So did she. It was warm, then warming. She traced her tongue along her top lip. The truth is the taste of alcohol is nice.

"Where've you been all this time Georgia? You disappeared. Like vanished. I sent you a hundred messages. I thought something had happened to you."

"Alright," said Georgia and exhaled. "First of all, my real name is Courtnee Marie. And I met Billie in prison. I was in prison; she was a prison visitor. I was 24, in with a bad crowd, stoned. I drove a car, not mine, into a lamppost and it killed a cat. I got 2 years suspended. I didn't think you'd give me a job if you knew."

"2 years for killing a cat?"

"It was a pedigree. That judge was a cat person."

Kavya laughed out loud. And then Georgia laughed too.

"Alright, so Courtnee Marie," said Kavya and grinned. "Sorry but –*Courtnee Marie?*"

"Why d'you think I changed it? By deed poll when I was 18. It was the name of a character in some American soap my mum watched when she was pregnant. And if you met my mum, you'd know the meaning of chav. She was the original pramface. She got up the duff so she could get a council house. So, short story. I never had anyone who gave a damn about me, except Billie."

Kavya was staring intently at Georgia. What if John walked in now? It was foolish to have left the door open.

"After our argument, I got triggered and I fled. That's what I do, that's my pattern. What you said went deep and I slid back into my old ways. I cut off everything and .."

"You ate. You ordered takeaways and ate."

"How do you know that?" said Georgia with a frown.

"I got that guy Tariq from Mo's place to find you. He tracked you down on the computer. He told me you were eating and eating."

Georgia nodded slowly.

"I was staying at Billie's place and yeah, I went on a bender, ordering takeaways and eating my way through them. It's no different to being an alcoholic."

"I wouldn't know."

"And when I'm like that, I don't know if it's the sugar or what, but I get delirious, almost semi-conscious," said Georgia staring at Kavya.

"I've seen documentaries about it. Sugar's evil."

"I told Billie that you'd put the police on to me. And maybe I was crying or screaming. Anyway, she got really angry, and she left. She's supposed to be on these heavy meds, for her physical condition, but when she leaves them off, she goes mental. And I haven't seen her for days. I just wondered if maybe she came to see you?"

"No," said Kavya both palms open and a frown on her face. "No, she never came here. I'll tell you if she does. I definitely will."

"Ok cheers," said Georgia.

What if John came in right now, holding Milan's hand and pointed to Kavya and said----?

But what can he say? That witch abused me and attacked me. John knows that, he knows it even if he didn't see it. Anyway, that woman, that racist was crazy. *I* don't know where she is. Shut up. You know exactly where she is. Don't ever lie to yourself Kavya. That woman is deep in the ocean.

But wait, what if she isn't? What if she survived it? People do. What if she didn't die and she came ashore, and she's walked here? What if she's here right now, outside the window, dripping? Trying to talk, with her Godawful speech impediment, her dead whirly eyes. Tapping on the window like a ghoul…

I'm going off my nut, thought Kavya. These are insane thoughts.

"Want another one?" she said pouring herself one.

"That's enough for me," said Georgia but she didn't get up.

"Don't fret George, she'll turn up," said Kavya taking a sip. "People always do."

Georgia nodded and said, "Yeah. Maybe. Ok, I'll have another."

Chapter 38

It was getting dark outside; they were talking and drinking.

“Why d’you say it was like being an alcoholic? Eating like you do? It’s not the same, is it? Alcoholics can’t stop.”

“Some can.”

“But do you really know any?”

“Yeah, my dad.”

“How much did he drink?’

“Two bottles of whiskey a day. And beer and whatever else on top.”

“Jesus Christ. How could he even afford it?’

“He stole. And he drank cheap whiskey.”

“And he stopped? Just like that?”

“Yep. Never touched a drop again. He gave up when I was three years old. He left when I was seven, but in those years he never drank. He was still a bastard, but he wasn't drinking.”

“But did he have a job?”

“All the way through. He was a manager at Argos. Always got Employee of the Month.”

Kavya snorted with laughter.

“Why do people drink though? I mean if they could figure out the reason…then they could.”

“It’s no mystery. It makes you feel good.”

Kavya stared at Georgia.

Feel good? You're an idiot, she thought.

"But it is a problem for a lot of people," said Kavya. "They have to see doctors and go to AA and well, it's a long struggle, isn't it? Alcohol Withdrawal Syndrome they call it. When they stop, they get mad hallucinations and seizures."

"Not really. You can control it if you want. You for instance. You like it too much. You don't want. And why should you? It's your life, isn't it?"

"I can stop whenever I want."

"Ok."

Kavya stared at Georgia. In a funny way, she liked her. She had a strong character, a point of view and interesting tales to tell.

"Are you coming back to work? I mean, please come back."

"Sure," said Georgia in an expressionless tone and stared at the desk.

"George! Are you about to cry? I'm no good with all that-"

"Nah. It's just that—I hope Billie's alright. I never met a person like her. She's really done a lot for me. I owe her my life really. But most of all she lets me be myself—I didn't know who I was even until I met Billie. She showed me who I was."

Kavya nodded.

"And who are you?"

Georgia grinned. "Not a clue."

They both laughed and raised their glasses at each other.

Kavya had once asked someone that question and they had said something sappy like "I am multitudes." Now what did that even mean? Georgia was a straight arrow, no bull. Kavya liked that. I like to think I'm a good judge of character. I hired her when no one else would. I didn't ask for references. I liked her. So, what if she was in prison for killing a cat? It was bad luck. It was a mistake.

"I'm sure she'll turn up. Or maybe the police will find her."

"Not necessarily. Lots of people go missing and they're never found."

What about the ones who drown, thought Kavya. But she didn't drown. She was already dead when you dragged her in there. Alright then, what about the ones who float? But do they float, or do they sink? In any case, don't they eventually wash up on the shore? That's what happens, she thought. There were always local newspaper stories about it. Well, alright then. But there still wasn't anything to connect her with Billie. Nothing except John. The way he had stood in the open door under the porch light with Milan gave her the shivers. What was he doing there anyway eavesdropping?

"By the way, can you tell that bloke to back off?" said Georgia.

"Who?"

"That phone guy. He's making a right nuisance of himself phoning up all the takeaway people."

Kavya snorted and poured herself another. It was convivial sitting with Georgia having drinks. She started giggling.

"I thought he was doing it all remotely, with…computers."

"He's an idiot. He doesn't fix anything you know. He makes out he's a big tecchy, but he gives all the phones and computers to a guy who works in the back, behind the black curtain. He's another refugee. Iraqi or Syrian, one of them. Can't speak English but he's an IT genius. You should have got him on to it."

"It's like Russian dolls. Maybe the Syrian one is giving it to another one, and another one…it's possible, isn't it? No one really knows how their phones get fixed. They all go into a black hole. And they could be fitting them with tracking devices to advertisers or Bill Gates, how would we know? Actually, I don't even care. They can."

"Listen," said Georgia with a serious face. "I don't want anyone digging up stuff about my past. I left that world behind. I'm rehabilitated. I'm not going back. I told you, Billie's the reason I have a good life now. I'm a better person now. I haven't had anything to do with my mother or my siblings for years. They've tried to contact me, but I've never replied. I don't want to know them. I wouldn't mind if they were dead. I'd like them to think I was."

"Don't say that!"

Georgia shrugged.

"I'll call him off. I promise. Bloody fraud. Sorry George. I apologise. And I understand, I hear you. But I had to know. I was... worried about you."

"The thing is you were right."

"About what?"

"You thought John was having a secret fling with me, and you tried to set him up to expose it, right? I'm sure you've got your reasons. I get that. I mean, it was lame the way you went about it but, you also got the wrong girl."

"What?"

"Right idea, wrong person."

"George! What do you know about it?"

"That's for me to know."

"You'd better tell me."

"Nah. That information aint for sale. It's priceless," said Georgia grinning in a way Kavya found intolerable. The cheek of it.

"What's so funny? You mean John's really been…cheating on me? Who is it? Georgia, you've got to tell me. Just give me a clue."

Georgia crossed her arms and thought it over.

"Alright. I'll just say this. Check his mileage meter."

Atima Srivastava

Chapter 39

After Georgia left, Kavya stayed in her chair. She didn't want to leave the computer room. She needed time to process. Damn Georgia, she thought. John's mileage meter? Right idea wrong person. So there *was* another woman after all? Now I must find out who it is. It made her feel so weary.

The smell of casserole drifted in. She woke up with a start. The time had passed for goodnight kisses. Milan had been put to bed and John was setting the table. Marymary had cooked one of her Anglo-Indian treats, a casserole of lamb and potatoes spiked with worcestershire sauce, cumin, soy sauce and tamarind. Kavya put the glasses and cutlery on the table and sat down.

John's hair was wet. He had shaved and showered. He was wearing a black t shirt and black jeans. She looked at him through hooded eyes thinking, wait till I tell Naani about this. Now she'll have to believe me. She thinks John's so good but look at him all dressed up. Going where? The thing is I've got to have evidence. I've got to check that bloody mileage meter although what that's going to tell me I have no idea.

After the casserole, there was coffee.

"You didn't eat much dear," said Marymary sadly.

"I'm on a diet remember. But it was very tasty. It's your signature dish. If you go on MasterChef, it's the one that will be a winner."

Marymary giggled with pleasure. Kavya noticed John's eyes were fixed on his plate, he never once looked up to find her.

Marymary put away the leftovers in the fridge and John sat down in front of the dishwasher with the manual. There was something wrong with the rinse cycle. Kavya washed up the dishes by hand and then announced that she was going to the computer room, and good night to all. She had been in there for less than 15minutes when there was a knock on the door.

"Who is it?" she said pointlessly.

"Me," John answered.

She got up and went to the door and unlocked it. John was standing there white as a sheet in his black clothes.

"I'm going away," he said not coming in.

"Going where?"

"I've got to go."

"You mean. Do you mean, you're leaving me?"

"Yes."

She stared at him.

"Like, for good? Walking out?"

He nodded.

She walked back and sat at the desk, picked up her glass and took a sip. John closed the door behind him but stood there looking at the floor.

"Separation. Divorce?"

"Separation anyway."

"You're just --? Out of the house, out of the marriage, out of our lives?"

"Yes."

She was stunned. Something drained out of her, and she felt sober.

"Well, what's the reason? Aren't you going to tell me?"

He didn't answer.

"What are you going to tell everyone? Naani and Marymary and people in the village. And what are you going to tell Milan?"

"I'm not going to tell anyone anything. Ever."

"Tell—*what?*"

Her heart began hammering. That sentence frightened her.

"John..." she said and he looked up and faced her. His eyes were dull shrouded pools. There was an expression written on his face that she had never seen. It was fear. Was it possible that John who used to bite off the rim of beer glasses as a party piece was scared of his little Indian wife? Was it fear or was it horror? Or disgust?

"Why land it on me now?" she said feeling panicky.

"Because I have to go. Tonight," he said.

Oh you *have* to go?

"Can't you at least wait till tomorrow? What will I say to Milan, to everyone? What will I do? They'll all think---I mean is that what you want, for everyone to pity me? Laugh at me. Is that what you *want*?"

She heard her voice sounded strangled, and he softened.

"No. I don't want that," he said and bowed his head.

He was a fool, she thought bitterly. Look at him. Like an awkward teenager. Both his arms were like useless appendages, they just hung there. Everything he feels is on show all the time. It's because he was bought up without a mum and dad, at the mercy of those weirdos in the childrens home, he's not normal, is he? That's always been his problem. Wears his heart on his sleeve.

And that's dangerous.

"Then wait till tomorrow. Can't you at least? ---"

"I understand. I'll go tomorrow. I'm going to sleep in the spare room tonight."

Good. And don't forget to lock your door, she thought.

"Have you said anything to Marymary?"

"I haven't said anything to anyone."

"What are you going on about?" she cried and strode towards him and punched him in the chest, once then once more.

He didn't flinch; he took the blows. He just kept on looking at her with those sorrowful eyes.

"Haven't said anything, haven't said anything, what is there to *say*? Hints and threats! Hints and threats! Spit it out, why don't you spit it out?"

"I won't say it. I made a promise to stand by you. You're my wife. In sickness and in health ---That's why I've got to go away, so--"

"But you're not standing by me, are you? You're running away. Far from me."

"It's the only way I can think to do it Kavs," he said quietly.

"For God's sake John!"

But he turned and went out the door.

She went to her desk and poured herself a drink. She hadn't wanted to have a drink tonight but now this... The thing about men is, they say they're going to do all this standing by you, protect you, be strong but they aren't. First chance they get they get lost, they die and run away, I mean die or run away. He's never appreciated me; he's never understood what I've done for him.

And now, leaving like this. Running to some woman. I'm going to have to explain everything. And within hours, minutes probably, it'll come to the ears of Lalita Sharma CBE. And then it'll be phone calls and the wide-eyed looks in the High Street and Marymary's pained expression. And what's going to happen to Milan? What am I supposed to tell him? Hasn't he suffered enough? You say you want to be a male figure in his life and then you disappear so how's that going to affect him? But she remembered something now. Talking to Georgia at the foot of the stairs. John standing in the circle of light in the porch. He had heard her.

He had heard her say she had never met Billie.

Kavya slipped out of the computer room, rummaged in the chest of drawers next to the drinks cabinet, found the spare keys and went outside, closed the front door behind her quietly, and walked to Johns car parked in the side street. The car door wasn't even locked! Honestly! She opened the door and sat down in the driving seat.

On her birthday he had taken her for a long romantic drive ending with them sitting in the parked car under a tree with a bottle of champagne and she had hung her head and said I'm an old lady of 39, and he said you're no lady and she'd clouted him one. Those 'couple-y' things seemed idiotic to her now. I'm glad he's going to clear off. Save me the trouble. Now, what?

She switched on the button that said mileage meter and a screen lit up. What am I supposed to learn from numbers?

And then a series of sentences blinked on.

Friday 5th: You drove to Mamble Wafre BarclaysBank ATM, then to BarleyBarton Mowgli Restaurant at 17.15

Friday 12th: You drove to Mamble Wafre BarclaysBank ATM, then to BarleyBarton Mowgli Restaurant at 17.17

Friday 19th: You drove to Mamble Wafre BarclaysBank ATM, then to BarleyBarton Mowgli Restaurant at 17.13

There were 15 sentences. All the same. Once a week, same time, same place. What the hell was John doing visiting Mowgli's before it opened? She took out her phone and went to online banking to check the ATM withdrawals.

£300, £380, £401, £503

Fifteen withdrawals between £290-£560. Grand total—she couldn't quite do it in her head, but it ran to several thousands of pounds.

Now, I've got him, she thought.

He's been stealing from our joint bank account. And going to see that horror Devaani who owns Mowglis. So it's true. It's all true. I knew it. I *knew* it. And he has the front to say he's walking out on *me*?

Atima Srivastava

Chapter 40

I hardly had anything to drink last night, Kavya thought as she lay in bed staring at the ceiling. But I feel awful, in pieces as though I've had three bottles of the stuff. Maybe it's something else after all? I'm 39, Asian, stressed, my husband's having an affair, maybe it's diabetes? All the Asians get it. Or hypertension. Kidney. Could be my heart! It could even be early menopause.

She felt trapped in the clutches of something invisible but fatal, like gas slowly filling up a room. By the time you came to smell it you were dead and if it was that other one, the one you needed to put up a box in the kitchen for, then you couldn't even detect it. But that wasn't gas, that was…fumes? Carbon monoxide is fumes. What's the difference? They still find your body the next day.

There's something very wrong with me, she thought. No way could I feel like this because of drinking, I don't drink enough for that. I could stroke out anytime. And I can't eat anything, it tastes like licking a tin. And I'm exhausted. Last night, just coming back from the car and climbing up the stairs was like climbing Everest. No, no, I've got to get to the quack today, got to. Oh, that bloody Devaani thing…I've got to sort that out as well.

Just the thought of having to go to that restaurant and confronting that woman…it's beyond my dignity, but anyway I physically can't do it. I haven't got any strength.

I'd like to curl up and sleep all day if I could. My brain's working fine, it's the body that can't cope. And if drinking was the problem, my mind would be all over the place.

Maybe I've picked up a virus...On the news they said there's a killer virus coming. They've already got it in China. Name of a Mexican beer. I'm not a beer drinker! Maybe I got it from one of our students? That's most likely what it is. I've had my flu jabs anyway so I should be fine against any Mexican Chinese virus.

She lifted her hand and it was shaking. "See, that's physical," she thought grumpily putting it back under the duvet.

I must go to that Dr Moody and see what she can do. It could be a simple course of anti-biotics, although if it's a virus there's nothing they can do. Have to let it go through my system, but she could give me vitamins and maybe some alternative therapies. I like the name Dr Moody. I wouldn't be as keen if she was called Dr Feelgood.

As soon as she got out of bed the ceiling started swirling; she staggered into the bathroom and bolted the door. She vomited into the sink and turned the tap on, looking away. She turned the radio on because she didn't want anyone to hear. She opened the medicine cabinet and things fell out. She picked them up slowly. This is pure misery she thought as the smell of sick climbed up her nostrils. And I must be quiet. If anyone hears...

When she went back to bed she was shaking from head to foot. A common symptom of the flu. Those jabs are useless because it's a new strain every year. I'll stay in bed and close my eyes. But I've got to get up. I've got to investigate that humiliating affair with Devaani. And I haven't got the strength. I'll have to have a drink. I don't even want to.

She opened the wardrobe and took it. Then she went back to the bathroom, had a shower, washed her hair, cleaned the sink, and sprayed the Lavender air freshener. Then she rinsed with Listerine, towel dried her hair and put on perfume, lipstick and eyeliner and went downstairs. In the kitchen, which smelled reassuringly of toast, Milan, Marymary and John were sitting around the table.

She came up behind Milan and put her arms around his little bony shoulders and put her chin on his head. He started to giggle and grabbed her arms with his little hands.

"It's stuck!" she said pushing her chin down.

"Mummy, stop it!" he cried.

"But my head, I've got no control over it."

Marymary touched her arm and said, 'have some coffee dear,' so she took her chin off her son's head and sat down with a thump.

"You're alright," she said.

Milan nodded enthusiastically.

"Marymary thought I was hurting you. But you're a strong boy, aren't you?"

"Well..I..I..I," said Marymary looking helplessly at John.

"Yes, I am a strong boy," said Milan nodding and smiling.

"Tonight, we'll have an evening of magic, ok? You show me all the ones you've practised. And then we'll talk about school. Not the subjects, that's boring. Teachers, you'll tell me who's good and who I should avoid at the PTM. Now don't be late. Marymary will only get in trouble and blame me!"

Once Marymary and a giggling Milan had left, she looked daggers at John, but he didn't react.

"I've got to sort some things out today," he said. "Got to go to my workshop."

"Are you taking your car?"

"No. The brake isn't working. I've left it parked for now, I'll sort it later. Why, do you need a lift somewhere?"

"Yes, thanks but I've asked George to drive me."

He shrugged.

Kavya peered at him. He wants to know how come George can drive me when her car's disappeared. Why should I tell him?

"Goodbye then," she said and got up and flounced off into the computer room and closed the door.

She texted Georgia.

URGENT! Hey Courtnee Marie, y'all! I need to go places today y'all. Can you get a car?

Georgia texted back within seconds.

Give me an hour. Call me that again you die!

By the time Georgia arrived, John had long gone.

"How did you get a car?"

"I can get things," said Georgia.

She had her mane of red hair tied up in a ponytail and she was wearing mirrored shades, a leather jacket, and cut-offs. She's a cool dude, thought Kavya.

"You're my driver for the day, ok? Daily rate plus here's some cash for petrol."

"Where we off to?"

"Do you want something to eat first? Coffee?"

"I'm fine."

"Alright, so first stop---there's some new quack in Bobbins in the Beans, name of Moody. I don't know where exactly the clinic—"

"I know where."

They got in the car. It was a shabby blue mini that smelled of old people.

"Where'd you get this heap?"

"Jimmy's Car Hire in Saint Dorothy's at Cliffe. Under New Management, but still cheap n cheerful. Do you mind if I have a cigarette?" said Georgia adjusting the mirror.

"Give me one too."

"I didn't know you smoked?"

"Now and again, you fancy one don't you?"

When they started driving, Georgia turned on the radio and opera came out.

"OMG" they both said in disgust.

"John's always got that stuff on in his car. Find something else," said Kavya.

"I grew up on a farm and I've heard that sound before. Like when they killed a pig."

Kavya hooted with laughter.

"I always thought you had to be a gay man to listen to opera."

"Oh yeah? What are you saying?" said Georgia with a grin, her eyes on the road.

"What's that supposed to mean?"

"Nothing. Lighten up."

Chapter 41

Kavya opened her window and blew out perfect smoke rings. She felt humiliated having to ask but she had to. Bloody John.

"So, do you know this woman called Devaani? She owns Mowglis, it's an Indian restaurant in --"

"*That* bastard."

"Oh," said Kavya.

"She's not the owner! The owner's an Irish gangster from Belfast; he's got 'her' in there to make the place look authentic. She's on minimum wage."

"Really? And what else do you know about her?"

"Nothing."

Kavya frowned.

"Why the air quotes?"

"Seen the hands?"

Kavya stared at the dashboard. A fury was welling up inside.

"Why'd you tell me to—you *knew* that John's been seeing her."

"Not just seeing her."

"Alright, alright. He's been *paying* her. Going to the ATM, it's all in that car display. Why, what for?"

Georgia raised an eyebrow.

"What are you saying? She's a prozzie?" cried Kavya.

"Haven't heard that word for a while. Thought you was well bought up."

Kavya pushed out her bottom lip and went quiet.

I've got to *think.*

"But she's like a *hundred years old!* And – what? You're saying she's a *Trans*?"

"I know she is."

"She's a he. He's a man," said Kavya. "I knew it! I called it!"

Georgia laughed.

"But they want to be called women, don't they? They want to be 'her' now, you can't say 'him.' You must use the correct pronoun! Otherwise, they'll beat you up."

She's all woman, John had said and at the time Kavya had thought what does he mean by that?

Silence.

"How did you know…about the mileage?"

"How d'you think? I looked at it! He never locks it."

Kavya made an impatient noise. "What's the point of installing a top of the range mileage meter when the bloody car hasn't even got a security lock? He's been taking money out the joint account, you know? For three months!"

"Didn't you notice?"

Kavya didn't want to tell Georgia that she never checked her bank account. She just took money out the ATM and all the bills were paid like magic via direct debit. She didn't want to tell Georgia who lived from hand to mouth and week to week that she never gave a thought to the incoming flow of monies.

"Yes, I noticed but, if your husband's spending money you don't question him do you? It's for bits and pieces and things he needs for the upholstery business. You don't think about interrogating the husband, do you?"

"I wouldn't know."

"Never been tempted?"

"What, to enter an institution? No thanks. I've already been to prison."

Kavya laughed.

"Not into the soulmates thing then?"

"That's romantic bull. Sex is good and easy to get but the only reason women get married is to have kids, but then they get saddled with them. I might have done it if I had a full-time nanny like you do, otherwise no thanks. I like my independence too much."

Kavya nodded. She loved Milan, but the truth was he hadn't been part of the plan. She'd never wanted babies, but when her parents died, it just seemed the right thing to do to add to the world.

They drove in silence for some moments.

"Obviously I'm *upset,*" she said suddenly, in case Georgia thought her reactions were all wrong. She'd just been told her husband was seeing a prostitute who was also a Transsexual. She couldn't just be blasé about it. But I've got to play it cool, she thought. Don't tell her too much. "I'm very upset. I'm probably in shock. To be honest."

"Yeah."

"I appreciate you telling me about it George."

"Anything I can do to get that bastard into trouble, I'll do it."

Kavya looked sideways at Georgia whose eyes were on the road. Cold stony bitch eyes. She had never heard her be so candid before, or so profane.

"Why didn't you tell me before?"

"We weren't friends."

"We've always got on!"

"Right up to the point when you tried to make out I was having it off with your husband!"

"I *didn't*! Stop saying that."

"I didn't really understand you before," said Georgia. "I wasn't sure how you'd react."

"How was I going to react? Like any wife would react!"

"But after you tried to set me up."

"There was no freaking set up."

"Alright, after I *thought* you tried to set me up, I changed my mind about you."

Kavya threw her cigarette out the window. The breeze raked her hair back and she thought I've got to be careful what I say to Georgia. She's—I don't know, she's smart. She's smarter than me. I've got to keep it friendly, but distant.

"Yeah, and what did you think?"

"I thought, after that little scene, you might be interested in doing a set up for real."

"Huh?" said Kavya.

Georgia screeched the car to a halt.

"Well here we are madam. At the doctors."

The Bobbins in the Beans Private Medical Practise was a small glass fronted building with two large Bay Leaf trees in pots outside. It consisted of a Walk-In clinic and two other specialist clinics.

"I've changed my mind," Kavya said, sinking back into the car seat. "I'm feeling better."

Georgia's face was expressionless. It wasn't disdain. It was indifference. Kavya had to admit she admired it. She had been used to people looking out for her all her life, encouraging her, cajoling her…if it wasn't her family, it was the people she had picked to be friends, lovers, even husbands. No wonder she wasn't friends with any of her cohort anymore, she'd dropped them all one by one, so bored had she become with their one trick pony offerings. I've always wanted a lot from people, but once they give it, I'm bored.

A therapist might say I don't believe I'm worthy of love and so I get rid of the people who love me. Maybe a therapist *had* said that. They'd probably all said it. Intimacy issues. Trust issues. Anger issues. She used to sit back in the comfortable chairs in rooms full of books and think I'd like to issue *you,* with a gagging order! She had seen quite a few in her younger life, expensive ones, all spouting different theories; they all merged into one now. The talking cure. God help us. These people couldn't cure a thing, they just took pot shots with their theories hoping something stuck. Spaghetti therapists she used to call them.

Thing is, I've got to go in, she thought. Never mind anyone else, it's *my* health and I've got to get it seen to.

Chapter 42

Inside the waiting room several patients were sitting in comfortable leather chairs. She marched up to the reception desk.

"I don't suppose I can see the doctor now. I'm in a bit of a hurry so, no matter if--"

"You're lucky. Dr Moody just had a cancellation," said the receptionist and gave her the price list. "We offer 20minute consultations."

Kavya thought, well if they have cancellations that means this quack's no good. And what's Moody going to do in 20minutes? Turn water into wine? A waste of money. Private healthcare, what a complete rip-off.

"Please allow Dr Moody 10mins to access your medical details. Sign here."

Kavya took out her credit card, paid and signed.

Done like a kipper...

When she walked into Dr Moody's office, she was surprised to see an old white haired lady with an obvious facelift and painted on eyebrows. For some reason she had assumed it would be a young woman from California. This one had a comical gravelly Noo Yawk accent too. And some sort of hearing defect as she projected the words to the back of the room.

"Halo! I'm Moody! I've reviewed your file but not much to go awn. What's the problem? Why don't you tell me in your own words?"

Well what other words would they be?

"I mean…it's nothing really specific."

"Uh-huh," said Moody and took out her stethoscope. "Stand up please, let's take a listen."

She pressed the thing on Kavya's chest, then asked her to turn around and did the same on her back, listening intently.

This is a disaster. It's like she's playing at being a doctor. Kavya scanned the room for a certificate. It was hanging on the far wall. She squinted, thinking they've deliberately made it small so no normal person can read it. Probably says University of HawaHee.

"Just breathe normally."

"I am. Why?"

"You're wheezing. Can't you hear it?"

Kavya held her breath and then exhaled.

"Open your eyes wide," said Moody. She took out a large magnifying glass and stared at Kavya through it.

"I haven't been sleeping. That's the main problem," said Kavya feeling appalled. What's next, open your mouth, show me your foot. What is she a vet or a doctor?

"Uh-huh. What about your diet?" Moody said putting the magnifying glass away carefully in a drawer as though it was a gun.

"Fine. Three meals a day."

"Hot flushes? Sweating? Lack of focus."

"I'm too young for menopause. I'm still getting periods. I'm 39."

"Uh-huh."

Why does she keep making that ridiculous noise? It's like she's playing for time, or she doesn't believe me.

"And you've tested for diabetes? I don't have any results to show."

"Yes, yes yes in London. We don't have diabetes in the family."

"Alright but being South Asian you have a higher risk."

"Of what?" said Kavya rudely.

"Heart attacks, kidney failure, sight loss that kind of thing. Those conditions can lie in wait, undetected."

"I have the blood pressure of a 10-year-old," said Kavya boastfully. Moody checked the file and nodded.

"Now stand up and hold out your arms."

"I don't want to," said Kavya and sat on her hands.

Silence.

"Just give it a try," said Moody.

"I had a couple of drinks last night and I've got a bit of a hangover. I mixed the grain and the grape. I'm under a little bit of stress."

"Really? And what is the nature of that?"

"Oh, well. Just. Hmm."

Be careful. You were just about to say 'my husband is about to walk out on me, shouldn't I have a drink or two?' Keep your mouth shut, because Moody will ask why, why is your husband leaving you? Americans can be very rude.

"What would you like to tell me, about how you feel?"

"I'm not happy."

"Alright. How old are you?"

Why's she asking me *that*? She said she'd read my file! Did she forget or does she think I've got a memory problem? Maybe *she's* got the memory problem.

"39! … My mind is working fine. But –I think it's something in my body."

"Yes?'

"It feels like my body is sometimes uprooted. Like, there's no gravity. Just sometimes."

"Delirious."

"You mean it's all in my head?" said Kavya. "You think I've got some mental problem?"

"How much do you drink?"

"Well, that's relative and it depends."

"Ok so yesterday. You had a few drinks. How many?"

Kavya began to count on her fingers.

"And your hand is shaking though," said Moody.

It was a trick to see my hands! Well let her see them.

Kavya held out her hands and said "My hands do shake from time to time when I'm tired, very exhausted. Sometimes I do drink more than I should. I don't keep count."

"Don't worry, most people halve their intake when they report it anyway."

"I wouldn't do that."

"Ok, look I am going to give you a prescription. I want you to take these every day for two weeks. They're mild, but they'll help you sleep. And I want you to sleep for 8 hours every day. It's very important. 8 hours. How about your husband, can he take up the slack? With the household chores, with your son?"

"Oh yes."

"Good. Let's see you again in two weeks. And no alcohol at all."

Who is this fool, thought Kavya?

It's a well-known fact that if you stop drinking entirely it has a very detrimental effect. It's like those people who suddenly go jogging. They fall down dead.

"Ok, thanks doctor. What's wrong with me do you think?"

"We shall see," said Moody.

"What do you mean?"

"When you come to see me again, we'll have a better picture. And you'll talk more. And we will attack the problem. And look for solutions. In the meantime, I advise you to face things. Whatever is going on in your life, face it, Kavya. Face it, don't flee. Take responsibility."

Kavya came out of the practise in a bad mood.

"What was she like?" said Georgia.

"Total fraud."

"Now what?"

"Get away from this dump. Let's go and get the prescription."

"You'll never guess who I saw while you were in there?"

"Who?"

"Going into the GIC."

"What's that?"

"Gender Identity Clinic."

Chapter 43

Georgia drove. Kavya didn't speak.

"Was it definitely her?" she said finally.

"Can't miss her. She looks like a skunk. Or should I say skank?"

Kavya bit her bottom lip. The whole thing was preposterous, and yet...

"Is she *really* a prostitute?"

"Yes," said Georgia with a smile. "She's *really* a prostitute."

Kavya had never met her, but she had been in hearing distance once when she was standing outside Mowglis. Devaani had one of those IndianIndian accents, not as posh as Lalita's, more like Marymarys. So Devaani had probably been educated in English to at least High School level in India. She looked a bit like an old Indian prime minister called Indira Gandhi, with a broad white stripe in her hair. Not that it made much difference who it was…

The point was, there *was* a her.

And John was paying her. And Kavya could think of no reason other than the obvious one that would explain why John was giving regular cash to a woman. Or was she still a man? It was worse than an affair. It was worse than seeing a female prostitute. It was utter disgrace.

"I can't believe he'd do it," she said. "I'm in a daze. John. Of all people."

And yet, she had seen the evidence before her.

"It's more common than you'd think. Not just guys going to prostitutes, that's rife. I mean straight guys going to chicks with dicks."

"I don't think you're allowed to call it that nowadays."

Georgia nodded.

"Pre-Transition. That op's expensive. Not everyone can afford Caitlyn Jenner's surgeon. The designa-vagina don't come cheap."

"But why would a straight man? Does it mean he's gay?"

"I wouldn't know," said Georgia. Then she said: I suppose you could ask him.

No, thought Kavya. I, one hundred per cent could not.

"Yeah. I suppose I could."

"Want me to get it for you?" said Georgia when they reached BarleyBarton-on- Sea.

Kavya nodded and gave her the prescription and a £20 note.

"You look a bit—You gonna puke?"

"Of course not," said Kavya.

Georgia strode off down the street. She had strong powerful calves. How old was she again? Not even 30 yet. She wore the same heavy boots encrusted with mud all the time. There was something vital about her. I've always been tethered, thought Kavya miserably. To my family, to money, to houses, to the school, to a husband, to a child. To the past. To my choices.

Georgia's hair burned bright; a devil may care confidence in every nimble step. It contrasted with how Kavya felt. Heavy, despondent. Fearful. At every turn I must learn something new, something unpalatable, something I don't want to think about, she thought crossly. It's so humiliating. And how many people know about it? Mamble Favre is a small village and news will travel easily to BarleyBarton and beyond…

It was twenty minutes before Georgia came back.

"Nothing you couldn't have got over the counter," she said handing her the white paper bag.

"Is it?"

"No better than herbal pills. I could get you proper sleeping pills if you wanted. They'd knock you out."

"Moody's answer to everything is sleep."

"Sometimes that can work. I take pills to get off a bender. You sleep 48 hours solid and then you're good to go."

"Bender?"

Georgia looked at her.

"You didn't really believe I was a food addict did you? Ordering pizza and burgers and eating them? I'd be the size of a house."

"Well, what was I supposed to think?" said Kavya feeling annoyed.

"I can understand that little idiot jumping to conclusions, but you come from London."

"Well, yeah. So, what *were* you doing?"

"Drugs, obviously."

Kavya snorted with laughter; she couldn't help herself. Somehow this revelation felt like relief and put her at ease. Food addict indeed. Bumpkin provincial Tariq jumping to conclusions. He's no Sherlock. Bounty Hunter my left foot! I was in a bad way, I was preoccupied, that's why I believed him.

"So, the food delivery is a front for drug delivery. If we were in London I'd have realised right away, but this little snoring place."

"The little snorings are the best," said Georgia. "You can get away with anything. The police are like Keystone Kops. By the way you know that's an actual place, Little Snoring. Who *lives* in a town called that?"

"The same ones who live in Bobbins in the Butter Beans and Mable asks For a Favour."

"Padre Pervert's at it with Cliff!"

Both started laughing.

"Fancy coming for a drink with me? I need a drink," said Kavya.

"Sure, where d'you want to go?"

"I don't care. I've just got to have a drink."

"I know a place."

Georgia drove out of town and hit the motorway. Kavya stared miserably out the window at the skimming countryside. As the needle climbed to 80mph the white paper bag containing the prescription rolled off her thigh and hit the floor. She didn't really want to go for a drink with Georgia, but she didn't feel like drinking alone either. I could have asked her to drive me to Mowglis and have a showdown with that...*person*. I don't want to. I can't.

"Where the hell is this?" said Kavya.

They were in the middle of another nowhere, but this was scrubland, the kind of place that existed beyond England's green and pleasant land. Georgia stopped the car outside a concrete bunker. You expected scuttling lizards and a dust ball to come rolling along the deserted road, which had nothing but an incongruous little bus stop and this bunker.

"Irish pub. A real one," said Georgia leading the way.

Inside it was one large dark room with a pungent beery smell. There was a post in the middle of the room which had a lot of pointed signs written in a different language, Irish place names and kilometres, none of which Kavya could decipher. There was a bar and a fruit machine and a tv stuck high on the wall showing a hurling championship.

They sat down at a table and a waitress appeared.

"Sorry?" said Kavya.

The waitress repeated the question.

Kavya looked at Georgia and shrugged.

"What d'you want to drink?" said Georgia.

"Oh, I'll have…a vodka and tonic. A double. Make it, tell her to give me two doubles. To save ordering again. What about you?"

"I'll have a mineral water thanks," said Georgia addressing the waitress who nodded and went away.

"If they're going to employ Eastern Europeans, shouldn't they learn English?" said Kavya. "I've heard there's an excellent International School of English in BarleyBarton-on-Sea owned by an amazing..."

"She was speaking English. She happens to be from Ireland."

"Oh, my bad," said Kavya. "She'll probably spit in my drink now."

"Nah, they're a nice lot here."

Kavya said, "So? You seem to know her quite well. Devaani I'm talking about."

"Yeah, I know her."

"Tell me something more about her."

"I haven't got any more useful information."

"Useful for what?"

The waitress bought the drinks over and set them down. Kavya watched Georgia open the bottle of Ballygowan and pour it slowly into her glass.

"You said you'd love to get her into trouble. I didn't ask why. But let me ask you this. Did you ever make a plan to do it?"

"Yeah, but I couldn't do it on my own."

“What was it?”

“Better you don't know,” said Georgia.

“I don't understand why you’ve got it in for her,” said Kavya leaning forward.

Chapter 44

"Ok, I'll tell you. It was two years ago. I'd just come to BarleyBarton-on-Sea looking to make a new start after prison. I had nowhere to stay so I slept on the beach. I could see things going on. During the night men would park in a line on the road. The same way taxis do outside railway stations, only they weren't going anywhere, just waiting. You know what the beaches are like around here, no police, no surveillance, no witnesses. Frightened little men worried their wives would find out, but too cheap to go to the next town for it. Men are lazy bastards. I had no money. So, I went with a couple of them, just hand jobs. I wasn't planning to make it my career. I'd rather get my hands dirty doing gardening or cleaning."

Kavya sipped her drink. Her mind began to wander a bit. There's something very good about just sitting here, in this fuggy warm room with my hand around a cold glass, yes, even with Georgia. I can relax here, not think, let go. *No!* Keep your mind clear. You've got to. Don't get distracted. You've got to say it.

"I was asleep on the beach one night and this bastard comes up to me, starts screaming I had no right going on her patch taking her business blah blah blah. Off. Her. Nut. Takes one to know one, but I was never *that* bad. Her eyeballs were literally swivelling. And the words that came out of her pretty little mouth. I never heard a posh woman talk like that. She wasn't no lady! I tried to say I wasn't, but she didn't care, she just kicked the shit out of me and left me for dead. She might look like a woman, but she's still got the strength of a man. The hormones don't take that away. I couldn't fight back."

"George, that's terrible. What did you do?"

"Nothing, I passed out. In the morning I took myself to the hospital and got fixed up. They gave me painkillers, but I went looking for stronger ones. Those knocked me out for a week. I stayed in the homeless shelter. Then, I found somewhere else to stay. That was it, end of story."

"You didn't *report* her?" said Kavya wide eyed.

"Who to? The police? She's Asian, she's Trans, she's well-spoken and I was just out of jail with no money. Dropping my aitches all over the place. The police would assume *I* was the prostitute, not her. Plus, they don't want to be accused of Racism, Trans-Hate, whatever. She's got double whammy insurance, triple if you count her plummy accent. They would have arrested me in a heartbeat. I couldn't risk going back inside."

"So, what you just forgot about it?"

"I'll never forget. I've got the scars to remind me."

"Do you keep tabs on her?"

"Not really, I just keep my ears open. Anyway, she's a hardcore smack addict now, doubt she'd even remember me."

"Really? And what about you?"

"I told you. I'll go on occasional benders when I feel like it. I'll take any Class A, get out of my head for a week or two, then I'll clean up. I don't inject. I'm not a slave to it. I'm not an addict."

Kavya nodded thoughtfully.

"Don't you ever bump into her? BarleyBarton's a small town."

"If I see her, I ignore her. Make like it never happened. That's the only way to deal. I'm used to violence. I was born near a farm, and you see it close up, red in tooth and claw like they say. Nature is violent. Then I grew up in a violent home and prison was violent. You cave or you rise above. I trained myself to take it. It changes you. When you come through violence, nothing shocks you. You can do anything. It's like a superpower."

"I've never known violence," said Kavya shaking her head. "I don't approve of it."

It wasn't true. She had watched six racist men viciously attack a teenage girl. She had run home a quivering panting coward and let someone else find Dinny. And Kavya had never told anyone. Even when she had let it slip to Marymary, she had made herself into the rescuer so Marymary could say 'it wasn't your fault.'

"Not everyone's that lucky," said Georgia. "You're still innocent. Violence changes you. I like BarleyBarton though, the name I mean. It's like a person's name. BillieBarleyBarton I call her sometimes, and she laughs. She owns that town; everyone knows her there. She hasn't been in here either, not for days, no one's seen her. She's the only real friend I've ever had. Really hope she's ok."

We're going off track, thought Kavya sipping her drink.

An impatience was building inside her, almost a desperation. It felt like her last chance, but she couldn't quite nail it. The idea had been fermenting in her mind ever since the drive to the medical centre.

"I want another drink. D'you want one? Tell her to put it on my tab."

"Sure," said Georgia, got up immediately and went to the bar. Kavya could only see her from behind, and even though she hardly moved, Kavya could tell she knew the place, the waitress, everything. Soon she was back with a tray holding a large vodka and tonic and a mineral water.

"You're not drinking?"

"Driving."

"Oh yeah. Hope you told her I didn't mean to be rude and---"

Georgia sat down and stretched out her legs, gazing in the distance.

"Don't worry I got you out of it. I told her you were 'a little slow so you were,' she said in a thick Irish accent."

"Thanks a lot!"

"She said you've got great hair. I said, yeah makes you sick, some people have all the luck. A lot of girls would kill to have long black hair like yours."

Flattered, Kavya ran her hand absentmindedly over her hair. She took a few sips and felt much better, clearer. She thought this one is my second double, or maybe it's my third, mustn't have any more today. Even if they're just herbal, I'll take those pills tonight. Get some sleep. Sometimes the most obvious thing is the answer. And if they don't work, you can get sleeping pills that knock you out.

"Listen George. What Devaani did to you, was a crime. She should have been arrested tried and convicted. What do they do with someone like that, put them in a men's prison?"

"Probably, especially if they still got a dick."

"She'd probably get the shit kicked out of her in there wouldn't she? Or worse. Good!"

"Yeah."

"Too harsh?"

"Nothing's too harsh."

"What would be perfect," said Kavya carefully. "Is if she was –if she was arrested but for *something else*. Like, if she was caught taking money. That's soliciting, isn't it?"

There it was now. Out in the open. She had said it.

Chapter 45

"Like set a trap for her, you mean?"

"She *is* taking my money. It's not a trap if it's true. It's just proof."

"Not sure it would be so easy to prove though."

"Why not? We already know he goes to the restaurant on a Friday."

"You want to barge in there and accuse him?"

"No! What about…taking a picture of them on my phone?"

Georgia sniggered in a way Kavya found disrespectful.

"That might work in a film, but in real life …Even if you got it, what's the point of a picture of two people meeting, even if one of them is your husband? I suppose if you caught them at it, you could Tweet that out. But who would care, they're not famous."

"Ugh gross! Ok. Stupid idea to set a trap."

"Not necessarily. You've got to think it through. They have to be seen together but not at the restaurant—too public and–He's allowed to give her money. Bad luck for you but that's not really against the law."

"Oh." Kavya felt deflated.

"You've got to make the meeting in a different place. A flat or a house in the middle of nowhere, no people, no network, where you can control the situation."

"Moghul House!"

A river of relief flooded through her as if finally, after a long arduous struggle she had found the light.

"Yeah, good. The catch is you must get *both* of them there at the same time."

"Impossible."

"No. Just needs work."

"It still doesn't prove anything. Even if he *is* giving her money for…"

Kavya couldn't bring herself to say "sex". She didn't want to know if Devaani was a biological woman now courtesy of the Gender Identity Clinic or a pre transition, she didn't want to know anything about what happened between them, she just wanted him disgraced. "They want to be called 'her' now, you can't say 'him' Georgia had said. But Kavya had used the correct pronoun.

Because she didn't mean Devaani. *She meant John.*

"Yes, it does," said Georgia. "It proves she's on the game and he's unfaithful."

No, thought Kavya.

Neither of those things are illegal. What's more important is it proves he's a freak and a liar and a cheat and so if he says anything to the police about me, it won't be worth the paper it's written on. She had seen enough thrillers on tv to know the first thing you do is discredit the witness.

"How would you get them both there?" she said.

"SMS."

"Huh?"

"Send him a text from her, and her a text from him. Easy. You get them both there at whatever time you want them."

"No, because they probably have each other's numbers, and the display will come up."

"That's easy too. Use a burner. Explain the 'unknown number' by saying their phone got stolen or some other excuse."

"So, you use a burner to send one from him to her, saying meet me at Moghul House...and then you send one from her to him. I don't get it. Then they're both getting texts from an unknown phone. That's silly!"

Georgia sighed.

"No, it's not silly. Listen carefully.

1. You send a text (from the burner) pretending to be John to Devaani's real number. 'It's me John, my phone got stolen/hacked. Text me on this new number. No phone calls. I need to meet you at Moghul House tonight. It's urgent.'
2. Devaani texts the burner phone, which she believes is John's new phone. 'Why do you want to meet at Moghul House?'
3. Remember, John's not getting this message. *You're* getting the message on *your* burner. So you reply something like 'Something's come up. Will explain then.' Ok, now Devaani's in place.
4. Next, you text John, *from the same burner phone*, with the same message. "Hello John, it's Devaani, I

lost my phone, and this is my new number for a few days. Can I please meet you at your Moghul House tonight. It's urgent. I'll explain when we meet." Ok so now John's in place.

5. Conclusion: Both parties have been set up to meet at a time and a place of your choosing. They both think they're texting each other, but in reality, *you're* controlling the conversation, everything that's being said. Just close your eyes and think about it."

Kavya closed her eyes and put her hands over them, trying to picture the logistics. One, two, three, four and five.

Yes, she got it now.

"When you say "you", you mean you right? Because I'm not texting anyone. You're just explaining what *you'd* do. How *you'd* set them up."

"Yeah, I'll do it. I'll do all the texting."

"But what's in it for you Georgia?"

Georgia smiled.

"To mess her up. Put her in trouble with the police and everyone else. Expose her for what she is. She's got an image, a reputation as a respectable restaurant manager. Once your reputation has gone, you can't build it back."

Kavya nodded. She noted thankfully that Georgia didn't ask what was at stake for her...

"It's kind of like catfishing, but on a burner."

"Exactly," said Georgia. "Only in catfishing it's a one-way street, one person dupes another. Here, both parties are being duped."

"So, you'd be conducting the text conversation from the same burner?"

"Yes. Only *you'll* write the text from him to her. Just on paper. Like a hard copy draft. I'll copy it out and do the texting part."

"But why?" cried Kavya. "Why can't you write them both?"

Georgia looked at her calmly.

"Because I'm not going to do everything. You could drop me right in it. But if I've got a piece of paper with your writing on it, that's my insurance. Then we're both in it. Anyway, it's your husband, you know how he writes text."

"But I don't want to! I can't, I don't know what to say!"

Georgia shrugged, as if she couldn't care less.

"Alright *alright* I'll do it! I just mean I'm no good at writing things. What would *you* write? From her to him."

"Something like, 'Need to see you urgently. I'll meet you at Moghul House at 6pm tonight. Be there.' Short and sweet."

"But it's our house! She's never even been there! Why would she...?"

"Even better. So now he *has* to meet her. He didn't even know she *knew* about the place. He's in a panic. I can add something like 'Come alone. I'm not using my phone. Risky. Don't call me. Text on this number. I'll explain later' " That might be better than saying 'I've lost my phone'—yeah that's better."

Kavya nodded slowly, imagining John getting that text. It was melodramatic but it would work. He wouldn't ignore it. He had too much of a sense of responsibility.

"But, as soon as they meet and start talking, they'll know it's a wind up," said Georgia.

"Oh," said Kavya, stricken. "Yes, they'll know immediately!"

"But we can work on that. I could make sure she takes some gear. I'll leave some out for her, she won't be able to resist it. She'll walk in, see it, snort it straightaway. Addicts are very predictable. Then she'll be out of it when he arrives, and he'll have to shake her up before they can talk."

"Drugs...? No but, he'll never stand for that. He'll leave immediately. He doesn't approve. I don't think it'll work," said Kavya shaking her head.

"Yes, it will. You haven't heard it all. You won't have to do much; I'll do most of it. I'll get you the other burner for the phone call."

"Who do I have to phone?" cried Kavya.

"The police of course."

Chapter 46

"You've lost the plot now. What am I phoning the *police* for?"

"Just listen," said Georgia looking into her eyes. "Stop interrupting."

Kavya's heart thudded.

"Ok."

"Now this is important, can you drive?"

"Of course, I can drive. What d'you think I am, a moron?"

"I don't mean have you got a licence. I mean if we're going to do this, you must keep a clear head. Can you?"

Kavya stared at her glassily, feeling a bit annoyed.

"Yes."

"When's the last time you were behind a wheel? Sober."

"For God's sake, I don't drink and drive! I haven't driven since we moved here but I drove in London all the time. I've been driving since I was 17. I'm an excellent driver. But why do I need to drive?"

"I'll get to the driving part in a minute. So, this is how it'll work. Your text from him gets her there for 7pm. Tell her to let herself in with the key under the flowerpot. My text from her gets him there for 8pm. The gap is to give her enough time to get wasted. And when he arrives, there's got to be confusion."

"But he'll still be normal---and like I said he'll leave."

"No, not if he's been---sedated."

"Ridiculous. How's that going to happen?"

"You suggest he takes Milan to the circus—arrange a playdate. Then, while he's there, he gets the urgent text from his girlfriend."

"Don't be gross."

"I know, more like grandma. Ooo what big eyes you've got?" said Georgia and laughed. "Anyway, so he says to the friends please look after Milan, I've got an emergency. He might even say it's Moghul House, there's been a break in, the alarms gone off…I know there isn't an alarm, anyway, he'll say whatever he needs to say. He'll call you as well to tell you some story about why he's going to be late home. Let it go to voicemail."

"Milan could have a sleepover with Shanta's grandkids. That's do-able. She'll jump at it, and he wants a sleepover."

"There you go. The point is, John's got somewhere safe to leave Milan."

"I get it. But he's got to be sedated or something by the time he reaches Moghul House, to create confusion. But how? I'm not going to be there."

"You give him something *before* he sets off for the circus. Put it in his tea. Slow release. I can get it for you."

"You're a regular pharmacy, aren't you?" said Kavya staring at Georgia. "Slow release. Does that really work?"

"Of course, it does. Chemicals. They're 100% predictable. There are all kinds of sedatives. It'll take about five hours to start working."

"Wait, that's not the... *rape* drug, is it? Rohypnol?"

"No not that one. This one causes tiredness and sleepiness, not memory loss."

"This is crazy. Too many variables."

"Yes, but take it step by step. They realise they didn't send any texts to each other. What are they going to do?"

"Leave. Phone the police. Phone someone."

"No bars. No reception. And phoning the police is not the first thing they're going to think of let's be honest."

"True. But he'd just leave, he'd get out."

"He can't. I've locked the door from the outside."

"Then he definitely knows something's wrong ---"

"Yeah, but now it's too late. They're trapped. It's been 10 minutes since he got there. Fine, that's all the time I need."

"For what?"

"To pump in the gas."

"Pardon?"

"That's why you need to drive. You've got to hire a car from Jimmy's, drive to Moghul House, see them both in there-- they'll be unconscious-- smash a window to let the gas out, call the police anonymously, destroy the burner, drive back, leave the car and go home on the train. The police will be at Moghul in 15 minutes, they've got nothing else to do. They'll find them both groggy with a smashed window, and Class A. They'll ask them to explain what's going on, but they can't remember anything. It's a mystery!"

"Ok, go on."

"Well, the broken window suggests burglary, but nothing has been stolen. And John is the—"

"Co-owner of Moghul House," said Kavya.

"Right. Private citizens are allowed to get high and have sex, in their own home, and the police *might* have turned a blind eye but there was a phone call from a concerned citizen, and so they must follow it up. It's on record. The police will want to question them both, Devaani for sure. She's got Class A running around her brain and ---"

"And what's John going to say?"

"Very little I'm guessing. If they take them both in, their little secret will probably come out. She might blab that he's been giving her money for services. But even if she doesn't, the whole thing is fishy, even though there's no actual perp. No one has broken in, nothing is missing. They'll have to charge Devaani with possession and, they might want to investigate her living off immoral earnings. They'll let John go. Or maybe they'll detain him. Either way, *you'll* get a visit from plod, reporting that your husband has been involved in an 'incident', maybe plod also tells you that your husband's been giving this ladyboy money, and maybe you'd better check your bank account and then you can act all OMG, no Wayyyyy. The betrayed wife. Duh duh *Duh*"

For some moments they sat in silence.

"Let me ask you something Georgia. Were you in prison or a *freaking* loony bin?"

Georgia didn't laugh. She just stared at Kavya in a way that was not pleasant. And all at once, Kavya felt insecure. She couldn't have Georgia turn against her now.

"Sorry, I was just trying to be funny. Didn't mean to offend you. Or upset you."

"I'm not offended. Or upset."

"I just meant," Kavya lowered her voice. "It's such a crazy scheme. It's so convoluted. There's so many ifs and buts."

"Like what?" said Georgia pursing her lips.

"Like…where do I start? It's such a long list. And you're going to pump *gas* in the house? How is that even? And I must drive to a timetable…and call the police...? How am I supposed to remember all that? And gas? That's bloody dangerous."

And yet as Kavya heard herself speak, it all seemed possible, in exactly the way Georgia had explained it. In the sparkling dust in the beery darkness, she could see it all unfold like a movie. John arriving at Moghul House, shaking Devaani awake, trying to fight off his own tiredness. Jimmy's Car Hire outside Saint Dorothy's at Cliffe station. 10minutes driving on a deserted road. And then she saw her own face looking in through the window of Moghul House. Smashing the window. Hello, I want to report a robbery. Driving back into the night. This wasn't something Georgia had made up on the spot. She had spent a great deal of time figuring it out. Like she said, she needed someone else to put it into practise. She might have spent hours thinking it out.

Her own earlier 'plan' seemed idiotic to her now, hanging off the thread of an old Indian biddy and her conservative views to make some vague assumption and then carry it as gossip to Lalita who would then what? Approve of Kavya divorcing John? ...What utter pointless wilful absurdity had taken a hold of her for thinking that could work? And back then, the stakes had been less than zero.

Now, they were the highest they could ever be.

Chapter 47

As if she was reading her mind, Georgia said, "The thing is, if you want to do something, you must plan it out. Doesn't matter how wild the plan is, the wilder the better because it means no one can guess what really happened."

"But this is beyond--"

"It's all negatives with you. Don't you want to do it now?"

"Why d'you keep saying that? I want to. I do. But I'm allowed to ask questions! For instance, you never said anything about gas before. What's that for?"

"To make sure they're found together. You know, like lovers. Romeo and Juliet."

"Romeo and Juliet killed themselves!"

"Ok, but that's a film. These two are just going to be sleeping. Until the police arrive."

Kavya opened her mouth to say it wasn't a film, then closed it again. Georgia's education was not her priority in the moment.

"How are you going to pump gas in there?"

"Through the air vents. I know how to do it, it's easy."

Georgia sipped her water. She was supremely relaxed, Kavya noticed. She remembered asking Georgia once if she was freaked out by something and Georgia had looked at her blankly, then said, 'nothing freaks me out' and Kavya had wondered if the girl was fearless, a bullshitter or a sociopath.

"Remember one time we were talking about travelling?" said Georgia.

"Spain?"

"Driving through France. It was this English couple with a motorhome. They hired me for three weeks as a cook and driver. They were quite well off, but they didn't want to stay in hotels. This motorhome was huge, like those American ones. And in the parks where we stopped for the night there were loads. It's a whole thing, a community. We travelled all around the French Riviera where the footballers and celebrities have massive villas."

"Oh yeah—" said Kavya nodding, although she had no recollection. The memory's been letting me down. I should have mentioned that to the quack.

"And one morning we woke up and everything was gone. Laptops, iPhone, passports, jewellery, wallets, handbags, cash, the lot. And none of us heard a thing. We'd all been asleep. Even the dog didn't bark! We couldn't figure it out, how that was possible. And then we heard of other people it had happened to. Even celebrities in their villas! It was all in the newspapers. And the police said some kind of gas was pumped in through the air vents. It knocked you out but didn't kill you like normal gas. The locks had been broken but no one heard a thing."

Kavya stared at Georgia. Her heart began to flutter.

"But that's not the full story," said Georgia.

"So, what really happened?"

"Well truth is...*I* didn't exactly get burgled."

"You mean you were the burglar?"

"No, not the burglar. I was, the 'inside man.' It was a French gang. They did it exactly as the police said. They did it up and down the Riviera for the whole summer. It was a perfect scam. And in the end, insurance had to pay out, so everyone was happy. Victimless crime. No one got hurt. In some cases, so they told me, people contacted them to do the burglaries so they could claim insurance. Designer burglaries, all the rage!"

"Did you know them from before?"

"No of course not, it was random. I met one of them at the beach and started talking, they wanted information about where the air vents were, how many motorhomes were in the same park. They cut me in. I didn't do anything. I just gave them information."

"But then …did you get knocked out too?"

"Yeah, I had to. Otherwise, it would have looked too suspicious. Of course, I knew it was going to happen. We all woke up at 5am, bleary eyes and saw the motorhome had been ransacked. What I knew was, the gas had been pumped in at 4am and we were all in a deep sleep by 4.20am when the gang entered and by 4.45am they were long gone. Of course, I pretended to be in shock same as my employers. We couldn't believe it, we asked the other motorhome people, we called the police.

It was bold. The gang would be sunning themselves on the beach during the day. Fit young French guys, they looked like surfers or beach bums, blending in, they'd even chat to some of the people they had burgled the night before! They had Russian contacts, and all the stuff was out of the country within hours. A massive diamond got stolen from one of the villas owned by a racing driver. The newspapers called it The Pink Panther Robberies."

"Oh, because of those old movies. Inspector Clouseau."

"Who?"

"The Pink Panther was a diamond."

"Ok, well anyway. So, I got to know those guys and they taught me a few things. You'd be amazed how easy it is to get hold of cannisters of chloroform gas. It's got a name. CGAc12. It's used in hospitals by anaesthetists, but theirs is stronger obviously, it's for operations. This is a small cannister and all you need is a pipe to attach it. It's simple. It works fast and it wears off fast."

"An hour. It works for an hour. That's all?"

"It makes things easier all round. A burglar doesn't want to go into a house that has normal sleeping bodies and dogs, because they wake up with guns and baseball bats."

"And what about surveillance cameras though?"

"No, I don't think anyone had them. Not in the motorhomes. But if they had them in the villas, maybe they weren't turned on. Or they turned them off. Anyway, they wore balaclavas and gloves. But that's not what I'm talking about here. Those blokes were professionals. I just learned how to use the gas from them."

"Oh, right," said Kavya.

"So, in this case, in Moghul House, you'll have a time window of an hour max, between me pumping in the gas, you smashing the window, making the phone call and the police arriving. It's not the end of the world, but after an hour, they'll wake up so it's better if they're found sleeping."

"Are you sure the gas won't …."

"Kill them? No way. I told you; I've experienced it myself. It's not like gas from the oven. It won't kill, but it can make you feel sick, so".

"So, if I break the window, it'll be weaker."

"Exactly."

"But it'll definitely work?"

Georgia shrugged.

"Nothing's 100%."

Atima Srivastava

Chapter 48

"Cheer up," said Georgia. "If it doesn't work and they wake up before you get there, they'll just think it's a wind up and you can turn back, and we can try it again—nothing will have happened."

"No but...I've just got to get the sequence of events right in my mind. I don't feel like writing it down."

"You don't need to. Just use your head. It's like this. You reach St Dorothy's at Cliff by train. You hire the car from Jimmy's at 7.40pm and you wait. The gas goes in at 8.10pm. I text you GO. You start driving. I leave the scene. Just to be safe, I'll go the other way, along the beach, towards the lighthouse. I'll just walk and take a bus. Don't worry about me. We won't see each other."

Kavya nodded.

"It's less than a 10-minute drive. You arrive at Moghul House at 8.20. Park the car, come down the steps, look in the window. You see the two figures in there fainted on the floor. You smash the window around 8.30 and drive back to the station. You leave the car at 8.45 and catch the train back to Mamble Favre at 9 pm. If you're early, catch the 8.50. Loads of time. You can have a coffee, or a drink on the train."

"When do I phone the police?"

"At 8.35. As soon as you get back to the car. You're a concerned citizen. You were walking on the beach, and you saw a smashed window in the onion house at the end. You thought it might be burglars. You left the scene, you were afraid. Because you don't want them to ask you to wait for the police."

"What about the smashed window? What do I tell them about that?"

"Nothing. They'll assume the burglar did it."

"And as soon as I've made the phone call to the police, I cut up the sim and destroy the phone. I've seen that in tv shows."

"Yep."

"But…even with the burner? Won't they know it's me?"

Georgia laughed scornfully.

"You'll be talking to some call centre, not Scotland Yard. And muffle up your voice. It's easy. They get random reports all the time from people who don't want to get involved. That's the majority of tip offs they get. It's normal."

Kavya stared at the grain on the table, imagining the whole train of events in her mind. Burners, drugs, hiring a car, a tight timetable, a phone call and then wait for the police to come knocking to tell her about her husband. This happens, then this happens then this happens…she could see it all clearly.

"I have to think about it," she said. "I don't know if I can do it."

"It all depends how much you want to do it".

Kavya nodded.

But it's not a matter of want, she thought fearfully. I *must.*

"We should probably go," said Georgia. "I've got to go and meet some people and then get the burner and the other things."

"Yes," said Kavya as if in a trance. She staggered to the bar to pay. As she inserted her card into the machine, she thought I can't go home right now. I've had too much to drink. Marymary will be there, and Milan. And John will have come home too. He only had a few things to do at the workshop. He won't leave before seeing me. Maybe he'll pack his things.

They walked out of the bunker into bright sunlight and it stung Kavya's eyes. She got in the car and stared at the white prescription bag on the floor. I could say I'm not feeling well and that's why I've come home from work, and I must go to bed right away. Right away! It's my home, I'm allowed to go and sleep in my bed when I want to. Marymary would tell Milan to be quiet and she would let her close the door and get some rest. But John would stare at her with those blue eyes.

And that earnest, tortured man wouldn't leave her alone. She was quite sure of that. He wouldn't believe she was ill. He'd come knocking on her door. He might even phone the doctor without telling her about it. Doctor Moody.

And what if I am ill, she thought with a fright. Then I'll be helpless, I won't be able to move, and he'll find the bottles in the wardrobe inside the rucksack. He'll find the wet clothes and he'll tell everyone that I killed that old witch and dragged her into the sea.

"I want food," Kavya said suddenly as Georgia was driving homeward. "We could go to the café by the lighthouse on BarleyBarton beach. Oh, but we just missed the turning. We can't go now."

"No problem," said Georgia, "I can take the next one."

"Ok," said Kavya coldly.

At 5pm she had a few more glasses.

She ordered a plate of fried whitebait and squid rings that they shared. The tartare sauce was homemade. They were in the sun trap, on what the locals called the "sunset strip" sitting at a plastic table on the decking outside the café Bar near the lighthouse looking at the sea. The sky was slashed orange and purple and lavender. Spectacular sunset, as usual. And it was still warm outside.

"No, I won't thanks," said Georgia when Kavya offered her wine from the bottle she had ordered. "After I've been on a bender, I stay dry for a few weeks. Then I'm fine."

"A few weeks? You said it was. A few days."

"It is. But the days that follow you must be careful too."

"Pretty bad days I bet. Cold turkey."

"Not really. Because I'm fit and healthy."

"I'm not," said Kavya. "I've got fat. Always used to be so skinny when I was younger. Now I'm on this new diet, it's mainly protein and I've been thinking of cutting out the booze altogether. Or cutting down. Maybe just have a couple in the evenings."

Kavya stole a look to see if Georgia disapproved, but Georgia had no expression on her face. She sat looking at the sea with her red hair ablaze, looking young and energetic and alive. Yeah…thought Kavya, that's what I'll do. Dry out. The first three days will be the worst like she said, and then I'll see, I'll get through it…

It was dark suddenly.

"Let's go," Kavya said.

"So do you want to go ahead with it?"

"I think so," said Kavya.

"You've got to be sure. I don't want to end up in a bad situation."

"Was it like that when you met that gang on the beach in the French Riviera?"

Georgia nodded. "Yeah. I had to say yes or no to helping them. They couldn't be left holding the bag. I was scared, but I went for it. To be fair, I didn't have that much to do. You'll have to do more."

Kavya nodded.

"Ok, let's do it. I'm still not convinced it's going to work though. I doubt either of them will even go there."

"We'll see."

They drove back to Mamble Wafre along a quiet winding lane with green fields on either side, and Kavya fell asleep. When she woke up the cool evening air caressed her face and she felt melancholy, but she told herself it's fine, it's fine.

Georgia dropped her home and drove off.

When she entered the house, John and Milan were coming down the stairs together laughing as they bumped into each other deliberately. A routine they had started to do after Milan had asked what "rubbing shoulders" meant. Kavya found it annoying, it was too blokey, too physical.

She stood under the light in the hallway and held out her arms. Milan jumped the last step and made to come towards her but then looked over his shoulder to see if John approved. He's taken my own son away from me, she thought. We never have a laugh anymore, no good times or jokes. Because he's always with him.

"Hey, do up your shoelaces please. Then, go and set the table," said John and Milan immediately squatted down and started to do up his laces into four bows, the latest thing.

With all her heart, Kavya resented the air of authority John had over Milan, and her son's ready acceptance of it. She stood watching him, the man she had replaced Kishore with, because her vanity had made her succumb to a handsome blonde, blue eyed man who adored her.

John was wearing a stylish navy denim jacket she hadn't seen before. It surprised her because he was usually oblivious to fashion and tended to wear the same old.

"Why are you all dressed up?" she said.

"Lalita gave it to me. It's Paul Smith. And Milan got new trainers."

"Hmm, she likes to buy presents so she can justify her own spending. *Oh, I've got to phone her,*" said Kavya slapping her head and walked into the tv room and snatched up the land line.

Chapter 49

"I'm having dinner in my room. You said you would call at 5," said Lalita in a sharp tone.

"So sorry Naani. My battery died. I've just got home. Room service at the White Sands? Snazzy. Can I come by tomorrow afternoon?"

"Of course—I'm at a private view in the morning but my timetable is clear from 3pm, come anytime. You sound upset, anything happened?"

"Yes. It has. I'll tell you about it tomorrow."

She hoped John had overheard her grim tone, and it would worry him. When she put the phone down, she saw him standing in the hallway, and it seemed to her she was always seeing him in the shadows, in hallways and doorways and under the porch light, where he wasn't wanted, looking pale and hurt and haunted.

"Kavs, can we have a talk about me going away?"

"What now?" she demanded exasperated. "I've only just got in!"

"Ok but you've been out all day and then there never seems to be a right time."

"John, I'm not very well. I went to see the doctor today. I was going to go to bed. Or do we have to have this urgent talk now?"

"I could move out and go to a B n B…"

"You're so desperate to get away. Can't you just wait a couple more days? For Milan, and for, well so I can make some arrangements? I really don't feel well John."

He sighed.

"Ok, I understand. I'm sorry you don't feel well."

But there was this cold look in his eyes. He isn't bothered if I live or die, she thought bitterly and she felt her heart pop. It terrified her.

"I just need to go to bed and try to relax, maybe watch some Netflix rubbish, a comedy."

"Take my laptop from the bedroom," he said. And she thought he assumes I'm going into the spare room. I am, but he doesn't have to assume it. So, he was going to go without taking his laptop. That's big of him.

She locked her door and stood debating if she should take a drink. She felt overwhelmed with hopelessness, queasy with fatigue and sadness. A drink would perk me up she thought, but it doesn't always do that. You can't depend on it— That wasn't good, she thought. That was important to make a note of. Used to be she could count on four or five drinks to see her through the night but now---

There was a knock on the door.

Not again! Why won't he leave me be?

"Who is it?" she said as if that might send him away.

"It's me," said Marymary in her little wavering voice.

"Oh, Marymary," said Kavya, her own voice softening as she unlocked the door.

Marymary stood looking at her with such concern that Kavya almost burst into tears.

"I'm alright," she said as she saw Marymary's lips tremble. "Come in, come in. Sit."

"No, I won't disturb you. Johnny told me you needed to rest but you wanted to watch something. I have a code for Hayu. I came to give you the code."

Marymary had written it out in her perfect tiny handwriting on a small piece of paper. All week she collected the empty envelopes from the correspondence that came to the house and on Sundays cut them up to create a pile of blank paper to make lists on.

Kavya smiled.

"That's all Reality, isn't it?"

"Yes. I recommend Selling Sunset, about Real Estate agents in Los Angeles."

"You sly dog! I didn't know you subscribed."

"Oh, I don't. It's a—friend of mine. She gave the code to me."

"Ok. That's perfect. Thankyou darling. What would I do without you?"

"Get some rest," said Marymary, patted Kavya on the shoulder and left.

Kavya smiled. Marymary and her secret life. It didn't matter at all. Let her have her secrets. And if she had a secret lover, good for her! The support and solace Kavya had always felt in the presence of Marymary and Lalita knew no bounds. My own mother, it wasn't her fault, was cold, thought Kavya dispassionately. Sometimes she wondered if her mother had suffered depression after giving birth. They had never talked about it, but Kavya had a memory of being very small and her mother backing away from her when she was crying. It had stayed that way. I could never talk to her because she could never talk to me.

And yet, the chambers of the heart were many. What she had received from these other women in her life had compensated for all that she had not received. So much so that she had never felt badly towards her own mother. Infact, she had admired her, been in awe of her intelligence. There had never been a cross word between them. With these pleasant thoughts pitter pattering across her mind Kavya felt light and happy; she didn't need a drink. She got into her soft pyjamas and left the door unlocked which made her feel good.

Marymary bought her a tray with soup and a roll, and she curled up in bed watching episode after episode, sipping the gruel-like home-made vegetable concoction with a sense of security. The shenanigans of the show made her giggle and sometimes laugh out loud. How did these girls walk in those heels? Who lived in such expensive houses? The nourishing soup and bread tasted better than anything she had eaten for weeks. And no drinks, she thought. I need this! Calm and peace. She took out the bottle of prescription pills and read the instructions. One every night before sleeping.

Repeat if needed, after an hour. She read the small folded up paper that they came with, looking for side effects and contraindications. She was very curious as she had never taken a sleeping pill in her life. She hit pause on Selling Sunset and shook the bottle to hear the pleasing noise.

A strange thrill went through her body at the prospect of the magic this chemical would perform. You take a pill and in return you get uninterrupted sleep for 8 hours. It was incredible when you thought about it. How would they make her feel she wondered? She had never taken any hard drugs in her life, what they called Class A. Weed was all she had ever imbibed, and she hadn't much enjoyed that sleepy blurred feeling. But what if they didn't work at all? Georgia had said they were very mild.

I'll wait till bedtime, perhaps 10, or 11pm. Marymary knocked to get the tray and then Kavya settled down to serious binge. Netflix didn't even ask you if you wanted the next one, so she was surprised to see that she had finished the entire Season. She paused it and listened to how quiet it was. It was an unusual evening for her. No one came to bother her, there was no noise, and she was in bed, like a virtuous snug little bug. No booze, not even wanting booze, just waiting patiently to take the magic pill. She giggled remembering that Georgia had thought Romeo and Juliet was a film.

At 10.15pm she got up and got herself a glass of water and settled back in. She loved wearing the plaid pyjamas, so sexless and innocent. I'll take one now and carry on with Season 2 all the time monitoring what happens. She carried on watching and monitoring and while she felt a bit sleepy it wasn't anything big. She checked the time, and it was 11.20 so she popped another one and within a few minutes she felt a wave of tiredness engulf her and she started yawning repeatedly till her jaw ached.

And then she seemed to fall into a settled pre sleep, and she thought it's working, it's definitely working and paused the laptop and set it on the bedside table and curled up under the duvet.

Chapter 50

It was 7.30am when she woke up. She'd slept for almost 9 hours. I haven't had this much sleep in decades. I feel amazing! Never felt better in my life. It was a new start for her, she could feel it. Now that I've stopped drinking everything will be different, she was sure of it. I just need two or three dry days… At 4pm I will have done 24hours of no booze. Wait what's at 4pm? No, 12pm. Naani. I'm visiting her at the White Sands.

The burden descended on her again, all the complications and the spectres. It was worse now she felt better and balanced in her head. If John opened his mouth about the old witch, it would be serious trouble. Why didn't I call the police myself? she thought, disgusted with herself. I couldn't have done a worse thing than what I did and now. Now if the body's found and John talks, it'll look like----

It would look like murder. What she had done was perfectly simple, justifiable and correct. That woman had attacked her, and she had defended herself. I think I hit her twice but that's not the point, in self-defence you don't know what you're doing. But the point is, what matters is that I—*disposed* of her in that way. I acted like a guilty person. Like a murderer.

There were still the wet clothes inside the rucksack and the monkey wrench and this morning in the light she could see exactly how dangerous they were to her. Someone else could turn up she thought, feeling her throat constrict. For all I know, someone else has already turned up, gone to the police and told them about Billie because they knew she was going to Moghul House to look for me.

What if that someone wouldn't leave the police station unless the police paid me a visit? And they'd come and ask me if I'd ever seen Lady Billie and if indeed, she had ever got to Moghul House. And if she said no, there would be John standing in a doorway to say yes. Police would search the house and they would find the wet mouldy smelly clothes and the tell-tale wrench covered with DNA, mine, and hers.

How can I explain? she thought, in rising terror. Oh God. Everything I've done is exactly what a murderer would have done. Oh God, O God that's what alcohol does to you. I've got to manage it properly, carefully, or else it's the end. Total collapse and downfall.

If it wasn't for John, she thought, I could handle everything. I'd get rid of the clothes and the wrench and then I'd just deny whatever they said. It would be my word against who's, no one's because no one else was there. I'd just say I never saw the woman. And after all, I've got a bit of status here. I own the school, we've won some awards. And, although it embarrassed her to even think of it this way, the fact was, the "Race" card could be played both ways.

Even if it was a small town, and even if they had all voted for Brexit, the truth was they were against Eastern Europeans here, not Asians. She was liked, her School was liked and there would be many who would give her character a good reference. And the police won't go after me, she thought. Billie was known to have some 'challenging' views, everyone knew that. She had supported UKIP and she was well known to be anti-immigration.

Alive they might have kow-towed to her but now that she was nowhere to be found, they might think differently about her. You could never downplay the politics of envy in England thought Kavya. I could manage it all, I could play it…but then if my own husband spoke against me...I couldn't fight that.

And that's what he's thinking about. That's what he intends to do. And he knows that I know. That's why he's wary of me, that's why he looks at me with that look in his eyes. Locks his door. Wants to go and stay in a B n B. Then he can easily go and talk to the police because I won't know when or how. He's afraid of me because he knows I know he's going to betray me. How can I stop him?

She looked down and saw her hands were shaking uncontrollably, her face and back and belly were dripping with sweat, it was falling off her eyebrows. And back came that repellent feeling of sick in her throat, giddiness, headaches, despair, and degradation in her bones, that old familiar cycle back again. Just when this new era was about to begin, a new start full of light and hope….

If I could just have one day free and clear. Just one day. And then I could handle it all.

I've got to tell Georgia it has to be done tonight, the thing.

Then, by tomorrow John will be a completely unreliable, discredited witness. Nothing he says will matter or have weight. And whatever he says against me will be seen as malicious, wicked, and spiteful. Twisted. Which it is. But I haven't *got* a day free and clear. What if the police turn up *today*—because someone, an unknown someone, has made a statement to them? I won't have time to get rid of that rucksack. I feel sick, violently sick and it's all backed up, stuck in my throat. I didn't want to have a single drink today. I was feeling so well, so healthy…I don't want to, but I've got to.

She took just two shots of vodka, and like medicine, it helped to steady her nerves. I'll take the rucksack to the office, she thought. And if I can get John out of the house…. oh but he's got to get the text from "her". Ok, but how early can he get that text? I'll have to consult with Georgia. But whatever happens, I've got to get him *out of the house*! To the circus. When the police come, he won't be here, and the rucksack won't be here either.

Her brain was functioning properly. She bought out the wretched rucksack full of the wet clothes; it smelled a bit so she sprayed deodorant all over it. She locked the wardrobe and left the bottles inside, full, and empty, and went downstairs. John, Marymary and Milan were there as usual.

"Did you have a good night's sleep dear?" said Marymary.

"I really did, thank you for asking," she said with a big smile. "Listen, I've had a great idea. John why don't you take Milan to the circus today? You too of course Marymary? It's an extra special day because they've got a Russian trapeze act; Shanta Acharya is taking her two grandsons and I thought you could meet them there. It'll be fun! For Milan, don't you think?"

"Well, my car isn't working and—" said John. "I've got to sort some work things out and."

"No problem! Georgia can drop you all off!" said Kavya.

"Please Johnny. Please!" cried Milan jumping up and down.

"Yes John. Please don't disappoint Milan. You're self-employed, you can take a day off to spend with your son! You can make some arrangement to come back—by train or maybe Shanta will give you a lift, anyway, it's a great chance, isn't it?"

Kavya was proud of herself for saying that, it would melt John's heart to hear Milan called his son.

"Ohhh, a circus," said Marymary eyes lighting up and clapping her hands. "The only time I ever went was when I was a child, with my younger brother in Goa."

"Why don't you come too?' said John unsmilingly.

"Well, I've got to work John! I told you we're doing a presentation in Calais to get their cohorts from the schools, and I have to go and do it in person in a few days so I have to prepare! That School doesn't run itself you know? It takes hard work. And dedication," said Kavya pompously.

Milan was slapping the table in front of John and for once Kavya didn't tell him off.

“Mate, why don't you go with Marymary? You don't want me along, it'll be---”

Kavya's face dropped. But she needn't have worried because Milan became insistent. She could see he didn't want to offend Marymary, but his little eyes were beseeching John now.

“But I want to go with you Johnny. I want you to see the circus. With me! You said you never saw one when you were my age. You came from the childrens home to Saint Dorothy's at Cliffe for the day but there wasn't enough money to take any of you to the circus. And you cried on the bus home!”

“Mate you've got a great memory, but now you've blown all my cred. Don't tell everyone I cried on the bus! Men must have each other's backs.”

“But it's good to cry. We all need to do more of it. It releases stress,” said Milan importantly and they all tittered.

“They learn it all in School. Empathy lessons,” said Marymary with a giggle.

“I didn't mean to be rude Marymary. I want you to come too. But I want Johnny. He's my best friend.”

“Of course, little one. Not rude at all. I want Johnny too,” said Marymary and flashed John a rare full set of teeth smile. “Johnny has been a very good friend to me too.”

Has he now, thought Kavya?

“Ok, I'll go,” said John.

“Hooray!” said Milan and punched the air.

Chapter 51

"Brilliant," said Kavya. "Shanta will be delighted. Marymary you can liaise with her about what time to meet at the circus, there are lots of food stalls too apparently. Georgia's coming to give me a lift to work…and then I've got to go to see Naani at White Sands… I'll tell her to pick you all up around…2.30pm, so have a good lunch first. Yes so, you'll get to the circus at 4pm. Bound to be a long queue. It starts at 5 and it's on for about 2 or 3 hours, I think. So, I'll see you all back at home in the late...evening. We'll order pizza whenever you all get home. Perfect plan! I'm going outside to wait for Georgia."

"Your organisational skills are second to none!" said Marymary. "Don't you agree Johnny?"

"Yeah."

"A great thrill for me," said Marymary smiling all over. "A great thrill. It was the last time I saw my brother. That was the last time I went to a circus."

Kavya smiled. *She* was happy, unlike some people. But the smile froze on her lips because if Marymary should ever find out….

In the hall Kavya picked up her yellow rucksack and threw it over one shoulder. It seemed that she had been carrying this damn thing forever and a day, this bag containing shame and danger. It had gone here and there, back, and forth, like a guilty man searching for justice.

Georgia was waiting outside with the same car.

"Listen, you've got to send both texts today."

"Ok," said Georgia.

"What if Devaani doesn't get it or –her phone's not working…or."

"Relax. I'll make sure she gets it. So, when do you want to do it, tomorrow?"

"Tonight."

"No. Tomorrow's more practical. Things to sort out."

"Well, it's too bad," snapped Kavya. "I've arranged the circus trip. It's got to be tonight!"

"Why?"

Georgia was looking at her like she was crazy. Even *she* could turn against me, thought Kavya. Especially if she knew what was in the rucksack.

"Because I must go to Calais tomorrow! For *work*!"

Georgia nodded slowly. "Ok, I think we can manage it for tonight."

"I forgot my sunglasses."

"Go and get them then. What are you doing, you can leave your rucksack here."

Kavya pretended she hadn't heard. She couldn't leave that bag anywhere. She hauled it over her shoulder and walked past the kitchen door and saw the three of them still sitting there, went upstairs, found the sunglasses, trudged downstairs again. Everything she had to do was laboured and agonizing and her body had lead weights pulling it down.

She got into the car again and Georgia drove off.

"I told them you'll give them a lift to the circus at 2.30pm."

"What d'you do that for?" said Georgia irritated. "I've got loads to do. Got to get the burner, the gear, and the pills--"

"Sorry, I didn't think---"

"Alright, I can probably manage it…If I drop them at 4pm, I can leave the car somewhere and still get to Moghul House for 6 by train which gives me plenty of time before Devaani gets there."

"Oh*!* I've got to go to see Lalita at 12 and then I'll go back to work so I can't give John the sedative! I've messed up! Georgia, now what?"

"Don't worry, I'll handle it."

"Really?" said Kavya with relief. "But how?"

"On the way to the circus I'll just stop at the petrol station and get us drinks and sweets. I'll buy him a bottle of Vimto, chuck the pills in there."

"You know that's his favourite drink?"

"Yeah, I know. He can't resist it."

"How do you know that?"

"He told me. Vimto was their big treat in the Home, and you didn't get it if you'd been naughty."

Something in Kavya's heart turned. That's my husband, she thought. Everyone knows everything he likes. He shares his most intimate feelings with…

Well, she didn't want to think about her husband now, not anymore, not ever.

They drove for a time.

"I'll come to ISEE around 11.30am, to get the note."

"What note?"

"I told you. You've got to write the note from him to her."

"No! I can't do that."

"We've already been through this," said Georgia. "What's your problem?"

"I'm dyslexic!" blurted out Kavya.

She avoided writing anything. She hadn't written anything for years and had got out of the habit. "My handwriting is like a five-year-olds."

Georgia laughed. "Doesn't matter. It's just for my insurance. No one's going to see it. We hope! Just write the words. And then I'll text them. You crack me up, you're mental. And talk about vain!"

Kavya pushed out her bottom lip.

"Can't you write it out for me and then I'll copy it out and then you'll still have a note with my handwriting on it and then you can text it."

"Well no."

"I don't want to write it," said Kavya stubbornly.

It hurt her that Georgia had unwittingly used the word "mental" infact it made her livid. She supposed it was what they called a trigger.

"Do you want to call it off then?" said Georgia lightly. "Alright, we'll call it off."

I can't call it off, Kavya thought. I've got to make sure John is totally disgraced and discredited before the police. It doesn't matter how much I don't want to do it, how exhausted I am, how honestly ill I feel. I've got to go through with it.

"Georgia," she said in a strangled voice feeling the desperation in it. "I physically can't do it. It's not just the— it's that. I'm not well. My hand. A pen. It won't hold it still. My hand won't stop shaking."

"Then we'll call it off."

"Alright," said Kavya after they had been driving for a few moments. She knew that Georgia knew she wasn't dyslexic. It's just that her hands shook so often, she avoided writing. Well, she'd have to do it somehow. "Alright, *alright* I'll do it. Come to the office at 11am. I'll have it ready for you."

"Found your balls," said Georgia with a smile. "Good. And I'll bring you the burner. Sure, you're up to this?"

"Yes," said Kavya nodding. "Don't worry. I know what I must do. The note, the driving, the phone call, all of it. Oh."

"Yeah?'

"What if, I mean what if John goes there *earlier* than 8pm? It'll mess up the sequence."

"Why would he?"

"Because. After he gets the text, he won't bother to even go into the circus, he'll buy their tickets, make the arrangement for Marymary and Milan to stay with Shanta, maybe even sleepover...and then what if he decides he may as well get to Moghul House earlier than 8pm? I mean much earlier. 7pm? Just because she's told him meet her at 8pm, that doesn't mean he'll follow it to the letter. Remember he thinks he's going to meet her *outside,* not inside, so he might deliberately go early..."

"Relax," said Georgia. "I'll just send him the text as late as possible. So he won't have time to get there earlier."

"Ok, that's good. And you're sure the gas won't be fatal. That's important."

"Chemicals are 100% predictable. Relax. Don't freak out."

"But if it all just goes tits up? Then what?"

"Then nothing. They can have a big paranoid chat with each other about unknown people plotting against them. They won't tell anyone, no one will believe they were set up. They can't prove it. No motive. Even if nothing happens, the main thing is, you'll have proof that John and Devaani do meet in secret. That all you wanted, wasn't it? You can keep it behind your ear while you're watching telly together and use it whenever you want."

The thought of John sitting next to her was terrifying. Georgia doesn't know about Billie, thought Kavya. She doesn't know the damage that John can do to me if he wants.

Chapter 52

She asked Georgia to drop her off on BarleyBarton seafront saying she would walk to work from there. And yes, she would have the note ready at 11.30. As soon as Georgia had driven off, she bought a quarter bottle of vodka from the supermarket, shoved it in her jacket pocket and checked into a small B n B called The Lazy Days for 24 hours under the name Indira Gandhi from Bradford without even thinking about it.

The lady who owned The Lazy Days, a trim white woman in her sixties wearing an apron, stared, and then smiled encouragingly at Kavya for some moments and then blurted out, “Welcome to BarleyBarton Indeeeera. We love a curry. We have one every Friday.” Kavya lugged her rucksack into the room, locked the door and lay down on the bed and closed her eyes. Someone was hoovering somewhere, and the room smelled of bleach.

She got up and went to the desk. The window above it looked out to the sea, and she stared at it for a while. Then she took out one of the letterheaded sheets and stared at that. What an old-fashioned little place this was, stuck in the 1950’s, and she had never heard of a B n B having headed notepaper.

“What am I supposed to write?” she said out loud in desperation. “I can’t do this. I just can’t do it.”

Every ounce of drive and determination drained out of her. Her limbs turned to stone and her vision became blurred.

Everything was a chore, having to go back and forth, back, and forth relentlessly, like a trapped rat in a maze. She could hardly think. Her brain seemed to have shut down. She folded her arms on the desk, put her head down and started crying quietly.

But if this didn't happen tonight, the other would happen. The police would come or John would go to them. Her sobs turned into low animal moans. I've got to lose this freaking rucksack, just get *rid* of it, she told herself between moans. Face it Kavya! You've got to get yourself *out* of it. You've got to be done with the whole thing!

She despised and dreaded the thought of a drink, but she had to try. Just one small sip to see if it would give her magic strength and focus. It nearly made her vomit, but she still managed to get it down, and in a few moments, she felt surprisingly better. I've got to channel this energy, she told herself. But it had to be a fast channelling because she couldn't count on it, it might disappear as quickly as it had come.

She started to write painstakingly, her left hand holding her right wrist.

Hi Devaani. It's me John. Something very serious has happened. URGENT. You have to, absolutely must meet me at my house 1 Beach Drive, Saint Dorothy's at Cliffe at 7pm TONIGHT. It has an onion top. Use the key under the flowerpot and let yourself in and wait for me. I am bringing a lot of cash for you. It's really really important so don't ignore this message, please.

That'll do, she thought reading it over without interest. Good enough. That sounds like him. Maybe I'll take the uppercase off, men don't really use that. The handwriting was atrocious. She copied it out again on another headed notepaper, scrunched up the original and chucked it in the bin. The words she couldn't be bothered to change but the writing itself she felt, was shameful; Georgia was right to have called her vain but it looked like it was written by her left hand. She checked the clock on the wall. Plenty of time, it was only just past 9am.

Maybe I'll try it again, write it slowly this time, she said feeling a bit worried in case the alcohol wore off. Then she realised there were no more headed notepapers and went into a panic. But you mustn't write it on headed notepaper *anyway,* what's the matter with you? Georgia is going to keep it as insurance, she needs *my* handwriting, but it shouldn't have any indication as to *where* it was written. Just in case. It should be anonymous. It's more information than is necessary.

She decided to keep the one she had already written and carefully tore off the top and the bottom where the address telephone number and email of The Lazy Days were printed. Then she looked in horror at the bin, took out the scrunched up one and tore it up into tiny little pieces. Now where was the ashtray so she could burn them?

Searching manically for the ashtray made her think again of how laborious it was, how relentlessly she had to do everything back and forth. She looked up and next to the clock was a sign that said *We ask you to not smoke. There are smoke alarms fitted.* Great! She took all the paper pieces in her fist and stuffed them in her jacket pocket and did up the zip. A few fell down on the brown carpet like confetti, but they didn't matter. She looked back again at the clock, and it still said a minute past 9. She took out her phone and groaned. It was almost 10.30. She must have been crying for an hour; she couldn't remember.

She hailed a taxi with the yellow rucksack on her back.

"Coo-eeee," trilled the lady who owned the Lazy Days. She was watering her hanging baskets of anemones out front while her husband sat doing the Daily Mail crossword. "Off somewhere nice with your heavy bag?"

"Oh, um just got to take some things for my grandmother who's in town. I'll be back later."

"And what's Bradford like?"

"What. Is. Bradford. Like?" repeated her husband looking up.

Kavya stared at them both smiling at her. Tolerant smiles, she thought. Lalita had said back in the 1960's that's how the ones who said, "I'm not racist, some of my best friends are Black," used to smile at you. That's why he was speaking slowly, and she was shouting. Well meaning, maybe. Yet even though it must surely be clear to them that Kavya was British born and bred, they felt the need to talk to her like she was Johnny Foreigner. Back in Naani's day, Kavya thought, Indians would have felt small; today it was these backward gnomes that seemed small. Left behind, tiny dinosaurs.

But still, thought Kavya as she got in the taxi pretending, she hadn't heard. How could they not *know* she was bred and born in the UK? Didn't her accent alone tip them off? Did they only see the colour of her skin and think it foreign? So maybe it wasn't just the Eastern Europeans they hated but loved the Asians; maybe there were degrees of white hatred? But, she reasoned, they were being quite nice, it wasn't hatred, it was just ignorance. Intelligence must make concession, as Naani liked to say. Intelligent people must make allowances for the stupid.

Anyway, she had no time or energy to dissect everyday racism. She sighed and sat back. Why hadn't she just told Georgia to come and meet her at The Lazy Days? All this back and forth, again. But the thing was, she didn't want Georgia to know that she just needed to be on her own in a place where no one knew where or who she was. There was no clear and free day but at least she had the room in The Lazy Days where she was someone completely else. Indira Gandhi from Bradford.

When she reached the office, she blustered through into the small room before anyone could stop her. As soon as she'd sat down among the folders and files (they seem to use this place like a junk room, maybe they don't realise it's supposed to be my office!), there was a knock on the door.

"Someone's come to see you," whispered Mrs Flinders.

"Who is it?" said Kavya warily.

"That one who used to be the cleaner here." She lowered her voice. "She looks very odd."

"Oh yes, she's...no it's all fine now. Let her in, let her in."

Kavya told Georgia to close the door behind her. Mrs Flinders was right, the girl looked white as a sheet, which was saying something, as like most red heads she was already pasty looking.

"You alright?" said Kavya with a frown. "You're not coming down with something are you?"

"Have you done it?" said Georgia briskly taking out a phone from her pocket. It was an old phone. The kind Tariq mended and unlocked. She put it on the desk.

Kavya took out the envelope with the folded-up notepaper and gave it to her. Georgia took it out and read it.

"What's funny about it?" said Kavya. "What are you laughing at?"

"Nothing. Don't give up the day job. And what are you saying please for?"

"You can change it," said Kavya sheepishly. "In the texting."

Georgia's face was like stone. It crossed Kavya's mind that she might be on something.

"He's polite. I thought he'd say please."

"I'll do the edit in the SMS. The main thing is, you've got the time right. So Devaani will get there when we want. You can leave the rest to me. Now, you do know how to get the sim out? Destroy it and the burner after you've called the police. And don't forget, you'll need to show some ID to the car hire place. You can use your ISEE identity card. They don't bother to make copies, it's just a visual."

Mrs Flinders knocked and came in with some papers and cheques for Kavya to sign. Georgia wasn't fazed, she just stopped talking and stepped back with a glazed expression while Kavya attended to the admin. But it's alright for her, she thought resentfully, I'm the one with the burden. I'm the one with the bloody rucksack, the trembling hands, the fear, and misery. Mrs Flinders went out again.

"Where do I leave the car? Don't I have to give the key back to the car hire place?"

"Post the key through their door. Just leave the car in the street if they've gone home. They've got trackers on them, just need to leave them in a 1mile radius."

"Trackers!"

"They just get activated when the car's stationary. They don't record the journey. Their cars are pretty old too. I've got to leave now to pick your lot up and take them to the circus."

"You're sure there'll be no danger from the gas?"

"I told you. It's not that kind of gas. When I do something, I do it right. I don't fail."

"You're very sure of yourself."

"Because I'm a planner."

"And what do I say to the police, I saw someone breaking into my house?"

Georgia sighed.

"God no, don't identify yourself. You're not calling Scotland Yard. It'll be some kid in a call centre. You saw the window was broken, and there was a smell of gas. You're worried so like a good citizen you're phoning the police. End of. Ring off. Ok, any more questions? Can I go now? Have you got it?"

"Yes, got it," said Kavya.

Chapter 53

"Flying visit," said Mrs Flinders and Kavya made an inaudible noise.

"Just, hum, yeah,"

She was all over the place. She knew it. Everything she was doing was weird, strange, out of place. And the worst ordeal lay before her. Meeting Naani. She looked at her phone. She had a half hour to spare. As she walked out of the ISEE building with the rucksack hiked over her shoulder she felt like bursting into tears again. I've got to pull myself together. But if I have a drink, will it help me? Or will it make me worse? I just don't know.

One thing she knew was she couldn't eat a thing. Where could she go then to kill 30mins, she didn't have time to go back to The Lazy Days, and the only place where she could be quiet and at rest was a bar. Among people. Even if she could have gone back to that bleach smelling room and smiling owners, she didn't want to. She wanted to be where there was some atmosphere, people. I could have a shandy in a bar, she thought. There's some health in that.

As if on cue a text came through from Lalita.

Shit shag and shampoo! I've got caught up in meetings with the Arts Council. Can you come a little later? Say 3pm?

Kavya giggled at grandad's catchphrase, and texted back 'no problem' and dived into a bar she hadn't seen before. She didn't want to sit at the bar because her feet didn't reach the floor and she had to make sure the rucksack that she despised like sin, was close to her, touching a part of her body, and so she went to sit in a booth. She knocked back two double vodkas and then took a taxi to The Lazy Days. When she got out of the taxi, she was very aware that she must look extremely drunk. She was swaying.

And yet—I'm not! I can drink twice or three times what I've had today and be perfectly normal. It's not the booze, it's the other matter...She let herself in to her room, dropped the rucksack and jacket to the floor, fell on the bed with her face buried in the pillows where she started sobbing inaudibly and after a while, fell asleep.

When she woke up it was as though the magic wand had sprinkled her with fairy dust again. She reached down into the pocket of her jacket to check the time on her phone and her fingers came out stuck with a confetti of torn paper. That was ok, she knew what to do now. The phone informed her it was 2.15pm. She lay back and took a breath.

Then she got up, took her jacket to the bathroom, and flushed the torn paper down the toilet, added the bleach, and flushed it again. Good riddance. She peeled off her clothes, put her hair in a high ponytail, pulled on the provided shower cap and took a quick shower marvelling at the tiny soap and shower gel, observed her puffy face in the mirror as she towel dried her body, put her clothes back on, picked up the damn rucksack and went out in the street.

“I don't go there,” said a taxi driver sourly.

For God's sake, it was a one-horse seaside town and a six- or seven-minute ride. You’d think she was asking him to take her to South London.

“The White Sands Hotel?” she said. “It’s just up the road?”

“I know what it is.”

“Just drop me by the park then, I’ll walk the rest.”

“Nope,” said the taxi driver and drove off.

How dare he talk to me like that? Totally racist. Nakedly so. No pakis or blacks or eastern europeans or dogs in my cab. The disdain on his face said it all. Any non-white person could see it. *But how could you really prove that?* There was no other sign. And to whom would you have to prove it? Did white people see differently to non-white people? Nothing’s changed, it’s just more subtle.

She’d never noticed that shade of racism in London, where it was either overt or absent. By the seaside it had a particular nuance. She stood rigid, struggling against the fury that shook her. She wished she had grabbed his collar and punched him in the face. Kicked his car. No! Calm down, she told herself. You’re getting upset because you’re upset about the other thing. Stay cool, compose yourself.

She raised her hand. A taxi careered past, slowed down, saw her face, and then drove off at top speed. Kavya’s jaw dropped. Two in a row? She raised her hand again. Another taxi drew up and she grabbed the door handle, got in dragging the rucksack, sat back and then told him where she wanted to go, so he wouldn't be able to refuse. They drove off. I need her to understand and support me, thought Kavya as she sat hunched in the back. If only she'd take my side, unconditionally. As they approached The White Sands, a dark despair filled her entire body.

Lalita's approval was essential to her, necessary. It was food and air to her. But she's so fixed in her ideas. She thinks John's an angel, he walks on water as far as she's concerned. She could care less about the truth. And now, when I need her the most, she's likely to be narrow minded and impatient and completely insensitive. Just when I need her the most.

Lalita opened the door to her suite.

"There you are," she said, casting her shrewd sharp eyes over her granddaughter. She was dressed in a magnificent silk orange and pink shalwar kameez embroidered in the Kashmiri style with an arresting burnt orange cashmere shawl, what they called 'ring' shawls because you could pull them through a ring they were so sheer.

"Here I am," said Kavya with a sigh and put down her rucksack.

"Where are you off to?"

"Nowhere. It's just paperwork and stuff I have to work on for my presentation, for my trip to Calais. For the School. Sorry I'm late Naani, there was traffic. Or should I say shit shag and shampoo?"

"You like that don't you? Alliteration, my dear, alliteration. One of your late grandfathers' little quips."

Kavya tittered.

"I know. I wish I'd known him. This suite is unbelievable Naani, better than the Dorchester and the Ritz! In little BarleyBarton-on-Sea no less. Russian owned?"

"I'm sorry I had to mess up our schedule sweetheart. Now come in, and let's relax. Yes, or Chinese."

They walked into the large drawing room.

"Wow," said Kavya. "Chinese owned! Look at those silk curtains."

"Yes, I think Chinese, yes. I know it's ridiculous, but I am simply a patron of the Arts, but Mick Jagger wasn't in town. The suite was empty."

Kavya looked at her grandmother with an amused frown.

"He's, my generation. If you don't mind. I've met him twice I'll have you know. Your grandmother can rock it with the best of them. I was at the Flamingo in '63, their first gig! Your grandfather took me for my birthday. We were very International you know?"

"Wow," said Kavya. "Impressed."

"Come on, shall we have a little cigarette together? What about a cocktail? There are these marvellous ready mixed ones here. None of your dreary M & S ones in a can. They make these up in the bar downstairs in these lovely glass bottles. Negroni. Let's have?"

Kavya nodded and took one of the cigarettes offered. She took the Negroni and had a sip.

"So, tell me what's been going on. You sounded very upset on the phone."

"I am. I've had a shock."

"Milan?"

"No, he's fine. It's John."

Catching a glimpse of her grandmother's automatic resistance to anything said against John, in the form of her closed lips stretching back, sent Kavya into a slightly desperate spiral of mania.

"There's no point in hiding it…anymore! I didn't want to tell you. I didn't know how ...What's the use, you don't – you've already made up your mind so there's nothing, nothing I can ever say about John that you will believe. Nothing ever!"

"That's not true," said Lalita. "It's just that you're tired of him and when you're tired of people you tend to become. Well, ruthless."

"That's a horrible word! Who have I ever hurt? So unfair."

"You've hurt a great deal of people Kavya. You're indifferent to them once they lose an appeal for you."

"Alright, I'm a terrible person. That's the end of it. I'm wicked."

"Did I ever use those words?"

Chapter 54

"You don't have to! That's what you think! You think I have no feelings and I don't get affected, I'm insensitive—"

"Talk to me," said Lalita calmly.

"What's the point?"

"Come on now. All I mean is that I don't want you repeating silly gossip and rumour that these small towns tend to specialise in. If there was anything serious then…"

"Oh well depends on if you think that my husband sleeping with a prostitute is *serious*. And not only that! A *trans-sexual* prostitute! He's already given her four thousand pounds of my money. That's not silly gossip or rumour, that's a fact!"

"Kavya, what are you saying?"

"This is exactly what I mean. You won't listen. You can't even allow the possibility of the great John Ashworth."

"Calm down, calm down. How do you know this?"

"I've seen the evidence!"

"But who is it?"

"Her name is Devaani. A loathsome cartoon. She's the manager of Mowglis, a repulsive bad taste Indian restaurant. He goes there every Friday and gives her money. Shameless. I say *her*…we don't know if she's even a--"

"Oh, Devaani," said Lalita.

"*What?* Don't tell me you know her?"

"No, but Milan has mentioned her."

"My Milan?"

"He's been to the restaurant with John and Devaani ordered a special biriyani to be made especially for him. Apparently, she's a Bollywood Goddess."

"Unbelievable—"

The door rang and Lalita said 'come'.

A waiter came in with a trolley. It had a large stainless-steel dome covering a large platter. He lifted the dome and underneath was a hill of ice upon which were draped prawns, cockles, mussels, and clams.

"Compliments of The White Sands. We appreciate you staying with us."

"Thank you so much Abdul," said Lalita and tipped him handsomely; she always tipped non-white waiting staff handsomely and was unapologetic about it. *If the likes of us don't, who will darling?*

As soon as the man left, she said,

"I'm not at all keen on seafood, but it's all fresh and local. Would you like some?"

"Not hungry. In fact, I can't eat a thing. I've got some medical problem, went to the doctor. I'm so stressed out with this *thing* I'm never hungry!"

"Well, me neither now. Kavya, have you spoken to John about this?"

"No, I have not. He'd just deny it. And then there'd be a big drama where I'd be the villain."

"But shouldn't he have the chance to explain?"

"Oh, he's going to get this chance," said Kavya darkly.

"What do you mean by that?"

"Tonight, he'll be exposed. You'll see. Everything I've told you about him is true. And you'll see."

"What are you going to do?"

"Something you won't approve of."

"All the more reason to tell me."

"No! He's made a fool out of me; he's humiliated me and for all I know it's the talk of the town."

"Oh, a little melodramatic, people have other things to—"

"But tonight, he's going to meet her and there will be witnesses. He's going to be caught in the act! I've arranged it like that."

"Kavya! No! But what have you arranged?"

"What should I do Naani? Be one of those silly women who buries their head in the sand. Why should I? I won't!"

"Look, don't do anything hasty. If you have grounds, then talk to a solicitor. Do it properly. I have a good one."

"He's stolen from me; he's ruined everything between us, and he might have even given me a disease! He can't be allowed to get away with that."

"But darling you sound so bitter…"

"And why shouldn't I be bitter? I'm not sorry. He deserves to be publicly disgraced."

"Look let me talk to him…"

"No! I'm going to handle this myself. He's my husband Naani. Give me some credit. I have agency, I have a mind. You have no idea. No offence but. It's a different world to your day. There are no Gentlemen's Agreements and playing fair. If you don't have an advantage, you end up crucified."

Lalita became very distressed, and that made Kavya feel good, strong, and confident.

"I don't like the way you're talking."

"If I don't take control of the situation, I become a victim of it. And women should be tough when it comes to defending themselves. That's what you've always said."

"Well." said Lalita. She was quiet for a moment, her perfectly manicured hands clasped together in her lap. She doesn't blame me, thought Kavya. She knows it's the right thing to do.

"But if. If it doesn't happen the way you say. Then what will you do?"

"Then I see a lawyer. But Naani, I need to know you'll stand with me on this. I've got to know you're on my side."

Lalita sighed; her brow furrowed. "I wish you would do this another way, but yes. Yes, I will stand with you. I always will."

"That's all I wanted to hear," said Kavya with a sigh.

She got up and they embraced. Lalita put her hand on top of Kavya's head, just as she had done when she was a child. Her grandmother was her uniting force, her conscience, her anchor. Once she gave her approval, all darkness lifted from Kavya's heart.

"There won't be any violence involved will there?"

"Only when I kick him out on his arse. Literally!"

"You must remain dignified. Think of Milan."

"I am!"

Kavya moved towards the door.

"You forgot your rucksack."

And immediately, the solution popped up.

"Do you mind if I leave it here? You're staying for a week, aren't you? I could pick it up in the next few days."

"Don't worry, I'll look after it," said Lalita.

Now that burden was lifted too. The situation had unfolded like a dream. It was the perfect place to leave it. Kavya trusted her grandmother completely. Even if the rucksack had been open, she would never look inside.

I've got the go-ahead now; she thought feeling elated as she stepped into the lift. Everything is going to be alright from now on.

Chapter 55

She bought herself a Vogue and a Grazia at the corner by The Lazy Days. In the Italian restaurant next door, she got a takeaway box of salad, cold roast chicken and a bottle of Gingerino. And then, just because she felt like it, she went into a cheap (everything was made in China but had a label saying Made in Italy) fashion store and bought herself a pair of joggers and a hoody top as well as a long coat to wear over her jacket so she would have lots of pockets. She didn't want to carry a bag tonight.

In the room she put on the table lamp and sat down to eat and read. She had no alcohol, didn't need it. The bleach smell had been replaced by a pleasant smell of geraniums. An air-freshener she supposed but not too synthetic. She hung up her coat, took off her trousers and top, threw them in the bin, took another quick shower (all the little mini things had been magically replaced) and pulled on her new garments. The atmosphere, the simple pleasures, reminded her of when she had felt best. Travelling in Europe in her twenties.

She looked back on those truly halcyon days now and wondered what had happened to her. The woman she had been before her first marriage. Those days were suspended in formaldehyde like an exhibit. It was like an inversion of that dead shark. Lalita had taken her to a special Invite Only showing at The Saatchi Gallery to see the sensation. In The Physical Impossibility of Death in the Mind of Someone Living, Hirst is challenging us to comprehend death. *He's telling us we can't fathom the eternal slumber known as "death," even though we are face-to-face with a dead animal.*

At the time Kavya had found it hilarious, but now her life seemed the exact opposite: The Physical Impossibility of Life in the Mind of Someone Dead. She couldn't fathom that time when she had been alive, really alive, really living, even though she had so many memories, photographs, screengrabs, souvenirs.

But I'm not dead, she thought. My mind is not dead.

As she turned the pages of the magazine, she felt resolute and composed. I've got the go-ahead, she told herself. Naani did that. Now I can be sure I'm doing the right thing. The only thing. She had left behind her that degrading life of empty bottles, dangerous rucksacks, and all that constant anxiety and suffering. She was free of all of it now. Returned to a natural state of calm. It was entirely possible that she wouldn't see John again after tonight. I won't even let him into the house, I'll change the locks and I'll never let him see my son.

She felt incredibly relaxed, not at all restless and when it was time, she got up. The half-finished bottle of vodka she decided to leave on the table. She'd buy a new one! It seemed a perfect symbol of having discarded the old ugly life. Leave it behind, walk into freedom, an end to all the interminable locking and hiding and worrying. But then she had second thoughts and slipped it into the inside pocket of her new coat.

She took a taxi to Saint Dorothy's at Cliffe Station.

I'm early, she thought with a satisfied smile as she stood outside the station with the cool misty breeze rolling in from the sea. When you're early, you really do feel good. The sun was setting, and the sky had a lilac sheen. In her jacket pocket she had her phone and purse and in her inside pocket, zipped up, she had the burner. It was 6.50pm. No one was around. I wonder what would happen, she thought if I bumped into someone I know?

Well so what, let them say hello. Why am I here? I don't have to answer that.

She imagined being interviewed by a famous broadcaster on American prime time television.

"And where were you at the time of (broadcaster consults notes, camera moves in close)"

"I was in Saint Dorothy's at Cliffe. I have a house there."

"And did you know about the meeting at your holiday home between your husband and"

"I did not."

"Are you sure."

She would say nothing.

"Was your marriage happy?'

"At no time"

"And were there rows?"

"No"

"Could you tell us the basis of the unhappiness in your."

"I prefer not to answer."

The wind rolled in cool and salt and wet, and it was exhilarating. She took a deep breath and walked across the road to the car hire joint that was not Jimmys anymore.

She pressed the buzzer.

"Yes," said a voice.

"Hello, I want to hire a car. Can I hire for a couple of hours or does it have to be for the day."

"Minimum you have to pay for 5 hours."

The voice had a heavy Asian accent. She tried to look into the office, but it had vertical blinds. The cars were held in the lot behind the building.

"Ok, I'll take one for 5 hours please."

"No."

"Hello?" she put her head near the Entryphone. "I want a car."

"Can't do it."

"Why not?"

"No keys"

She made a gesture of impatience; this guy was killing her buzz.

"Alright, can you open the door please?"

He buzzed her in.

A young, bearded man was sitting in the office. There was a table and an old-fashioned desk top computer. The entire place smelled of stale curry.

"Can I hire a car for 5 hours please? I used to know Jimmy."

"Jimmy sold it. Now my cousin owns it. Can't rent. He got keys."

"He's got the keys for all the cars?"

"Yes"

"Where is he?"

"Mosque."

"It's not Friday. It's not Eid."

"He is praying. His father died."

"Oh. Sorry to hear that but. I'm in a hurry."

"Where you want to go? I am mini cab driver. I take you."

"No, I don't want that. I want a car."

"Let me drive you."

She looked at her phone. It was 7.30pm.

"I'm in a big hurry."

The man looked her up and down expressionlessly.

"I said, I want a car," she shouted.

"And I say no."

Chapter 56

Blind rage overtook her.

"Yes, I know you TOLD me. Now I'm telling YOU. You must have a spare set of keys. I just want to hire a car for a couple of hours. Can't you just do it?"

"Why shouting? Don't tell me like that. I told you no."

She sighed.

"I still want a car. And your lot has got cars. Just get me one please. It's very important. I need a car. I'll pay extra if that's what you want."

The man stared at his phone and then got up and went somewhere. He came back with a set of keys and a form to sign.

Leave it there, Kavya told herself. Leave it. You've got things to do. But no, how *dare* he waste my time like that? She started to write down her details.

"Driving licence"

She handed it over. He took it somewhere in the back and came back quickly, as though he was only pretending to photocopy it.

"Why did you do that?" she said aggressively. "Why waste my time, when you had the key all along?"

He just looked insolently at her.

"What's your problem?" she shouted. It was his face she couldn't stand.

"I don't like way you tell me. I don't give you car," he said nastily.

"What? You can't do that!"

"Yes."

She took a deep breath. "I'm very sorry. I am stressed out. I must drive somewhere. It's for my family. You can understand that. We will do anything for our families. It's very important. Please. I'm very sorry, very sorry."

She hung her head. He threw down the keys, face still insolent and mean.

Having to apologise to this creep made her sick. For no reason other than to be awkward, he had refused her... Because he wasn't used to being spoken to like that by a woman, and an Asian woman at that! If it had been a white woman, he would have taken it, he wouldn't even have tried to play that pathetic power game. Anyway, doesn't matter. She would have liked to punch him on the nose, but she disciplined herself. You've got to be sensible; you must be ready and waiting for Georgia's text.

"Thank you very much. Sorry again for raising my voice. Where is it?"

"Outside in the street, grey Renault. I go to mosque at 8. You post key in letterbox. Leave car in 1mile radius. Cash. Regards to family."

"Won't you take a card?" she said aghast.

"Cash only."

"Oh God," she spun around looking for an ATM. "Alright, alright wait there. I'll be back in a few minutes."

She ran across the street to the ATM praying it would dispense. It was now 7.40pm, still in good time but what if the ATM failed? What sort of Mickey Mouse outfit only took cash for hire cars? As she stood in front of the machine waiting for the display, she couldn't help thinking it had been a much more professional place before, catering to a yearlong stream of foreign students and English tourists. But over the years, business had got slow. Jimmy must have cut his losses sold up and gone. And now this crew! It was obviously a taxi and car hire place, and they probably didn't declare half of their income. No wonder English people hate immigrants she thought ruefully. They bend rules. They ruin it for the rest of us.

Fresh banknotes were ejected. She pulled them out in triumph. She hadn't asked for a detailed bank statement, but it gave her one anyway. She shoved it in her pocket and ran back to the car hire place. The man had been leering openly at her from in between the vertical blinds, and she was dying to give him a piece of her mind about disrespecting women but what was the point? And she didn't dare risk it.

It was a cheap old Renault, a make she had not driven before. Now she was nervous about her driving. She positioned the mirror and looked around. The street was empty, and the car hire looked closed, even though she knew it was open till 8pm. Although she supposed he left by the back door, so he might as well leave now, it didn't matter to her. Now just get comfortable, she told herself. 7.55pm. She opened the glove compartment and found a slim torch.

She tried it, yes it worked. Excellent! She needed a torch, a good idea!

How could she have forgotten to buy one? A piece of luck! She took it out and put it in her jacket. Then she took out the burner and placed it on the dash. She checked the battery was charged and it was. She waited. The minutes ticked by silently and flipped. 8.05pm. What was Georgia up to? She should have set the gas off by now. What's going on? Or was it 8.10 the gas would go in? Yes. She took out her own phone and put that on the dash as well, to make sure the time was synchronised.

Seconds ticked by. What the *hell?* There was no text. Why? Her heart started beating a little fast. She picked up the burner and put it down. 8.15. I can't wait any longer. I've got to go there; I've just got to *go*! Maybe something happened…maybe...? Reception! No bars! If she's set off the gas and she can't text me…? That's bad. Go. Go. Go. Just go. Stick to the plan. Do what we agreed. It's 8.16, you'll get there by 8.26. But I must wait for her text. I just don't know…

She turned on the lights and started the car feeling jumpy. She hadn't driven for a while and her eyesight felt ropey. She squinted and things came into focus. It was dark and the road was empty, at least. You can do it, it's muscle memory she told herself. You're a superb driver. The wheel was stiff, no power steering. Ugh. Her hands felt curiously light on the wheel. She wanted a drink.

She drove away and slowed down at the petrol station. The wind was blowing steadily now and the whole area looked weird, like a charcoal drawing against a flat sky. There were flares in the distance. No one was about. Saint Dorothy's at Cliffe was a strange creepy town.

The thing is, she thought, would a drink make me better, or worse? She didn't know the answer. It might make her better, it might make her sleepy, it might make her puke. She didn't *know*. I'll wait, she thought. Later, if it gets too bad, then I'll have some on the way back...

And then, the text came through. GO! She stared at it, exhilarated. It was only 7 minutes late. She took a deep breath and put her foot down. This is it. We are *on*. It's less than 10 minutes to get there. I'll park it just by the steps, there'll be no one around, no cars for sure. I'll run down, make my way around the house, and look in through the window. I'll see them lying there, I'll smash the window, then I'll make my way back quickly up the steps, phone the police.

It's a straight road all the way, she thought. The "GO" had gone out, but the fact of its existence urged her on. She felt connected to the action. Georgia had done her part, now she would do hers. She hunched over the steering wheel and drove. Just keep going, and soon it will be over.

Chapter 57

But that wasn't true.

John could still talk. Tell them about that old witch. Let him do it! She would deny everything. What woman, never heard of her, never laid eyes on her. And then, all that would remain would be the word of a husband who regularly had sex with a transsexual, for money.

And what if he talked to the police about the text? And what if Devaani talked about the text *she* was sent, the one Kavya had composed? What if they showed those texts to the police who would see they had come from the same phone number? So, what, let them talk about the texts. And if the police ever forced me to admit it, then yes, I'd admit that I did set a trap to incriminate my husband! What do you expect, my husband was deceiving me in the worst way possible, with a prostitute, with a …

And all at once a pure light came on in her head, like the crack of lightning in the dark that for some moments illuminates everything. She did not believe John was deceiving her. He never had and he never would. If he had gone to Moghul House, it was because of a mean conniving trick that had been played on him. You only had to look at him; the light of honesty shone out of his eyes. He only had to speak, and everyone would believe him. The world would know he was innocent. He couldn't help but tell the truth.

Kavya could see John telling Naani, shaking his head, not wanting to say, but Naani would make him tell the truth.

"I saw Kavya kill that woman. I saw her get the monkey wrench and strike her down, and when she was struggling to get up, Kavya struck her again. Kavya hated me. She wanted to get me out of her life. She sent a text pretending it was from me, to set a trap for me. She conspired with Georgia who gave me a drug to sedate me, and then gassed me. Kavya wanted to destroy me. She wanted to kill me."

The car swerved wildly out of control and narrowly avoided smashing into a tree. Kavya shut off the engine and started coughing, leaning forward. She couldn't catch a breath; her windpipe had closed up. No air came from her lungs. Her neck grew thick. Her left arm went into a paralysis. O God…. This is it….

This is dying, she said.

She tried to wrench the bottle out of her inside coat pocket, coughing and spluttering, shaking from head to foot. She got it out, and she couldn't unscrew the top. With those hideous quaking hands, she slammed the neck of the bottle against the window frame, but it was too feeble. She tried again and this time broke it; she took a swig and gagged and threw it up. She took another swig and kept that down. She was still gagging, coughing, but in between the spasm she forced down the liquid.

She leaned back, struggling for breath, taking a sip and then another. Hurry up, she told herself. You've got to get this over with. Hurry up. *Jaldi kar, jaldi kar.* It was like speaking in tongues, rasping Hindi words flew out of her like flying knives, Exorcist style. But she couldn't move, not just yet.

The trees swayed in agreement above her, bent back by the howling wind, and the roll of the waves roared in her ears, going back and forth, covering, and uncovering the beach like the tide inside her own lungs, which was she realised, the sound of her own fitful breathing. She drank some more and stopped. Drank again and stopped. The tightness in her chest turned to panting and then to exhalation because whatever it was that had grabbed her by the throat finally, mercifully, let her go. She let out a great long sigh and then threw the bottle out of the window and started the car.

How long had that lasted?

A spasm. Some sort of epileptic fit. A panic attack? Never mind, keep going, almost there. A seizure. A heart attack? A blood sugar plunge? I don't know. I feel cold and light, as though I might drift away like smoke…. Anyway, it was something very bad whatever it had been.

She didn't dare drive fast. Her hands felt too numb and shaky. Take care take care. *Sambhaaal kay, sambhaaal kay.* She got there. She stopped the car and got out; she started going down the wooden steps to the beach. Be careful, she told herself holding on to the rail.

When she got down to the house, she was surprised to see there were no lights on. She had assumed the light would be on in the lounge. The house seemed to be in darkness. But why? What were they doing? Where were they? She remembered the torch and quickly took it out, switched it on and pointed the beam at the lounge window. Thank God I have this.... but the room was not only in darkness, but exactly as they had left it. Confused, she turned it off and moved deftly along to the next window which was the small one in the kitchen diner, and peered in.

She turned the beam on.

And there she was, face down on the lino, her long black tresses spread out on the white squares like a dark mermaid. To see Devaani's body fainted like that, shook her to the core. Kavya's breathing quickened and she automatically stepped back. They're *in* there, *he's* in there, passed out. She couldn't bring herself to look again. The smell of gas escaping through the cracks in the walls crept into her nostrils and made her choke and cough, feeling claustrophobic. Without thinking, she automatically smashed the corner of the window with the heel of the torch; the thin glass shattered instantly making a small hole.

She turned quickly and ran back up the steps, pulling herself up, holding on to the rail and got into the car and started driving steady and vigilant. Just as she was passing the petrol station, she remembered she had forgotten to phone the police.

O God! *You had to do one thing.* Discombobulated and in a gasping panic, she stopped the car, pulled out the burner and punched in the number. Her breathing was erratic, and she coughed repeatedly to clear her restricted throat. She wiped the clammy sweat off her face with the back of her hand and interrupted the voice on the other end.

"I want the Police! Get me the police!"

"Just a moment caller."

Hurry up, hurry up, hurry up.

"You're through to the Police."

"Hello?"

"Hello! Police!" She put her hand over the mouthpiece. "There's been an accident in one of the houses on Saint Dorothy's at Cliffe beach. That one with the Onion tops, the one at the end. A woman was lying on the floor unconscious. I smelled gas very strongly. I broke the window. I was only passing by!"

"Alright, I've made a note. I know those houses. Are you there now?"

"Is that important?"

"Can you give me your name and address please?"

"No, I don't want to," said Kavya.

Chapter 58

The train home was a breeze. She sat in an almost empty carriage with the bright lights speeding past outside the window and it seemed a great passage of time was going by, but that felt fine. She didn't know if she felt tired, but she knew she felt a kind of stillness inside, a settling. No racing thoughts, no urgent matters to resolve or remember or reproach herself with.

Because it's done. Whatever happens now, happens, but it is done, and I can't do any more.

At Mamble Wafre station, she got a cab home. As she sat in the back she kept thinking 'it's done'. The driver was smoking so she asked him for a cigarette and sat back making smoke rings. Like a distant memory, she remembered how in that time of anxiety she had started spouting exclamations in Hindi. The brain was a crazy mysterious place; after all she didn't speak Hindi fluently, only when she had to and then she had to think about it. In the car, she had been raving, regressed to some earlier primitive self, something in the DNA. That attack…she shuddered at it now. But she'd come through, even though it had delayed her a bit, it didn't matter. In her mind's eye she saw herself coming down the steps to the beach, holding on to the rail…

The police would come. Sooner or later. Once they both came round, they'd be taken to the police station. Would they arrest Devaani for possession of drugs? Would they let John go? They would probably detain them both. Question them. They would want more information about the suspicious circumstances. It would come out about the payments. And then, when the police came to her, even if they knew it was her who made the phone call, she would tell the truth. Simply.

Yes, it was me that reported the burglary. But didn't I say it was an accident? Well, whatever I said, I'll say I was in shock. Seeing them together in Moghul House, at night. Lying unconscious. What was I to think or do? I was in shock. Shock, as everyone knows, makes people do inexplicable things. The odd thing was she hadn't felt any shock at seeing Devaani lying on the white kitchen floor.

Once the cab had dropped her off, Kavya stood at the end of her drive and looked at her cosy home. The two windows were lit up by the table lamps within, the porch light was on casting a halo on the welcome mat. The garden was in beautiful repose, shimmering emeralds under the moonlight. A form of tranquillity in recollection. Everything about the scene pleased her; it was serenity. Home, hearth, safety. She sighed a long deep sigh of contentment.

As she walked up the path, Marymary opened the door.

"Kavya…!" she cried, a horrified look on her face.

"Hello Marymary! Lovely evening, isn't it? Full moon."

"What…has happened... to you?"

Instantly she was scared stiff. What had given her away?

"Your mouth."

She walked inside and caught a glimpse of herself in the hall mirror. Her entire face had changed; it looked misshapen. Her top lip was cut and swollen twice the size.

"Oh," she said putting her hand on her bulbous lip. "I walked into a wall and cut my lip."

"I thought you had been attacked," said Marymary, her little face looking terrified. "I thought you had been…been…beaten up…in the street."

"No," Kavya sucked her lip and felt the cut with her tongue. It hurt. Now it began to hurt in earnest.

"Let me put some TCP on it!"

"No, no, it's fine I'll take a paracetamol later. It's just a swelling. Come on let's have drink."

Kavya walked into the sitting room and made a beeline for the cocktail cabinet.

"Please sit down," wailed Marymary. "I'll get it for you."

"No thanks," she said and bent down to see what was there.

She was used to Marymary being over solicitous as a rule; she had always put it down to an "Indian" thing. Indian people in paid employment didn't regard themselves as equals to their employers, the way say someone like Georgia did, or even Eastern European cleaners or a secretary like Mrs Flinders. Indians were all Uriah Heep with their employers, eager to please, more was always more. It was to do with the pernicious Indian caste system, she thought pompously although she couldn't be bothered to analyse it further.

Then she thought, I can think of nothing better than to pour myself a drink, in my own home, without having to hide it from anyone, without having to lock the door in that cramped computer room. Just have a drink. What could be more normal and natural than that?

"Kavya," said Marymary looking increasingly worried. "Your top has blood on it."

She looked down and saw the sweatshirt had large dark red stains. Blood must have spilled when she drank from the bottle; she couldn't remember any of the episode now.

"You don't look well at all. Let me take care of you," said Marymary patting her shoulder.

For a long time, it seemed to Kavya nobody had worried about her welfare, no one had noticed the turmoil she had been going through, the heavy burden she had been carrying. The whole sorry tale would be told soon enough, about John and Devaani found on the floor unconscious, caught together in a despicable liaison. He might have bought money to give her, and that too would be found.

"You're right darling. I'm not well," she said sadly.

"What's the matter? Please tell me. Sit down and tell me," said Marymary earnestly.

Kavya poured herself a vodka, plenty. She took a sip. There was no harm in telling her.

"Do you know a person called Devaani? She's the manager at Mowglis."

Marymary stared at her. Then she bowed her head.

"Yes," she said in a small voice. "Yes. I know her very well."

Atima Srivastava

Chapter 59

Poor Marymary. John must have involved her in some way in his shameful... ...he'd already got Milan in on it. "Well, I know that John has been seeing her. And she's not a her. She's a –well she's a prostitute and he's, her client."

Marymary's head shot up like a meerkat.

"No. That is not true. You are wrong," she said sharply.

"He's been taking money out of our joint bank account and giving it to her. Driving there every Friday regular as clockwork."

"No. No No No. You have misunderstood. He did that for me. I couldn't face it. He has been doing it for *me*. I transferred the money into your joint account, and he would take it out and give her the cash every week."

"What?"

"Devaani is my brother you, see?"

"*What*?"

"He---She—ran away from Goa because my father beat him one day when he saw him wearing a sari in secret. He was only 14 years old. Father beat him to a pulp. You see, us girls..all seven of us, we were too afraid to do anything."

"So, he wasn't beaten up by hoodlums? You said he was beaten by hoodlums! For wandering the street, for nothing..and the police did nothing."

Marymary hung her head, shaking it in shame.

"Yes, we said that. To protect our father. Also, our mother. We were all so very afraid of what the village would say, and afraid of Fathers anger, so we did nothing. We did worse than nothing, we directed the blame away. We protected the perpetrator. Our Father. And Lionel, he became isolated in his guilt and shame. He had no one to rescue him. Seven sisters. All cowards. We all betrayed him. He was only 14 years old.

He ran away. Left his family and went into the unknown world. To this day I do not know the ravages he suffered, what predators he encountered, what devils he had to meet to make a life, to make a living. A 14-year-old boy, confused, alone, afraid. We didn't see him again. We became seven sisters with no brother.

I missed him so much. Every baby I looked after was Lionel. I poured all my love into those babies I cared for. Dinny was one of those babies. Because you see, I had come home to Goa when Lionel was born, to help my mother take care of this prince who had finally blessed our house. A boy at last. We only had him for 14 years. After he left us, life had to go on. I worked, I took care of other babies, other children, I led a strict religious Christian life, I tried to be a good person. Inside I was dead.

And then the Mukherjees told me a little baby had been born to Kishore and his wife in the UK, and I was needed. I've always wanted to be needed you see. I wanted to be of use, as I had never been to my dear brother Lionel. And then Fate took over. When I came to London to work for you, I found the nearest Church and that's where Lionel found me. He worshipped there. God had reunited us. I don't know how. Remember my church in Marylebone, yes, we would meet there. He was still a practising Catholic and the nuns had been very supportive to him.

He was 22 years old, and I was 45 but he had already lived several lifetimes. He was living at the seaside where he was transitioning. He would come to London where he made friends, good friends who did not stand in judgement, who supported him. Her. She was Devaani now. Had always been Devaani. She was having painful operations, gender re-alignment when we were in Marylebone. Now for the last year she has been taking hormones.

They are from Switzerland and very very expensive. She's had a terrible time. An awful period of life. I wanted to do something to help her future. My little sister. My little brother, my little child. And now she has a job, and the hormone cycle is over. She is not yet 28 years old. I know she looks much older, but that is a side effect of the hormone therapy. I'm very proud of my Devaani. Now she can live happily with a real future ahead of her. She is a most courageous person. She has earned her happiness. It was my money. John just took it to her. From me."

Kavya slipped down on the sofa holding her glass with both hands. An unbelievable exhaustion was growing in her, pulling her down with its weight. To hear this about Devaani was devastating. Absently, her hand went to her joggers' pocket, and she pulled out the ATM receipt. As she suspected, it had a list of incomings as well as outgoings. Marymary's regular deposits were there, she didn't need to check; she crumpled it up and put it back in her pocket. It had never occurred to her to check incomings, only outgoings.

But she thought. Even if John's been the saintly helper in this situation, he still did it without telling me, and how was I to know he was taking money that Marymary was transferring in? Who could blame me for finding it all highly suspicious? Who wouldn't jump to the conclusion I jumped to? She took another long sip. And Marymary, she's so upright and full of her own feelings of guilt and reproach, how does she know nothing untoward was going on after all?

They could still have been having sex, for all we know. Devaani never told her about how she attacked Georgia on the beach, how she was working the beach. She doesn't know that Devaani is a prostitute! No, Marymary doesn't know the half of it. What she's told me doesn't really make any difference to the facts.

"Kavya," said Marymary. "I'm sorry but I need to speak to you about something important."

"Hmm, what is it darling?"

"You aren't well but..I'm…this is why you see me so terribly flustered tonight."

"What's happened?" said Kavya sharply.

"You see…. it's Milan."

The earth shifted under Kavya's feet.

"What about Milan?" she said, curtly.

"He's not here. He went out with John earlier in the day and. They've both gone."

Kavya frowned.

"I don't understand."

"It's as I say. We came home and John said he was taking Milan somewhere, to the shops, I don't remember what he said, but I had a nap and..."

"Hang on. Hang on. What do you mean *when you came home*? I thought Milan was staying with Shanta after the circus—wait, just explain this. Please."

"No, the circus was evacuated. There was a terror threat, something, anyway they wouldn't let us in. So, we decided to come home. Georgia had dropped us and gone so we just came home on the train. We had a snack, John took Milan out, I went for my nap and. I've looked, he didn't take his car, so I don't know *where* they are. I'm so sorry. I just don't know."

"I don't understand what's happening," said Kavya. "What is happening?"

"I called John's phone many times, it went to voicemail. I called Shanta Acharya; she also went to voicemail. I called the school, and they said you had come and gone. I called you, but it went to voicemail. Many hours had passed. So, I called Lalitamam. She's on her way. I didn't know what else to do!"

"I don't understand," said Kavya. "What are you *talking* about? This is not happening."

"I think we should call the police Kavya."

"Why," said Kavya unsmilingly, taking a long sip and putting down her glass, pouring herself another. "Because my husband has left me?"

"No, Kavya. No."

"But yes. It's exactly what he said he was going to do. And now he's gone. And he's taken my son. My only child. He's taken Milan."

My son is dead, thought Kavya.

Chapter 60

"Kavya dear," said Marymary. "It's almost midnight now. Shouldn't we ring the police? I'm very sorry. I should have been with Milan, but so many times he and Johnny go out, I didn't think anything of it."

Kavya was sitting motionless in the chair.

"No," she said. "We're going to wait."

"I think..are you in shock? I think you are in shock. Can I help?"

"No," said Kavya staring at the wall opposite.

She was waiting for it to hurt. But she was numb. She couldn't feel any part of her body. John had gone to Moghul House as per the text, but he'd taken Milan with him. When Georgia set off the gas, Milan was there, and Milan had passed out with them. It was dark in Moghul House. My little boy. He must have passed out quickly, painlessly. *But he wouldn't survive that gas.* He's too small. His little lungs and throat and button nose. He couldn't survive the gas. Any moment now, they'll bring him to me. In a grey ambulance.

Dinny lay in a bed with a brain haemorrhage. Kishore collapsed with ischemic heart disease. Mum and Daddy instantaneously in a car crash. No, we burn our people, we don't have graves to visit. That's a shame dear, said the woman in the florist. We went to the same Asian funeral parlour, I think they're in Wood Green, it's hard to drive there it's all one way. They do a mix of Indian and Western. Kishore's coffin had to be the most expensive, his parents insisted. Well, I haven't seen *them* in years. I don't want to look for a small coffin.

Suddenly she looked at Marymary and couldn't work out what she was doing, and then she realised she was counting her worry beads. She's waiting too, like me. The strangest thing Kavya felt was the numbness. It wasn't in her extremities, it was her heart, her actual heart had turned to stone. No blood was getting through, no oxygen, no plasma, and yet she was brazenly, presumptuously alive, her organs were somehow functioning, but what for? *What for?*

When he was a baby, I was so proud of him. He was a delight. I didn't want Kishore to even pick him up, he was mine. You've played your part; you can go now I thought. She was a mother. That would always be more important than being a wife. It irritated me that he was taking credit, shaking hands with the Hospital staff and I thought, why what did *you* do? In the hospital ward Milan never blinked, he kept staring at me from his crib as though he had something he wanted to tell me. I thought, and she could remember it exactly now, if I concentrate hard, I'll read his mind. But Milan was enigmatic. Maybe all babies were and that was their power over adults.

Robust. That's what they all said about him. Mum and Dad, my gentle lovely ghosts were with us in the room giving him their aashirvaad, their blessings. He was a tough little boy. And no trouble. It was ridiculous how little trouble that little boy was to me. Marymary came from Goa and even as a baby he ran rings around her, he always had. *No,* I said. I don't want another. I was an only, and he'll be an only. So, he won't want to share his toys, why should he? But he did. He'd give all his toys away to the other kids at nursery. Strange unreadable self-possessed generous kind and lovely boy.

Drinking? she thought. I never drank during the pregnancy. When I travelled, I used to drink alone in bars, but that was Europe, they do things differently there. It was Kishore who really got me into it. We'd leave Milan with Marymary and go out carousing in Soho, walk there in our flip flops. When he got rat-arsed Kishore loved to run down the English race (even though he'd only been in England five minutes, courtesy of me) and tell them how great India and Indians were, in his loud annoying bark.

A couple of those pubs banned him for being drunk and disorderly once too often. But there were so many pubs, bars, membership clubs, late night knock on the door dives, we had endless choices. We always drank, cocktails and beers and wine and voddies and we got home late and fell into bed. All our friends were people we met in bars. Everyone drank. Kishore could drink for India, but he was a lightweight in the end, I could drink him under the table. I'm a Brit I told him; you can't outdrink me! But never like this, never drinking in the morning…Never all this *secrecy.*

She heard the screech of tyres on the road outside.

"It's the police," she said.

"We didn't call the police," said Marymary shaking her head slowly, like those dogs in the back of cars.

Kavya got up before the doorbell rang.

"I'll get it," she said.

She was ready for the interminable admin that had to be gone through. She was an old hand at it. Mum and Dad. Kishore. Such a business. Forms to sign and details to listen to. She didn't care, she didn't care about any of it. None of it mattered to her, except she was concerned about the sort of expression she should have on her face. What would be appropriate? As she reached for the door lock, she knitted her eyebrows together and made a ditch in her forehead. *"What....? What did you say...?"*

She opened the door and Lalita Sharma was standing there.

Her hair was coiled in a perfect Indian bun. She was in civilian, meaning not Indian clothes, grey trousers, beige cashmere cardigan, a Liberty silk scarf and a long smart grey dress coat. She was wearing court shoes.

"Have you heard anything?"

"Nothing so far," said Kavya.

"I bought your rucksack," Lalita said putting it down by the stairs. "I didn't want to leave it unattended at my hotel. I wasn't sure how long I'd be here."

She walked on into the front room and sat down next to Marymary. She took her hand.

"It's alright. I'm here now."

"Mam," said Marymary reverting to the word she had used when she'd come to London and both Kavya and Lalita had told her no, they didn't like those kinds of formalities, in the UK everyone was on first name terms. "Don't you think we should call the police?"

"Let's discuss the situation first," said Lalita in Hindi, for reassurance. "Before we trouble the British Police."

She took off her silk scarf and folded it up, put it in the pocket of her coat, and then took off the coat, and folded it over a chair. Then she smoothed her cardigan and sat down next to Marymary again, leaning forward. Now she switched to English.

"Did you uber it?"

Lalita looked up at Kavya with a slight hint of irritation.

"Yes, I ubered it. What does that matter? Now, listen to me both of you. I don't believe John would just disappear. We must make sure we have thought of everything before we raise any alarm. Now think Marymary. You were all together and then you came home. And then, he told you they were going out. And then? A message. A text we may have overlooked. A note he might have left."

"There's nothing. I've thought of everything Mam. I've called everyone. I looked everywhere. There is no note of where they have gone. And they are missing now for almost 6 hours."

"They are not missing. They are somewhere. How about Georgia? Didn't she drop you all at the circus? Let's try her."

"She's gone. Her number doesn't work."

Kavya who had been standing sat down silently on the large sofa chair.

"Gone where?" she said.

"I don't know. But when she dropped us at the circus, she said she was going away. Packing up and leaving town and didn't know when or if coming back. She was very upset about Billie. This very morning, she had gone to the police station to identify her. Billie was her shelter you see? She lived in her flat and I think Billie had saved her life once. Neither of them had any other family. They were like a mother and daughter."

"What happened to this Billie?" said Lalita.

"She was found dead early this morning by the bridge in Saint Dorothy's at Cliffe Bay. Washed up on the rocks below. The police said she had been in the water for several days."

"What a tragic accident," murmured Lalita.

"No. Not an accident. They told Georgia she had been hit on the head and died of a brain haemorrhage or a stroke. And then, they think she was pushed off the bridge."

Chapter 61

Kavya was sitting very still staring at the carpet, her hands underneath her thighs. The numbness in her body had disappeared, replaced by a watchful animal consciousness. The damn rucksack had come back, she thought. Like a dead body that keeps bobbing up it just won't die. I've got to get it out of sight.

"Local gangsters I expect. Well, the police will find them," said Lalita and with that she tilted her head and began to think of something else. Billie, a stranger who had died, was of no interest to her. "Now Marymary dear. Do you remember what John said when you went to the circus, and it was evacuated? Anything he might have mentioned?"

There's no danger now except for the rucksack, thought Kavya. Nothing else. And why would the police want to search the house in any case? There's no link to me. Unless Georgia told them something. She looked weird when she came to the School today. *She'd already been to the police and identified Billie.* Well, she didn't say a word about it did she? Not to them, and not to me.

Why, because she doesn't *know*. Only John knows. I've just got to follow the plan and stay cool.... everything will be alright. After all, I am sorry about it. It *was* a tragic accident really. She was aggressive and shouting at me; she tried to hurt me, and I retaliated. My brain went into a red mist. It was a mistake; I didn't mean to do it. And then she was dead, what else could I have done? I'm very sorry about it.

"Kavya," said Lalita. "You don't look well. What has happened to your face?"

Kavya said, "I don't feel good. I've had a shock. I walked into a wall." And then she thought of how she could do it. "Maybe I'll go and wash my face upstairs before the police arrive."

And take the rucksack with me.

"No," said Lalita facing her now. "As I've just been saying to Marymary, I'm not sure we should call the police just yet. In my experience they only muddle things up. If God forbid, there had been an accident, we would have been informed by now. And if not, then let's wait a bit longer."

"But..but," wailed Marymary. "I don't want to say it but, what if they were abducted?"

"By aliens?" said Kavya.

Lalita gave a little smile. "But if they had been kidnapped Marymary, it would be a strange thing, wouldn't it? Who would kidnap a man and a little boy?"

"Yes, yes" said Marymary dazed.

Lalita took a deep breath and looked at Kavya.

"There's nothing to start worrying about. John loves Milan as if he were his own biological child. There is nothing nefarious here. He would never wilfully harm your boy. I give you that guarantee. Alright?"

"Alright," said Kavya.

"Good, now let's the three of us sit down and put our heads together. John is naturally cautious and capable, so something must have happened for him to leave like that. What might that have *been*?"

Lalita looked at Kavya questioningly.

"I don't know," said Kavya.

"Oh, where can they be? Where are they?" cried Marymary.

"I wonder if... doesn't John have an ex-wife?" said Lalita.

"Yes, but they got divorced 14 years ago," said Marymary.

"What about family? Friends? Colleagues."

"No one…John works alone and although he is well liked in the village, I've never heard him talk of any friends. Kavya, have you?"

Kavya shrugged.

"And family…no, except maybe a boy he grew up with. In the Home. He is a schoolteacher in Brighton. In the Montessori School," said Marymary.

"Well, that's something. What's his name?" said Lalita bringing out her phone. "I'll google him. It's late but it's important. I'm sure he won't mind."

"I'm feeling rough. I think I'll go up and lie down for a few minutes," said Kavya.

"Hmm?" said Lalita looking up. "Yes, alright darling. You go up."

"Can I make you a Horlicks?" said Marymary jumping up.

"Look at her pretty face hmm," said Lalita to Marymary. "My girl. Only you could make an accident look like botox. You have the bee stung look!"

Marymary chuckled and nodded. Lalita looked indulgently at her granddaughter.

Kavya felt herself light up in a smile. Her lip hurt a bit but it felt so good to have them both actively care for her, look at her. Like sunshine on her entire being. These two wonderfully kind and good women who had been the mainstay for her life. She smiled at them both and bent down to pick up the rucksack when the doorbell rang. Lalita moved like a hare past Kavya and opened the door. They've bought Milan, thought Kavya feeling her heart stop. They've bought him home.

"Kavya," said Lalita returning to the lounge. "It's a policeman."

"What does he want?"

"I don't know. I told him to wait at the door. Look, whatever news he has come with, you must face it. We're here. We are with you. Just stay calm. Alright, I'm going to tell him to come in."

Face it Kavya, someone else had said that.

"I'd like a drink I think," said Kavya nonchalantly.

"Well…but now?" said Lalita.

"Yes, now," she said breezily and walked over to the cocktail cabinet and poured herself a large vodka. She carried it back and looked at Marymary and Lalita.

"This is Sergeant Mike Robinson," said Lalita.

Mike Robinson was a tall well-built man in his fifties wearing a suit and tie. He looked like a policeman, with his short crew cut hair and large feet and an air of authority.

"Hello, Ms Kavya Sharma? I apologise for disturbing you so late at night. I've come from the Sussex Division. And excuse me, I've come directly from a black tie leaving do for our Inspector. I'm not usually so smart."

Kavya stared at him and sipped her drink.

"Sussex division?"

"That includes the Saint Dorothy's at Cliffe borough."

"Oh ok. Have a seat, Sergeant. Do you want a drink? I've got one already."

"Thanks. No, I don't drink."

"Oh," said Kavya and pulled back her lips.

"Should we go into the kitchen and leave you alone?" said Lalita.

"Well, I think Ms Sharma might prefer to speak to me alone."

"No," said Kavya. "I want them to stay. If it's alright with you?"

She had to have them there, she needed them to keep her feet on the ground. Was it about Billie? Or was it about Milan.... She wished fervently there was ice but she was glad she hadn't added a mixer. But drinking neat vodka was not good for your liver.

Chapter 62

Sergeant Robinson sat down opposite Kavya on the tall back chair. She was in the sofa chair, so he naturally loomed above her. Deliberate, she thought. They probably have techniques like that for interviews, where the police keep the upper hand over the suspect. Only I'm not a suspect.

"Ms Sharma."

"Kavya."

"Kavya, thanks. I was given your details as the person who called Sussex Police station about an incident in Saint Dorothy's at Cliffe Beach tonight."

"Yes," said Kavya.

So much for that stupid burner. They *can* trace your call. Maybe I said who I was though, I can't remember. In any case she felt relieved. It wasn't about Billie. Whatever the police asked her, she had all the answers. I'm completely prepared, she thought.

"After you made the phone call you took the train back here?"

"Yes."

"Can you describe this incident for me? As much detail as you can," said Robinson taking out his notebook and pen.

"What happened was, when I reached the house, it's was all totally dark. So I switched on my torch and in the kitchen I saw this—woman—lying on the floor. I could smell gas, it was strong, so I wasn't sure what to do but I just reacted, I smashed the window with the torch and the glass shattered.

And there was a hole. To let the gas out. And then, I ran back to the car and phoned the police."

"And you could tell this woman had been overcome by gas?"

"Oh yes. It was obvious."

"You didn't go inside the house?"

"No! I told you, I was shocked, so I acted on instinct. Smashed the window."

"You're the owner of the property, aren't you?"

"Yes."

"It didn't occur to you to enter your property and turn off the gas?"

"No! I wouldn't even know how to *do* that. Don't you have to get the gas engineer out to do that sort of thing?"

Robinson nodded and wrote something.

Kavya felt it was going well. She had answered every question truthfully. And who turns off the gas? Trick question.

"Earlier, before you got to the house on the beach---forgive me, was there any particular reason you went there tonight?"

"No reason."

"Really?"

Kavya didn't look at her grandmother because she was sure Lalita was looking at her with keen interest. And the policeman would be watching to see every facial expression;

wasn't that how they often deduced things rather than from forensics. Or was that only in cosy murder mysteries? Modern crime was all about the hard evidence. Well, there wasn't any.

She shrugged. “It’s my house. Sometimes I go there in the evenings.”

“Yes, the beach can be beautiful at night. Alright, so. I’m a little confused as to why you didn't drive there in your own vehicle.”

“I don't own a car. My husband has a car and it’s not working.”

“I see. Anyway, you went there by train and then you proceeded to hire a car at.” He looked at his phone. “Saint Dorothy’s at Cliffe Car Hire and Taxi. Formerly Jimmy’s Car Hire. Correct?”

“Yes.”

“Alright. And you had quite an acrimonious discussion, with the agent there, is that right?”

Acrimonious? Where had he got that word from? Certainly not from that moron.

“No, it wasn't a discussion. More a case of bullying. I wanted to hire a car and that man, for reasons of his own, pretended he didn't have the keys. Obviously, I stood my ground and said I didn't believe him and so eventually he gave me a car. Maybe he didn't like it, that I stood my ground, but I wouldn't say it was acrimonious.”

“Uh-huh”

That noise again, thought Kavya.

"Alright, but if all you wanted was to go to the house, why not get a taxi?"

"I didn't want to," said Kavya. Then added, "I might have wanted to stay a while and then drive somewhere else. So, I wanted a car."

"Where would you go?"

"Well, I don't know. I wanted the option. And anyway, it was just as well that I did, because if a taxi had dropped me, and I had seen what I saw…then how would I have come back? There are no ranks there. I would have been stranded."

She felt triumphant, but she kept her face straight.

"But was there maybe another reason you wanted to hire a car?"

"Like what?"

"I don't know. You tell me. It's quite a lot of money to hire a car just for a short period."

"Well, I wanted to be alone," said Kavya carefully. Saying "I can afford it," would not go down well.

This was important. She was glad Lalita and Marymary were listening. Because this was a crucial part of the story, and she wanted good witnesses.

"Why was that? Was there something you expected to find at your house?"

"I don't really want to say," said Kavya looking at the floor. "Do I have to?"

"You don't have to answer that, but if I was advising you, I'd say you should. It'll be better for you."

"It's...quite personal. And so, I'd rather not."

"Alright," said Robinson. "That's fine. Would you be willing to make a statement at the station, saying that when you reached the house, you saw a woman lying unconscious on the floor, you smelled gas very strongly and you broke the window, and then you phoned the police. You never entered the premises?"

"Yes," said Kavya in a small voice.

"Are you sure you don't want to reconsider any part of that statement?"

"I'm sure."

Robinson nodded and closed his notebook. He looked like a detective in a Miss Marple episode with his suit and tie. His eyes were glassy, but his mouth. It was mean like a jailors mouth.

"The thing is, Kavya. The woman on the kitchen floor was not unconscious. She was dead."

Chapter 63

Kavya took a sip of her drink. She opened her mouth, but no words came out, so she closed it.

"Did you hear what I said?"

"I didn't know that" she said in an even quieter voice.

"Did you have keys to the house?"

"Yes."

"And it didn't occur to you to go inside?"

"I didn't want to disturb anything."

"Why, did you think it was a crime scene?"

"No. I just thought – I thought they'd committed suicide."

"Why did you think that?"

"I assumed. When I saw her lying there."

"Did you know who this woman was?"

"No. She was a stranger to me. I was in shock."

"Didn't you wonder why she was in your house?"

Sergeant Robinson looked at Kavya and waited.

"Why did you go to the house this evening?"

"I—I told you it's a private thing. I can't talk about it."

Sergeant was watching her, she knew that. Her hand was shaking as she took a sip, but what could she do about that?

"Alright. Let's talk about something else. The drive from the car hire place to the beach. Would you agree it's 10, 12 minutes at the most. On a clear road."

"Yes."

"So, let's be generous and say 12 minutes there, 12 minutes back. And you said you went down to the house, saw what you saw, broke the window and ran back to the car, drove back, left the car, posted the key through the letterbox, and waited for the train."

"Did I tell you all that? About posting the keys?"

"You don't have to. There's CCTV at the petrol station and the railway station. We have your movements at different points on video. And the car has a tracker. You made the call to us when you reached the petrol station, not at the beach. And then you left the vehicle and walked. We have you at the train station at 9.15pm. You caught the 9.20 train."

"Ok."

So, they didn't have footage of her disposing of the sim and the phone. Because she had done it while walking from the car to the station. That was lucky. She was sure she had got the 9.00 train, but she didn't want to mention it. What difference did it make?

"The round trip should have been 34 minutes if you count 10 minutes at the house. And yet, it took you almost an hour. Why was that? Did you go somewhere else before you went to the house. Or afterwards?"

"Oh!" said Kavya. "No, I was delayed. On my way to the house, I ..had a sort of fit. I had to stop the car. I tried to take my medicine but the bottle broke. That's why my lip's swollen. And then I blacked out. It must have been for about 15 minutes. I felt fine afterwards."

Robinson nodded.

"Who's the doctor that prescribed this medication?"

"Dr Boody," said Kavya, but the word came out in an American accent. "As in Boody call."

She was surprised by how it came out. Why had she said that? I'm under a lot of stress, she told herself. When Naani finds out, and when Marymary finds out what I've had to put up with, they'll understand. When this ordeal is over. I've lost Milan. I can't come to terms with it. My mind won't let me.

"What's the address?"

"I don't know. She's American. It's a practise in Bobbins in the Beans." Usually whenever she said that, she would giggle but she didn't think she would ever laugh again.

"Kavya, why did you leave the scene? Why didn't you phone the police there and wait for them?"

"I was scared, and it was dark. I wanted to get away from there."

"Sergeant, if you don't mind me interrupting," said Lalita. "Can I ask if you know the identity of the woman who was found?"

"Yes. It's a woman by the name of Devaani D'Souza."

"No....!" cried Marymary. "oh..."

"Do you know this person?" said Robinson turning to Marymary.

"She was my sister. She's dead?"

"I'm very sorry. I didn't realise. I wouldn't have said it like that. I'm very sorry…Ms.." said Sergeant Robinson quietly.

"Miss Mary Fernandez," said Lalita quietly.

"Did she kill herself?" said Marymary. "Was it suicide?"

Sergeant Robinson assumed his sympathetic face.

"I'm sorry but this is going to come as a shock Miss Fernandez."

"Is going?"

Marymary looked like a character in a pantomime. One hand was on her heart, the other raised uselessly in the air.

"She didn't kill herself Miss Fernandez."

Marymary's hand came down and sat uselessly in her lap.

"Then what was it?" she said wearily.

"I'm afraid your sister was killed with a knife. She was stabbed."

Lalita got up and went to her.

"Oh…" she said. "You mean, she was murdered? Are you sure?"

"I'm very sorry." Sergeant looked at Lalita who shook her head imperceptibly, and he understood.

It was very common for people who heard the news of the killing of a loved one, to ask 'are you sure' as a way of processing denial. There was no need in the moment to tell Miss Fernandez that her sister had been found in a pool of blood with what was classified as a zombie knife lying on the floor. They had the weapon, and the fingerprints and DNA would soon come from the lab. There was no need in that moment to tell Miss Fernandez that Devaani had taken over 2 hours to die from a wound so deep in her belly that it had ruptured her internal organs. She had died alone, writhing in agony.

"There's no doubt about it I'm afraid. I'm so very sorry," he said gently. Marymary became limp like a rag doll and Lalita held her tight.

There was an ominous silence.

Chapter 64

"What about the gas?" said Kavya.

"There was no gas turned on in the house."

"But when I got there. I smelled gas. It was a strong smell of gas," she insisted.

"We had officers at the scene within 11 minutes of your phone call. There was no gas."

"Then it must have all escaped! When I broke the window."

"There was no odour of gas at all. If there had been, even with the window open, it would have been perceptible."

Kavya frowned; she remembered a detail.

"But some gas has no smell. Chloroform gas. Isn't it?"

Sergeant Robinson pressed his lips together. There was a slight impatience that he covered up. The same as when a doctor heard patients self-diagnose via Google.

"That's a myth Kavya."

"What?"

"If you're referring to the motorhome robberies in the south of France, I know it was an internet viral sensation last year, but it's just another conspiracy theory. The robberies happened but the rest is an urban myth. There was no gas pumped into the properties. No such gas exists. It's impossible. You would need a truckload of such a gas to immobilise anyone in a house, even a motorhome."

Bewilderment was beginning to rise in Kavya's mind like light on the edge of a town. She wanted to close her eyes and hide away but it kept on becoming less dark.

"I'm going to get a drink," she said getting up.

"No Kavya!" cried Lalita.

"Please sit down Kavya," said Robinson. It was a clear order. "Someone else will get you a drink."

But neither Lalita nor Marymary moved.

"If it's alright, I'd like to meet with your husband," said Robinson. "Mr John Ashworth."

"What?" said Kavya.

"I know it's very late. But I'd like to talk to him. Now."

"I don't understand. Didn't you find him?"

The light was suddenly blinding.

"Find him? Where?"

"I've simply got to have a drink, Sergeant. Naani? Marymary, please."

"Just a minute," said Robinson. "Answer the question please. Where is John Ashworth?"

"He's not at home," said Lalita.

"Where is he?" asked Robinson.

"That's the thing. We don't know. We've been worried."

"Can I please have a drink?" said Kavya.

"You don't seem to have comprehended the severity of the situation Kavya," said Robinson.

"Yes, pay attention Kavya for goodness sake!" said Lalita.

"What haven't I.?"

"Your account of this evening isn't satisfactory," said Robinson.

"I've told you everything. It's not my fault if it doesn't satisfy you."

"You haven't explained why you went to the house at that time."

"It's *personal*!"

"And why you said you smelled gas."

"I did smell gas!"

"And why you didn't go inside your own property."

"I've already told you. I was in shock, and I was scared. I thought police always say don't touch anything!"

"And why you went to so much expense and trouble to rent a car for a half hour."

"But we've already been through this. I've told you everything."

"I'm not satisfied."

"Why not? I've told you everything!"

"I'm going to have to ask you to come down to the station."

"What now? Wait, are you saying you think I had something to do with what happened to that woman? You think *I* stabbed her? You think I could do that? You're accusing *me*?"

"Please stay calm. I'm not accusing you. I just want a better account of the events."

"What else do you want me to say? It's never going to be better because this is it."

"Alright. So, we need to go to the station so I can formally interview you. I'd appreciate it if you would come with me now."

"Alright alright alright," cried Kavya. "I don't care what I've got to do. But I've got to have a drink first."

"Better not Kavya," said Robinson.

"This is my own house! I can't have a drink in my own front room. What is this, a police state?"

"Kavya, *please!* Stop behaving badly. I'm sorry Sergeant," said Lalita.

She looked at them all. No one was giving her any sympathy. She wasn't well. Her hands wouldn't stop shaking. And the light, like needles in her eyes. If I go to the police station, she thought suddenly, and they lock me up even just for the night, how will I get a drink? *How will I get a drink?* Her body seemed to go into a mild spasm. If only I could throw off my skin, she thought. And let my soul go free.

"We should go now," said Robinson.

"No…wait. I'll tell you who killed that woman."

"Do you want to make a statement?"

"Yes. But I want a drink first."

Marymary suddenly rose.

"May I get it for her?" she said in her sweet little voice. "I'd like to keep busy. I like to be useful."

"Er... yes of course. Thank you very much Miss Fernandez."

"Bring the bottle!" cried Kavya as Marymary started walking across the room towards the cocktail cabinet.

The doorbell rang and they all turned like meercats to look at the lit-up hallway.

"I'll get it," said Robinson. "Please all remain seated."

As soon as he was gone, Kavya sprang up and moved toward the cocktail cabinet, bypassing Marymary.

"*Kavya!*" said Lalita.

Kavya poured herself a large vodka, swallowed it, then refilled the glass.

"Kavya," said Lalita. "You've got to get your act together. This is very serious."

"It's fine Naani. I had nothing to do with it."

There were footsteps and rustling out of sight by the front door. Presently, Robinson came back accompanied by a young woman officer.

"This is Sergeant Pukowski. She'll take down your statement. Please come and sit down."

Kavya lit a cigarette and blew a smoke ring. He must have texted the station earlier. That sergeant came quick. Obediently, Kavya came back to her seat, holding her drink and an ashtray.

Chapter 65

"Mrs Kavya Sharma Ashworth. You want to say that you know who killed Devaani D'Souza Fernandez?" said Robinson while Sergeant Pukowski had a Samsung notebook open. A microphone was attached.

"Yes, I do."

"Why do you think so?"

"I don't think so, I know so. I saw her."

"Excuse me? Who?"

"Georgia Galton aka Courtnee Marie"

"And who is that?" asked Robinson mildly. Kavya had the feeling he knew exactly who it was.

"She's a young woman who works for us. A kind of Jill of all trades. Cleaning, gardening, driving. She works for other people in our village of Mamble Favre as well."

"And you saw her stab the vict—" Robinson corrected himself. "Ms Devaani D'Souza"

"No. But I know she was there. She made sure Devaani went inside the house."

"How would you know that?"

Kavya took a large swallow of vodka.

"Because we'd sort of arranged it like that."

"Please expand."

Kavya bit her bottom lip.

"I'm afraid you have to tell us now," said Robinson gently.

Yes, thought Kavya. I must tell everything. I don't want to wind up in a prison cell.

"Alright. I knew that Devaani was going to meet my husband there."

"Why was that?"

"Because he had been meeting her…"

"What did you arrange with Georgia Galton?"

Kavya wished she could get so drunk that she wouldn't be able to speak. How peaceful it would be. To just be quiet. It had been a long time since she had been that drunk.

"Georgia was going to go there first, and leave some..drugs...I don't know what it was…something for Devaani to take so she would be, unconscious."

"For the record," said Robinson. "No such substance was found."

"Well…and then my husband was supposed to meet her there. And Georgia would lock the door so they couldn't get out."

She could hear the words tumbling from her mouth and how ludicrous it all sounded.

"Go on," said Robinson.

"And then, Georgia would text me and I'd come along and see it all."

"And what was going to happen then?"

"Nothing. I…I would just see them together."

"Kavya? Had you arranged with Georgia Galton that Georgia would pump chloroform gas into the house, so that both parties would be found unconscious together? Was that the plan?"

Kavya's face was burning.

"No! I never said that!"

The lady protests too much, that's what he's thinking she thought furiously. And that gas is all made up. It's impossible.

"How did Ms Devaani D'Souza enter the house?"

"I don't know. Probably took the key from under the flowerpot."

"Alright. And you went to the house to see this rendezvous happen. But I'm confused. Why would Devaani D'Souza go to the house in the first place? You said she and your husband had meetings. But these meetings weren't at the house I assume. So why this time? And at that specific time?"

Kavya's leg started shaking and she pressed her knee down. I can't breathe she thought. I'm frightened she thought. If only it would all go quiet in here. In this room, in my head.

"You say Georgia Galton went to the house and placed substances, and then later, locked the door. But is there any evidence for this? It's only your word, isn't it? No drug paraphernalia was found anywhere."

"What? Of course, it was her. This is like a cross examination. I don't need evidence. Anyway, her fingerprints will be there, everywhere. Georgia planted the drugs to ...I promise you."

"Let's look at it a different way. These meetings. You suspected your husband had been seeing Ms Devaani D'Souza. You thought they were having an affair?"

"No," said Kavya carefully.

"What then?"

"I don't want to say. Now I know differently. I know that she was a relative of my Marymary. So, I don't want to say anything more."

"It's necessary."

"Alright, alright. I'm sorry. But I heard rumours, and I knew he was giving her money. I didn't know what it was for. All I knew was he was giving her money. Regularly."

"You assumed she was a prostitute? Because it was a regular thing?"

Kavya nodded.

"I know now that the money was for something else. But."

"Again, for the record," Robinson looked at Pukowski. "Let me state here that Mss Devaani D'Souza was well known to us. She was the manager of Mowgli's Indian restaurant and not only an upstanding citizen of BarleyBarton-on-Sea, but she was also on our Police Advisory Panel. Along with other local people who have been helping us to co-ordinate training and awareness of Drug issues, Trans rights, and combatting Racial profiling. At the Gender Identity Clinic, she was automatically tested for drug use every week. I can categorically state that she did not use drugs. And may I add for the record, I will refer to her using the name she wished, which was Devaani D'Souza. She did not recognise her father's name of Fernandez."

The room fell into silence.

Kavya had the sensation of her knees collapsing. I'm falling, she thought. She couldn't quite piece it all together but…what part of the story was true and what part was false? If she wasn't a drug addict…if she wasn't a prostitute…then Georgia didn't leave any drugs and then... Then?

Sergeant Robinson got up and went out into the hallway.

"Mr Ashworth. Please come in."

Chapter 66

So, John was here. How long for? Since the Pukowski woman came in? Of course. Robinson hadn't called her; she had come with John. He must have heard everything. How much had she said, she couldn't remember? And something, something very important was there. She couldn't touch it, but it was finally there. When John entered the room, it was as though she hadn't seen him in years and yet there he was. Risen from the dead. She opened her mouth to speak.

"Milan is fine," said John meeting her eyes. "He's at Shanta's house with her grandkids. Milan is fine."

Kavya exhaled. That was it. The very important thing.

She squinted at John. His was all in black. His blonde hair was matted. His face was ashen. He didn't look at her, or anyone. He just looked directly at Sergeant Robinson. She'd never seen John looking so old. His blue eyes, even they were submerged in his ashen face.

You've got lines, mister. No amount of moisturiser will fix that. Me, no. I might be older than you but black don't crack, brown don't frown, white turn to pasty face clown. But there wouldn't be any bants between them now, not ever. He would tell Robinson everything he saw, all that he knew. Honest John with the baby blue eyes, he won't be able to help himself, thought Kavya. That's how they taught him to be in that home. Always tell the truth. The truth will always set you free. In the end, the truth always wins.

I'm sunk, she thought.

Sergeant Robinson took out his phone and showed the screen to John.

"I'm showing Mr John Ashworth who has now come into the room, a screen shot of the text message found on the phone belonging to Ms Devaani D'Souza. Can you read this Mr Ashworth?"

"Yes," said John.

Kavya was mortified. She could hardly remember what she had written in that wretched Lazy Days B n B when she was trying to write in John's voice. When she had shown it to Georgia, she had laughed and said don't give up the day job. She said she'd shorten it when she texted it. And Devaani had received it. And now, it was a screenshot.

"Have you seen it before sir?"

"Yes," said John. "I wrote it. It says John at the end."

"You wrote this text?"

"Yes," said John again.

Kavya thought: Oh God. I just want to get very very drunk.

"In this text you ask Devaani to meet you at the house on the beach and you stress the importance of it. So did you also arrive at the house at 7pm?"

"Er…no." said John with a frown. "No, I didn't go there."

A lightbulb came on above Kavya's head.

Georgia never texted John. She never meant to. And she didn't drop any pills in his Vimto. And so, he never needed to be sedated because he never went there. It was all a ruse and a fabricated story to get Devaani there so she could kill her.

"Why didn't you meet her as per the text you say you sent?" said Robinson.

"Well…I intended to. But it turned out to be a strange day. We were turned away at the circus so we, that's me and Milan and Marymary, we came home on the train. Milan was pining because he wanted to play with Mrs Acharya's grandsons – they had a video game he was keen on. He was very upset. The thing is, he really doesn't meet any other Asian kids in Mamble Wafre, he really is the only "Asian in the village", child I mean, and so I didn't want him to miss the chance.

So, on a whim, I said OK champ, let's go back. My car wasn't working, so we hopped back on the train. Mrs Acharya lives in a suburb between BarleyBarton-on-Sea and Framley. It's called Digly. I left a note for Marymary in the kitchen, she was napping. It must have fallen on the floor. We got to Framley and we took a taxi to Digly from there but—it wasn't a lucky day—there was a snarl up on the road. A water pipe had burst. We were stuck in traffic for over 2 hours with no reception. Anyway, finally we made it to Digly. I…I was so relieved that I just forgot all about meeting Devaani at Moghul house.

The kids were allowed to stay up and Mrs Acharya said she would organise the sleepover, she had extra clothes and all the rest. Mrs Acharya had her daughter and her husband there too and they all insisted I stay for dinner. One of them would drive me back. And so I had dinner with them in their conservatory and the kids played upstairs in the bedroom…. We'd all left our phones in the kitchen, and then after dinner we saw all the missed calls. And –"

"What domestic bliss!" snapped Kavya.

Why had she said that? She couldn't understand the bitterness she felt. Or the jealousy. John having a happy time in such a *desi* setting, with Indian hospitality and Indian food, an Indian setting that he was naturally a part of and welcomed in to.

"Did you ever intend to meet with Devaani D'Souza?"

"Yes, obviously. I wrote her that text, didn't I?" said John. Then, "I'd let you see my phone to prove it, but I texted her from my work phone. And my work phone, I think I left it somewhere. It's an old one. Doesn't work well."

My fucking God thought Kavya. He's lying through his teeth.

"That's alright Mr Ashworth. What I'd like to know is, do you think your wife was jealous of your meetings with Devaani? Did she think you were involved in some way?"

"No, not at all. I'm sure she didn't think so. She's not that kind of person."

"She told us that she thought you were paying Ms D'Souza for sex."

John blinked.

"No, that was just a misunderstanding. She didn't really think that. We're very happily married."

Kavya looked at John as he talked. He was so believable. He didn't look like he was acting or lying. And yet, she knew how much it cost him, because he was. I remember now, she thought mildly. When she had met him on 'sunset strip' that magical part of BarleyBarton beach that was a secret suntrap, and the light seemed to be shining out of his eyes, for that split second she had seen into his soul. Quite simply, he was good. Goodness was in his DNA like the words in a stick of seaside rock. And she had loved him instantly.

"But you didn't want your wife to know about this meeting? At the house on the beach."

"She wouldn't have minded. It was just administration – I was a go between, a facilitator for Devaani and her older sister Marymary here. Miss D'Souza was as you know, undergoing hormone therapy and her sister wanted to pay for it. It was easier for me to give her the cash, that's all."

"Mr Ashworth. Do you have any information about Ms D'Souza's death?"

John was quiet for a moment. Then he said, "First I want to say I'm sorry and shocked and I want to give Marymary my condolences, because Devaani was a good person and didn't deserve this."

"Thank you, Johnny," said Marymary in a quiet voice.

"Thank you, Mr Ashworth. And what would you like to add?"

"Well. I want to be careful what I say. But. I'm sorry to say it, but I must. Georgia Galton hated Devaani, with a vengeance."

"How do you know this?"

"I witnessed Georgia pick a fight with Devaani once. In the middle of the street, in daylight. She just came up to her and pushed her down, totally unprovoked. She repeatedly called her the "c" word. It was aggressive and nasty. Anyway, a small crowd formed and then Georgia went off and Devaani didn't press any charges. I asked her about it, and she said it was because Billie, that's Wilhelmina Brown, had been Georgia's mentor and helper after she came out of prison, but when she was on the Police committee--"

"Yes, Lady Brown is on our committee too."

"Well, Billie wanted to help Trans Rights. Devaani convinced her of it, she was such a powerful advocate. Billie felt it was right to help every cause that she saw fit, even if the causes were sort of opposed. I mean, Billie supported UKIP, but she also gave money to Momentum, so go figure. She was an adamant European, half her family is German, but she campaigned for Brexit. Georgia depended on her in a lot of ways, but when she saw her getting close to Devaani, not just in political campaigns, but as close friends, Georgia saw red. It was really a sort of sibling rivalry if you ask me."

Chapter 67

"Are you aware that Lady Brown was found this early morning too? Washed up by the Saint Dorothy's at Cliffe Bridge."

"Oh," said John. "No, I didn't know that. I'm sorry to hear about it. I heard she disappeared a while ago. But can I say what I think happened with Georgia?"

"Alright, go ahead."

"I think. Because she hated Devaani so much and because she was convinced Billie would begin to favour Devaani, I think she planned to use my wife Kavya in a scheme of her own. She found out about the money somehow, and I think she persuaded my wife that something dodgy was on. And I think she went to Moghul House specifically to kill Devaani. And she fixed it so that my wife would come along later and be blamed for it."

"Do you know how Devaani was killed?"

"No," said John. "But Georgia used to have a lock up in which she stored a load of junk to sell at car boot sales. She was secretive about it, although she took Milan to look at it, and once I went there and I saw she had a zombie knife stashed there. And I told her I didn't want Milan going anywhere near that place. I didn't say anything about it, but there's only one thing those things are for.

Georgia was a troubled girl. My wife gave her a job and at the time I thought it was a good idea because everyone deserves a second chance. She was good with us, but I monitored her closely from day 1, because there was Milan to consider. And she never put a foot wrong. The mask never slipped. She was a hard worker; a good gardener and she did a lot of driving for us. But then. I don't know, maybe something snapped?"

Robinson turned to Kavya.

"Is that how it was?"

John's got me out of it, thought Kavya dully. I didn't ask him to do it. I didn't even want him to do it. But he's got me out of it.

"Yes, more or less."

"Tell me again then, what did Georgia tell you that you would find in the house when you went there?"

"My husband and—Devaani. I've already told you."

"And was there a plan between you that Georgia would pipe in this chloroform gas?"

"No! I already told you. The reason I said it—maybe I read it on the internet. A lot of times, you read something, and you think it's true. Like you said, it's an urban myth. I just assumed..."

"But you said you *smelled* gas. Very strongly, you said."

"I honestly thought I did. Because maybe she put it in my mind. Or I read it on the internet. Maybe I –I don't know. But I *did* smell gas. And that's why I broke the window. Maybe the mind...has a mind of its own, I don't know. I can't explain."

"So, when you saw Devaani on the floor, what did you really think had happened to her?"

"I don't know. I panicked. I didn't care in the end, I was scared and I just wanted to get away."

"Did it ever occur to you that Georgia, who had told you she would be there to put the drugs in, to lock the door—none of which she actually did by the way because the door was wide open and there were no drugs, and you would have seen the door was wide open if you had gone into your own house where a stranger was lying on your kitchen floor--- Didn't it ever occur to you that Georgia might have killed Devaani and fled?"

"No! Because for a start I didn't know she was *dead!* How many times?"

It had never crossed her mind once, not once, that Georgia might double cross her. Not in a million years. It was my own prejudice, my own blindness, she thought. My snobbery. My privilege. My utter stupidity. It never occurred to me that Georgia who was uneducated and had been in prison was *smart* enough to fool me. And yet, I did know. I felt the sparks of her cleverness, out the corner of my eye. Now, she remembered how clever Georgia had been. She had understood Kavya's psychology far better than Kavya had understood hers.

Kavya could not have understood the complexities of Georgia Galton nee Courtnee Marie because she had not lived that wretched girl's life, which was a study of survival. She had a mean streak alright. Maybe she'd always had it, maybe she had developed it. How could you ever know what a person was really made of? Most people were weak, and only a few were strong, and sometimes it was the bad ones who were strong. And yet, in a funny sort of way, she had

had the best time with Georgia, sharing a drink and talking as friends do.

I never understood you before, she had said.

Once you go through violence, you can do anything.

She done me like a kipper, thought Kavya. I believed everything she said. Everything. The whole story about the gas…the story about Devaani beating her up….and all of it was just so she could get Devaani to Moghul House and kill her. There must have been a lot more to it than sibling rivalry, maybe more than the revenge story, a lot more between them that she never told me about why she hated Devaani. To have plotted and planned to kill someone in cold blood the way she did. She knew I'd be in it up to my neck, the police would have pinned it on me. And if it hadn't been for John speaking up for me, I'd be deep in it.

If he hadn't said what he said about the text, and about Georgia hating Devaani, and about the knife…. If I've got out of it now, all of it, it's because John knows everything. He knows the whole ugly truth of it all, and still he's lied and lied, to save me. But that, she thought listlessly, that's what makes it all so much worse. When a good person lies to save the guilty, the guilty are damned forever.

Suddenly from the kitchen, came three blood curdling screams.

Chapter 68

"Who the hell is that?" cried Lalita Sharma. "Who's in the house? Who?"

She got to her feet and started looking around. Kavya had never heard her grandmother sound so angry, so out of control, so incoherent. So fearful. She had never seen Lalita Sharma afraid. She's an old woman, she thought suddenly. For all her perfectly dyed and arranged hair, her manicure, her perfect figure, and the appropriate clothes, she was after all an old woman.

John stood expressionless averting his eyes from Kavya. Pukowski looked to her superior and Robinson strode out of the lounge and disappeared into the kitchen. There was no need this time to tell everyone to keep still; no one was going anywhere. In those few moments while Robinson was out of the room, Kavya said, "Milan? He's alive."

John nodded. "He's safe. He's got no idea about any of this."

Kavya nodded.

Robinson came in carrying the yellow rucksack. Behind him was Marymary, sobbing.

"I'm sorry..." she wailed. "I like to be useful. I like to be busy."

"It's alright Miss Fernandez," said Sergeant Pukowski, patting her on the back. Who could have imagined this tiny little Goan woman had produced those three tremendous blood curdling screams?

O, thought Kavya. It was Devaani who must have given her the black kimono, and the Netflix code. Of course.

"I picked up the rucksack and I took it to the kitchen because it was wet and I didn't want it to stain the carpet. I opened it and there were wet clothes and they smelled so I started to take them out to put in the washing machine..in ...in"

"Shh, it's ok Miss Fernandez," said Pukowski, her palm on Marymary's back.

There it is, thought Kavya staring at the rucksack in Robinsons hands. That damn rucksack.

"I put my hand in and this slimy...ohhh...*thing* climbed on my arm and I. I'm sorry. I think I became hysterical."

"It's alright," said Robinson, his face grave. "It was just a length of seaweed."

He put on a pair of plastic gloves. Then he took out the sodden jacket and held it up.

"Who does this belong to?"

"That's mine," said John.

Robinson put down the rucksack and took out the wrench.

"And who's property is this?"

"That's mine too," said John.

Robinson looked at the wrench. There was a congealed dark substance encrusted at one end.

"Why are these items in your rucksack?" he said looking at Kavya. No one had to tell him the rucksack was hers.

"She won't know. I was working on my car, and they're just my dirty clothes and things," said John. "I put them in my wife's rucksack because I was going to wash them at some stage."

Kavya couldn't answer.

"I happen to know this wrench belonged to Lady Wilhelmina. It's a rare German brand and she's had these tools for a long time. This wrench belonged to her father, Lord Brown of Sutton. She was a first-class mechanic."

John shrugged. "Someone lent it to me, someone in her workshop."

"Lady Wilhelmina was struck on the head twice with a blunt instrument. Kavya, when did you last see Billie?"

"I never saw her. I don't even know her," said Kavya.

"Mrs Sharma. Did you ever see Billie at your house on the beach?"

"No, I never did."

"I'm going to need a better explanation for the contents of this bag," said Robinson.

That damn rucksack. I knew it would finish me off. Now I'm Mrs Sharma. I've known for a while now. A long, long time; I just didn't want to face it. Everyone has told me to face things, ever since…I can't remember ever since when. It's like I've been in a fog, a dream of a fog, walking blindly.

"It's getting late. I think we would all like to conclude this. I repeat Mrs Sharma, Lady Billie was struck on the head with a blunt object and then thrown off the bridge into the water. What do you know about this?"

I'm almost at the end of it now, thought Kavya with an inward sigh.

"She wasn't pushed off the bridge. I dragged her into the sea."

Marymary made a strangled sound, but no one looked at her.

"Billie came to the house shouting and screaming, and she fell. It was dark and we thought—we thought," said John.

"No, Johnny," said Kavya. "I did it. I hit her on the head with the wrench. I think I hit her a couple of times and she fell. And then, she was dead. Later, I dragged her into the sea. To make her disappear."

"*Hai Raam*!" cried Lalita Sharma. "My Kavya! No. No!"

To hear Naani's voice like that was the guillotine on her own conscience. It was the end of any belief she could ever have in herself because she had slid into the mud in her grandmother's eyes. Now she had lost her respect, she had lost all hope.

"Mrs Kavya Sharma Ashworth I am charging you with…"

"Yeah, yeah yeah," said Kavya. "Let me just finish my drink and then let's go to the police station."

"You have the right to…"

Kavya knocked back the dregs of her glass. The thick lip stung. It hurt bad. She was glad in a way. She ran her tongue along it. It was like when you went to the dentist and the injection wore off.

John came towards her and grabbed her hand.

"Listen," he said urgently. "I will swear in any court that you had too much to drink that night and you had no idea what was going on. You were not responsible. You'll plead diminished responsibility. Don't say another word now. Wait for the lawyer."

"No, it's ok John," she said without emotion. "Thanks. But I was responsible. I did it. Thanks for trying to help me, Johnny."

Their eyes met.

In his desperate, earnest face she could see the endless deep ocean of his love. She could see his heart and she could feel his soul. She knew he would go to the ends of the earth for those he loved. Not only for her, but he would also do it for Milan. He would even do it for Lalita and Marymary.

But I don't want that, she thought with a mild surprise.

She looked across at Marymary; she meant nothing to her. And then she looked again at her grandmother and was a little surprised to see an old woman who would be dead soon. And Milan? She never wanted to see him again. She felt the opposite to "I am Here". I am not here, she thought. I no longer exist. There's nothing left of me. It's all turned to stone.

"Hold on Kavs. Look at me. Listen. We'll get the best lawyer," said John. "Just be strong. Just wait. We'll get you the best. Don't say anything. Wait for the lawyer."

"No Johnny, please don't. I don't want it," she said quietly.

She didn't even want to look at any of their faces. I'm so sick of it, so tired and bored of it all. Wait? For what?

Chapter 69

"Before we go. Can I please go up to my room? Alone?" she said.

"Afraid not," said Robinson. "But Sergeant Pukowski will come with you if you want to get a few things."

It was beginning to get light outside.

She got up and stumbled. She was drunk. Pukowski came and took her elbow.

"Sorry," she smiled. "It's procedure, I've got to come with you."

Now I'll have to think of something else, thought Kavya. I'll have to be quick. I've had a lot to drink tonight, and I know what's going to happen. Very soon, the nightmare will begin.

It's happened before. I'll get sleepy, and my body will ache. But they won't let me sleep. They'll keep me up and ask me the same questions over and over and over. I won't be able to answer, even the ones I've answered already, even if they've recorded them, they'll ask me again. And I won't be able to keep awake. Not without a drink. And they won't get any sense out of me, so they'll tell me to sleep it off in a cell. And in the morning...

But it wasn't like that. Sleep didn't deliver you. Sleep didn't refresh you. Sleep was like entering a blacker nightmare full of fitful wakings. The shaking, the nausea, your whole body numbing and throbbing and your blood full of chills. The pain in your ribs, in your heart and your thighs and the drilling behind your eyes in your head, deep inside there, the hammer in the middle of your brain. The dread of things you couldn't even name. Just an exhausting endless spasm of wretched existence.

"I need to go to the loo," she said.

"Sure, of course. But you must leave the door open."

"Ok," she said.

After she finished, she said "Can I brush my teeth please? I know you're in a hurry."

"No worries," said Pukowski with a smile. "Take your time. Brush your teeth."

Kavya opened the cabinet, took out her electric toothbrush and dropped it behind the bin.

"Sorry officer, I can't bend because of my back. Would you mind?"

"Sure," said Pukowski and stooped down.

In that split second, Kavya took a razor blade from the pack in the cabinet and put it in her pocket.

She took the toothbrush and turned it on, holding it to her gums.

As it whirred, she thought I'd get off with manslaughter at the very worst. Naani would get me the best lawyer. She knows them all. I'd get bail. And they'd find a great defence, they could even get me off. If you're rich, you don't have to serve.

But then what? Come back here? I never could. Go to London and start again? How would I ever look at John? I could never face touching Milan. He deserves better. Both do. And Naani? No, I could never look at her. None of it would ever be any good, none of it could ever heal if I was a part of it. I couldn't ever look at Johnny and all he has done for me, gone against his nature for me. For us.

She went downstairs with Pukowski and Robinson took her elbow. They went outside to the waiting car.

"I hope you catch Georgia," she said.

Robinson grimaced.

"I like to think we will, but I suspect she's long gone."

Pukowski got behind the wheel and Kavya and Robinson got in the back. It was a beautiful sky, pale pink. A new day, a new beginning.

After all, she thought she could even get off. A good lawyer would do better than manslaughter. A good lawyer would plant doubt. Maybe use the Race card? She was rich, anything was possible. And then, they could go to the Bahamas if they wanted. Sell up. Go away the three of them, John, Milan, Kavya and start a brand-new life. Rich people did it every day. Or if I wanted, I could even do what I dreamed of. Go and live by myself in Great Titchfield Street in a flat high above and do what I please all day long.

But then, I'll have to wake up the next day, and the next day and the next.

They'll make me go to AA or give me something to stop me drinking. They're bound to. They won't let me drink. And even when I know it's no good, it's all I'll want to do. And even if they get me out on bail today, by tomorrow, I won't be able to stand it. I won't be able to do one night in a cell. I just can't. I'm too afraid of what I know will come. The terror. And what's the point of it all, really? If I do it on my wrist, it'll show and it'll take too long. Where then? It's got to be the throat. But slicing across the throat is too hard.

I'm sorry for Milan. He'll miss me. But John will take care of him. He'll devote himself to my boy. And he'll only ever tell him good things about me. He'll tell him how happy we were, and he won't say I broke his heart. And Marymary and Naani and Shanta and her grandchildren, and even the people in the Mamble Favre, they'll all take care of Milan. And they'll take care of John too. They'll all take care of both my lovely boys. Everyone will be sad, but they'll carry on. And it'll be more stable without me in the picture. John will meet a nice girl, he should. Naani will be devastated but she'll carry on for the sake of Milan. And she'll make sure John is alright too, she'll love him like a son. And he'll get all the properties and the investments, and he'll never ever be poor again which is only right. I want that for him.

My brave little girl, Naani used to say to me. She always called me her brave little girl. Losing my parents. Losing my husband. Brave little girl. Was I really ever brave? I don't know what I was. If anything, I was a coward. I didn't face anything. Right to the end. Things came easy to me. They'll burn me, but if they had a tombstone for me, I think it could say 'things came easy to her'. And they'd be right.

Georgia was right too. When you go through violence, it changes you. Maybe I changed a long, long time ago but I never realised. Maybe that's why I liked to be alone, so no one could see my shame, my cowardice. All those issues those shrinks talked about, maybe I had them all. I've been loved all my life, yet it didn't redeem me. And I did kill Billie. I killed her. I didn't realise, or maybe I did realise, but it changed me. I was different after I did that. Even when I was dragging her in the water, I was thinking I could stop this now. But I didn't.

It's got to be somewhere on the throat. The razor blade cut her hand, but she hardly noticed. She was slumped to the side by the window. She took it and cut deep into the skin under her ear. She'd seen that on a show once. Then she cut the other side while she still had the strength for it. It was hard but not painful. The alcohol in my blood is a permanent anaesthetic, she thought.

"What's that?" said Sergeant Robinson who had been busy scrolling his phone screen. He had over 54 messages and emails for work. "I didn't hear what you said. Say again?"

He turned to see Kavya crouching against the window, a muffled gurgling noise coming from her. He moved her shoulder and then took a sharp intake of breath.

"Gosia, turn the car round asap. We need to get to the hospital."

The car swerved and Kavya felt the bump and then skidded, and the gravel flew.

Robinson put on the siren.

Almost out of consciousness, Kavya saw the dark and light of the winding road flitting by; they had to go into BarleyBarton A&E, but BarleyBarton Hospital, inexplicably, was in the next town of Framley. Kavya was aware of something, perhaps a handkerchief or a scarf, that Robinson was pressing against her ear.

And then through the double doors, the lights overhead. They gave her a blood transfusion. She lay on a narrow white hospital bed with a cold white light above her and sank into death. The doctor and the nurse were standing by the bed talking to the policeman. She couldn't hear it all, her soul had been cut loose at last and was drifting away into the infinite beyond.

Sergeant Robinson put his phone away in his pocket. There were 20 emails he had to answer and the paperwork for this would take him till breakfast. He didn't mind, it was the job. He shook his head sadly and a small sigh came out.

"We did all we could Sergeant. It was bad timing. Some minutes more and we might have saved her," said the doctor.

"I just don't know why she did it," said Robinson.

"There was a very good chance she would have got off. It was all circumstantial. Her husband's evidence completely exonerated her. And she had it all, money, a loving family, a support network. Everything to live for."

The two men stood in silent respect for some moments.

A great commotion began happening downstairs in A&E. Two ambulances had arrived carrying heavy casualties from a bomb blast. Nurses and doctors fled to the scene.

"I'm going to have to move this lady," said the nurse briskly. "I need the bed."

Dark Waters

Printed in Great Britain
by Amazon

23456767R00258